Historical action

TAMANRASSET
Crossroads of the Nomad

by Edward Parr

2025
Edwardian Press
New Orleans, Louisiana

"TAMANRASSET," as well as the text, characters, story, and illustrations are © 2025 by Edward Parr and Edwardian Press (New Orleans, Louisiana). All rights reserved. This is a work of fiction. Any similarities to persons or entities, living, dead, or undead are entirely coincidental.

First Print Edition 2025

ISBN-13 9798999644619
LCCN: 2025917687

CONTENTS

Map of Morocco, Algeria, and Tunisia, 1900

Prologue	1
I – Across the Maghreb	11
II – A Death in Fez	107
III – The Siege of Taghit	173
IV – Expedition to Tamanrasset	319
V – The Ruin of Casablanca	471
Epilogue	523
Notes	527
Epitaph	529

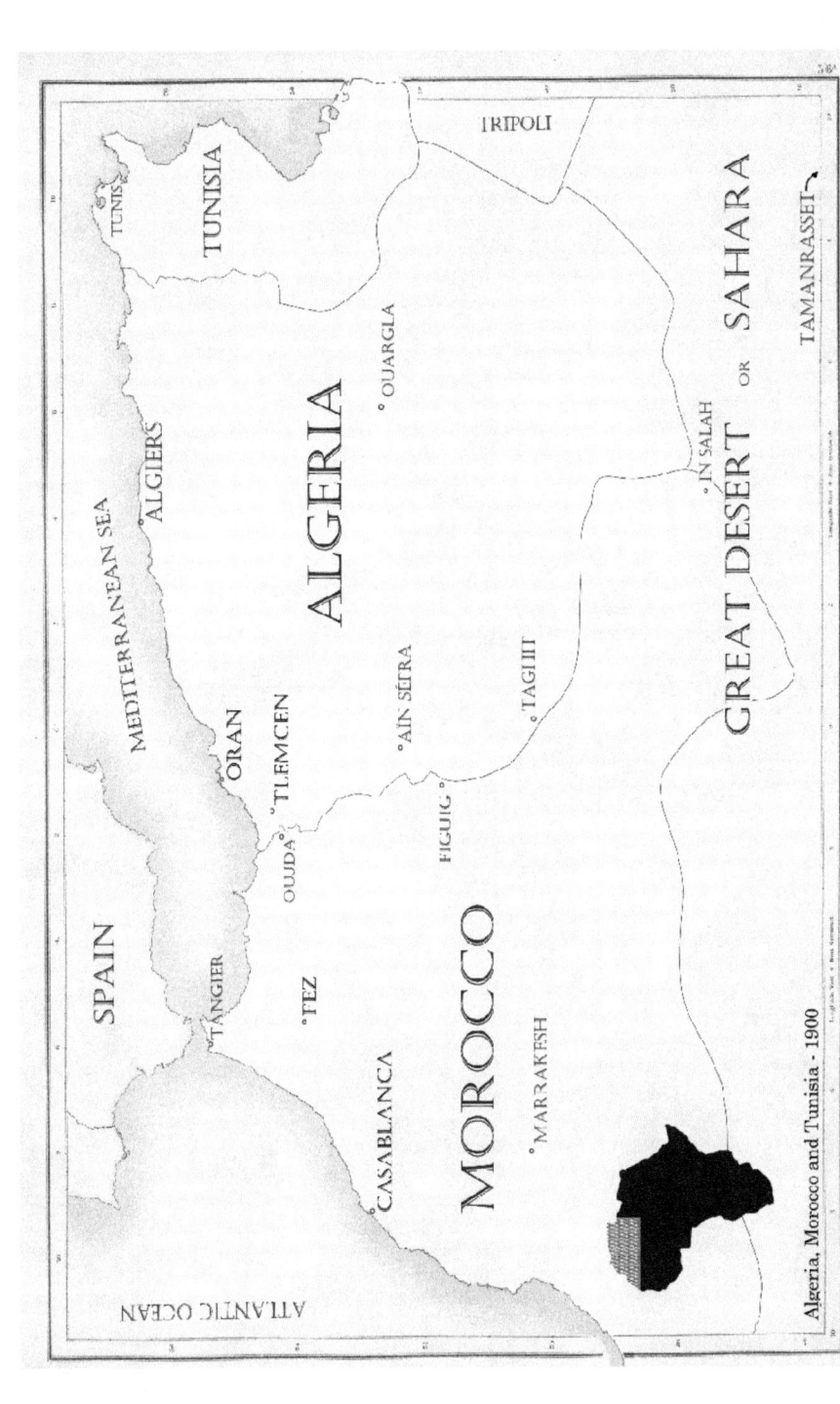

Algeria, Morocco and Tunisia - 1900

Prologue

Having arrived at the port of Oran, we stand beneath the canvas canopy on the wooden deck of our steamship with French and British tourists, each of us maneuvering to catch a breath of fresh air as we eagerly await our turn to disembark. Even at this early hour, the rays of the Sun are intense, and the raw smells of the dock saturate the air. The tourists step one by one onto the whitewashed metal gangway grasping their *Baedeker's* tighter than a Holy Bible, excited to investigate this exotic and ancient land but apprehensive of the dangers that may be posed by the unfamiliar customs of its native inhabitants. By contrast, the French military recruits who have already disembarked from steerage, dressed in rags and standing in a line on the dock as they wait for their transport to the Cercle Militaire, by and large look bored: Whatever drove them into military service has by this point been left far behind, and all they see ahead is hard labor, strict discipline, and the perils of war.

A cacophony of voices in unfamiliar languages arises from the port to assault our ears. We descend the gangway rather unsteadily after a week at sea and are met at the

Tamanrasset

customs house by disagreeable French port officials busily warding off a large throng of porters in white djellabas and turbans—Arabs, Berbers, and Black Africans—who are all seeking employment. We approach a wooden desk where a sleepy customs official stamps our papers without glancing at them. The natives are then released and rush towards us. We grip our suitcase tightly and hang on lest it be wrested away by one of the more aggressive candidates. These are all fine-looking men, tall and thin with clean-cut features and oddly pointed teeth whose unfortunate circumstances have made it necessary for them to plead for work. Most speak French and Arabic with some interspersed words of Sabir, the contact language heard around the Mediterranean. There is no foolproof method for locating a dependable guide, so we look each gentleman in the eye and ask slowly and clearly whether they can take us to the Gare Centrale. Our choice is of little consequence since we are not staying over in Oran. For a few sous, a soft-spoken older gentleman with a lengthy white beard, straight white teeth, and large brown eyes agrees to carry our suitcase and accompany us safely to the station.

Following our guide uphill into the New Town, we cross broad new avenues lined with Turkish hazelnut saplings and black enameled cast iron streetlamps. Parisian-style buildings with iron balconies and tall windows are set well back on wide boulevards open to the full heat of the Sun. Walking slowly uphill, we overhear conversations in French, Italian, English, and Spanish, but with occasional shouts of Arabic and something else, possibly one of the native Berber languages. Dark-skinned African children run playfully through the streets. We pass the notorious stone edifice known as the Chateau Neuf, the "new castle," which was built in the Fourteenth Century by Sultan Abu al-Hasan. Now at the dawn of the Twentieth Century it flies the Tricolore of France and is home to a French military prison.

After cutting across the wide avenues, we are led into an older and denser part of the city, the Quartier de la Kasbah. It is a labyrinth of shadowy narrow streets lined with neatly painted townhouses and orderly storefronts displaying Arabic signage. The smell of unfamiliar spices in the still, warm air is overpowering. Muslim women dressed head to toe in black scarves which cover their face and neck avert their eyes as we pass, but there are also uncloaked Berber women from the south with olive complexions, jet-black hair, and piercing black eyes which stare at us provocatively, much like the feral cats who stretch themselves in every small patch of daylight.

We emerge onto the Boulevard Marceau just across from the Gare Centrale somewhat relieved to be out in the open air again even though the Sun is nearing its zenith. This modern train station has a style intentionally reminiscent of classic Moorish architecture: The foundations are yellow sandstone topped with smooth white limed walls, and horseshoe-shaped arches are decorated with colorful geometric tiles and windows of stained glass. Despite its striking appearance, the station is uncomfortably crowded with French soldiers headed south to areas that remain under military governance even after decades of French rule. However, now is not the time for a lengthy history lesson as the train's whistle indicates we must board for our imminent departure. We thank our guide and pay him for

Tamanrasset

his excellent service, take our suitcase, and climb onto the train.

Our seat is reserved but we find our first-class compartment already occupied by two officers of the Armée d'Afrique. We stow our case on the rack and take our place upon the thinly upholstered bench as the train begins with a bang and jolt to move out of the station. With a great deal of grunting, Capitaine Poilievre of the Chasseurs d'Afrique closes the window since the movement of the train draws dust and smoke into our compartment. He then retakes his seat and gives us a skeptical but silent evaluation before crossing his arms and closing his eyes. The other officer introduces himself as Lieutenant Dumarché. He is an easy conversationalist and shares anecdotes of his service in the Maghreb (the name of that portion of northern Africa which includes French Algeria and the French protectorate of Tunis as well as the countries of Morocco and Libya, he explains). The Lieutenant has been stationed in Oran as a liaison (although he fails to clarify with whom he liaised) and tells us of his time in Algiers where he accompanied a French archaeologist on a desert expedition to the ruins of an ancient Roman city. This helps to pass the time as our route on the narrow-gauge railway takes us quite slowly through endless farmlands of wheat, olive trees, and grape vines growing in the rich, red soil. We notice that habitable dwellings appear further and further apart. After several hours, the train climbs into the gently folding Tell Atlas mountains. As the ambient temperature declines, Capitaine Poilievre awakens and becomes more conversant. He tells us he has a new Italian wife in Oran, but, sadly, his leave was cut short and he has been ordered to report to his Regiment.

Early in the evening we arrive in Sidi Bel Abbès, headquarters of the First Division of La Légion Étrangere, the renowned French Foreign Legion. Many of the soldiers on the train will remain in this small city, but some will continue with us in the morning, destined for more remote military outposts and forts in the south. We take down our case and step out onto the platform as the Arab, Berber and Black African passengers exiting from third-class are brusquely dispersed by French railway officials into the darkening alleys of the city. The well-laid streets and parks are bustling with Legionnaires, local merchants and farmers both French and Spanish. Nearly every edifice in this city is daubed with yellowed plaster. The dusty streets, smelling of jasmine in the evening twilight, are wide and lined with mature palm trees. The muezzin at the mosque nearby is calling to the faithful in Arabic: "Allah is most great. I testify that there is no God but Allah. I testify that Muhammad is the prophet of Allah. Come to prayer." We have a short walk to the Hôtel des Voyageurs and are welcomed by a friendly French proprietor who shows us to a clean, comfortable room.

After sunset, the town becomes quite dark, but we step out to a café nearby where we are served a fine local Burgundy-style red wine and, to our surprise, a French breakfast of eggs, toast, cheese, and tomatoes which is comfortingly familiar. The "Street of Seven Delights" in the livelier district of town (which we are told is strictly forbidden to the Legionnaires) is where most of the Legionnaires spend their evenings. Nevertheless, there are a few French officers who sit nearby enjoying their wine and quiet conversation in the cool of the evening.

Tamanrasset

In the morning, we board a far less comfortable train and continue south across the bleak "High Plateau" to regions which remain under the governance of the French Bureau Arabes. Our train stops first at the small dust-swept village of Le Kreider. Some of the soldiers disembark to report at the small fort there. We learn it was built in 1881 after the massacre of the local Spaniards during the rebellion of Sheik Bou Amama. We then continue south across the dry salt flats through the towns of Mécharia and Naama and pass over the jagged and barren Jebel Antar mountain range.

After two long days of stifling heat aboard the train, we come to the current terminus of the French railroad located in the town of Aïn Séfra, a busy regional center for pan-Saharan trade situated in a wide valley between eroded sandstone mountains. The town benefits from standing bodies of clean water connected to each other with irrigation canals. Sandy brown buildings are bisected by sandy brown streets. The lovely square minaret of the main mosque which stands proudly above the town is painted yellow and green; the mosque is named for Abd al-Qadir who many years ago led the struggle against the French colonization of Algeria. There is greenery everywhere in the form of trees, palms, and grasses, but the native people look somewhat exhausted and malnourished. Fortunately, we have sent letters ahead to reserve a room in the Hôtel de la Paix which has only two guest rooms. The hotel is filthy, and we are provided with a meager meal of kouss-kouss, a small portion of roasted fowl, and a few beans. Across the street is a plain mudbrick barracks for the Legionnaires that looks much like a prison.

Crossroads of the Nomad

There is as yet no train south from Aïn Séfra, and we must make alternative arrangements to continue our journey. Our Italian hotelier refers us to a "trustworthy" local guide named Ayoub who can take us south across the valley and through the Saharan Atlas mountain range for an extortionate fee. This also means an extra night in Aïn Séfra, but at Ayoub's suggestion we spend it at the house of his brother Mohammed rather than the awful hotel. The house is a sparsely furnished riad with interconnected rooms around a glass-covered central courtyard. After a dinner of more kouss-kouss, onions and roast goat with a bottle of imported Bordeaux (an indication that we are perhaps overpaying Ayoub), we are led to a clean room furnished with rich camel-hair carpets, blankets, and pillows and invited to sleep.

It is a brief rest: Shortly after midnight we are awakened by Mohammed's young son, a lanky fellow who is still learning to speak French. In the courtyard, his wife, dressed all in black, hands us a cup of hot mint tea; we walk circles around the courtyard as we drink and shake off our exhaustion. Ayoub asks us to prepare for our two-day journey by camel. These animals appear as dazed as we are to be awake at this hour. We are told it is preferable to travel during the coolest part of the day; indeed, it is quite cold at this hour. Our camel is named "al-Haml" (although we later learn that this is a common epithet for any camel that wanders around the desert without a master—a reference perhaps to our poor control of the creature). Ayoub explains the risks of our journey which include robbery, torture, disembowelment, dismemberment, and death but then

Tamanrasset

assures us that our route is often traveled by merchants and French soldiers so we "probably" won't encounter trouble.

We set off long before dawn and endure hours of bouncing uncomfortably upon the mischievous al-Haml. The camel's "pace," its unusual side to side gait in which both legs on the same side move together, is frankly nauseating, and, as the Sun rises, there is nothing to see but the hamada–hardpacked, tan-colored dirt–as we pass through mountain valleys one by one. Soon the Sun is beating down on us, so we stop to set up our camp and drink our fill of warm gritty water from leather waterskins. Ayoub erects a lovely tarpaulin tent for us, and we rest on a cot until the evening. At sunset we emerge from the tent to see a sky on fire in shades of yellow, red, and orange while behind us the cloudless blue sky is deepening to violet. We smell the pungent smoke of the camel dung fire; its black smoke rises into the night. As darkness draws a blanket over us, the sky erupts into countless dots of light arranged mostly in a wide swath across the open sky. We wonder how we could have ever overlooked such a sight before. Supper is announced. Our meal consists of kouss-kouss, of course, plus beans and goat meat again cooked in a pan over an open fire, served with unleavened bread and eaten with our fingers. A jackal barking nearby requests the leftovers. We note that Ayoub and his son are quite satisfied with some bread and dried figs and an occasional drink of water for their entire day's food.

Collapsing after dinner, we sleep until it is time for our departure shortly after midnight. The next day we are very sore and very tired and the ride is tedious and hot. But then, after two long days riding across the high plateau and through wind-etched gorges past caves whose walls still bear the engravings of Stone Age nomads, we come suddenly down from a wide valley and arrive at a small unnamed village.

Unwilling to suppress our excitement any longer, we leave Ayoub to arrange our accommodations as we walk into town. The hollow-eyed and silent inhabitants view us with both curiosity and enmity, with ingratiating smiles from those eager to take our money and hostile glares from those wary of Westerners. The village has little food or water, and half of the dwellings have been swallowed by the encroaching desert sands. It is a thankfully short trek across the town. We climb a large mound and at last lay eyes upon our final destination: The great Sahara.

We gaze out at the massive waves of fine yellow sand, and a hot gritty wind blows in our face. Before us, as far as our eyes can see, is an immense and lifeless void, a vast emptiness greater than we could have conceived. This unknown and unexplorable region remains utterly silent but for the nearly constant hush of gently shifting sands. We stand upon the outer boundary of human domains, and to those who reside along the edge of the abyss, be they settlers or soldiers, emirs or explorers, the Sahara remains a silent, encroaching peril shrouded in myth and mystery. But let us indulge in no romantic fantasies: No one would enter this vast emptiness unless pressed by great need or unnatural desires. There are no maps, no points of reference, no roads, no landmarks. The desert's currents are known only to the dangerous Tuareg warriors who migrate east and west and to the mysterious Berber traders whose caravans range north and south.

Tamanrasset

To enter the Sahara is to be swallowed up by a place utterly indifferent to our presence. Our words are met with silence, our footsteps disappear instantly in sands that are endlessly replaced by more sand. The bleached bones we see scattered on the ground are all that remain of beasts or men who died years or months or possibly only weeks ago, a constant reminder that all things are reduced to dust in time. Our slow, almost reverent steps take us forward between enormous crests of sand to an aptly-named hollow that is silent and totally removed from the lives of our fellow men. We feel our singularity, our uniqueness.

We then come to the disturbing realization that we are unable to precisely identify the direction from which we came. The Sun is now directly overhead, and we cannot discern east from west nor north from south; the path in every direction looks identical. We struggle to climb a sand dune to gauge our bearings, our feet backsliding in the loose grit, and achieve the summit at last only to see dunes and dunes and more dunes as far as the light reaches. Heat radiates both down from the sky and up from the ground stabbing at our flesh. Panic seizes us. No one hears our cries for help. There is no path, no shelter. We climb crest to crest, the direction hardly matters for it is all the same.

Heat and dehydration and exhaustion deplete our strength. We lay down to rest. The unyielding rays of the Sun blister our skin, scald our eyes, boil our brain. Our memory of the past is obscured by a mist. Our hope of locating an oasis evaporates as we succumb to madness. We are seized by the urge to flee this inhuman realm, but a fine dust clogs our eyes and lungs. Our lips crack, our gums bleed, our tongues swell and blacken. We pray for rescue, but the dreadful consequence of our misadventure has already been written.

I – Across the Maghreb

Sergent Jacques Demoreau wrenched open the gate of the fort and urged the exhausted stragglers of his Company to make their way inside before they were all killed. He wiped the sweat from his face with one grimy hand as the bullets of their pursuers randomly struck the walls above and about him. Flecks of stone and shards of metal rained down. Although tall enough to be a conspicuous target, Demoreau was a slim man, hardened by his many years in the scorching desert under the rigid discipline of the Foreign Legion, still strong, only beginning to gray. The Sergent's deeply lined face was red from the day-long retreat and from shouting orders at his men in the unrelenting desert Sun. His head and heart were pounding and his mouth was parched, but at least the blood on his dusty white trousers and blue jacket was not his own. The 6th Mounted Company had been fighting a rear-guard action since that morning when they had come under attack by four hundred mounted tribesmen of the Doui-Menia, and Sergent Demoreau was determined to get the remainder of his men into the fort before nightfall.

Demoreau was the highest-ranking member of the Sixth still on his feet. Lieutenant Claussen, who had been acting commander of the Sixth, had been wounded that morning; he had been brought to the infirmary but there was no doctor to treat him. Those Legionnaires who had already withdrawn into the fort and were physically able—only Keppeler and Walders, Mora, Britten, and Rivoli—climbed the walls overlooking the village to provide covering fire for their comrades who were still retreating from the bloodthirsty tribesmen. The Company's Sergent-Fourrier, Kurtz, had been among the first to reach the fort that afternoon. He found a Tirailleur light infantry Company was already stationed there, Arab, and Berber units highly regarded for their fierceness and tenacity, which were raised in the pacified northern parts of the country and commanded by French officers. Their commander was a brash but untested French Lieutenant. He brought the Tirailleurs out to relieve Demoreau and hold off the attacking tribesmen while the rest of the Sixth withdrew into the fort.

The Legionnaires trailing Demoreau were finally making their way up to the gate. Most had wounds which slowed them considerably. Legionnaire Andreev and Caporal Dupont were the last two to arrive: Dupont had a bloody saber wound on his right leg and was barely conscious. Andreev, a massive Slav from Odessa, carried the Caporal.

The Doui-Menia had not broken off their attack: It seemed the tribesmen intended to surround the fort and continue into the night, but the stronghold at Taghit, Le Fort de L'Eperon, had high, impenetrable walls. Sergent Demoreau took a last look at the scattered positions of the enemy before entering. For a moment, hatred welled up inside him, and he felt a deep desire to stand and face the ruthless barbarians that had attacked them, but then Demoreau took a deep breath and held it as his mind and heart sharpened: He had been through many battles during his long years of service to the Legion, and each encounter had made him harder and colder. He also had to admit he had grown a little more protective of his Legionnaires. He released his breath, stepped into the fort, and barred the gate.

Demoreau's Company had been stationed in Igli for the past few months, about seventy kilometers to the southwest. It was barely a village—just a few acres of mudbrick buildings in the river valley, or wadi, of the Saoura river on the western edge of the Sahara. Still, it was an improvement over where they had been. Last year, the Company, with a nearly full complement of two hundred-forty-five men, had been attached to Colonel Bertrand's 1st Foreign Regiment, a force of over two thousand men and twenty-eight hundred camels sent to pacify the Touat region. In the spring, after many months moving from village to village, the 6th Mounted Company, reduced by then to one hundred-sixty-four men, had been sent back up to Igli to take a defensive position along the Saoura river. They were stationed there at a fort that faced empty desert in every direction.

Most of the year, the Wadi Saoura was the mostly-dry valley of the Saoura river, but the rainy season brought plentiful water and flooded the valley's plains. These waters refreshed an aquifer that sustained huge date palm groves and fields for grains and grazing livestock. The locals tended to avoid confrontations with the French and respected an uneasy peace. However, while Igli was not as far south as In Salah, it was close to the border with Morocco. Nomadic tribes from Morocco regularly migrated from the nearby Atlas Mountains to graze their livestock in the Wadi Saoura, and they viewed the French as hostile invaders of their territory. Tensions between the family-based tribes, part of the confederation known as the Doui-Menia, and the French soldiers had been rising for years, and it was not uncommon for the tribesmen to attack individual Legionnaires and small work parties, called "corvées," and sometimes even larger "pelotons" of Legionnaires that were caught out after dark. The soldiers, for their part, knew that any man captured by these tribesmen would be subject to terrible tortures and mutilations followed by a slow and gruesome death. That was the fact of life in the Wadi Saoura.

During the months spent at Igli, the Sixth lost another thirty men to such attacks, and the Legionnaires spent weeks racing back and forth across the desert chasing the tribesmen with little success at making the region any more secure. When the depleted Company was finally told they were being sent back north to their barracks in Saïda to take on and train replacements, the Legionnaires all breathed a sigh of relief. But then they had to wait three more weeks for another Company to come garrison the fort, and in those three weeks, summer settled over the region like a hot blanket. Temperatures soared to well over 110° Fahrenheit. More men were lost while on patrol. Both the Company's commanding officer, Capitaine Roubec, and his Adjutant were ordered to report to Algiers, and the Capitaine left the Company under the command of the only surviving officer, Lieutenant Claussen. Claussen was himself a replacement who had recently been sent down from Tlemcen. He was a graduate of the French military academy at St. Cyr and an able officer, but he was young and had no experience with desert warfare. The Legionnaires began to express their concerns aloud. A fresh Company finally arrived from Saïda to replace the Sixth just in time to prevent several Legionnaires from going "en pompe," as they called deserting. And so a greatly depleted 6th Mounted Company was obliged to depart Igli during the height of the summer heat.

The morning of their departure, the sky had begun to lighten although the Sun remained hidden behind the massive sand dunes to the east as the Company stood assembled "en ligne" and prepared to march north. The air was dry but still very warm having never fully cooled off during the night. Sergent Demoreau reviewed his Section proudly–they were good men he knew well and trusted. Both the Legionnaires and their mules were fully packed. Of the large Kabylian mules used by the Legion, forty remained able to make the long journey; they snorted impatiently and stamped their hooves on the loose, sandy soil. Of the Legionnaires, there were only one hundred-thirty-two men able to make the journey, and all of them were eager to begin as well–eager to start off during the cool of the night knowing that it would get much, much hotter. They stood silently in the uniform of the "Campagne d'Afrique": Gleaming boots and clean puttees, grey-white pants with a dark blue sash around the waist, dark blue long jackets with the tails buttoned up to the back waist, gleaming brass buttons, criss-crossed with gleaming leather straps, the kepis on their heads covered with a worn white havelock to shade their ears and neck, each with a full pack and a trusty Lebel rifle.

The reduced Company had been reconfigured into two Sections, one commanded by Sergent-Fourrier Kurtz, the other by Sergent Demoreau, but the men stood in one long column, four across, first the men on foot and then those mounted who would ride, all awaiting the commander's order to march. As usual for a Mounted Company, the Legionnaires would alternate marching and riding at one-hour intervals, but it was to be a relaxed first day: Lieutenant Claussen planned to cover the first stage of the journey from Igli to the French fort on the ridge overlooking Taghit, or in other words from the Wadi Saoura to the Wadi Zousfana, in two days. Most of the Legionnaires, Demoreau included, wished they had departed hours before sunrise and had made the journey in one long day.

The Lieutenant at last gave the order to march, and the bugle brayed. "En Avant—Marche!" Kurtz ordered. He led off half the men. Then Demoreau, accompanied by the Lieutenant on horseback, followed with the remainder. The sun began to rise over the enormous sand dunes to the east as the Company quietly marched away from Igli into the dry gulf between them and safety. The plains here were only dotted with brown grass, and the Company was able to quick march parallel with the riverbed for several kilometers.

After a time, the day began to warm considerably. Demoreau blew his whistle and there was a stop. "Easy on the water," he yelled. The men sank to the ground beside the small domed tomb of a long-forgotten holy man. A few minutes later the Sergent blew his whistle again. "Changez, Montez!" Those who had been riding exchanged places with those who had been walking. The air was hot and still as they regained their places in the column. The whistle was blown, and the march resumed. Demoreau had trained these Legionnaires himself and they had been together for well over a year, some much longer than that, both in training and on maneuvers. The Sergent was very satisfied with their conduct and their morale, but then of course the Legionnaires knew they were marching away from danger, not towards it.

The Company continued northeast away from the riverbed and into a series of sand-etched gorges that provided cover from the morning sun and the sandy, dry wind of the desert. The morning wore on, and after a quiet two hours, the canyon opened up into a broad plain of hardpacked wind-swept dirt. Marching across the "hamada," keeping to the usual route along the eastern edge, it was time for the riders and marchers to exchange places again, and Demoreau raised his whistle to his lips when a guttural war cry suddenly pierced the air.

From the ridgeline to the west, at least a hundred horseback riders, their faces obscured by scarves, bore down upon the Sixth in a cloud of dust with wild howls of "Allahu Akbar!" Some of the riders discharged their rifles, and the whine of bullets through the air was like the excited hum of angry hornets. Other riders waved their long, curved scimitars or brandished spears or pikes in the bright, merciless sunlight.

The Legionnaires froze and looked around as they brought their Lebel rifles down from their shoulders, shocked to see the avalanche of tribesmen emerge from over the rocky crests to the west of the Company. Each rider wore a turban and cloak, a "burnous," which blew in the wind like a banner of war.

"Halte! Formez le carré d'infanterie!" The Sergents ordered the Legionnaires to draw together and form square.

The men pulled the mules down in front of them to provide cover from the riders' fire, and Demoreau had the Legionnaires affix their bayonets. The experienced soldiers, now veterans of many skirmishes, were ruthlessly efficient at forming what ended up as more of a long rectangle. The tribesman quickly closed the gap between them and their intended victims. "Feu à volonté!" Demoreau shouted to his men to fire at will, and the Legionnaire's well-aimed rifles began their staccato bark that cut mercilessly into the attacking wave.

Unable to penetrate the Legionnaire's close formation, the tribesmen broke off their charge and split to encircle the Company and cut off any retreat. Many of the enemy riders and many horses were wounded, but the Legionnaires suffered losses as well. Then another wave of horsemen, and another and then another, came over the western ridge and rushed to join in the attack. The tribesmen's spears landed among the Legionnaires and wounded more men than did the riders' bullets. The French steel bayonets and accurate firing kept the riders at a distance, but eventually the defensive formation became untenable as gaps began to open. The Legionnaires were able to repulse several further charges by the tribesmen but these attacks now ended in gruesome hand-to-hand combat.

Demoreau knelt beside Lieutenant Claussen. The Sergent had been in plenty of actions during more than twenty years of service in the Legion: The sun beating down, the barrel of his rifle smoking and hot from constant firing, the taste of sand and sulfur in his mouth as he and his comrades fought off their enraged enemy with nerves of steel and cooler heads. "Que voulez-vous? C'est la Legion!" A part of him relished it. He had a calmness of mind gained through years of experience and training. As he raised his rifle to aim at the advancing tribesmen, he recalled to his mind the melody of a fine composition, the death waltz by Saint-Saëns, which unrolled in his inner ear, turning his blood to ice. He hummed the tune as his rifle fired and his deadly accurate shooting dropped one rider after another.

Claussen was a good Lieutenant and had plenty of courage, but that did not mean he couldn't benefit from Demoreau's experience. The Sergent turned and faced his commander: "We're being overwhelmed and losing too many men, Sir: We can't maintain this position. We must move east onto the ridge where there's cover among the rocks."

"I know, but it may be too far, Sergent," Claussen replied.

"Yes, it might," the Sergent agreed, "but we still have to go: We'll certainly all be killed if we stay here."

Claussen looked distraught, but as he looked Demoreau in the eyes his nerve was hardened. Everything had to be done "par règlement" in the Foreign Legion. He nodded: "Yes, give the order, Sergent. Withdraw to the ridge; smartly, now."

There seemed to be fewer riders involved in the attack at that moment, so the time to move was ripe. Demoreau and Kurtz passed the orders on to the men, and then Demoreau blew his whistle and the surviving Legionnaires arose "en masse" to grab the wounded and the surviving mules and make a desperate rush across the hardpacked ground, firing behind them and dragging what supplies and comrades they could. The enemy saw the movement and rode urgently back towards the Legionnaires, firing wildly. The race was on.

Tamanrasset

Demoreau and Claussen brought up the rear. With a handful of men, they stopped, turned, and knelt to fire at the pursuing riders. It was enough to give the enemy pause, all too brief a respite though it was. Yard by yard the Legionnaires raced back across the plain until the quickest of them reached shelter among the rocks on the eastern edge. They started shooting at the tribesmen and provided covering fire for their retreating comrades. With many casualties, the survivors of the Company at last reached the small cover provided by the rocky terrain of the eastern ridge of the valley.

It was fully mid-day by that time, and the sun was bearing down on the wicked and the innocent alike, boiling the men alive. The Legionnaires' ammunition would soon run low and they would have to engage in a desperate retreat, either north towards Taghit or back to Igli. To go south would put the men back into the canyons where they would be easy targets for tribesmen who could fire down on them from the ridges. To go north, they would need to stay on the eastern ridge as long as possible but then fight their way yard by yard to Taghit and the safety of the French fort.

Demoreau crept to Claussen's side. The young officer was exhausted and scared. "I know, Sergent. I must make a terrible choice."

"Yes, Sir," Demoreau replied. "Igli or Taghit. But we are Legionnaires, Sir: Every one of us here volunteered to fight, and every one of us fights for his honor and the honor of the Legion. We are prepared to die for France. There is no wrong decision."

Claussen looked at Demoreau with gratitude, set his jaw and opened his mouth to shout: "Legionnaires! We proceed north to Taghit. Maintain good order. Leave no wounded man behind."

A wicked smile crossed Demoreau's face as he shouted: "You heard the Lieutenant! Off the ground and move! Now, you worthless dogs!"

The Legionnaires, to a man, grabbed what they could, helped their wounded comrades to their feet and began their trek. The enemy was relentless, but by this time somewhat chastened. They continued to come, but more carefully, in bands that inaccurately rained bullets down on the Legionnaires as the beleaguered soldiers scrambled across the rocky ridge.

Claussen remained in the rear, urging Sergent-Fourrier Kurtz and Demoreau to push the Legionnaires northward. The surviving mules, who had been largely ignored by the tribesmen since they were considered potential booty, followed aimlessly across the ridge. The Legionnaires leapt from the cover of one boulder to another, dodging bullets with each step. And then suddenly, as he turned to help up a wounded Legionnaire, a bullet struck the Lieutenant. His hand went to his gut as thick, dark blood flowed down his pant legs. Gritting his teeth, Claussen fired back with his pistol and saw his attacker fall from his horse. Demoreau lifted the groaning Lieutenant onto one of the mules and had him led away as quickly as possible.

The survivors of the Company reached the end of the ridge, and to their immense relief found a narrow gully pointed roughly in the direction of Taghit. This meant that for some kilometers still they had enough cover from which to repel their attackers. And then the Legionnaires realized they were in a gradually expanding grove of date palms.

That meant water, and the presence of water could only mean that they had entered the southern end of the Wadi Zousfana just below Taghit. And then there was an actual river, and it was thankfully shallow enough to ford. Sergent-Fourrier Kurtz led the remaining mules, the wounded, and a number of men to the fort at Taghit to get reinforcements as Demoreau and his squad maintained defensive positions amidst the grove of date palms on the edge of the village to hold the enemy at bay.

The stand-off in the grove continued for what felt like an eternity. The still hot air grew thick with smoke and the acrid tang of gunpowder. Demoreau had to move the men back yard by yard, until they were on the outskirts of Taghit itself, but it was only a matter of time before they were outflanked by the enemy. Exhausted, the remaining Legionnaires could only hold their position and wait, and half of the men had no ammunition left at all.

Then shots rang out from behind their position, and Demoreau raced back to see whether his men had been surrounded. But by some unlooked for grace, the Tirailleur light infantry from the fort arrived at that very moment. They had been sent by Kurtz and were well-armed and led by the brash French Lieutenant. Demoreau and the remainder of the Sixth were finally able to retreat into the fort as the infantrymen held off the relentless attackers.

At long last, as the sun was setting across the town of Taghit, Demoreau brought the remains of the 6th Mounted Company behind the high stone walls of the fort. The battlements bristled with armed marksmen. Sporadic shots from the Doui-Menia riders persisted through the night, but they no longer had sufficient forces to breach the well-defended walls. By dawn, the enemy had melted away into the desert.

Without a doubt, it had been the largest and best organized attack that Demoreau had experienced in more than twenty years of service in French Algeria. Twenty-six Legionnaires were dead, Claussen among them. Seventeen Legionnaires were seriously wounded and would never fight again. Kurtz awakened briefly but was still unable to speak coherently. He had "le cafard," literally "the cockroach" but in the parlance of the Foreign Legion it referred to the madness brought about by heat and sun and dehydration: It was said that a man felt as though there were cockroaches inside his skull. Yes, Demoreau thought, it sometimes felt like that's just what they all were, cockroaches scurrying about in the desert, trying to avoid being stamped out one by one. But the Legionnaires of the Sixth, he thought, had at least behaved like well-disciplined cockroaches. They had fought honorably side by side and survived that gruesome day.

* * *

Isabel Pedersen entered the Kissaria marketplace from the main road that went through the neighborhood where she resided in the city of Fez. At once, the crowded Moroccan market stalls and rush of strangers awoke her sense of alienation. Her eyes welled up briefly, and she stopped and wiped her face with a lace-fringed handkerchief, the last of those she had brought with her from Sweden. She pulled the top of her black scarf forward to better obscure her face, took a deep breath, and bravely continued into the medina.

The morning sun shining through the wood trellis overhead made a dappled pattern on the stone-paved alley, but the air was warm and still; the strong scents of spices—rose, jasmine, and verbena—were cloying. There were many men in the market that day; usually there were more women. The men tended to stare at Isabel when they noticed her pale face and blue eyes. Most assumed she was one of the mysterious and haughty Tuareg women from the desert. Isabel was careful to avert her eyes, especially since the old-timers sometimes thought she was giving them the "evil eye" and spit at her. But she was in no mood to be friendly to strangers regardless.

She passed one overflowing souk after another that had gorgeous displays of herbs, spices, rugs and carpets, silks, shoes, brassware, leather goods both tan and dyed, perfume, or clothing. She slowly moved down the alley towards the meat market, careful not to disturb anyone or knock anything over. She allowed herself to be easily distracted, hoping to find one thing or another that might give her a moment's pleasure. She finally stopped in front of a shop that had colorful dresses on display. They were kaftans decorated with gold filigree, jewels, and beads—not her style but there were a few of a more European style, the sort of thing she might have worn as a girl in Sweden. Some of the dresses were really quite pretty, not at all like the plain deep brown djellaba she had on. But it wasn't a sense of longing or envy which stopped her but merely nostalgia for a time that seemed so far removed from her present. Now she was alone, and felt it keenly.

Isabel finally reached the souk where the halal meat was sold. She had been told to buy goat, but it looked like the goat meat was all sold. She approached the butcher—a large, muscular man with a waxed mustache: "Asalamu alaikom, peace be upon you, Hassan" she said, looking down.

The butcher squinted at the young woman standing before him and paused briefly. "Wa alaikom salaam, peace be upon you," he replied at last. "What do you want today?" His manner was cool and unwelcoming.

"Have you any more goat meat? Majida sent me for goat," she said; "Omar is having a colleague from the university come for dinner tonight."

"It's important then?" He asked with little interest.

"I am certain Majida would say so, yes," she replied.

"Hmm, well," he said at last, "do you know Hamza, the baker?"

"Yes, sir."

"He has goat that he bought from me earlier today, but he will let you have it; you can bring him a chicken and pay him for the goat. He will understand. Omar needs the goat more than Hamza does. Does that sound alright to you?"

"Yes, praise Allah, Majida will be very grateful to receive the goat from Hamza," she replied. Isabel looked up at the butcher and saw an expression of cautious curiosity on his wide face. He went down to his cold cellar to get the roaster and wrap that up for her in paper while she waited. People were still getting used to her, she thought with mild exhaustion, even though she had been living with Omar and his wife Majida and their daughter Faiza for several months. She was still considered a foreigner even though she dressed and spoke like a native. She was able to read Arabic well, but she had only learned how to live in Morocco and how to speak and how to behave when she began to live with the Benayoun family and, recently, to take classes at the madrasa. She also began to pray with the family at the small neighborhood mosque.

Hassan handed over the paper-wrapped chicken, and Isabel gave him a silver dirham. "Go in peace," he said before turning his attention to the next customer.

Isabel sighed with relief that the encounter had not been too awkward. She continued down an alleyway. She had already planned to visit the baker's souk on her way back to the house. She continued to browse as she passed through the market and stopped briefly for rice and onions and spices along the way. Unlike the meat market, Hamza's bakery always smelled lovely, notwithstanding the towering bags of grains and flour which lined both floor and walls. Despite being surrounded by this dusty granary, the baker always smiled and remained cheerful. He was remarkably clean; at most, you might see a bit of flour on his hands as he handled the bread. His wife Ala, who lived upstairs, was said to have suffered a terrible accident many years ago, although Hamza never discussed it. Ala stayed inside their home above the souk and was said to not receive visitors, yet Hamza remained kind and polite to all his customers.

"Asalamu alaikom," Isabel said, looking down.

"Wa alaikom salaam," the baker replied.

When Isabel explained the situation, Hamza understood right away that Isabel should have the goat meat for Omar and went upstairs to his home to get it. Isabel gave Hamza the chicken as a gift and paid for both the bread and the goat meat. Omar could afford the extra expense—he had an important job and was well paid.

As Isabel walked home, she thought of how generous Omar and Majida had been to allow her to live with them, asking nothing from her. Even before her "iddah," or mourning period, had ended, Isabel had volunteered to help Majida with chores around the house, and she began to go to prayers with them. Yet Isabel still felt sad, lost, and lonely. She sometimes felt she should just return to Sweden, although there was nothing for her there.

Isabel had come to Morocco with her husband, Erik Pedersen, two years earlier. He had been a young scholar of religions at Lund University, and shortly after they married he was given a grant to study at the University of al-Quaraouiyin in Fez, the oldest university in the world. She had lived a sheltered life in Fez helping her husband with his work in their small home and all their needs were met by servants. But then, eight months ago, Erik had gotten ill with a high fever and almost instantly had died.

In her disabling grief, Isabel had been unable to care for herself. Erik's colleague at the university and his wife took Isabel into their home and cared for her. They treated Isabel as a member of their own family. She had become a companion to their young daughter, Faiza, who called her Swedish companion "Bella." Isabel respectfully practiced Islam with the family, and she appreciated the constant demands that the religion made on her attention. She enjoyed reading at the madrasa. However, she had not actually declared her faith, the statement of belief that is central to Islam called the "Shahadah." She could say it, of course, but she wasn't certain she meant it. And she was also not certain whether it was proper for her to be living in the home of an unrelated married man; that wouldn't have been acceptable in Sweden either. She had been meaning to discuss that problem with her host. On the other hand,

Isabel could not imagine returning to Sweden and trying to resume her pre-marital life, moving back into the house of her bourgeois parents, and acting as though none of the major events of her life had ever happened. That made her even sadder because it felt like a betrayal of her dead husband and of all the things she had learned. And then she wondered whether she would ever again feel like she really belonged anywhere.

It was almost noon, so Isabel hurried back with the shopping just as Omar and Majida were preparing to walk to the mosque. As Isabel entered the house, Faiza ran up and hugged her. The girl had just celebrated her eighth birthday and sometimes went to prayers with her parents, but she was still young and learning how to behave in the mosque. Majida was Faiza's mother, but she was Omar's second wife and just a few years older than Isabel herself. Majida was delighted with the purchases Isabel had made and asked Isabel to help with the cooking when they returned home after prayers; Isabel was glad to help with whatever Majida needed.

Omar was quite a bit older than Majida, and, while a rigid academic at heart, he was very soft-spoken and considerate. He generally wore a European-style black three-piece suit and spectacles, and he kept his grey beard quite short. He entered the cooking area to collect Majida as it was time to go to the mosque, but he stopped when he saw Isabel, evidently remembering that he needed to speak to her. He looked at her very carefully for a moment and then addressed her formally: "Madame, for your sake, Majida and I have tried to limit the number of outsiders we have invited into the house these past few months, so as to spare you any disturbance. But, as you know, I am having a guest to dinner tonight, a colleague who has just joined us at the university. He is an important scholar of Islamic law, and I've asked him to contribute an essay to a new volume I am preparing. His name is Muhammad al-Kattani. Have you heard of him, by any chance?"

"Certainly, I have," Isabel replied. "Erik mentioned him often, and I have just finished reading Sayyid al-Kattani's book regarding our duty to the descendants of the Prophet. Do you think he will agree to draft an essay for your book? That would be a wonderful addition."

"Well, yes, I hope he will, yes, although al-Kattani's writings are sometimes controversial, and in fact the Sultan's new decree has shut down our printing press at the university and there is to be a judge now to decide which books may or may not be printed, and I'm not certain whether al-Kattani's essay would be acceptable."

"You're not going to agree with such censorship, are you, Sayyid?"

"Well, no, no, certainly not, or at least not if it can be avoided, no, and my guest has some ideas for how to bypass the decree, and I have asked him to discuss with me what he has in mind."

"It would be very interesting to hear him," she said, almost too quickly. In truth, Isabel was excessively excited at the thought of being able to listen to some intelligent conversation, she had spent so many months alone in the company of the quiet Majida and the child Faiza. "Erik and I always enjoyed discussing academic issues together. Of course, I know not to question your guest, but may I be allowed to listen?"

Omar frowned and looked at his watch. The muezzin could be heard calling the faithful to prayer. "Well, hmmm, I suppose you may attend, yes. But that raises my main concern, Isabel, the real matter we need to discuss: That is, how to explain to a man who (let's be honest) is quite strict when it comes to the laws of Islam, that a pretty young widow from Sweden is living in my home."

Isabel looked down and blushed. "I've been thinking about that myself, Sayyid," she assured him. "I wouldn't mind if you want to tell him that I am a servant to Majida. Unless, perhaps, you would like me to call you 'my father'?" Isabel replied, looking up modestly.

Omar chuckled and smiled kindly: "That is a lovely suggestion, Isabel, but unfortunately you are not my child, so it would not be proper. Still, you do give me an inspired idea: I wonder whether I could be appointed as your guardian, 'sponsor' might be a better term to your way of thinking. We will have to ask the Imam this afternoon whether that is permissible. I believe it would be, I do, but only if you are serious about pursuing your religious instruction here in Fez."

"I think I am," she replied, feeling somewhat less certain than she sounded.

"Oh, yes?" Omar asked with obvious pleasure, a wide smile on his face. "Yes, yes, Allah be praised, I am very happy to hear it, Madame; that is very good news indeed."

Isabel admitted to herself, even as she prayed in the small nearby mosque that mid-day, that she was still not prepared to commit to Islam. She knelt on the wool prayer rug, and the intricate geometric and floral motif in reds and blues captured her eye. She looked around at the room at the many other women beside her and the passages of the Quran written on the walls above her. A decorative screen made of wood separated her from the domed room where the men prayed, but she could see the mihrab that indicated the direction of Mecca to which they were expected to pray. She had always believed in God, but she also believed that the warm glow in her heart she was feeling at that moment came from the simple pleasure of being welcomed into the community of the kindly people around her. She also loved to learn, and she loved to read Arabic, even if the belief part seemed sometimes rather unnecessary to her. Then she thought, this was the best she had felt for many months.

Afterwards, she and Omar spoke to the Imam. He was an older man and known for being very strict, but he was not overly discouraging. He accepted that Omar, because he of his senior position at the university, could be Isabel's sponsor as long as she was truly serious about converting to Islam, and he decreed that she could only live with Omar and Majida as long as Majida accepted responsibility for Isabel's care and conduct. If the Imam was skeptical of the young Swedish woman, she believed he meant it kindly, as a sort of challenge. She was determined to show him that she could behave properly and be a part of the "jama'ah," the gathering of people who were united in faith and practice, what Westerners would have called the "congregation." She wanted to be accepted by these people.

That evening after dinner, Isabel was permitted to sit and listen to Omar and his colleague as they talked about work; Omar introduced her merely was a Swedish widow returning to Islam under his family's tutelage. Muhammad Bin Abdul-Kabir al-Kattani was a handsome man, several

Tamanrasset

years older than Isabel but vigorous with an intense and energetic manner. She could see, in his eyes and voice, that his mind was excited by ideas and finely honed by logic, but he was also argumentative to a fault. The two men went back and forth about Omar's book and the essay al-Kattani wanted to write about the parable of Solomon's horses. They also discussed what might have prompted the Sultan's new edict on printing, and al-Kattani said that he was looking for a printing company in Spain or Portugal since there was no reason for the Sultan's edict to be obeyed outside Morocco and there was as yet no ban on the import of books printed abroad. Isabel found it a fascinating discussion, and for the first time in many months she felt a little less lonely.

* * *

Ahmad ibn Mostepha al-Haybah crouched atop a sand dune overlooking the village of Igli to carefully count the French Foreign Legionnaires standing below in the murky pre-dawn twilight. The soldiers stood in a long column, four across, awaiting the order to march. Each man carried his pack and rifle while more rode behind them on the large desert-bred mules that the French mercenaries purchased from the Berber traitors in the north. The French commander, a tall white man with sand-colored hair, was apparently the only one allowed to ride a horse. The tails of Ahmad's tan "keffiyeh," or scarf, fluttered in the morning breeze. The wind was picking up and bringing with it the smallest grade of sand. Ahmad wrapped the cloth across his nose and mouth and pushed himself back and down into the trough between the dunes where his small but muscular horse stood patiently waiting for him. Most young men could not afford to own a horse, but Ahmad's father was an important leader in the region, a Sharif who led the Ouled Abadla and had brought together a coalition of many tribes, the alliance known as the Doui-Menia. The tribes had many warriors who wanted to oppose the French invasion of the Wadi Saoura, Wadi Zousfana and Touat regions. The Sharif had entrusted Ahmad, his oldest son, with this reconnaissance, and the young man galloped proudly north to report his findings while his father stood ready with nearly four hundred tribal horsemen. These riders (most were Arab but there were Berber and Black African riders as well) had come from as far as Bechar and Figuig to join the Sharif's haraka, and most considered themselves to be Moroccan rather than Algerian. After the rainy season each year, however, they, and countless generations of their families before them, had harvested dates and grazed camels and goats on land that they owned or leased in the Wadi Saoura. Almost all had lost land, livestock, silver, or family to the French. While their tribes were now herding their animals back up to the mountains, the strongest of the men had stayed behind to join in the effort to push back against the recent French incursions. Most knew only that a large group of French soldiers would soon be marching from Igli, and the tribesmen had waited many days for the chance to attack them in the open desert.

The excruciating summer heat had given the men no relief during the short night. The riders had not camped but merely assembled loosely along the Saoura riverbed in small bands, or further northwest where the Saoura merged into the Guir river, mostly separated into family groups where they could find water for their horses. Most had flintlocks, but some had the more modern breech-loading rifles that had been showing up in the medinas; all had a sword, spear or pike honed with a lethal edge. To avoid detection, they had maintained a fair distance from the route regularly used by the Legionnaires to travel up to Taghit, a route which continued north to Beni Ounif and Aïn Séfra, and from there, it was said, all the way to the sea. The Legionnaires traveled mostly in well-armed regiments which they foolishly believed would keep them safe from attacks by the local tribes: Sharif Moulay Mostepha al-Haybah intended to show them otherwise.

A pale pink glimmer in the east grew and grew until the morning star dissolved but the Sun still lay well below the horizon just as Ahmad reached his father's encampment on the riverbank overlooking a deep pool of still water. The Sharif had a large tent made of goatskin draped over short wooden poles, but with two tall poles to raise the center high enough for men to stand. The finest sheep's wool and camel hair rugs and pillows, most with intricate geometric patterns dyed with the deep red of the madder root, were on the ground for the men to sit upon, all to create a space sufficiently prestigious for the Sharif to meet with the representatives of the tribal families: Sharif Moulay Mostepha had been preparing for several days. Ever since his tribesmen had learned that the already-depleted force of Legionnaires would be marching north, he had been able to summon many additional tribesmen to join the haraka.

As the Sharif's oldest son, Ahmad was admitted to the tent by the guards without question, and he listened respectfully as the men from the Idersa tribe argued for a dawn attack; one could sense their impatience. Sharif Moulay Mostepha, wearing a bright white turban, was seated cross-legged on a pillow slightly higher than the other men. He listened and stroked his long grey beard while some of the tribesmen agreed and others disagreed. Ahmad liked how his father gave each man a chance to explain his thinking. The Sharif countered that to defeat the Legionnaires it was necessary to catch them out on the desert plain, for if the soldiers were attacked too soon, they would simply retreat to Igli where many innocent residents would be put at risk. He further stated that no one had yet been able to force the Legionnaires out of their stone fortifications, some of which, like the fort at Igli, were equipped with cannons. Therefore, he said, the attack needed to occur after the soldiers were unable to return to Igli. Furthermore, a place had been identified in the wadi where, once the French soldiers were caught out, it would be almost impossible for them to reach a fort or summon reinforcements. That was the place where they would attack, the Sharif declared. The tribesmen nodded their agreement and praised Allah for the Sharif's wisdom. Ahmad smiled and nodded too, since he had scouted the route and selected the location of the attack himself.

Sharif Moulay Mostepha next called for Ahmad to report on the Legionnaires' numbers and equipment. Ahmad stepped forward, a tall and modest young man who was liked by all even if he was barely old enough to be permitted to join in such a dangerous enterprise. He was very much at his ease, however, as he explained exactly how many of the French mercenaries were marching and how many were riding and how they were each armed. Ahmad's report was well received, and then he was dismissed. He knew he was not yet viewed by the tribal leaders, or even by his father, as

Tamanrasset

a great warrior or leader; he was still young. And, in the past, he had perhaps advocated a bit too loudly for negotiating with the French. But the days when a peaceful resolution was possible were long past, and now Ahmad was determined to be part of the planned attack and to show his courage in battle, if Allah willed it.

At dawn as the blood-red Sun emerged over the horizon, hundreds of horsemen, who were all, by and large, Muslim, knelt together, each on his own small rug, and prayed. Ahmad was beside his father as they faced east towards Mecca and the rising Sun. Many members of his family, the Ouled Abadla, joined them. At the end, they turned and faced each other to finish the prayer: "May the peace and mercy of Allah be upon you," they said.

The Sharif smiled at his son. "I sent you to count the enemy because you are clever, Ahmad. It may yet prove that your intelligence is the best way for you to help our people. Therefore, do not attempt to prove your courage to me or anyone else today by acting rashly. Do you understand?"

"I do, my father," Ahmad replied, "but I must say the same to you. These tribesmen must not lose a leader with your wisdom."

"Thank you, my son," the Sharif replied, "but if I could not lead the tribes into battle, then I would not have the right to lead them at all. My fate today has already been written."

The time had come to move. Tribe by tribe, the riders mounted their horses and walked them slowly northeast in the early morning sunlight across the dry Wadi Saoura and up onto the rocky ridge that overlooked the Legionnaires' usual route. Ahmad found it an awesome sight to see the hundreds of Arab horsemen in line stretching back beyond sight. His heart raced with excitement.

The haraka was roughly assembled at last behind the ridge that bordered the desert plain, prepared to attack in waves as the Sharif had commanded. The breeze had died and the sun had risen to make the day extremely hot, so the riders were eager to get the attack begun. Ahmad sat upright on his horse beside his father and loaded a round into the breech of his new German-made rifle; he was an excellent marksman.

On the other side of the ridgeline, the column of Legionnaires was marching out of a lengthy rock canyon and onto the open plain; they could soon be easily cut off from their only path of retreat. Ahmad's heart raced, but his anger and hatred of the French mercenaries neutralized his fear.

With a flourish of his curved sword, the Sharif signaled for the first riders to attack. The men reared their horses and charged forward, some brandishing their swords or spears and some firing their guns into the air, screaming "Allahu Akbar!" They galloped over the ridge, their cloaks waving wildly, coming at the French soldiers like a sandstorm under the searing desert sun, bearing down upon their enemies. The eyes of the Legionnaires were seen to widen in panic, and the mercenaries appeared ready to scatter: The riders fired their rifles to feed that fear.

However, all too quickly the French commanders were able to get their men back under control. As the riders charged forward to close the gap with the French line, the disciplined Legionnaires came together in lines, their mules pulled down in front of them for cover, the gleaming bayonets on their rifles bristling in the sunlight. They held their fire until the riders came within range, and then carefully the Legionnaires began to pick off the charging riders one by one.

The riders' horses couldn't be forced to charge into the mass of French bayonets and gunfire so the riders split to either side to encircle the French. Small charges were made with sword and spear, but those with rifles did the most damage as the riders rode in a circle about the mass of foreigners to contain them and prevent their retreat. Ahmad stayed close to his father as they fired at the mercenaries who fought for the French invaders. Few of the riders and few horses in the first wave were shot, but there were wounded men on both sides.

Sharif Moulay Mostepha withdrew to gather his riders and with fresh waves repeatedly charged the enemy mass, inflicting many casualties. After some time the sun had risen high in the sky and the horses had been drained by the heat, so the Sharif began sending small groups back to the river to water their horses. It was during one such lull in the attack that the Legionnaires suddenly made a break. They were up and dragging their wounded and the few remaining unhurt mules back toward the eastern ridge of the valley, seeking cover among the scattered rocks and depressions as they returned the riders' fire. The Sharif's men continued to attack to wear down the enemy and force them out of the rocks along the ridge.

Both men and horses were suffering in the burning sun, and the day was wearing away. Ahmad could tell his father was angry and frustrated, and suddenly the Sharif galloped straight at the French. Ahmad and a dozen more riders raced after him. The Sharif was shooting wildly, and suddenly Ahmad spotted the French officer, the one whom he thought was the commander of these Legionnaires: The pale, sandy-haired man was dragging his horse up onto the rocky ridge. The Sharif raised his rifle and aimed carefully as he charged forward, firing at the last possible second before pulling up. Ahmad saw the French commander shot; he was swaying, and then he staggered and dropped to his knees; he allowed his horse to run off. As soldiers rushed to crowd around the wounded man, the French commander raised his pistol and fired back at the Sharif. The Sharif reached for the wound in his shoulder as he fell from his horse and landed hard upon the stony ground.

Ahmad was the first to reach his father. He jumped off his horse and dragged the Sharif behind a boulder where Ahmad could inspect his father's wound. There was a lot of blood, and Ahmad used his scarf to bind the wound and stop the flow. The Legionnaires began to draw off towards the north.

Ahmad called to an older rider nearby, the head of the Ouled Youssef tribe who was one of his father's most trusted followers, and instructed him to gather the tribesman and pursue the French soldiers for as long as possible. Ahmad stayed with his father. He cried and prayed to Allah asking that the Sharif not die.

* * *

Doctor Renwick Francis Villere, FRS, FBA, took a seat upon a shaded Byzantine column cast down upon the scattered remains of the Basilica of Douïmès. The sun had risen high into the midday sky, but a breeze from the sea was cool and refreshing. Ren had been working diligently all morning on his survey of the basilica which had been built by the Byzantines atop the ruins of Carthage. These lands were once the center of a great empire and a flourishing city with a population of nearly a million people. Here were the remains of Stone Age nomads, Egyptians, Numidians, Phoenicians, Romans, Byzantines, Berbers, Umayyads, and Barbary pirates, and mingled with their bones were the ashes of lost empires and the relics of the many great civilizations that had washed across north Africa. Beneath the thin veneer of soil lay the works of great sculptors, the treasures of monarchs, and the bones of human sacrifices, saints, and crusaders. To be here, in Carthage on the outskirts of Tunis in the French Protectorate of Tunisia, was to become a traveler in history. As Ren sat upon the column, he looked out towards the sea across a narrow stretch of land that had again and again contained all the richness, all the beauty, all the misery, and all the triumph of mankind.

Those who worked in such dry and dusty fields uncovering ancient civilizations were literally digging up history, establishing previously forgotten facts, and ruthlessly demolishing fanciful theories and myths. Yet as Ren well knew, interest in the science of archaeology was as varied as the shades of green across the continent of Africa. A lack of funding had long impaired the excavations at Carthage, and most of the city, like the Basilica of Douïmès, had never been carefully studied. The site remained a natural museum, uncharted and uncatalogued, with treasures so thick in the earth that not even a spadeful of dirt could be thrown aside without risking the loss of some priceless artefact.

Crossroads of the Nomad

    The Reverend Père Alfred Delattre had been in charge of the archaeological site of Carthage since his appointment by the Archbishop of Algiers in 1875, long before Tunisia had even become a French protectorate. For twenty-five years, Père Delattre had been scratching at the surface. Valuable artefacts found there were instantly removed from the soil and taken to the "museum" run by the Archdiocese. When items of rare beauty were found–items which could be ornaments for houses or adorn a museum in another country–and if such items were deemed "duplicative" (as was very often the case), they were allowed to be taken out of the country. Some were even sold privately for the benefit of the church. Such practices, although traditional in the realm of archaeology, especially when the excavation was financed by a wealthy individual or institution, were now strongly discouraged by the professional archaeological societies. The leaders in the scientific field argued that the environment of each discovery must also be considered by trained men so as to add to the complete reconstruction of the civilization of which the things unearthed are merely tangible evidence. No excavation was to be undertaken without a sufficient staff of experts to supervise and record the work. As a middle-aged Priest and missionary with no formal archaeological education, Delattre had done amazing work in Tunis, but his methods had increasingly been subject to criticism by the international societies and his stewardship of the site had been deemed unsustainable. For Ren, it was frustrating that so little had been uncovered about the ancient city of Carthage. Père Delattre had been working diligently to restore the ruins of the early Christian period, and he had done much more single-handedly than anyone might reasonably have expected, especially since

Delattre had no outside funds to draw upon other than a modest annual grant from the Institut des Antiquités in Paris. Under his purview, miracles had happened: The Basilica of St Cyprian and the Damous El Karita were all saved for posterity. Yet other eras in the long history of Carthage had frustratingly been "reserved for future study."

That's where Ren's interest lay. Doctor Renwick Villere had studied at Cambridge and completed his doctorate at University College London. He had worked for many years with his mentor, the renowned Edwards Professor of Egyptology Sir W.M. Flinders Petrie, on important excavations in Egypt and Palestine. Ren was in Luxor with Petrie in '96 when the infamous Victory Stele of Merneptah was unearthed: The stone slab contained one of the only instances in which the ancient state of Israel was clearly acknowledged in an external source. Ren, like all of Petrie's students, was indoctrinated in his mentor's exacting methodology, painstaking recordation, thoughtful evaluation of artefacts, and dedication to site preservation. Their work had revolutionized the science of archaeology and was the foundation for everything being done in places like Palestine and the Valley of the Kings in Egypt.

It had been two years since Père Delattre had first approached Ren about coming to Tunisia to be the Field Director of the Carthage archaeological site and to impose much-needed rigor to the work. It had seemed a perfect opportunity for Ren to get out from Petrie's shadow. And, indeed, Ren had significantly improved the work being done at Carthage. He had even become an ambassador for the project, traveling to England and France to lecture on the work being done at Carthage, a city which he described as "the center of a world empire" before becoming a Roman then a Vandal, a Byzantine, a Berber, and finally an Arab trading center. These lectures had helped to raise awareness of Carthage in the archaeological community.

From such trips, Ren returned to Tunisia with enthusiasm. But then it was back to work, and the work was more frustrating than ever. It was still pretty much just Ren and Delattre with whomever Ren could cheaply hire to dig. The work was slow and unremarkable. Ren was already in his mid-thirties and had not yet gained a name for himself: He had not personally made any great discovery or been the first-named author on any important academic paper. He still hoped to find something in the excavations at Carthage that would allow him to turn it into a noteworthy site and to achieve the level of personal recognition that he felt he had earned after years of solid work and important research.

The Basilica of Douïmès site was quite lovely (and fairly peaceful considering the dozen native workmen who were lazily taking measurements and digging pilot holes at Ren's direction) yet it was not a place for great discoveries. He thought about the Byzantine necropolis behind the basilica which seemed such a promising site; unfortunately, Père Delattre had reserved it for his own excavations. Ren wondered how much it would cost to drain the flooded marsh in the Salammbô district nearby where the Temple of Tanit was rumored to be located.

As he walked about and reviewed the work of the native diggers, Ren became increasingly irritated. Ordinarily, he thought, the Tunisian diggers preferred to do anything but work—they showed a greater interest than the professors in the minutest fragment of pottery and would stand around listening in awe to an academic discussion of a thing they'd never heard of before. Their picks moved with a balletic slowness of motion intended to keep even the most delicate relic safe from harm.

Ren had to remind himself again that he was lucky to have earned this position: He had no surviving family, his father had been no one of importance, he had been raised on money left for him in trust. He was lucky to have ended up in England after being orphaned, lucky to have worked with Petrie in Egypt, and lucky to be in Carthage. Nevertheless, he chafed at Père Delattre's pedantry and the slow pace of the work.

The diggers finally finished their pilot holes (merely a yard deep) and were slowly sifting the dirt to capture anything of interest. They had already confirmed for Ren that the basilica's floor marbles had been removed many centuries ago. Ren sighed. He placed his wide-brimmed hat on the stone beside him to wipe his brow with his handkerchief and then checked his pocket watch. It was nearly noon, so he allowed himself a few generous sips of gin from a silver flask he kept in his back pocket. With one more sip he was prepared to join Père Delattre for their daily luncheon. Ren stood and began to walk the short distance to the cathedral alone as he again considered the nearby marsh. Could it be drained? How much would it cost? Would anyone give him the necessary funds?

St. Louis Cathedral, only recently completed, was a magnificent Catholic edifice of mostly red brick, and it was connected by walkways to a small building behind which had become the local museum with laboratories for artefact analysis and offices; there was also a seminary there where

Ren lived like a monk. Over a luncheon of boiled chicken, rice, herbs, and red wine, served on an old oak table, Père Delattre ate his lunch as Ren watched. Delattre was lethargic: He had no ambition but to spend his final years parsing through the tombs of early Christians. He was already grey haired, and his face was tanned and etched by the sun after many years of slow shuffling in the dust of Carthage. As they ate, Ren felt his heart pounding and his leg would not be still.

"I've been reading Audollent, you know," Ren said, "his newly published work, 'Carthage Romaine'—are you familiar with it?"

"I've only just received my copy from Docteur Audollent and haven't begun to read it yet."

"There's a story I found fascinating, of a Roman Carthaginian in the First Century named Bassus."

"Tell me, please," Delattre asked quietly while sipping his soup.

"It was in the year 65, a clever Carthaginian Roman, Bassus was his name, suggested to emperor Nero a way to vastly enrich the treasury of Rome. At that time, Nero's coffers were almost exhausted (his manner of living was such, as you know, that he urgently needed more funds all the time). Bassus reported that he had found gold in a cavern near Carthage and he was close to locating the infamous treasures of Dido, the founder and first queen of Carthage. Nero listened rapturously and agreed to fit Bassus out with an entire expedition including some three hundred soldiers to dig wherever Bassus directed. When they reached the site, (somewhere in Tunisia, we have no idea where) the soldiers did not supply enough labor and the civil population was also drawn upon. Months and months passed, but all the work and vast expenses were in vain; no treasure was found. Bassus returned to Rome, so the story runs, to report his lack of progress to Nero. The emperor became so enraged by disappointment (and was so seriously in need of funds) that he angrily sent Bassus back to Tunisia to try again. Only, this time, Nero sent a number of additional soldiers who were instructed to watch over Bassus and his men, to keep them at work, and, failing success, Bassus and all his men were to be crucified. They found nothing. The legend credits Bassus with committing suicide during a fit of severe stress, but the workers were all put to death. Such was the science of archaeology at the time."

"I've met Docteur Audollent, and I very much doubt that he wrote so colorful a tale."

"I admit to some embellishment of the story. I don't suppose you've found Dido's treasure in all your years here in Carthage, have you, Father? And hidden it away in the museum somewhere?"

"Dido's treasure? No—I fear it is from the time of myths. But you would like to seek for the treasure yourself, I suppose?" Delattre asked, baiting Ren.

"As you say, it is only a myth," Ren replied casually, "not that a bit of treasure wouldn't ease some of our constant financial constraints."

"Alas, we find many more artefacts than treasures."

"Still, such ancient tales, like pearls, are often founded upon a grain of truth. But as for treasures, I find much more credibility in the stories regarding the Emeralds of the Garamantes," Ren observed. The Garamantes were an ancient people descended from prehistoric Berber tribes who held power among the nomadic northern Sahara people for nearly two thousand years. "No one has found emeralds in this part of the world nor identified any plausible source for them, but the existence of the Emeralds of the Garamantes is noted in multiple texts from several different civilizations."

"Indeed, and I agree the Emeralds did likely exist; I know of two ancient eyewitness accounts which mention them. Undoubtedly, they would be priceless, but I very much doubt they will ever be found, and only then if the Lord wills it," Delattre intoned.

* * *

Sharif Moulay Mostepha was alive, thanks be to Allah. The wound to his shoulder was healing, but he had lost a lot of blood and was still very weak. He lay in bed asleep, covered with a thin wool blanket in a cool, dark room. Ahmad sat beside him. They were in a small townhouse belonging to the Sharif in Abadla, a town on the Guir River about sixty kilometers northwest of the place where the attack upon the French Foreign Legionnaires had begun.

After the Sharif was wounded, Ahmad stayed to care for his father through the night and had not joined the pursuit of the French mercenaries to Taghit. In the early morning, after the attack was abandoned and the riders returned, his fellow tribesmen helped Ahmad lift his father onto his horse and bring him gently west to the Guir river where they rested until sundown. After dark, they traveled onwards, all through the night, to reach Abadla by dawn the next morning. Ahmad had perhaps not proven himself to be a leader during the attack as he had intended, but his father would live and everyone agreed that Ahmad had displayed both courage and skill in the front line of the attack on the French mercenaries.

After news of the Doui-Menia's action spread, Sharif Mostepha's reputation rose. Men came from all over the region to show him their respect. The attack was never intended as a battle to be won, Ahmad would tell them, but rather to show the terrible price the French would have to pay again and again for their incursions into the Doui-Menia land, and in this they had succeeded. While there had been losses on both sides, the tribesmen had fared better than most had expected: Many had been wounded, but few were dead. While Sharif Moulay Mostepha rested and greeted visitors over the next few days, Ahmad rode to Igli and Taghit to gather information. There was a great deal of talk about whether the French might attempt a counterattack, but Ahmad didn't think it was likely: The surviving Doui-Menia riders were scattered over a wide area and difficult to find. No one would willingly identify them. More importantly, most of the riders had returned to their homes in Morocco, and no one believed the French were prepared to engage in a large-scale invasion of Morocco for the sole purpose of revenge. Yet, that was exactly where things had begun to get complicated.

Ahmad shook his father's good shoulder. "Asalamu alaikom, my father; I apologize for waking you," he said. It was just after midday. "There is a man named Abu Abdulah who has arrived to speak with you: He says he was sent by the Sultan."

The Sultan, Abd al-Aziz, was the ruler of Morocco, but he did not have strict control over every part of his country.

Certain regions were largely autonomous, and these included most of the areas south and east of the Atlas mountains, including the Wadi Guir, Wadi Saoura and Touat areas that Sharif Moulay Mostepha now controlled.

The Sharif yawned and rubbed his cheek. "Wa alaikom salaam, my son. Abu Abdulah, yes, I know of him; he was probably sent by Ba Ahmad, the Grand Wizier," he said angrily. "He always questions when the Southern tribes act without consulting the Sultan first."

Ahmad helped his father, who was still struggling with his wound, to get up, and servants came in to dress the Sharif. He asked his son: "Have you learned anything about how the invaders will respond?"

"The French soldiers we attacked still haven't left the fort at Taghit and additional troops have come down from Sidi Bel Abbès to reinforce the forts at both Taghit and Igli," Ahmad told him, "but, Allah is gracious, they are not as numerous as we would expect to see if the French were planning to launch an attack on every town along the border with Morocco. However, we must expect the size of the garrisons at the French forts to be increased permanently: The French are determined to stay."

"As long as they stay inside their stone walls, we will not need to kill any more of them," the Sharif replied.

They found Abu Abdulah, the short well-dressed Arab envoy of the Sultan, in the lush inner courtyard of the house and exchanged greetings.

"We had heard that you were mortally wounded or dead, Sayyid," the envoy said. "Allah be praised for sparing your life. And it is a pleasure to meet your oldest son; peace be with you, Ahmad. I have been sent by the Sultan, and there is much I need to tell you. May we be seated?"

"If you wish it, although, when you say that the Sultan sent you, I know you mean the Grand Wizier, since he is the Regent during the Sultan's minority. And I already know what the Regent would say to me," the Sharif said accusingly.

"I am sorry to inform you, then, that Ba Ahmad passed away quite recently; there was a cholera outbreak in Meknes. Rather than replace Ba Ahmad, the Sultan has claimed his majority and no longer has a Regent."

The Sharif appeared saddened and expressed his remorse at the death of the Grand Wizier, although his son felt he was too obviously just being polite; his father had never been fond of the man.

"Well, then, perhaps we should sit; I can see you have much news to share with us," the Sharif said. He clapped his hands and servants brought floor cushions and rugs, as well as low tables and mint tea. A space was prepared in the courtyard, surrounded by green plants and a small pool of water. They were shaded from the sun in the courtyard, and although the air was hot and dry, it was fresher than any of the rooms inside the house. "Come then, please, be seated, but be succinct for I am still recovering my strength," the Sharif requested.

"I'll get right to the point, then; yes: Sultan Abd al-Aziz bin Hassan sends you his greetings and respect, and he wishes you to be informed that he has received strong protests from the French Ambassador. France very strongly objects to the recent intentional and organized attack by so-called 'criminals' upon French soldiers in Algeria. The

Sultan, of course, denies that any such actions, if they did occur, were authorized by the Sultan or his government, and those acts, if they are proven to have been perpetrated in Algeria by Moroccans, are most heartily condemned by the Sultan."

"I am not a criminal," the Sharif objected.

"Nevertheless, you are now deemed a criminal in Algeria by the French government, and to that characterization, in Algeria where the Sultan has no jurisdiction, he has no power to object."

"And does the Sultan now serve France instead of his own people? I grant you it has been long since the Sultan pretended to exert any dominion over the parts of Morocco which fall on this side of the Atlas mountains, but I assure you: You are in Morocco, not Algeria."

"It has only been four years since the Sultan brought an army south to occupy Marrakesh and quell the rebellion in the Atlas Mountains," the envoy replied.

"The Sultan came to collect taxes because Madani El Glaoui threatened a revolution unless he was paid. Without Madani El Glaoui as Qaid of the High Atlas, Sultan Abd al-Aziz would lose control of an entire third of his country. Every honor and beneficence have been bestowed upon the Glaoui family, and their allegiance has been bought with gold, guns, ammunition, and cannon. The Sultan ignores the Tafilalt, Guir, Saoura, Zousfana and Touat regions because he believes his family's ancestry here ensures our fidelity. But now the French have marched into the Wadi Zousfana and occupy Taghit. They have marched into the Wadi Saoura and occupy Igli and Beni Abbès. Their general has marched soldiers into the Touat region, and they occupy In

Salah. These are all areas that traditionally have made obeisance to the Doui-Menia. Would the Sultan prohibit his own people, even those like myself who are descended from the daughter of the Prophet, would the Sultan bar us from protecting our rights and managing our own affairs in Morocco south and east of the Atlas if he will not?"

"The Sultan has sent me to inform you that, after this most recent attack, he has given his permission to the French government to maintain peace and security in the Zousfana and Saoura valleys, including the Touat region, and as far west as the Guir river. The Sultan has decreed that the French soldiers are no longer to be attacked or molested."

The Sharif and Ahmad were both shocked.

"We are to be governed by the French?" The Sharif asked, biting his words.

"No, not governed, no, but it has been decreed that local leaders, such as yourself, will meet with the French Deputy Governor of Algeria in Taghit later this month to discuss the new arrangement. If you choose to attend that meeting, I recommend you come with a better explanation for your injury than having been shot during the attempted massacre of the French Legionnaires."

The Sharif seemed ready to explode at this insult. Ahmad stood and rested a comforting hand on his father's shoulder. "My father is a religious man, not a politician," he said to the envoy. "It is difficult for us to understand. Can you explain why the Sultan has made this arrangement with the French?"

The envoy shook his head. "Were I to speculate as to the reasons, I might suppose that the Sultan is concerned that he lacks a military force sufficient to secure his country from both foreign and domestic enemies. He must collect taxes to train and arm soldiers, yet he cannot collect taxes without first obtaining soldiers to protect the tax collectors. There is only one answer to this conundrum: He must borrow money with a promise to repay from future taxes. Who will loan the Sultan the money: Great Britain, Germany, France? In the newspaper it was said recently that an arrangement has been made for French banks to loan the Sultan more than seven million Francs. Very generous of the French, don't you agree?"

"So the Sultan set up an auction to sell us, and we have been bought by the French, is that your theory?" Ahmad asked.

"I believe the Sultan would say: If the French want to waste their money and their men to preserve the peace in this wretched wasteland, they are welcome to do so," the envoy replied, "as long as they continue to recognize the Sultan's sovereignty, and it is all the better if France simultaneously gives the Sultan the means to keep the 'Makhzen,' his government, under his control, pay his debts, and maintain peace in his country."

After the envoy left, Ahmad helped his father return to his bedroom to rest.

"I am exhausted by this terrible news. What do you think, Ahmad, my son?" The Sharif asked, as he pulled the blanket over his legs.

"I don't think it changes anything, my father," Ahmad replied.

"No?" The Sharif asked, genuinely surprised.

"No," Ahmad said plainly as he again sat next to the bed. "We already knew that the Sultan has no political authority in this region, and now he has admitted it. He believes he has given authority to the French, but he had no authority to give them. You are the only power that the people recognize between the Guir and Zousfana rivers. It seems to me that the French will only ever have as much control of this region as you grant to them. They just don't know it yet."

The Sharif nodded. "You must come with me to Taghit for this meeting to which I have been invited, my son. Peace be upon you."

Ahmad sat beside his father and watched as he struggled to get into a comfortable position and fall asleep. Ahmad believed his father was a great man, that he had shown how different tribes, even those that had long-held disputes, could be brought together to address a serious threat like the French. The haraka had done exactly what the Sharif had expected. As long as his father held the respect of the tribes, they would be bound together. That gave them power. It was the Sultan who needed the Doui-Menia, not the other way around, for how else could the Sultan maintain his territorial claims to the southeastern half of Morocco without the support of his people. There were some who said that a jihad should be declared against the French, but only the Sultan could declare a holy war in Morocco. Abd al-Aziz would not do so, yet a war had begun, whatever one chose to call it.

* * *

Isabel had spent the morning reading and playing with Faiza, and then had put on her hijab and gone to the mosque for prayers: The Imam had made it clear that if she wasn't actively preparing for her "reversion" to Islam, as the Muslims call it, there would need to be a serious discussion about her situation in Fez. It was unclear just what the Imam expected, but Isabel didn't want to cause trouble for Omar and Majida or do anything to harm their reputation. She tried to pray often at the mosque to let the neighbors and the Imam see her, and she tried to engage in conversations there. She was still working on being accepted in the community.

Isabel had some free time before her meeting that afternoon with the Alima at her madrasa, so she walked through the medina, greeting those she knew, and visited the bookseller's souk to admire the leather-bound volumes on sale there—they were much too expensive for her to buy. She next stopped to look at the intricate and beautifully decorated fountain in the Place al-Najjarine, glittering with blue and green ceramics, and then walked around the great walls of the Royal Palace of Fez, the Dar al-Makhzen. The gorgeous high walls were decorated with Arabic texts from the Quran. Majestic white-turbaned figures squatted near the gates, their pale faces ringed with curling beards.

Isabel stopped to admire the massive bronze gates of the palace, three or four times the height of a grown man. It just so happened as she passed that Court attendants in white robes and crimson-peaked fezzes were emerging from the central gate. Isabel stood with a throng of onlookers rapt as trumpets sounded and a band of shrill pipes and drums burst into song. Banners and spear-bearers followed. Black African grooms led horses saddled and caparisoned in colorful silks and gold embroideries. Then came the Sultan himself, a young though stately figure dressed all in white on a white horse trapped in green and gold. A great flat parasol of red velvet and gold was held over his head while beside him attendants waved white scarves to keep away the flies. The Sultan was followed by his Wiziers, portly gentlemen swathed in soft white hanging garments, and then more Court attendants and slaves. As the Sultan passed into the square, the public stood stupidly in awe of the obscene display of wealth. The procession approached a waiting delegation from the British consulate. The Sultan advanced, accompanied only by his Grand Wizier and two attendants. The British Consul bowed, the Grand Wizier presented the Consul to the Sultan, the Sultan bid him welcome. The Consul handed over his credentials, wrapped in silk. The Sultan took them, holding the "infidel's" papers between the folds of his cloak rather than touching them with his bare hand. Then the Sultan turned his horse and retired calmly into the palace amid the booming of cannon and a shrill blast of music. It was a magnificent show which, Isabel was told, was repeated at least once a week.

Her meeting at the madrasa was to discuss the books she was reading. Isabel had decided to learn Arabic while still in Sweden when her husband, then a student at Lund University, told her that he was doing his doctoral work on the relationship of early Islam to Judaism and Christianity. She wanted to help him with his research, and learning the language of Arabic had come easily to her. Indeed, she felt the writings were beautiful to look at as well as poetic. While she became an avid reader of Arabic, there were unfortunately few texts available to her in Sweden. It was Isabel who had first suggested a trip to Morocco so Erik could conduct research at the most famous Islamic university in the world. That suggestion had eventually led to a generous grant for Erik to live and study at the university for up to two years. It also meant, she often reminded herself, that it was her fault they had ended up in Fez where Erik had gotten ill and died.

Her husband would bring home books from the university library for Isabel to read, but it was the madrassa's library, and its accessibility to women, which had initially drawn her to the school, even before Erik had left her. Yet, in the few weeks since she had become a student there, Isabel had already read every book in the building. She entered the long, interior main hall where students listened to their teachers read from the Quran, the holy book which contained the code of laws, both religious and civil, that formed the rules of Islamic life. That afternoon, there were only a handful of boys in their white shirts and pants, wearing white knit caps, sitting barefoot on mats reading very silently. No doubt they were being detained after class as a punishment. One of the boys could not resist looking up at the woman who had entered the room. He was a large boy, fourteen or fifteen years old, whom Isabel knew was named Driss. He looked at her with a low level of voracity, as if he would like to eat her. Isabel shuddered and quickly passed through to the study room beside the main hall.

An Alima is an Islamic scholar, specifically a woman with an extensive education in Islamic subjects, and the Alima at Isabel's madrasa, Mu'mena bint Hassan, was an elderly and highly-respected scholar who only worked with the older students, those who were quite advanced and didn't require discipline. Isabel found Mu'mena sitting at a table in the study room and greeted her: "Asalamu alaikom."

"Wa alaikom salaam," the thin, elderly woman replied as she stood.

Ordinarily Isabel would kiss another woman on the cheek as part of her greeting, but the Alima was so old and so severe that Isabel was afraid to approach her.

The woman looked at Isabel piercingly for a moment. "Well, Madame Pedersen," the old woman began, "I have in the past assisted other women to return to Islam, but, of course, those women were born here in Morocco. I have never worked with a woman who came to us from a northern, Christian country. Is it difficult for you, being here in Fez?"

"I am trying to learn the right ways, Madame," Isabel said.

"Yes, I know you are, and you are doing admirably. Omar and Majida are taking care of you and looking after your lessons, yes? You spend a great deal of time with their daughter, Faiza, do you?"

"Yes; it's a small way for me to assist Majida."

"I have several thoughts about that," Mu'mena replied somewhat icily. "Firstly, since you are not yet a professed Muslim nor adequately trained, you can only do harm to the girl by teaching her bad behavior and bad thoughts."

"But I am only playing with her, in the house," Isabel objected.

"Secondly," Mu'mena continued undisturbed, "as you know, we have no more books in our library here at the madrasa for you to read, but you are a very bright young woman and your studies should be encouraged. Maybe one day you could become a fine Alima yourself, if you choose to make that your path. Have you considered that?"

"I ... well, no, that hadn't occurred to me. My husband was the scholar."

"When he made you his wife, you also took on his work as your own, didn't you? But I merely mean that with adequate study you could improve your understanding of Islam and perhaps become a source of wisdom to women in the community, perhaps even spread the wisdom of Allah in your home country."

"Thank you, Madame," Isabel replied modestly.

The Alima became suddenly impatient. "We need to find you additional material to read, do we not? You know we are just around the corner from the university."

"Women may not study at the university," Isabel countered.

"Third, your period of mourning is over. You must become more engaged in the community outside of the Benayoun house if you are to stay in Fez and return to Islam, as you say is your intent. Is that truly your intention?"

"It is, yes," Isabel stated flatly.

"I happen to know a faqih, a scholar of Islamic Law, at the university who needs a reader to assist him with his work."

"Are you suggesting that I apply for work at the university, Madame?" Isabel sputtered in surprise. "What an idea! Is this scholar someone you know well and trust?"

"You would be working for the scholar, not the university, but in that capacity you would be given access to the university library and a private space there to read and write notes. The scholar is someone I know very well, and I've been told that you've met him: Muhammad al-Kattani."

"Oh," Isabel said, somewhat deflated. "Would an important man like that want to hire someone like me."

"You did similar work for your late husband, didn't you?"

"Well, yes, I did, but—"

"It's the same work. In any event, I have already arranged for you to have the position and you are to begin immediately. It will get you out of the Benayoun house; in my opinion, you have been spending too much time with their daughter. At the university, you will meet others and make new acquaintances. Sayyid al-Kattani will treat you with respect. If you mean to return to Islam, as you claim, then you must live as a Muslim. If not here in Fez, where would you go—Stockholm? Are there many Muslims in Stockholm?" She chuckled.

Isabel stared at the Alima a full minute, her mouth ajar. She was shocked that someone had simply told her what she was going to do, but at the same time she was relieved that she did not have to figure it out. Moreover, Isabel had no income of her own and could not rely on Omar's generosity forever; she needed to make money, especially if she was ever to leave Omar's house. "I want the position, yes," she said. "I want to stay in Fez. Your guidance is deeply appreciated, and the logic of your arguments is uncontestable. 'Baraka laho fiki;' may God bless you, madame."

"Whether I am blessed or not will now depend on your behavior, Madame Pedersen," the Alima replied. Isabel understood her to mean: "Do not embarrass me."

Crossroads of the Nomad

* * *

The sun was rising over the sand dunes to the east of the massive French fort atop the ridge overlooking Taghit. Although the new walls of the fort were solid and high, reconstructed within the past year by native workers overseen by Legionnaires, the interior of the fort contained old wood buildings and blockhouses that were centuries old. Sergent Demoreau stood upon the wide brick battlement, from which the entire valley could be viewed. To the west lay the river, the village, and the hamada, dry flat ground that stretched as far as the eye could see; to the east were the great sand dunes, the ergs, which came from across the great desert. Demoreau cast his grey eyes over the crest of the dunes for any sign of movement. The Legionnaires who had just come on watch were dependable men, but the Sergent still wanted to take a look for his own peace of mind. The desert had a way of making men see things that weren't there, and just as often ignore things that were.

Demoreau stood upright, his face bearing a questioning or skeptical expression, his cheeks freshly shaven, his sandy brown hair disguising a few new streaks of grey. His Legion uniform was clean but unquestionably aged: The worn brass buttons and gold braid shone on his mended blue jacket, and his formal red trousers (worn because of the visiting government official) had cuts and holes that were sewn and patched; his gun straps and leather belt gleamed, and his kepi, the traditional round box-like cap in the light blue shade worn by the Mounted Companies of the Legion, was placed at an angle on his head. He was a stern and demanding Sergent, but with the intelligence to understand the difference between a leader and a bully. He had been known only as "Sergent Demoreau" to both enlisted men and officers alike for many years.

Legionnaire Fedir Andreev, who had carried Caporal Dupont and was among the last to withdraw into the fort during the attack, had been promoted to Legionnaire First Class. A great, hulking man, he stood watch on the battlements as Demoreau approached.

"Your report, Legionnaire?" Demoreau inquired. By asking for information, the Sergent was granting permission to his subordinate to speak.

"No sign of those pigs, Sergent," Andreev reported; even after nearly five years in the Legion, his speech was still heavily inflected with his native accent. "No one could move within a dozen kilometers of this fort without us seeing, and the townsfolk are still quiet as mouses." He gestured back towards the town which lay spread across the valley to the west of the fort. The entire town, every building, was made of the same tan clay found in the banks of the Zousfana river, with one square tower slightly higher in the center, the mosque. All still lay in shadowy darkness. On the other side of the town was the river, lined with palm trees and vegetation that, to the south, became denser and darker, finally becoming the valuable date palm groves.

"I hope they do shoot at us," said the new Caporal, Hans Mueller, short, burly, and flat-faced, as he walked over to join them. He had come with the reinforcements that had been sent from Sidi Bel Abbès. "Their aim is shit, it wastes ammunition, and it gives away their position."

Andreev replied: "I had always believed the guns they've got were poor, like flintlocks and garbage a hundred years old, but I was surprised to see that many now have newer rifles, and there was no lack of ammunition."

"Those devils have no fear of death," Mueller added.

"It shows you just how valuable this land is," Demoreau said with a sweeping gesture to the mountains of sand looming nearby, "and the wonderful trade that goes through these oases up to Aïn Séfra, the delicious dates, camel skins and whatnot ... well, it's awfully hard to put a cash value on that kind of thing, I suppose." He looked at Mueller and Andreev and could see in their expressions that they understood Demoreau's understated sarcasm. Yet he reminded both men: "But none of that matters to us: We're Legionnaires. We've been told to protect this fort, this route, and the people who use it. That's what we're going to do, yes?"

"Yes, Sergent," the two Legionnaires replied crisply.

Mueller asked: "If you don't mind, Sergent, is that why that fat French bureaucrat downstairs came from Algiers? Just to talk about trade?" It was highly unusual to have a French official of such importance come to a place like Taghit. The Legionnaires all knew that natives in the area had been invited to meet with the man from the Governor's office, but they expected it was for the French government to lay down the law and tell the locals who was in charge now.

"You know they don't tell us Sergents anything, Caporal," Demoreau barked, "and anyway there is no damn reason why I would tell you. Get back on watch, both of you. Rassemblement à huit heures."

"Yes, Sergent," the two Legionnaires replied. The Sergent turned and descended the steps.

In the aftermath of the attack, Demoreau had remained in command of the Legionnaires inside the fort for a week. He was an able commander and notorious for his exactitude when it came "le règlement," although tempered by many years of serving in French Algeria. Nevertheless, he was relieved when Capitaine Mitterand arrived with reinforcements and took command of the fort and all those inside it. Mitterand was as lean and vicious an officer as the French Foreign Legion could muster, and Demoreau knew him by reputation as a hateful and dangerous man. But, there were limits to what Demoreau himself wanted to manage. Twenty odd years in the Legion had taught him his own limitations. Furthermore, the years of sun and heat had taken a toll on his body and his mind. It was really for the best that the Company was stationed in Taghit where the constant demands of the service and threat of enemy activity could occupy his thoughts. But, after the reinforcements arrived, two more weeks had passed. In that time, three more men had died of wounds sustained during the attack. There had been little news from the locals and only vague rumors about the tribesmen who had attacked the Legionnaires. Efforts to find the riders had been called off after two Legionnaires failed to return from a search of the nearby caves. They were found alive but with their abdomens cut open and filled with sand and camel dung. They thankfully did not survive for long.

The Legionnaires wanted to strike back, and there was constant talk among the men about where the attacking tribesman might be found. As a result, the Capitaine was forced to order that no one leave the fort without specific instructions. Then a communique arrived from the

Governor's office stating that no reprisals or punishments were to be exacted either in Taghit or Igli, nor were the attackers, believed to be Moroccan, to be pursued: The French Minister of the Colonies in Paris had expressed the government's firm position that under no circumstances was Morocco to be "invaded."

The Legionnaires were incensed. Many spoke of going after the tribesmen regardless of orders: Some of the attackers were rumored to be in Bechar, a large town nearby in Morocco, and several Legionnaires said they were willing to hunt down the riders even if leaving Algeria was deemed desertion. Demoreau knew better than to offer himself for such an unauthorized mission, and, although he sympathized with those who wished to go, he had had to put a stop to it.

After leaving Mueller and Andreev, Demoreau descended to take his morning coffee: Perhaps the only evidence of his age was the Sergent's absolute intolerance of any change to the schedule that might imperil his morning beverage. He strode into the empty mess hall inside the fort and went directly to the urn where, on his instructions, "Le Jus," boiled coffee grounds, were kept simmering day and night. He dipped a tin cup into the urn; the coffee was hot enough to scald. He sat alone at a table to sip, oblivious to the heat of the cup. His sunburnt face showed none of his emotions, assuming he had any. His eyes were open but not looking at anything. He hummed a little piece by Schubert, "Die Forelle," the quintet variation.

The Sergent planned to conduct a brief inspection prior to the morning assembly; he was still acclimating the men to their new Capitaine. All the Legionnaires of the 6th

Mounted Company who survived the attack remained his responsibility since Kurtz was still in the infirmary. The new Lieutenant for Demoreau's Section, Hansen, was an inconsistent disciplinarian, and Demoreau hated to see any man punished for infractions that could easily have been avoided.

As Demoreau entered the barracks, someone shouted "Garde-à-Vous!" and the tightly crowded Legionnaires who had been polishing their brass and leather with spit and candle wax quickly jumped to the foot of their cots and stood at attention with hands at their sides and feet together. Most of the men were at least partially dressed; all had remembered to wear their red trousers with short leather puttees and the long blue sash wrapped around their waist. Some already wore their blue coat and their brodequins, the heavy hob-nailed boots which were worn and repaired and worn again and again and handed down from one Legionnaire to another for decades. Demoreau had been with some of these Legionnaires for the twenty months since they had left their Second Regiment barracks up in Saïda. In this room and the one next door were the seventy-eight Legionnaires who remained of that original Company. There had been casualties in Touat, Igli, and Taghit, as well as a few sent to the Penal Battalion and a couple who had gone en pompe. The Sergent would be comfortable saying, if pressed, that those who remained were among the most dependable men with whom he had served. Unfortunately, many of them were also nearing the end of their term of enlistment.

Having corrected some small infractions, he reached the end of the hall and turned to face the men: "Rassemblement à huit heures," he said clearly. "Oui, Sergent," the Legionnaires shouted in reply. There were a hundred languages spoken in the Foreign Legion. French was, of course, the language of official business, but almost no one spoke French at any other time. Demoreau gave orders in French, but ordinarily he spoke English. Most people supposed English was the Sergent's native language, although it did no good to think about where a man came from. It only made you think about what a Legionnaire's past might be, and what might have forced him into La Legion. Certainly, a Legionnaire could tell another man about his past if he chose, but questions were never appropriate. As Demoreau understood it, the original idea behind the Foreign Legion, when it was founded in 1831, was to give a man who had committed some error in judgment a chance to rehabilitate himself. No questions were asked when a man enlisted (or, if he was asked, the answers were not expected to be truthful), and most Legionnaires served under a false name, a "nom de guerre." It made no difference where you came from or the color of your skin. Some Legionnaires had served previously in another army but, for one reason or another, could not continue in that service any longer; they chose to become professional soldiers. A few were adventurers who sought action in undiscovered lands, and some were impoverished and saw the Legion as a final opportunity. One or two might even admit to a broken heart. But there were also murderers, rapists, embezzlers, thieves, and forgers evading the law. All were equal in the Foreign Legion. They would march night and day. If a Legionnaire was dog tired and dropped by the side of the road, he would be left there, even if he happened to be in the desert, in hostile territory, miles

Tamanrasset

from any human habitation; they were not very sentimental about a man in the Legion and would let him die without a single scruple. Men would go mad with le cafard, and some would attempt to desert only to be murdered by the Arabs, Berbers, or Tuaregs, whoever caught them first, or the deserter would be recaptured and sent to the Penal Battalion or, in a worst-case situation, across the ocean to the horrifying jungle prisons of French Guiana. But a Legionnaire always knew where he stood in the Foreign Legion—all that mattered was how he conducted himself in the moment, that he obeyed orders and served with honor, that he was dedicated *only* to the Legion for the entire five-year term of enlistment. Some even re-enlisted, but many who did not have anywhere else to go.

In the large central courtyard of the fort, the soldiers formed a large inward-facing square two lines deep, the Legionnaires on one side and the Tirailleurs on the other. In the middle, Demoreau stood with other officers and NCOs, Lieutenant Hansen, Capitaine Mitterand, and the French bureaucrat wearing a grey woolen suit as well as the white silk robes of an Arab. Demoreau, as the senior (standing) Sergent in the fort, took the roll call from each Caporal, and Lieutenant Hansen then read the change of the guard for the day and the result of the medical examinations of the soldiers who had reported themselves ill. Then the Capitaine, a thin balding man in a tight uniform and shining black boots, stepped forward.

In a clear loud voice, the Capitaine stated: "Those on guard duty within the fort today are expected to remain strictly at their stations, and all patrols outside the fort are now cancelled. All Legionnaires not on guard duty are confined to barracks until further notice, effective immediately."

The Legionnaires looked at each other in confusion and began mumbling. "Garde-à-vous!" Demoreau shouted angrily, and the men resumed their previous silent and formal demeanor. Capitaine Mitterand's order meant that, except for a handful of men, every soldier was to be hidden away. Not a word was mentioned of the French bureaucrat who was already blotting copious perspiration from his thick pink face with his handkerchief. "Lieutenant, dismiss the men," the Capitaine stated coolly.

"Dismiss the men, Sergent," Hansen told Demoreau.

"Congédiés," Demoreau barked, and the men immediately broke out of their lines and began shuffling towards the barracks. There was a lot of quiet grumbling.

"Sergent Demoreau." The Sergent turned and saw that Capitaine Mitterand was looking at him with his piercing brown eyes. Demoreau stood at attention and saluted. "Oui, mon Capitaine," he replied crisply. The Capitaine's expression was neither cold nor hot, as if Demoreau barely even registered in the officer's consciousness.

"I am obliged to inform you, Sergent," the Capitaine stated with obvious distaste, "that you have been promoted to Sergent-Major once again."

"Thank you, mon Capitaine," Demoreau replied placidly.

"How many times is that, now?"

"This is the third time I have been promoted to Sergent-Major, Capitaine," he answered.

"Let us hope this time it sticks," the Capitaine said nonchalantly. Demoreau hoped he would not remain under Mitterand's command for long. The Capitaine continued: "As the senior NCO in the fort today, it is your duty to accompany Deputy Governor Cayard this morning to the home of a local merchant. You will select two additional Legionnaires to accompany you. The three of you will say nothing and do no more than strictly required to ensure that the Deputy Governor returns here safely when he has finished this ridiculous meeting. Is that understood, Sergent-Major?"

"Oui, mon Capitaine," Demoreau replied. It was not often that Demoreau had to interact with an officer with whom he had some history, but he had no recollection of ever having crossed Capitaine Mitterand. As long as he continued to properly fulfill his duties, Demoreau didn't care what the officers thought of him.

The Capitaine turned to Deputy Governor Cayard: "As you requested, Deputy, there are three Legionnaires to accompany you to your meeting at the merchant's house. This is Sergent-Major Demoreau, the senior NCO in Taghit. I must again voice my opposition to you attending this meeting without one of my officers present, but I have at least ensured that there will be no display of force or threatening conduct by the French soldiers here today."

Cayard was still wiping his face with a handkerchief: "Thank you, Capitaine, but, as I indicated, these men are trained to follow orders, and that is all I require. Sergent-Major, please fetch the others, and we'll be off."

Demoreau, now Sergent-Major Demoreau, found Andreev and another Legionnaire of the Sixth, an Austrian named Nachmann, and explained quickly what they were doing. Cayard would only permit the Legionnaires to bring their rifles as long as they promised to keep them slung on their shoulders. The three Legionnaires and Cayard then left the fort and walked calmly down the road into the town of Taghit. The morning was still young, but the heat was already excessive, easily over 100° Fahrenheit. The tan clay buildings all looked like ovens.

As they entered the town, Cayard stopped to ask for directions; he spoke Arabic fluently. An elderly local man pointed and led the group up the street and turned left and then took several more turns. Demoreau paid close attention. He didn't care to rely on Cayard to obtain directions back to the fort. If they did have to beat a retreat and got lost in the maze of alleys, the portly Deputy Governor would surely be the first to die, and that was something Demoreau definitely did not want on his record.

The group eventually arrived at a large wood door painted red. They knocked, and the door opened immediately: They were expected. There was a lengthy discussion in Arabic in the doorway. Cayard finally said: "Sergent-Major, you please come inside with me and tell your men to wait here beside the door. Everything will be fine."

Demoreau gave the order, then he and Cayard entered and were led through a short corridor to a large, sunny courtyard lined with potted lemon trees, the floor was white stone but the walls were covered with mosaic tiles. A dozen men who had already arrived awaited them. Cayard stepped forward and bowed to the men and immediately began to chit-chat as if they were all old friends.

Demoreau was surprised: He had expected a huge meeting with dozens of locals. The twelve men, elders of the region, wore pleased expressions and acted respectfully;

they each wore a colorful turban and a princely bisht, a more formal outer cloak, decorated with beads or gold and silver filigree. There were a few younger men as well; they generally wore a tarboosh or fez. The Sergent-Major immediately recognized two of the men present. One, an older man with his arm in a sling was introduced as the Sharif of the Doui-Menia. Demoreau knew him as the very man who had murdered Lieutenant Claussen, and here he was still protecting the shoulder where he had been shot by the Lieutenant. The second man Demoreau recognized was a younger man—he had been at the attack too and was probably the Sharif's son. With them was a third man, another relative of the Sharif's most likely, who wore expensive clothes and had a Western gold pocket watch. He and the Sharif seemed to dislike each other; they were arguing and the young man was trying to mediate, without success.

The others attending, mostly Arabs and Berbers, had come from surrounding villages, but there were also men from Béni Abbès, Figuig, Bechar and Aïn Séfra. Cayard and the men took their seats on pillows in a large circle. They were a crowd of large men, wealthy men, undoubtedly most of them were merchants or traders, the kind of men who cared little for who ran the government as long as money and trade was allowed to flow. Some were probably already figuring out how to profit from the French.

Demoreau stood behind the Deputy Governor. The Sharif's young son stood behind the Sharif. The Sergent-Major watched carefully and tried to follow what was said; his Arabic was quite poor despite his many years in Algeria, but he understood enough to get the gist of the discussion.

Cayard stood and began by saying that no one could pinpoint exactly where Algeria ended and Morocco began, but he assured the local leaders that France had no interest in seizing the land between the Zousfana and Guir rivers; France wanted its soldiers to remain in the territory that was indisputably part of French Algeria; and in Algeria, he said, the French government respected all established property rights. However, he added, the French had the absolute right to defend themselves if the tribes continued to attack French soldiers.

The old men had many complaints, and the Deputy Governor listened respectfully to all of them: Crops and animals had been stolen, women had been assaulted, children had disappeared; some who argued with the French had been arrested, land had been seized without compensation, taxes had been collected without authority. The list went on and on. Demoreau watched as Cayard took it all in, but he couldn't believe that the Deputy Governor gave a damn about any of it. The wounded Sharif remained silent, but his son spoke into his ear several times; their wealthy relative was apparently a merchant in Figuig and had many complaints about the tariffs that France had imposed on cross-border shipments.

At the end of this expression of anger, Cayard stated that it was clear that there were many problems in the region. He didn't dispute the allegations he had heard but pointed out that French citizens had also been robbed by bandits, that the goods of French merchants had been stolen, that French travelers had been murdered, and that organized attacks had been undertaken against the French military. "Obviously," he said, "it would be preferable if

French soldiers could disengage from interactions with the local residents, but the soldiers are not going to leave."

"Why have your mercenaries been sent here?" The Sharif finally said. "For hundreds of years, Islamic law has governed the people of this region, and the people have survived even as the waters disappear and the sand creeps into our towns. Those who remain here have chosen to do so because they are able to survive here. Who is France to impose your laws and your religion on these people?"

"The Sultan of Morocco no longer has the means to maintain peace and security through this region," Cayard replied. "It is your Sultan who has authorized the French government, on his behalf, to bring order, and France will do so. It is the fervent hope of the French government that the laws and customs will be applied in a manner that is fair to everyone. Can this be done without angry confrontations between the locals and the French soldiers? Yes, I believe it is possible."

"Whose laws? Whose customs?" The Sharif questioned.

His relative stood and faced the Sharif angrily: "It is hardly uncommon for local laws to apply when merchants do business in other countries, my brother. Algeria is French, that has long been settled, and we must comply with their requirements in Algeria. That our laws differ in Morocco is of no importance."

"I hope it will be of greater importance to you, my brother, when France declares that Figuig is on Algerian soil," the Sharif answered, "and compels you to obey their laws and pray to their Christ."

"You are ridiculous," his brother replied. "The French respect only one God, money, and I am pleased to take their money regardless of which laws apply. Laws and regulations are needed, yes, but thieves and brigands abound and still the Sultan remains on the other side of the Atlas mountains. You are not enforcing the law, my brother. Will you now do so?"

"Well, if I may," Cayard interjected. He was prepared with the proposal which Demoreau believed was, in all likelihood, the one he had been sent to Taghit to implement: "If I may interject, gentlemen, you have on your own reached a matter that I would like to discuss. Taghit is in Algerian territory, but Morocco is nearby. The maintenance of law and order throughout this region is crucial for your success and security as well as ours. If there is agreement on that point, then the Governor wants to know if the local tribes will help to maintain peace in this region, to keep the bandits and the haraka under control, and to allow collection of the tariffs due to the French government by law, and thereby eliminate the need for further French military intervention. You see, once the law is enforced to our satisfaction, then France will be able to invest in new markets throughout the region where your local products may be sold. We will complete the railway whose purpose is to bring food, clothing, medical supplies, building materials, and a host of new products to your people, and allow your crops, your hides and skins, your metal work, they can then be transported for sale throughout Algeria, across the Mediterranean, and even across the oceans."

Demoreau was impressed: Cayard had deflected the local leaders' concerns with vague promises about accountability and financial prosperity. None of it gave the leaders what they really wanted: An assurance that France would get out and stay out. On the contrary, the locals had been co-opted into working on behalf of the French.

* * *

The temple of the goddess Tanit might never have been found but for an audacious digger who made the mistake of selling an ill-gotten priceless artefact to an Irishman. Ren was working at the Basilica excavation one morning at the end of summer when he was approached by an anxious red-haired gentleman who was quite obviously a tourist. People often came to look at the excavations and the archaeologists were not generally advised in advance, but it was incidental to the work and helped to generate public interest. Unfortunately, it was also not uncommon for tourists to pocket some small artefact that they believe to be of no consequence, and Ren had on several occasions been forced to apprehend such thieves and demand that they empty their pockets. On this particular day, however, the Irish tourist was frantically looking for Ren and had in fact been sent to him by Père Delattre. It seemed the good Catholic Irishman had purchased an artefact of engraved stone from a local merchant in the marketplace, and he had approached Delattre to find out whether the object might have had some significance to the early Christians. The Priest was acutely sensitive to the frequent disappearance of early Christian relics, and he had sent the man, who was told his immortal soul was in jeopardy, to see Ren immediately so that the object could be examined. Ren was forced to leave the diggers under the supervision of his new, inexperienced archaeology student from Oxford, Thomas Childers; the entire day would be a loss, he grumbled. Nevertheless, the basilica dig had so far proven fairly unproductive, so Ren graciously packed his rucksack and accompanied the Irishman to a fine hotel, Le Grand Palais, hoping that perhaps a fine dinner might accompany his assessment of the supposed artefact.

At the hotel, Ren was shown a stele, a thin piece of grey limestone, incredibly fragile, approximately three feet high and one foot wide in the shape of an obelisk. On the front face was engraved the silhouette of a priest carrying a child. Above them was a crescent moon and the sun, both symbols of the god Tanit, and two dolphins to represent the "Celestial Ocean." Ren gasped. "As you suspected, it is indeed a priest, sir," Ren told the Irishman. "But he is a Punic priest from ancient Carthage. This stele is well over 2,500 years old. Will you please show me at once where you obtained it?"

They went to the souk in the marketplace where the Irishman had purchased the artefact. The proprietor said that a local man supplied such objects to his store, on consignment. Had many objects been sold in this way? Oh, yes, very many, Monsieur, but usually only one or two at a time; he had no more at the moment. When the legal consequences of such sales were explained to the proprietor, he became extremely eager to refund the purchase price. He claimed he had no knowledge of where the priceless item had been found.

The next day, at a time previously agreed upon, the proprietor met with the local man again to "split the money." Ren was watching and recognized the local man as a digger who had recently worked for him. The digger was followed surreptitiously over the course of a few days, and it was discovered that he was now conducting his own private excavation in the marshlands in the Salammbô district adjacent to the Gulf of Tunis, the very parcel of land that Ren had long considered a promising site. The digger, it was discovered, had for many months been taking artefacts from the marsh to sell.

It turned out that the entire marsh could be purchased at a reasonable price, there being no practical use for the property. Ren contacted a colleague from Cambridge who was now president of the archaeological society in Manchester. This colleague promised to provide both money and a crew of young archaeology students to assist in the excavation. Ren further discovered that donations from one individual or institution could be used to entice matching donations from another. A donation of one Franc was equal to six or seven Francs by the time it was received in Tunisia. In this way, Ren was able to collect enough funds to expand the excavation to the new site.

It was at this stage that a disagreement arose between Ren and Père Delattre. Ren had early on suggested draining the marsh to see what could be brought up from beneath the water, arguing that the land was unlikely to have been disturbed for centuries. It was well known that the sea had encroached in that area, and in ancient times it had been above the water table. Père Delattre had shown little interest. Once money began to be expended upon the project, however, the French Priest expressed his preference that the money be spent on other sites. Ren countered, disingenuously: "If a particular site enflames the imagination of potential benefactors or excites the members of an organization, and they want to support work at that location, they have every reason to expect their donations to be spent on those sites." He knew that he had intentionally excited the interest of his colleague in the marsh site, ignoring for a time the need for donations to support the work at other sites around Carthage. "Still," he said to placate his employer, "I am certain that there will be adequate funds to support work at more than one new site. Why, from the front doors of the cathedral you can see Roman columns that you keep telling me need to be investigated. Shall we hire diggers to begin excavating there under your supervision?" Père Delattre agreed they would hire the new diggers, but Ren thought he seemed unhappy with the compromise.

Ren had been living in a small room in the seminary attached to the cathedral as a way to minimize the project's expenses, but he decided to lease a house which he would share with the new archaeology students coming from England. The "house" was in fact a palace (several hundred years old) that had once belonged to a Muslim prince. Ren renamed it "Le Palais d'Hamilcar" after the Carthaginian general and statesman of the Third Century BC: It was a large white mansion overlooking the sea, located in the prestigious area of Tunis which in ancient times was called Megara, the Phoenician suburb where Hamilcar had lived. The gardens contained cypress trees which made an avenue to a front gateway surrounded by bougainvillea, prim roses, and poppies, and the courtyard contained ancient marble columns and a fountain. However, most of the interior of the palace was very much like an old boarding school and merely comfortable. Once the archaeology students, a half-dozen of them, arrived in Tunis, Ren instituted a daily routine reminiscent of his days at Cambridge which included lectures in the evenings from colleagues whom he enticed to come view the excavations.

Ren worked the Salammbô site intensely with his students and a score of diggers under his direction. It was established that several distinct levels existed, each belonging to a different period in the history of Carthage. The earliest sanctuary or temple was dated from the very foundation of the city, and it continued in existence until the fourth level, at the destruction of Carthage. It was a temple for Tanit, the chief goddess of Carthage, of motherhood, fertility, wisdom, civilization, and of crafts. The remains of her temple were discovered beneath centuries of scattered Roman and Byzantine debris. The area had sometime afterwards flooded and remained untouched for more than a thousand years.

One evening, Ren sat in the "Great Hall" of the Palais d'Hamilcar which he and the students used as both a dining room and lecture hall. On its stone parquet floor sat a large round table which Ren said was inspired by the Arthurian Round Table myth. Large windows faced the gardens and the deep blue Mediterranean Sea. Above, a coffered ceiling was decorated with Moorish-style engraved plaster. On the comfortable upholstered chairs around the table sat a dozen young archaeology students and a colleague of Ren's from Egypt, another of Petrie's men. Ren always ensured that a generous amount of wine was available each evening. However, there would be no lecture that evening. Instead, a great matter was to be debated. It was one that Ren wished to understand more fully before he spoke to Delattre.

That morning, during the excavations of the Salammbô site's Temple of Tanit, a large cache of burial urns were unearthed, the first of what a quick survey suggested could be thousands of urns, and each of these urns contained the remains of a child. A handful were examined at the site, and it appeared that the remains were those of children ranging in age from newborn babies to around twelve years; there were also urns containing the remains of small animals. These had all been buried in the sanctuary and found at all four levels. Yet, unlike the remains of children found buried in Punic-era cemeteries nearby, these children had all been cremated.

The little commune that Ren had drawn together was full of excited conversation that evening. The significance of the finds that day was lost on no one. "If you would, please, all quiet down, we can begin," Ren announced. Slowly, the students and their guest complied. "I think," Ren began, "we are all aware of the potential implications of today's discovery. The urns, the first of what appear to be a substantial number, and their contents, are naturally disturbing. More so, I expect, because it has long been suspected, based on historical sources, that the Ancient Carthaginians practiced ritual child sacrifice. This is something the Romans and Greeks both said the Carthaginians did. Plutarch in his work on superstition, for example, speaks of a practice among the poor in Carthage of selling their children to the wealthy as substitutes for ritual sacrifice. Dionysius of Halicarnassus likewise refers to child sacrifices in his 'Antiquités Romaines.' I offer this quotation: 'It is said that the ancients sacrificed to Cronus *in the way that was done in Carthage for as long as the city lasted.*' Cronus, you will recall, was the Titan of Greek mythology who swallowed his children. And we all know what happened to Hasdrubal's children. These may be merely slurs against the oft-maligned Carthaginians, but our understanding of the Punic society is still being developed, and, at this juncture, the possibility of child sacrifice simply cannot be dismissed."

His colleague, a handsome fellow whose father was a British Earl, was quite disgusted: "There's no reason to believe that this site is any more than a cemetery for children who were stillborn or died young. In my opinion, a small, weak, or sick child would make a pretty poor offering to any god, and it's hard to imagine how the death of a child could count as the answer to anyone's prayer."

Another student chimed in: "We have to consider the elevated level of mortality among children in the ancient world. In the cemeteries of any ancient civilization, one should expect to find the remains of a great many children. That doesn't mean they were murdered."

"These are important considerations," Ren replied. "But we mustn't allow our personal revulsion for the practice of child sacrifice to alter our analysis. It would be inaccurate of us to project our morality onto people living in a completely different world than the one we inhabit today. We know that at regular intervals, intensified in times of national crisis such as in famine or war, human sacrifices have been offered in many early societies. Here in North Africa, Tanit was the goddess of wisdom, civilization, and war. She was the defender of the towns and homes where she was worshipped. The Ancients used her symbols as protection. So Tanit very much represents the sort of goddess to whom ritual sacrifices would traditionally have been made."

Another student pointed out that the Salammbô district was adjacent to both the military and the commercial ports of Carthage, the sort of places where people still pray to the gods for prosperity and protection.

"There's also the animals," a young man added. "Some of the burial urns contain the remains of small animals. You wouldn't expect animals to be buried in a cemetery with human children, I don't think. But some people might have sacrificed an animal instead of a child: People who didn't have a child, or people who couldn't afford to buy one."

In Ren's opinion, it was not possible (nor desirable) for the discussion to reach a final conclusion that evening, and much more evidence would need to be accumulated as the excavation continued. He knew there would be arguments on both sides of the issue and heated opinions were to be expected with regard to such a sensitive topic, but the initial discussion was fabulous: It was exactly the sort of community Ren had always sought to build, one with brilliant men and women engaged in scientific discourse, working and living together. He was proud of his students and the scholars he had brought together. Nevertheless, he worried that Père Delattre would be so outraged by the possibility of child sacrifice in Carthage that he might even attempt to shut down the work at the Salammbô site. Before the end of the evening, Ren would need to halt any further speculation about the nature of the remains that had been found. The work would need to progress significantly before a responsible scientist could reach any sort of conclusion, he would tell them. Yet at the same time, the finding was so sensational, it could hardly fail to make headlines around the world.

Tamanrasset

* * *

Isabel awoke at a quarter to four to perform the Tahajjud, the voluntary prayer, something she did not do very often. She washed herself and went to the room set aside for prayer. After praying, she lay down on the rugs to nap until the first mandatory prayer period of the day. As she lay quietly on the prayer rug, she thought of her husband, Erik, and couldn't help from fantasizing that he was with her, holding her, kissing her. The sensations she imagined were raw, intense. She imagined making love to Erik, and a warm feeling washed over her that calmed her racing heart. She drifted back to sleep until Omar, Majida and Faiza came in for Fajr. When they were all together and Faiza had settled down because she was always very fidgety, they stood facing Mecca with their hands raised and began. When they finished, they turned to each other and said: "May the Peace and mercy of God be upon you." Then Omar went to dress for work while Isabel, Majida and Faiza prepared breakfast. Faiza ran down the street and around the corner to the bakery to obtain fresh bread, while Majida prepared eggs. Isabel made the coffee; she liked it strong. They all sat down to have breakfast together.

Isabel now worked for Muhammad al-Kattani in the mornings, so she put on her hijab to accompany Omar on his walk to the university. Faiza went with them since her school was on the way. They passed the bakery and decided to walk through the marketplace to say hello to their friends: Hassan, the butcher; M'barek, an ugly old stationer who had lost an eye and refused to wear a patch—he simply shrugged and said it was the will of Allah; Saif Elarab, the clever young bookseller who had several new tomes he was eager

Crossroads of the Nomad

for Omar to buy; Jaloul and his wife, Safaa—a sad story there: Jaloul was a dress-maker, but Safaa, his wife, did most of the actual sewing; they had a daughter about the age of Faiza who had died, and since then Jaloul no longer smiled and often looked pained and Safaa would still cry uncontrollably at times. Majida wanted a new dress for Faiza but Omar did not like to have Faiza around Jaloul and Safaa too long because they scared her. Of course, such things are predestined, Omar would remind them, as they continued past the shops and out of the marketplace. Isabel did not speak back to Omar, but she had lost her husband and understood how Jaloul and Safaa must feel. She promised herself that she would come visit with Safaa.

As they neared al-Quaraouiyin University, the streets became even narrower and more congested with people and merchandise. Isabel felt people brush against her which always made her uncomfortable. She and Omar brought Faiza to the door of the madrassa, and Faiza went inside after she gave her "Bella" a kiss on the cheek.

The university was fairly unimpressive from the exterior, an enormous complex of grey-yellow buildings with few exterior windows and a green-tiled roof. The main entrance was a high arch with two ancient, iron-riveted wood doors. Above the arch was an ornate design of colorful tilework and an intricately carved wooden overhang also bearing the signature green roof tiles. Omar and Isabel passed through into a dark hallway. Omar there bid Isabel a pleasant day and went through a door into an area reserved for the university scholars. Isabel continued to the large open courtyard surrounded by countless white columns and covered arcades. It was said that whoever tried to count the columns of the courtyard would go mad. The ancient floor was tiled in marble squares of white, black, brown, and green, and in the center was a large fountain, but it was dry and out of use. There were a dozen or so men standing together in clusters about the courtyard, or just passing through, as Isabel walked to the library; the men generally ignored her although from time to time one might smile at her or say "sabah al-khayr," meaning simply "good morning." She would just nod and smile modestly.

There were quite a few men in the library that day seated at the rows of ancient wood tables, reading books, parchments, and scrolls. Isabel had exclusive use of a small niche near the back where she could sit out of view at a small table, but there was a window and excellent light for reading. Al-Kattani had recently given her a list of quotations from the Quran and a list of books to review to see whether the author had commented upon those specific quotations. It was amazing to Isabel that dozens of scholars might have commented on a phrase of a few words. Some of the books she reviewed had been untouched for centuries.

As always, Isabel was the subject of substantial curiosity, partly because of her European appearance but mostly because so few women were seen in the university. As she sat at her table, brightly lit by sunlight coming through the window, an unusually tall stack of books threatening to collapse upon her, she sensed that she was being watched. A casual glance confirmed that a young Arab man seated nearby was looking at her. This would not ordinarily disturb her, but the man's gaze was intense and persistent. She ignored him for a while and continued reading, but she caught him looking several more times. He was a younger man, but tall and fit; she thought he was quite handsome. The thought sparked a pang of remorse for she still felt a duty to her deceased husband, she still felt love for him. At the same time, she thought it was not the woman sitting in the library at that moment who loved him but some prior version of herself, like a role that she once played. That version of her, that character, still existed inside her, in her heart, but she was holding it there with gloved hands so that she and that character could no longer touch. But her husband was dead, and she was unable to play that role any longer even if she wished it.

As midday approached, Isabel prepared to leave to attend prayers at the mosque connected to the university, one of the most beautiful in Morocco. She took a last look at the young man, letting her eyes linger on him slightly longer than was proper. Their eyes met, and he appeared to blush. She knew much more of men than he likely knew of women, she thought. She stood and walked towards the exit of the library. As she passed, the young man said to her: "Française?"

Of all the things the young man might have asked, Isabel certainly did not expect him to ask if she was French. "La, 'ana lasto Faransia," she told him in Arabic; "no, I am not French." Somewhat flustered, she continued to the door.

Isabel walked quickly across the courtyard to the hallway. There, she went through the door which Omar had used and entered into a large, bright room with many desks. There were several men, mostly in European attire, standing and speaking with each other, and a few older men sat together at tables. Isabel walked modestly to a desk where a very elderly man was seated with a pile of loose paper. He looked up at Isabel.

"These are the notes Sayyid al-Kattani asked me to prepare today," Isabel said. She passed over her papers. The man added them on top of his stack. "You'll see that he gets them today, amee?"

"He always starts at the top," the man replied icily. Isabel noticed that the room had grown silent and everyone was looking at her.

"Thank you," Isabel said. She nodded and quickly returned to the hallway. She could already hear the call to prayer and decided not to wait to see if Omar was coming. Heading out to the square, she had only to walk around the outside of the building to reach the women's entrance to the mosque.

After prayers she walked home to have lunch. Omar was with colleagues that day, but Isabel found Majida at home. Majida was a few years older than Isabel but still fairly young; she was short compared to Isabel and seemed to hide inside her kaftan. She spoke infrequently but never appeared to be unhappy. Isabel had gotten used to her silence and had learned to simply talk at Majida.

"We had a pleasant walk through the market this morning," Isabel told her. "We stopped briefly to see the dresses at Jaloul's souk. Maybe you would like me to take Faiza there this afternoon? I know you want her to get a new dress."

"Yes," Majida said as she looked away. She would rarely look anyone in the eyes, even another woman.

"An odd thing happened at the library this morning," Isabel continued, "and I don't know what to think of it. A young man, out of nowhere, asked me if I am French. Maybe all Europeans look alike to a young Arab man, but is there any reason you know why someone would think I was specifically French?"

"Perhaps he is Algerian," Majida replied.

"Oh, I suppose that's it. I had not considered that he might have come from another country to attend the university. People in Algeria must think all Europeans are just like the French. They're possibly not wrong, although Sweden has no colonies. They did, in the past, but not for many years."

Isabel attended a class with other young women at the madrassa that afternoon, but there were few others she spoke with regularly, as the other women were young and unmarried, still children really. She also met with the Alima Mu'mena to review the books she was reading for her personal education. After her afternoon prayers, Isabel waited for Faiza and they returned to the marketplace together to visit the dressmaker.

Jaloul's souk was a large room lit by lanterns behind double wood doors. As Isabel and Faisa walked up the alley, they saw the doors were both open wide and decorated with dresses of many magnificent colors, as well as some in black and some in a shimmering white fabric. All were decorated with silver or gold filigree, beads, semi-precious stones, or colorful embroidery. Inside there were many more.

"Asalamu alaikom, peace be upon you both," Jaloul said to Isabel and Faisa. He looked very tired.

"Wa alaikom salaam," Isabel replied, not so much looking down as looking around the shop to see if Jaloul's wife, Safaa, was there. Safaa was seated near the back of the store with a lantern; she had a dress she was embroidering, it lay upon her lap, but she was watching Faiza who began to look at the dresses. "Majida asked me to help Faiza purchase a new kaftan; she's growing out of this one."

"Yes, of course," Jaloul said. "There are lovely kaftans in her size over here." He walked over to the other side of the shop. "After you've chosen one, Safaa can help her try it on behind the screen in the back to make sure it fits properly."

Faiza took a long time to choose a dress, and then she went to a small space set aside with a dark wood folding screen in the back of the shop with Safaa. Isabel wanted to speak to Jaloul about the loss of a loved one, having lost her husband, but she didn't think it would be proper for her to speak with him alone. She decided it might be best for her to step outside but hesitated a moment, intending to say something, and just then two more women came into the store. Jaloul went to help them.

After a very long time, Faiza came out from behind the screen alone; she still wore her old dress and looked scared. She went to Isabel and told her: "We need to go home now; the sun is setting." It was time for prayers. Safaa then came out of the back room carrying the new dress. She looked sad and had clearly been crying.

"Just a moment, please," Isabel said firmly. It seemed like something had happened.

Jaloul went to speak with his wife quietly, then came to Isabel with evident distress: "The dress needs a few alterations, but we will have it ready tomorrow morning. Will that be sufficient?"

"Yes, Omar will come pick it up," Isabel replied. "Thank you, Jaloul. Ma'a salaama." She placed a hand on Faiza's shoulder and led her from the store. They walked quickly up the alleyway and around the corner before Isabel stopped. She knelt and looked Faiza in the eyes: "Are you alright? Did Safaa hurt you?"

"She scared me, Bella; she's so sad," Faiza said and broke out into tears.

"I'm sorry that I took you to this store today, Faiza," she said, hugging the girl. "Your father will pick up your new dress tomorrow, and the next time you need a nice dress we'll find a new store, okay?"

"Yes," the girl said, snuffling.

By the time they got home, the event was forgotten, and they were late for prayers so they washed and rushed to the musalla. Dinner came afterwards, and then Omar read a passage from the Quran to his family and asked Isabel some challenging questions about it, just like she was one of his regular students, until he said it was time for Faiza to go to bed. Isabel wanted to go to sleep early too so she washed up and prayed the last time, the Isha prayer. That was plenty for one day, she thought, before falling quickly asleep in her bed.

* * *

Ahmad ibn Mostepha al-Haybah was born at the house of his father beside the Guir river. The Ouled Abadla was their family, and the family was a member of the Doui-Menia tribal confederation. Ahmad had many brothers; he was the oldest, although he had male cousins who were older. A descendant of the Prophet and a respected man, his father had been named as the Sharif of both the Ouled Abadla and the Doui-Menia. Many people came to see Ahmad's father and confer with him; he was both a civil and religious leader.

Tamanrasset

He instilled in his children a sense of piety and devotion to Allah. Ahmad was taught to read so that he could better obey the dictates of the Quran. Since he was a child, Ahmad was involved every day in the trades of the family: Camel breeding, goat herding, and wheat cultivation. The family also owned orchards of date palm trees, some as far away as Béni Abbès. Béni Abbès, they were told, was in Algeria. There was a "ksar," or castle, there which belonged to his family, but it had been taken over by the French as a fort and two of Ahmad's brothers who had lived there with their mother had been thrown out. There was another ksar which belonged to Ahmad's family in Ait Ayoub in the Atlas Mountains. Ait Ayoub, they were told, was in Morocco. As the oldest and arguably the cleverest son of the Sharif, Ahmad would succeed to his father's position one day provided he was pious, wise, and courageous. Ahmad had fought beside his father, and he prayed that Allah would force the French mercenaries from Algeria and leave his family in peace.

Following the meeting with the French Deputy Governor, Ahmad's father said that neither he nor the leaders of the community, many of whom were merchants like his brother who simply wanted to sell to the French, clearly understood what the French wanted in the Sud Oranais or why the Sultan of Morocco had given the French "carte blanche" there. Ahmad wondered whether it really was because of the alleged loans from French banks. The Sharif did not like to be confounded and misled. Moreover, the situation had been getting more complex, he said. He believed that the next leader of the Doui-Menia had to be more than a warrior: He would need a deep understanding as well. That was why the Sharif decided that Ahmad would be the first member of his family to go to school. At the end of the summer, Ahmad was sent to Fez to learn at the university there. It was the farthest he had ever traveled from his home.

In Fez, Ahmad lived with a relative who was a low-level bureaucrat in the Sultan's government; he paid little attention to Ahmad's activities. Ahmad didn't mind; he was a good student and was treated with respect by his classmates, although he missed his family and fighting the French. Every day he went to the university and was taught by some of the most important living scholars of Islam. He learned about Islamic law and the history of Islam. He learned math, engineering, and geography. And he learned the history of the Maghreb.

Ahmad was aware that people had lived in the habitable regions north of the Sahara since ancient times, but he knew nothing of the people who had come before him. The Berber people, he learned, were among the earliest to inhabit the region. The Pharaohs of Egypt brought law and central governance, but they were eventually replaced by the Greeks and then by the Phoenicians who founded the Carthaginian Empire. Next came the Romans who destroyed Carthage and built coastal cities all around the Mediterranean. As the rule of the Romans ebbed, they were replaced by the Vandals and they by the Byzantines. In the Seventh Century, the Rashidun and Umayyad Caliphates began the Arab conquest: The Byzantines were destroyed and the Queen of the Berber people, al-Kahina, was defeated in a great battle. Islam spread across the Maghreb. The Umayyad Caliphate was overthrown by the Abbasid

Caliphate, but the Abbasids were too weak to extend their authority over the western part of the Maghreb; those regions eventually fell under the control of various Muslim Berber and Arab dynasties. These all became loosely and collectively governed by the Sultan of the Ottoman Empire in Istanbul who, as leader of the Islamic people, all Muslims were required to obey. However, as the authority of the Ottomans weakened, Morocco became independent. The Alaoui dynasty had ruled Morocco for over two hundred years, although Spain asserted a protectorate over some coastal cities where they engaged in trade. Algeria had been a semi-independent country when it was conquered by the French, almost by accident, in 1830. Tunisia had been weakly managed for many generations by a "Bey," a local governor, on behalf of the Ottomans, and it had become a haven for pirates and criminals. In 1881, Tunisia became a French Protectorate to promote the capture and imprisonment of those criminals. Only Libya remained under the loose control of the Turkish Ottomans in Istanbul.

Thus, it seemed to Ahmad, the Maghreb was destined to be conquered again and again by powerful invaders. He felt a great anger for the futile aims of these men. They lived far from the people that they sought to control and govern. They did not even understand the lives of the people who struggled in such a difficult environment to survive. Eventually, after these invaders had enriched themselves at the expense of those on these fringes of society, their power would weaken and the Maghreb would be left to rot. All that came from their avarice was grief, Ahmad concluded. The consequences of European colonialism would surely be the same.

Crossroads of the Nomad

Of course, there was much more to the history of the Maghreb, and Ahmad learned those details in his classes. He spent most of his days at the university, although he believed it was also his duty to befriend students and scholars: These were people who were worth knowing in the future, on whom he could rely, and who taught him the customs and concerns of other families and even other lands. These experiences exposed Ahmad to a much wider world than he previously imagined, especially regarding people and events around Morocco, Algeria, Tunisia, and the Ottoman Empire, and about European countries like France and Great Britain.

There was one other matter of concern to Ahmad which he considered as he sat in a small hall of the university listening to that day's lecture. He had been studying in the library the day before when he saw a woman there reading an impressive collection of books. Her skin was pale as cream and clear of lines and blemishes like porcelain, her eyes were the bright blue color of the midday sky, her hair, what he could see of it, appeared to be a dark brown like rich soil, and her lips looked like they had been stained by the red juice of the pomegranate. As he looked at her shamelessly, there was only one thing which Ahmad believed could ruin her great beauty–if she was French. He summoned his courage to ask her. She said she was not French, and she spoke Arabic although she was clearly neither Arab nor Berber. Was she a Tuareg? Some Tuareg women had pale skin and blue eyes. But Ahmad thought she looked European. The blueness of her eyes remained fixed in his mind. But he had not come to Fez to find a wife, and he had to work hard to put the woman from his thoughts.

* * *

Tamanrasset

Long ago, the city of Saïda had been the site of a Roman outpost. In the 1800's, the city remained an important crossroads. It had been occupied by the Muslim resistance leader Abd al-Qadir during the French conquest of Algeria; it was he who burned the city to the ground in 1844 when the French finally sent overwhelming forces against him. Due to its strategic location in the High Plateau of northern Algeria, the French rebuilt the city, and it became home to the Second Foreign Infantry Regiment of the French Foreign Legion, one of the most important stations in French Algeria. It was there that the Mounted Companies of the Foreign Legion were based and commanded by Colonel Eugene Rabat.

And in Saïda, "Rosalinda's" was the most popular wine shop, even though the shop was located in the forbidden quarter of the city. The large, darkly lit room was packed with Legionnaires shouting, drinking, smoking, and singing in several languages amid a din of clinking bottles and glasses; only wine could be sold to soldiers. Most of the men (and a few working women) were seated on benches at old wooden tables. Others stood beside a long wooden counter. On a chilly night in December, the air was thick with the heavy bluish smoke of Turkish cigarettes. Many of those present were new Legionnaires who were still in their preliminary training; of course, quite a few of these men had previously served in the military of some other country. There were also a few non-commissioned officers of the Foreign Legion in the shop, and there were some who served in one of the other French military services in Algeria such as the Spahis or Tirailleurs. But the soldiers in the shop had grouped themselves mostly by their native language. A large assembly of Germans by the door were singing loudly, a few English-speakers were conversing at the counter. There were small groups of Slavs, Scandinavians, and Spaniards, and many French-speakers. Some of these were from France and were tacitly being permitted to serve a five-year term of enlistment in the Foreign Legion under a nom de guerre in lieu of a prison sentence for some minor crime. However, the vast majority of French-speaking recruits had been born on German soil, specifically, in the Alsace-Lorraine region that had belonged to France until the Germans seized it during the Franco-Prussian War. Many young Frenchman living there preferred to join the French Foreign Legion to fight for France and earn French citizenship than comply with Germany's mandatory conscription order and serve in the German Imperial Army.

Virtually all the new Legionnaires present, "Les Bleus" as the recruits were known, expected to eventually be posted out or transferred for advanced training. Their days in Saïda were invariably the most difficult for these men to bear since their time was spent doing little more than marching, cleaning their uniforms, and polishing their equipment, activities that, even when fully mastered, still took ten or twelve hours each day. The men were also forced to endure the uncertainty of where they would be sent next: Many would be assigned to stations with active combat or to remote regions of the Sahara. With a little accumulated pay in their pockets combined with the self-assurance that their training was sufficient to meet the minimum levels of competence expected of a Legionnaire, it was not uncommon for some of the men to get into trouble. Unfortunately, the wine at Rosalinda's was particularly inexpensive at two sous per liter, and that for an excellent full-bodied Algerian wine.

Now that the depleted 6th Mounted Company had returned to its barracks in Saïda to take on and train reinforcements, it would be Sergent Demoreau's duty to prepare the new men for deployment. He sat with a small glass and an unlabeled liter bottle of red wine in a dark corner. He leaned back and gratefully took a hearty sip. He rolled the rich red Algerian wine around in his mouth and felt the tannins drying his tongue and palate, but more importantly his mouth like a sponge was absorbing every blessed drop of alcohol. With every swallow he could feel his shoulders loosen and his back unclench with the inrush of this vital fluid, so helpful, he thought, to balance the sun-bleached blood in his veins. But he would permit only enough to satisfy his need.

Demoreau was no more allowed to drink in Rosalinda's than any of the other Legionnaires, but he could at least sit upright with a certain formality that conveyed to his subordinates that he was not amenable to fraternizing. He was freshly shaven, wearing his old but well-repaired Legion uniform. The brass buttons and gold braid of his blue jacket were relatively polished; his light blue kepi sat on the table beside him. His tanned face showed none of his emotions, assuming he permitted himself to feel any, but his steel-grey eyes were actively examining the men in the shop around him. For years, Demoreau had trained Legionnaires in the Mounted Companies just like these for combat in the deserts, plains, and mountains of Algeria. Some of the new recruits in the wine shop that evening would be transferred into his Company, so he watched them carefully. He knew nothing of these men, and they likely knew little of each other. They would learn. Once they finished their preliminary training, these recruits would likely prove equal to the requirements of the Legion, but there were always a few who would meet the slow cruel death of the desert and drag some of their fellow Legionnaires down to Hell with them. What Demoreau had learned, and taught to the men under his command, was that a Legionnaire must constantly keep his mind occupied. He must maintain his professional demeanor at all times, even when his life did not hang in the balance. Tasks such as marching, cleaning his uniform, and polishing his equipment were necessary to occupy the thoughts of a mere recruit, but most Legionnaires had to eventually overcome their long-held prejudices and take strength from their duty and sense of honor and their trust in their fellow Legionnaires. But, even beyond that, Demoreau believed, each Legionnaire must cultivate the means to maintain a sense of himself to rely upon during the long periods of lonely isolation in remote fortifications and endless days-long marches in the vast empty spaces of French Algeria, otherwise, the desert and the Legion were certain to drive a man to madness.

As the Sergent-Major watched and waited for Caporal Mueller to arrive, a well-tanned older woman with a long braid of white hair and a faded blue dress entered the shop from the back room. She was carrying a lit cigarette, and the young men all said "bonjour" gaily to her. She surveyed her demesne and, eyeing Demoreau at the back table, approached him in her unsteady gait. In English with a gravelly Italian accent, she asked: "You are back, my sweet

Jackie? Staying in town this time, I hope? It has been so long since you came to see me."

Demoreau stood as she approached, and his wary smile greeted the proprietress. "I'm embarrassed that it's been so long, Rosa; I have missed you," he said as he took her tanned, leathery hand and bowed to kiss it. "Will you sit and share a glass with me?" He gestured to the empty chair beside him.

"I sit because you flatter an old woman," Rosalinda replied and eased herself onto the wooden chair. She took a deep drag on her cigarette and continued, "but if I am honest, Jackie, I did not expect to see you in here again." She gestured to his glass of wine: "You promised me, did you not?"

"I've been behaving, I swear it. You have been very patient and forgiving with me, Rosa. Training these younger fellows takes much more out of me than it used to."

"Ahh, but you're certain to be going down south again, won't you?"

"Oh, there, or somewhere else. We're not paid to stay in the barracks," Demoreau said, "but I expect to have some money for you before I go away again. You know I am awfully sorry about having busted up the place that last time."

Rosalinda gave a rasping laugh. "See that tall one," she said, pointing at a tall blonde Legionnaire with a black eye and bruises on his neck and forehead, "he's a Swede, maybe, or Norwegian. He gets into an ugly fight almost every time he comes in here, doesn't know when he's lost. He owes me quite a lot of money. But that is simply part of the business, my dear. I would never kick out one of you boys just because you got a little drunk and broke some furniture. I could never stay in business if I did that."

"That's why you've lasted longer than the others, Rosa." Demoreau said. "These men trust you enough to relax a little. Perhaps one day when I'm too old to be a Legionnaire, I'll buy your place here and have you teach me how to run it."

"Oh, yes, yes, you flatter old Rosa. Now, you take care of yourself, Jackie, and maybe I'll just leave this old place to you in my will," Rosalinda said as she casually dropped her cigarette to the ground and crushed it beneath her shoe. She stood and leaned over to pat Demoreau's cheek in a motherly fashion and then walked to the counter for another cigarette.

Demoreau saw the husky Caporal Mueller come through the doorway. He slowly made his way across the room towards Demoreau with many handshakes and greetings along the way—Mueller was well liked. "Ah, there you are, Sergent-Major!"

Demoreau rose. "Have a seat, Caporal; I'll get you a glass." He stepped to the counter to take a couple additional glasses and then he returned to pour the wine.

Mueller spoke quickly: "I've been trying to find out which of 'Les Bleus' will be transferred to the Sixth. This drove of pigs is especially filthy; most can't keep their uniforms clean," he said gesturing to the men in the shop. Mueller was known for his obsession with the neatness of the Legionnaires' uniforms. His own trousers and shirt were gleaming, and his blue woolen jacket and kepi were immaculate; the leather straps and belts of his uniform, and his boots, shone like polished glass even in the light of the oil lamps.

"Ha, then nothing has changed," Demoreau laughed. "You always say that about the recruits, Mueller. I haven't been able to find out exactly when we're being deployed again, we've got many men to take on and a lot of training to do. Have you found out who will be our replacements? Rosa was just warning me about that fellow over there. He's not one of ours, is he? He's probably too tall to ride a mule."

"Ja, he is unfortunately one of ours. His name is Larsen and he's a bit of a hot head, that is true, but he has had field experience in Europe and wants to be an officer so he'll probably get himself under control. There's a Belgian man next to him who I suspect was an officer in Europe, that handsome dandy over there. He goes by the name Van Hove. The one he's talking to now is Rutli. He will be a problem: He is very lazy. We've got one of the fellows over by the counter, the short one, Saratoff, and a couple Brits and there's another American in here somewhere," he said looking around carefully. "At least they're all experienced riders."

Demoreau looked around the shop. Saratoff looked like a hard case, but the English-speaking crowd was hard to judge. "Is the American here?"

"Uh, ja, the one that looks like a stevedore, shaved head, goes by the name of Lewis," Mueller replied. Demoreau located the man that the Caporal indicated, a great hulking man with huge shoulders. With a name like Lewis (assuming the name was genuine or close to it), he'd likely have come from New York. That would be fine. Lewis was listening to someone telling jokes in English, but it seemed he wasn't the laughing type.

"We also have a couple Americans being transferred over from the Ninth," Demoreau said. The Company usually had several Americans, most of them adventurers from the American West.

"Ja, Bennet and Jameson, you know them. They're also bringing over Vonheim; he'll be our new Sergent-Fourrier."

"I can work with him, decent NCO. I've known him for more than ten years."

"Now, look, you see that man standing next to Lewis right now, that is Henderson; he is one of our new Brits, supposedly the best marksman in Saïda right now. And the one speaking to him is the other Brit, Mills, an excellent rider I am told. I have no complaints with either of them, but they are both new to soldiery and will require some patience."

"I'm sure you and Dormayer have a good handle on all the new men, Hans." Dormayer was Demoreau's second Caporal. He'd also been assigned a new Sous-Lieutenant named Cauvain, a French Alsatian who'd been given a field promotion and acted like he was still a Caporal, but at least that put someone between Demoreau and Lieutenant Hansen; the Lieutenant had turned out to be an aggravating and inconsistent officer who was usually given too much latitude by the Capitaine.

Demoreau left Mueller talking with the men at the next table to go up to the counter and purchase another bottle of wine, taking the opportunity to listen in on the English-speaking group: Henderson and Mills, who were quite drunk, and the American, Lewis.

"You're a strange fellow, Lewis," Henderson slurred. "You really mean to tell me you've never been to a brothel? Why I'm sure even your father goes every week or two."

"I have not, no," Lewis replied in a cold voice. He was clearly unhappy that Henderson was baiting him. Unfortunately, Henderson had an accomplice in Mills to stiffen his spine, despite the fact that Lewis looked like he could deck a rhinoceros.

"Maybe the problem is New York, eh?" Mills said. "I hear the whores in New York are a bit hit or miss. There are no finer ladies than in Paris, yeah? You musta gone through Paris, right, Lewis? I mean, how'd you even get here? You musta come through France, dincha?"

"I enlisted in Tunis," Lewis replied icily, "not that it's any of your business."

"Oh, Lord help us, the poxiest whores of all are in Tunis," Mills said. "But what were you doing in Tunis, eh? Honestly, I can't imagine how anyone ends up in Tunis. Trouble in New York, you go to Paris, I understand that. But Tunis? You must have gotten yourself into something really bad to end up in Tunis. You don't have much to say for yourself, do you, Louie?"

Lewis was red hot and ready to fight; Henderson and Mills both looked like they were falling-down drunk. Demoreau decided he had better intervene. "Gentlemen," he said quietly, in clear American English, and with enough steel in his voice to get their attention. "In the Legion, a man is not asked about his past, and he has no obligation to share." He looked at each of the British recruits with obvious malice.

Henderson got the message: "Why, it's just as you say, Sergent-Major, and we're just heading back to the barracks now," he said.

"That's an excellent idea," Demoreau replied.

Henderson grabbed Mills by the collar and dragged him towards the door. Lewis looked at Demoreau with an expression more of anger than of gratitude. "You should find another place to drink," Demoreau told him icily, and he went back to his table with his second bottle of wine. The sooner they got out of Saïda the better, he thought.

II – A Death in Fez

It was Ramadan. The air in Fez was unusually cool and still, and the skies overcast. Isabel had gone to the mosque for prayers. She had not gone to work at the university for the past few days but she felt she absolutely needed to get out of the house and away from Omar and Majida for a brief time. Faiza had now been missing for six days.

As Isabel prayed, she heard a man near the main entrance groan as if he was suddenly ill, and then a woman behind her gasped. A low murmur spread through the men's assembly. Suddenly another woman cried out and began to sob. The woman next to Isabel placed her hand on Isabel's arm and told her the news: Faiza, the daughter of Omar Benayoun and his wife Majida, had just been found dead at the tannery, only a few blocks from their home.

Isabel felt a shock roll through her body and her heart stopped beating for a moment, and then suddenly there were tears coursing down her cheeks. It was everything she had feared.

A week earlier, Isabel and Majida were preparing iftar, a supper of lentil soup, roast chicken, and rice which they would eat after the day-long fast. Faiza was sitting nearby, obviously bored.

"Bella, can I go see my friend, Amina?" Faiza pleaded.

"Ask your mother," Isabel replied.

"May I go, please? Can I ask Amina to come for dinner?"

It was a small request that Faiza often made. Her friend Amina lived around the corner and often came to dinner, so of course Majida gave her permission. Isabel noticed that Faiza put on her mother's large black hijab, and that she took a large, heavy wool bag. Before Isabel could ask Faiza about it, Faiza ran down the hall and out the door.

When the dinner was ready a half-hour later, both Isabel and Majida began to wonder why Faiza was taking so long to return. Isabel offered to walk up to the corner and find out what was delaying Faiza. She put on her hijab and went outside. It was past sunset, and the street was becoming shadowy and dark. Fez was a grey city to begin with. There was a chilly breeze.

Isabel didn't want to say anything to worry Majida unnecessarily, but she had an uneasy feeling because Faiza had taken the heavy wool bag. It didn't make sense for Faiza to burden herself that way, and the bag wasn't going to be useful anyway. Isabel walked quickly up the street and around the corner. There was no sign of Faiza. The bakery across the street was already closed for the day. The door to Amina's house was shut and locked. No one came to the door. After a minute of knocking with no response, Isabel decided she had better tell Omar and Majida what was happening. Maybe Faiza had taken a different route home or had made an unexpected detour after running into someone she knew. Maybe she was playing a trick on her parents or hiding somewhere in the house. Isabel turned and ran back.

Majida was in the kitchen. Faiza had not returned. Isabel's first thought was that Majida would collapse if she was told that Faiza was missing. Majida was never a strong person and always assumed the worst. Isabel felt terrible already and considered whether there was any way she could go to Omar first; the last thing she wanted was to deal with Majida when she was distraught. Unfortunately, any other option was cut off when Majida asked innocently: "You're back at last, but why isn't Faiza with you?"

Isabel felt like a trapped animal; there was no escape from what she had to do. "No, I didn't see Faiza, and no one was home at Amina's," she said, trying to sound as calm as possible. "She must be with Omar or in her room, or perhaps she went somewhere with a friend, don't you think?"

Majida was still and silent for a moment as she looked at Isabel uncomprehendingly. "What do you mean?" She asked with just the slightest note of uncertainty in her voice, not uncertainty about whether Faiza was at home or with a friend, but whether she should be concerned about her daughter. "Faiza's not in the house; I would know," Majida said emphatically.

"Well, I only mean that I went to Amina's house and no one was there, so she must have come home or gone with a friend or something," Isabel replied as nonchalantly as possible.

"I would have heard her come in," Majida said. "She's not at home; I would hear her. Where would she go at this hour?"

"Maybe she's playing a trick on us; maybe she snuck into the musalla to pray with her father." Isabel immediately headed in that direction to check, but she could see the expression on Majida's face: It was exactly how Isabel felt.

Omar was alone and had just finished his prayers. "Have you seen Faiza?" She asked him. The "no" had barely escaped his lips before Isabel was rushing up the stairs to look for the girl. She ran from room to room calling out, but there was no sign of her. Isabel cried out in her head: Where could she have gone?

She went downstairs and found Omar and Majida sitting together in the room where they usually ate. Omar was holding his wife tightly. Both looked up at Isabel hopefully as she came into the room. "She's not in the house," she said gently. To her astonishment, Omar and Majida sat perfectly still and silent. "Do you want to check at her friends' houses, or walk around the neighborhood, to try to find her?" She asked tentatively.

Omar replied: "Faiza will come home when Allah wills it." Majida began to cry.

Isabel had been in Fez long enough to understand what Omar meant, but she still had to bite her tongue. Surely, she thought, Allah does not mean for us to do nothing but wait. Yet there was almost nothing she could do. Faiza knew a few people, of course, but it was hard to believe she would go to someone else's house without asking her mother or father first. There was no one her family could go to for help. There was no civilian police force; there were soldiers who guarded the imperial properties, government officials, and the muhtasib, an official appointed by the Sultan to enforce the Islamic rules and regulations. Isabel knew that no one would be at the mosque at this hour, but it was at least plausible that Faiza would go there. Isabel went to put on her coat.

"You will remain here with us," Omar said firmly when he realized Isabel meant to go looking for Faiza.

Isabel looked at Omar with an undisguised fury that clearly surprised him. She said nothing but merely turned and walked out.

She spent that first night wandering through the marketplace and sitting in front of the mosque. There was no moon, and the streets were black. It never occurred to her that she could become a victim herself in such darkness. She saw nothing. In the morning, she went to Hamza's bakery and waited until she could hear Hamza inside. He lived upstairs, she recalled. She beat on the door until Hamza came to answer. His hands and apron were covered in flour, and he looked displeased. "What do you want at this hour?" he said angrily. "I've only just begun the bread."

"Asalamu alaikom," she said brusquely. "Last night, Faiza went to her friend's house there across the street, but she never returned home. No one is answering the door. Did you see her? Did she speak to you?" She pleaded.

"You mean Omar's daughter, Faiza, that little girl?" Hamza asked. "I did not see her yesterday; I closed early when all the bread was sold," he said flatly and shut the door.

Isabel shouted at the door: "She was only walking up the street and around the corner—how could she have gone missing so quickly!" Isabel pounded on the door, then slouched down on the ground in the alley. She was shaking with anger, and it took some time to calm herself.

Over the next few days, word spread through the neighborhood that Faiza was missing. Isabel learned that Amina and her family had gone to visit relatives in Taza and had been away for days. Faiza must have already known that her friend was not at home. Had Faiza possibly lied about where she was going? She was not with a friend or relative, and still she did not come home. Yet, day by day, little was done or said about it. Occasionally, someone would mention to Isabel (or to Omar; Majida would not leave the house) that they hadn't seen the girl. Only twice was Isabel asked what Faiza was wearing when she had gone out; she described Faiza's dress, the black hijab, and the large, heavy wool bag. One older woman told Isabel that Faiza had probably run away.

One day, Isabel stopped by Faiza's madrassa to see if the other students had seen her. A young girl Faiza's age came up to Isabel crying because she missed her friend and was worried. Almost unable to speak, the girl took Isabel's hand and pulled her into a small storage room. She pointed at a pair of shoes. "Those used to belong to Faiza," she said, sobbing. "You should probably take them home."

The next day, an old rumor was resurrected that Omar was not Faiza's real father. Isabel was told that Faiza had been born early, meaning less than nine months after Omar had married Majida. There had been questions raised about the paternity–some said that Omar had only married Majida to save her reputation. At home, Isabel had never had reason to question that Faiza was Omar's child; he had always loved her very much. The rumor was simply a speculation that Isabel refused to even consider, but she was shocked that people would say such things about Majida and Omar.

At home, Majida had become unable to act. She sat frozen for hours with a vacant expression on her face. Omar had to hire a woman to cook for them. He tried to act normally, but he was unable to work. The three of them sat at home and said nothing to each other. Isabel went through all of Faiza's belongings—every piece of clothing, every bag and box and scrap of paper—and examined every hole in the walls of her room. There was nothing. Why had Faiza taken the large wool bag? Why had she put on her mother's hijab? Where had she really gone? How could she have gone missing so quickly?

Then, on the sixth day, Faiza's body was found.

Isabel ran from the mosque to the tannery which was only a few blocks from Omar's house. It was a large open courtyard containing dozens of stone baths in which animal hides were treated with chemicals and dyes. Isabel passed through the stone entry arch into the courtyard and saw a crowd of men standing in a tight circle on one side. They were animated, arguing. A red mass lay on the ground between them. Isabel walked up slowly, and several of the men turned and looked at her with animosity.

"You should not be here," one older man said. "Go tell Omar we will take care of the preparations for burial."

"Let me see her," Isabel insisted.

"No, it is not appropriate for a woman to see such things," the men objected.

"Why is she red?" Isabel begged as she pushed angrily into the crowd of men.

Faiza lay dead upon the ground. Her skin and clothes were a strange red color. Her body had been pulled from a red dye bath. Isabel knelt down and reached to turn Faiza's face. She had been badly beaten, her nose was broken, an ear lobe was ripped, and one eye was missing. Her clothes were torn, and her dress was pulled up. Her thighs were bruised. Her flesh was cool to the touch, but still stiff. It seemed like she had only been dead a few hours. That meant Faiza had been kept alive somewhere for days, Isabel thought, and the bruises on her thighs could only mean one thing.

A young man reached down and placed his hand on Isabel's shoulder firmly. "Everything will be done to preserve her dignity," he said. "Please, come away now and let these men take care of her. I will accompany you to the house of her family if you'll permit me."

Isabel looked at the face of the person speaking to her. She immediately recognized the young man who sometimes stared at her in the university library.

"Won't the police come, the *gendarmes*, soldiers?" She asked despairingly.

"No," he said softly.

"What is your name?"

"I am Ahmad ibn Mostepha al-Haybah of the Ouled Abadla," he replied. "I am the son of Mostepha ibn Ali al-Haybah, Sharif of the Wadi Guir and Wadi Saoura. You have seen me in the library at the university."

"Yes," she said, "often."

He blushed. "Omar Benayoun is one of the scholars with whom I study at the university. He is a mentor to me," Ahmad said. "Please, allow me to escort you back to his house."

Isabel looked down again at the lifeless body of Faiza. A man walked up with a thin white cloth and laid it on top of her. The red dye immediately soaked through the cloth obscenely. The sight caused Isabel to gasp.

Ahmad placed a hand under Isabel's arm and lifted her to standing. "There is nothing more you can do for her. Her family needs you now," he said.

"Alright," she said coolly. Isabel supposed she had known all along how Faiza's disappearance would end. It would have been better if the girl had not been found. She bristled at Ahmad's statement that she could do nothing, and his characterization of Omar and Majida as someone else's family bothered her: They were not merely her hosts and sponsors; they were her family in Fez, and she owed them a debt for taking care of her. She had begun to feel she was a part of their little community. The death of Faiza would ruin everything.

She allowed Ahmad to lead her by the arm from the tannery into the street. Her feelings of sadness were rapidly replaced by anger, not at Ahmad specifically although she dramatically wrenched her arm out of his grasp. Faiza was the child, not me, she thought; I am a grown woman and, as far as I can discern, I am the only person who seems to care that Faiza was murdered. Who is responsible for this awful thing, the torture, the abuse, the murder?

At the Benayoun house, Ahmad came in the door with Isabel and waited while Isabel went to find Omar. He later told Isabel that, in all his years traveling up and down the Wadi Saoura, in battles, facing death, and coming to Fez alone to start a new life as a student, he had never felt as scared as he did in the front hallway of Omar's house waiting for Isabel to get Faiza's parents.

Isabel came for Ahmad and led him into the courtyard where Omar and Majida stood side by side waiting. Omar was still dressed in his charcoal grey three-piece suit, Majida in the same kaftan she had been wearing for six days. Omar's arm was around Majida's shoulder, his other hand clasped with hers. Their faces were white with an expression of panic. Isabel stood between them and Ahmad.

"Go ahead," she said to the young man.

"Ya ustadh," he began respectfully, "I have been sent to impart the saddest news: Your daughter has been found. She is indeed dead. The Imam has been informed, and everything is being managed properly. The burial will take place tomorrow morning. Allah yi sabbarkoum; may Allah grant patience and strength in the face of death."

Majida began shivering and tears rolled down her cheeks. She fell to her knees and began to groan.

"Was it ..." Omar began, "was it the same as the others?"

Ahmad looked down. "I do not know," he admitted.

Isabel felt a bolt of electricity down her spine; her face flushed red hot with blood. "The same as *what* others?" She demanded of Ahmad, but he failed to raise his eyes. She turned to Omar: "Are you saying there have been other murders, other stolen children?!" She yelled.

Omar nodded almost indistinctly. "Yes," he admitted despondently, "many."

* * *

Weeks of repetition lulled Demoreau into a familiar and comfortable feeling of detachment. The schedule each day was exactly the same: "Réveille," the morning bugle call; "Rassemblement," or assembly; march out to the Champ de Tir to oversee shooting and artillery exercises; return to barracks; immediately after the return, "Rapport" in the courtyard; dinner followed by "Repose," cleaning up and getting ready for the afternoon exercises; assembly at the mule pens for marching, animal instruction, or riding exercises followed immediately by another Rapport which lasted until supper. The Legionnaires were then free until "Appelle." There was no bugle or whistle for the Appelle: At nine o'clock sharp an officer simply made the rounds to see that all those who had no midnight permission were in their barracks and to make note of those who were missing. The daily schedule was the same for those Legionnaires who were nearing the end of their terms of enlistment as well as for those who had just completed their period of basic training. After months in the Sud Oranais, the 6th Mounted Company had still needed a lot of replacements; some transfers were from the First Infantry Regiment, soldiers who had previously, for several reasons, been deemed unworthy or unable to ride a mule. Consequently, the newly complemented Sixth was a mess, and the training that Demoreau implemented had been both repetitive and difficult. Capitaine Mitterand blamed Lieutenant Hansen, who had gone from inconsistent to overly demanding. But these were minor concerns to Sergent-Major Demoreau, after so many years in the Legion. His Legionnaires would be properly trained, and they would know their duty.

After supper, Demoreau sat alone upon the bed in his small private quarters. It had been announced at Rapport that the "Musique Principale de la Légion Étrangère," the Legion's highly esteemed orchestral band, had arrived in Saïda and would perform that evening at the parade grounds. Demoreau had planned to visit Rosalinda's that evening, but he knew he should go to hear the music. It was both a pleasure and a torment for him. It was only a short

Tamanrasset

walk on a cool evening to the parade grounds. Sergent Vonheim and Caporal Mueller joined him along the way.

The concert began with a performance of "Le Boudin," the official march of the Foreign Legion. The Legionnaires' rolled blanket which lay across the top of their pack was supposedly the Boudin sausage referenced in the song, but most Legionnaires would have argued that they themselves were the sausage—meat stuffed into a skin that was prepared to be devoured for France, as described in the second verse:

> Our forebears knew how to die
> For the glory of the Legion;
> We have all prepared to perish
> In line with this tradition.

The program was predictable, but some of the new pieces by the American composer Sousa were warmly received by the Legionnaires; Demoreau had no complaint with the performances. He was distracted by the presence of Major Marie-Louis Vauchez, the Sixth's regimental commander who was almost never seen. The Major was accompanied by Capitaine Mitterand and the Capitaine's pretty young wife.

Mitterand remained cool and aloof to the Company he commanded, but some months earlier he had brought his wife down from Marseille and had purchased a small townhouse for her across from the city hall in the center of town. The Capitaine still spent his evenings at the café at the Hotel Vergnon with other officers drinking wine and playing chess, but at least he had his wife where he could keep her from trouble. Or so he thought. As the concert continued, Demoreau noticed that Capitaine Mitterand's wife spent an inordinate amount of time looking longingly at Legionnaire Van Hove, the handsome recruit who was quietly said to have a peerage in Belgium and had been transferred into the Sixth after finishing his basic training. It was Demoreau's firm opinion that any man who brought his wife to Algeria and left her alone in a city occupied by soldiers of the Foreign Legion was going to find trouble. He wasn't the only one who thought so. Later that evening, the Sergent-Major stopped on the way back to barracks for a few glasses of wine with Sergent-Fourrier Vonheim, who raised the subject first: "Have you any concerns about Van Hove? I doubt I was the only one to notice the attention paid to him by the Capitaine's lovely wife, no?"

It was not a matter that Demoreau chose to wade into. "Yes, I saw," he said unenthusiastically.

"Van Hove is in your Section, my friend," the Vonheim reminded him. "Mitterand will chew his head off and ship him to Devil's Island if he thinks Van Hove has even acknowledged the woman's attention."

Demoreau sighed, shaking his head. "Yes, I guess I will speak to him."

"Is she a provocateur, do you think?" Vonheim asked rhetorically. "Perhaps she delights in causing trouble, to gain her husband's attention? I have known such women, women who flirt with another man in order to rouse the emotions of her lover. It is an indecent ploy, to make a man her victim to secure another, no?"

The more he thought about it, the less Demoreau wanted to speak with Van Hove. This led him to postpone his return to the barracks and, consequently, drink far more than usual. By the time he left the café, he was furious and fairly drunk. He angrily threw open the door of the barracks and shouted for Van Hove to report to the hallway. The scared Legionnaire was good-looking in a way that made it easy to believe he had spent his previous life in fine clothes dancing in ballrooms across Europe. He was certainly not inexperienced with women.

"Legionnaire, you were no doubt aware of the attention paid to you by the Capitaine's wife at the concert this evening."

"Sergent-Major –" Van Hove began to object.

"Shut up," Demoreau said with a quite ferocity that took Van Hove aback.

Demoreau struggled to keep his body still as he continued: "You're an experienced fellow, Van Hove, and familiar with the sort of difficulties that the attentions of the wrong woman can bring to a man, even an innocent man. You'd agree that any woman with a powerful spouse is just the sort of woman you'd be wise to ignore. Capitaine Mitterand is not a man that you want to cause difficulties for you, for those difficulties will be extraordinary. The Capitaine is an exceptionally cold-hearted man: He does not resort to 'la course en rond' or 'le cellule' for punishment, as any ordinary officer would. No, the Capitaine will send a man off to the penal battalion at the slightest provocation; he will demand that his victim be imprisoned at Chateau Neuf or transported to Devil's Island. You do not want the Capitaine's attention. Therefore, I advise you to keep a good distance from his wife, at all costs. Is that clear?"

Demoreau saw the blood drain from Van Hove's face. "I never imagined I could end up in the Capitaine's Company, under his command, Sergent-Major; it's a fucking nightmare."

"You haven't caused any trouble yet," Demoreau assured him, slurring only slightly.

"You don't understand, Sergent-Major," Van Hove pleaded, his face in anguish. "I met Anne Marie Mitterand a year ago in Marseille, and we fell deeply in love. Capitaine Mitterand brought her here to get her away from her lover, but he doesn't know that I am that man. I joined the Legion because of Anne Marie, I followed her here to Saïda, at her request. My God, we are doomed!"

Demoreau stepped back, aghast at the stupidity of the man standing before him. He had sympathy for Van Hove, indeed, but the Belgian might have been the only man who ever thought of enlisting in the Foreign Legion as the way to get closer to the woman he loved. To end up under Mitterand's command, what a cruel twist of fate! It had been a gamble that no doubt seemed impossible to lose, yet here they were with all the power focused in the one man able to inflict the most harm.

"Have you spoken to her since you arrived in Saïda? Have you met with her behind the Capitaine's back?" Demoreau demanded.

"Yes," Van Hove replied, abashed. "We have … been together."

"And when we are sent to fight, what then? Did you plan to leave her here with her husband?"

"Anne Marie wants to leave him. We expected at some point he would be away from Saïda long enough for us to move her to a safe location, where she would be safe from him. The Capitaine is a violent man."

"And then, when she is safe, you intend to go en pompe?"

"No, Sergent-Major. I will do my duty to the Legion, I swear it to you, once Anne Marie is safe."

Demoreau thought "if she is not safe, that is partly your fault." He didn't say it, but Van Hove likely guessed from Demoreau's expression.

The Sergent-Major was silent a very long time; he was not thinking quickly. It had been many years since Demoreau had been in love and romance no longer played a part in his life, but the memory of love still existed somewhere deep within him. That memory was the only crystal of humanity, dusty and fragile though it was, that made it possible for him to still care about the world and the ridiculous people in it.

But Demoreau was now a Legionnaire, and over the years he had done many things as a Sergent to protect the men who had been assigned to his care. They were his responsibility. And when the life of a Legionnaire was at risk, it was not at all unusual to find that the Legionnaire himself had made the mistake which was going to cost his own life or the lives of others. Part of Demoreau's duty was to protect Legionnaires who had gotten themselves into such trouble and to preserve them so they could die when and where France dictated. Van Hove's situation in that regard was no different.

"I think," Demoreau began slowly, "you must get the woman away from the Capitaine as soon as possible—tomorrow."

"Yes, Sergent-Major."

"After that, you'll have to stay out of trouble. If the Capitaine seeks revenge, he'll need cause, and as for whether a punishment he demands is in proportion to the offense committed, that's something we'll just have to address if it becomes necessary. I hope it won't be necessary, Legionnaire."

"I understand, Sergent-Major, thank you." Van Hove was clearly relieved.

"Return to your cot, Legionnaire; tomorrow will be a busy day for you," Demoreau told him.

"Yes, Sergent-Major," Van Hove said and went back into his room.

In the morning, before Rassemblement, Demoreau wrote a letter to his colleague at the Champ de Tir outside the city. He gave the letter to Van Hove to deliver by hand with instructions to wait for a response. "Since I am taking the Section on a lengthy march today, I don't expect to see you until Appelle," Demoreau told him. It was plainly improper for Demoreau to hide a Legionnaire for a day, but he hoped that keeping all his men out of sight he might at least postpone a confrontation with Capitaine Mitterand and give Van Hove enough time to move the officer's wife, that is, if she wanted to be moved and if the Legionnaire genuinely cared to move her. If it was going to happen, it would have to be that day. Demoreau would do no more than spare a moment in Van Hove's schedule and make sure that the rest of his Section could not be implicated.

After Demoreau returned that evening after marching and riding nearly forty kilometers, a skinny Italian ran up to him outside the Legion's stables. The Sergent-Major knew the man as the manager of the seedy second-class hotel nearby, the Hotel de la Paix. "Signore, Signore!" The manager pleaded. "Please, you must come! He's going to kill them!"

Demoreau understood instantly: "The Capitaine?"

Tamanrasset

"Si, the Capitano Comandante is threatening to kill the Legionnaire and the woman; they are in the hotel! He has ordered the Polizia Militare to keep everyone out. The Legionnaire, he said I should find you if anything happened. You must come at once."

Demoreau dismounted quickly. He could not involve anyone else in Van Hove's little drama but he knew he had to go. They ran the few blocks back to the hotel. The Police Militaire were in the lobby and there were more on the stairs, but they looked unhappy and uncertain what to do. "Who is in command of this unit?" Demoreau demanded. No one knew. Capitaine Mitterand had brought them from the barracks, and he was upstairs in a guest room with his wife and a Legionnaire, he was told. Presumably, they were still alive, but the PM's would not allow Demoreau to ascend. He called up the stairs: "Capitaine Mitterand!? Capitaine, it is Sergent-Major Demoreau! You must allow me to come up, Sir!"

The Capitaine had been waiting for Demoreau to arrive and gave his permission instantly. The steps of the hotel were covered in a fading and threadbare rug; Demoreau went silently up to the gloomy first floor. He found Mitterand in a small, darkened room, sitting on a chair with a pistol. His wife Anne Marie and Legionnaire Van Hove, his arms shackled behind his back, were seated on the floor like hostages. Van Hove was bloody and bruised; he looked both angry and scared. Anne Marie Mitterand's face was bruised and she was crying meekly.

"Welcome, Sergent-Major," Mitterand said with exaggerated friendliness; "I believe this is your petit lost Legionnaire, the one you excused from duty today so that he could steal my wife from me. Is that not the case? I must now kill all three of you."

Demoreau stepped in between Mitterand and the man and woman seated on the floor, his fists clenched and a look of cold hatred on his face. "Capitaine, you're not going to kill anyone because your own head would be removed by the guillotine. Did you know it is said that the severed head of Anne Boleyn tried to speak to the assembled crowd when it was held up for all to see after her decapitation?"

Mitterand looked up at Demoreau with fury, and Demoreau struck him.

Van Hove later narrated in his court martial what had happened that day: "I had gone to Madame Mitterand first thing in the morning. I was gravely concerned for her well-being. It was known to me that Madame Mitterand was frequently beaten by her husband. When I arrived at their townhouse, I confirmed that the Capitaine had already left for headquarters that day. I knew I had to convince Madame Mitterand to come away. It took me all morning to convince her—she was so afraid of what the Capitaine would do to us. She finally agreed to submit to my directions and prepared a small bag of clothes to take with her. I took her immediately to the hotel, not the one the Capitaine drinks at but the other, although sadly it is quite unsuitable for a woman of Madame Mitterand's stature. It was a first step. She cried all afternoon and shook with fear. I foolishly told her over and over that everything would be fine. Then the Capitaine arrived with the Police Militaire, a dozen or so men. They broke in the door of Madame Mitterand's guest room and seized us both. I fought back, and they beat me. The Capitaine took hold of his wife and hit her. He called her a whore and threw her to the floor. He produced his pistol and ordered the PM's to go downstairs. He sat and berated his wife for more than an hour and accused me of stealing her and cuckolding him. I admit, I did steal her away from that cold-hearted villain. I would have attacked him, but I was afraid he might shoot Madame Mitterand. It seemed wiser to wait. Then Sergent-Major Demoreau arrived. He got directly between us and the Capitaine. He stepped forward and suddenly hit the Capitaine so hard that he immediately fell unconscious to the floor. The PM's then took us all into their custody."

In the aftermath of the event, Legionnaire Van Hove was sentenced to ten months in the Penal Battalion for dereliction and conduct unbecoming, Capitaine Mitterand was assigned to a desk in Algiers, Anne Marie Mitterand returned to France, and Sergent-Major Jacques Demoreau was sentenced to twenty-six months in Chateau Neuf for assaulting an officer.

* * *

Isabel's face turned red, and Ahmad feared she might leap forward and strike Omar.

"How many?" She demanded angrily. Omar had still not looked up at her.

"More than ten, perhaps more than twenty," he admitted. "There is no way to be certain."

Isabel looked like she had been kicked in the gut. "Jaloul's and Safaa's daughter: Is she a victim as well?"

"I believe so."

"And who is investigating these crimes?" She insisted.

"Children die, it is an unfortunate truth. Illnesses and accidents are not the only causes," Omar said.

Ahmad was prepared to intervene, if necessary, but he was afraid she would resent it. It was clear to him that Isabel was trying to decide what she wanted to do. Majida was crying loudly and groaning. Omar was fighting back tears. Isabel turned and looked at Ahmad. He had lost brothers and sisters and seen many people die, he was not disturbed by the death of a child but he very much cared what Isabel thought; she was the most unusual woman he had ever met, and not only because of her striking looks. All he could learn at the university was that she was a widow who worked for the scholar Muhammad al-Kattani and lived with the Benayoun family. He had seen her many times in the mosque at prayers.

"What do you want to do?" He asked sincerely.

She turned back to Majida and knelt down to hug her. They wrapped their arms around each other. After a long cry, Majida's tears and sobs slowly subsided. No one spoke or moved. The grief would not go away quickly, but Majida was exhausted and could cry no more at that moment. Omar finally extended his hand to Ahmad and thanked him for bringing the information; it was meant as a way of dismissing him. Ahmad said he would go to the mosque to check that everything was being prepared properly for the funeral.

"Please, let me go with you," Isabel asked as she released Majida.

"As you wish, of course," Ahmad replied.

After a few more hugs and expressions of sorrow, Isabel and Ahmad finally stepped outside. It was late afternoon. "Let us go to afternoon prayers, then we can speak to the

Tamanrasset

Imam," Ahmad suggested. "And on the way, will you share with me your name?"

Isabel started walking down the street, and Ahmad leaped after her.

"My name is Isabel Pedersen," she said; "as you know, I live with the Benayoun family. My husband was a colleague of Sayyid Benayoun at the university before you arrived. He died a little over a year ago."

"Where are you from? Are you Tuareg?"

She smiled, briefly. "No, I am from Sweden."

Ahmad had only recently learned of Sweden and other unimportant countries in Europe. "Was your husband from Morocco?" He asked.

"No, he was Swedish too. We came here so he could do his doctoral work at the university."

"He was a well-educated man, then?"

"Yes, he was," Isabel said.

"May I ask your age?" Ahmad inquired.

She stopped and turned to look at him. She looked both angry and amused.

"It's not polite to ask a lady her age," she said. Ahmad thought she was teasing him, but he didn't wish to press her. Isabel took another few steps then stopped again. "Let me tell you, Ahmad ibn Mostepha al-Haybah, that I mean to find out who is killing these children and stop them from doing it again. Is there any chance you'd help me do that?"

"I am ever at your disposal, Madame," Ahmad said earnestly.

She squinted at Ahmad in a sort of skeptical way that made him uneasy.

"Tomorrow, after the funeral, meet me at the bookstore owned by Saif Elarab. You know the one I mean, yes? In the marketplace?"

"I believe I do, yes."

Ahmad lost track of Isabel at the mosque since she had gone into the entrance for women. After the prayers, Ahmad spoke to the Imam and passed on further information from Omar. The funeral and burial were planned for the next morning, less than one day after the death of Faiza, as required.

That night, Ahmad thought about Omar's admission that so many young children, all girls, had been stolen and found dead. He supposed, from a European point of view, a Christian point of view, any loss of life should be prevented. Yet the French seemed prepared to murder any number of Arabs and Berbers and Tuaregs in the desert if it suited their needs. It was obvious that the French believed some lives had less value than others. It again made him wonder at the Sultan's outrageous decision to allow the French into the Wadi Saoura. Ahmad's own Sultan had granted permission to non-Muslim mercenaries to invade his homeland. It disgusted him.

But then there was Isabel Pedersen. She seemed a very devout Muslim although she claimed to come from Sweden. She had a sort of forceful character which excited Ahmad. She worked with Sayyid al-Kattani, one of the most respected Islamic scholars in the world. Ahmad was undecided whether to fall in love with Isabel or worship her. Then he thought, she will surely let me know which it should be.

There was great wailing and sorrow at the crowded Benayoun funeral in the morning, and it impressed Ahmad that so many people had affection for the young girl who had died. Isabel appeared worn. No doubt she had spent the night consoling Omar's wife. Many people praised Isabel for supporting the Benayoun family and helping Majida. Isabel was further known to be studying at the university under the great al-Kattani, and it was said she was going to become a great Alima. These statements confirmed Ahmad's own impressions.

After the burial, Ahmad walked to the marketplace. The small shop next to the bookstore where Ahmad often ate dinner was next to the souk that Isabel had mentioned. The restaurant was closed that day since it was still Ramadan, but Ahmad sat at a table outside to wait for Isabel. He saw her arrive and invited her to sit with him.

"Very sad, the funeral," Ahmad said. "I hope it is a consolation to Sayyid Benayoun and his wife that their daughter was beloved of so many people in the community."

"I know it is," Isabel said. She sat silently for a moment. "Do you really mean to help me, Ahmad?"

"If you wish it, yes," he replied eagerly. "It would be a great honor to serve you, Madame."

She studied Ahmad for a moment. "I asked Omar about you. He said that you are from an important family south of the Atlas mountains; is that right?"

"I suppose that is so, yes," he admitted. She watched him with her blue eyes, and he was embarrassed.

"There is a dressmaker around the corner whose daughter was also lost. He won't speak to me alone, but he may speak with us both if you come with me. I want to know when and where their daughter disappeared, what she was doing, if she had any friends in common with Faiza. All that kind of thing. Do you understand?"

"Yes, of course."

At the shop, Ahmad asked Jaloul if he would allow his wife, Safaa, to speak with Isabel about their daughter. The dressmaker thought it would disturb his wife, but he agreed to speak with Isabel and Ahmad himself. He sent Safaa to collect some bolts of cloth from their cellar. After she went down through the trap door, Isabel turned to Jaloul.

"Tell me about your daughter, Jaloul. She was abducted near your home, is that right?" Isabel asked.

"Sofia disappeared during her walk home from the madrassa a little more than a year ago; she was in the same class as Faiza. Sofia often walked around to see the surrounding neighborhoods or visit friends after school. That day, she never came home. I don't know anything about an abduction. About a week after she went missing she was found drowned in a fountain outside the R'cif Mosque."

"Was she drowned in the fountain or had she been killed before and then put in the water?" Isabel asked.

Jaloul was horrified by the question. "I don't wish to discuss that," he said. "Perhaps I've said enough."

"Please, Jaloul," Isabel said anxiously. "I know you wouldn't want any other girls to die. I promise you, I will find out who did this so they can't hurt our daughters again."

She was clever, Ahmad thought, to share with Jaloul the responsibility for all the children who lived in the area.

"I don't know how she died; I wouldn't know how to tell the difference," Jaloul said.

"Do you know how many girls have gone missing, how often, whether the deaths were all similar?" Isabel asked. It was a question she might have asked Omar, but it wasn't a suitable time to be asking him anything.

"I would say every year or two, a girl about this age disappears somewhere in this area. Then usually she is found a week or two weeks later, always dead. Always found nearby. How many? I have lived here my whole life. A dozen, two dozen? I think about two dozen girls that I can remember, over twenty or thirty years. But there are also older children that disappear and boys and women and slaves."

"Slaves?" Isabel asked.

"Some of the richer families in Fez have servants that they own–slaves, you would call them," he said plainly.

"Did your daughter ever dress up like she was older? Maybe she wore Safaa's hijab sometimes?"

"Sometimes, maybe; I never saw that," Jaloul replied.

"When your daughter disappeared, was she coming here or walking to your home?"

"We live upstairs, and Sofia was expected. She never came home," Jaloul said.

"You spoke to her friends at the madrassa?"

"No."

"Was there anyone, at the madrassa or in the community, you suspected?"

"No, of course not. No, there is nothing else to say."

"I want you to know how much I appreciate everything you've told me about your daughter, Jaloul. Sofia was a special child, and I am glad that now I can remember her too. Thank you," Isabel said. She bowed to Jaloul as a sign of respect. He clapped his hands, and Safaa came up from their cellar with a basket of fresh whole oranges.

"We are honored to have you here, Madame Pedersen," Safaa said. "Please allow me to apologize for my behavior when you were last here, with Faiza. You remember. I was upset that day, but I am doing better. Here, please, have these oranges to take away with you. I only wish we could do more to help. We are not accustomed to this sort of attention."

Isabel smiled at her sympathetically as she took the basket. "You honor me. May I come back tomorrow—would you help me to find a new dress, Safaa? One of the beautiful kaftans you make, something to make me look less like an old widow?" She cautiously peeked at Ahmad. He noticed, and blushed. It embarrassed him to respond so to this woman.

"Of course, it would be an immense pleasure, Madame. Whenever you wish."

When Isabel and Ahmad stepped out to the street, she was silent for a time. They walked around the marketplace, past the many souks, with Ahmad beside her. Finally, Isabel spoke: "Ahmad, I saw Faiza's body long enough to know that it was probably a man who abducted her. She wasn't murdered quickly; she was held and abused first. Even given that fact, there are still too many possible culprits for these crimes. It would be impossible to determine that all the abductions were committed by the same person: There could be many culprits, hundreds of victims. It is overwhelming."

Tamanrasset

"If I may suggest, Madame, we should focus on the deaths that we know for certain are related," Ahmad suggested.

"How can we even tell which are related? Children disappear, they are found dead, there is no autopsy or investigation."

"Faiza and Sofia, two girls about the same age in the same neighborhood are stolen. They are kept alive somewhere for a week, two weeks. Then they are killed," Ahmad checked to see if Isabel was shocked by his statements, but then went on: "Their bodies are taken to where they will be found quickly, none far from where they disappeared. These seem too similar to be unrelated. I wonder, how would the girls be kept quiet? Where were they held? How were their bodies moved?"

"If it was someone that neither girl knew, a stranger in the neighborhood, or different strangers that were only passing through, we would never be able to find the killer, but we know the girls were kidnapped and held for many days before being killed, so it must be someone who has a place in this area, and I think probably someone that they both knew, all of them, so it has to be someone who has resided here for many years."

"That is still very many people," Ahmad said. "You know the madrassa where both girls went to school. Is there anyone there that you suspect?"

She thought a few minutes. "There are a few boys who are capable, old enough to be interested in a woman perhaps," she looked at Ahmad and could see he understood what she was suggesting, "but none who could possibly have been doing the same sort of thing for the past ten or twenty years."

"If any of the young men have access to a private place where a girl could be kept, it would probably be a place known to many additional people, a meeting place. If so, there could be more than one person involved, a series of young men over many years?"

"I doubt such a thing could be kept secret."

"What of the adults at the Madrassa?"

"There's no one I have met in all of Fez who I believe could do such a thing, no one I have spoken to and felt soiled by," she said.

"Then it is someone no one would suspect," Ahmad observed.

That afternoon, Isabel had an engagement at the university to meet with her employer, Muhammad al-Kattani. Ahmad was returning to the university as well, and she invited him to come meet the renown Islamic scholar.

Muhammad al-Kattani was in his larger-than-average office niche in the hall where all the scholars conducted business. To Ahmad, he had an aura of experience, intensity, and energy he found compelling. He was a man to be revered, and Ahmad was almost rendered speechless by his admiration.

Al-Kattani was gracious. "It is a great honor to meet the son of Sharif Moulay Mostepha ibn Ali al-Haybah," the scholar said. "I know your father, Ahmad, and the stance he has taken to oppose the French in the Wadi Guir and Wadi Saoura. Your family is a very honorable. Please, come sit, both of you."

Tamanrasset

"I'm sorry to have been away a few days," Isabel said. "Omar and his wife have been in great distress. But, as you know, the child's burial was today."

"I have no complaint, Madame Pedersen, and I only wish to know whether you are prepared to continue with your readings."

"Yes, I am," she said cautiously.

"You hesitate. Why?" He requested.

"We, I mean Ahmad and I, are attempting to discover who murdered Faiza Benayoun."

"Why?" Al-Kattani asked.

"So that the person or people who hurt her can be prevented from doing it again."

"I see. Yet is it not said that only Allah can avenge the death of an innocent? It is for Allah to decide who will be punished, and which children will die."

"Vengeance doesn't enter into it," Isabel replied. "Does it not say also in the Quran: 'Whoever saves a life, it is as though she has saved the lives of all mankind'?"

Al-Kattani smiled. "Something like that, yes. And Ahmad, are you assisting my clerk?"

"If it is permitted, yes."

Al-Kattani nodded. "Yes, naturally. Very well then. If you could perhaps spare me a few hours in the mornings," al-Kattani said to Isabel, "you should continue with your investigation. And Ahmad, I have been told that you are an intelligent and hard-working student. If you should find that Sayyid Benayoun is unable to continue as your mentor, even for a little while, I would be please to instruct you myself."

"I am honored, Sayyid, thank you; I deeply appreciate your generosity and gladly accept your offer," Ahmad replied eagerly.

* * *

It was the last day of Ramadan. In the morning, well before sunrise, Isabel awoke and ate suhoor, a meal to sustain her through the final day of fasting. She washed herself and went to the musalla for the first prayer. Omar came in to join her. Majida remained in bed. Afterwards, Omar went to his private work room. Isabel had agreed to read for al-Kattani that morning, so she put on her hijab to walk to the university alone. She passed the bakery; it was closed now but Isabel expected that many people would come later in the day to purchase bread for the Eid al-Fitr, the celebratory meal that came at the end of Ramadan. She entered the Kissaria medina, full of market stalls and shoppers. The morning sun shone obliquely through the wood trellis overhead and cast dappled patterns on the stone walls. The air was cool and crisp. Many people now smiled at Isabel or said "nharek mebrouk," may you have a good day, or simply "sabah al-khair," good morning. She no longer had the sensation of alienation she once felt while walking through the city.

She passed the dress shop without stopping; Jaloul was busy speaking to a customer who was purchasing a special kaftan for the fast-breaking feast. Around the corner, Isabel ran into Safaa. She was directing a young man who was delivering bolts of cloth. A pavement stone had been swung up onto its side to reveal a staircase down to the souk's cellar.

"Asalamu alaikom," Isabel said.

"Wa alaikom salaam," Safaa said to Isabel. Safaa smiled; she was in a more lighthearted mood, perhaps because of the holiday.

"This new cloth you have is very beautiful; it will make lovely kaftans," Isabel said.

"Thank you, yes, I am very pleased with all of them."

"Do you keep them in your cellar? Is it not very moist?" Isabel asked.

Safaa laughed. "In Fez? There is no moisture, no, it is very dry, very good for cool storage. Good place for working, too. But you must have a new dress for Eid al-Fitr; please, will you come today?"

"I don't think Majida and Omar will celebrate this year."

"Then you must come this evening to the mosque. Jaloul and I will be there and many others. A feast is held each year, and all are invited; you should come. Bring something to add to the meal. And bring that young man who was with you yesterday; it is long past time for you to remarry."

Isabel laughed. "I promise I will come to the feast tonight. Thank you for making me feel so welcome, and for making me laugh. May I come by the shop after Dhuhr to try on a new kaftan?"

"Perfect, yes, I will help you. Jaloul has terrible taste in clothes," she confided.

Isabel finished her walk to the university and spent the morning reading and taking notes for al-Kattani. In the room for the scholars, just as she was bringing in her notes prior to the midday prayers, Isabel ran into Ahmad.

"Asalamu alaikom," Ahmad said. He looked excited to see her. "I've just been speaking with Sayyid al-Kattani; he

Crossroads of the Nomad

is expecting you. May I wait and accompany you to the mosque?"

"As you wish, yes. Allow me to drop these off," she said, indicating the papers in her hand.

As they walked around the block to reach the women's entrance to the mosque, Ahmad asked: "Do you wish to continue the investigation today? I have no appointments this afternoon."

"I have a few ideas. A person with a compulsion to do this sort of thing might have other weaknesses. There are probably a few people in the area who sell hashish, alcohol, child or female slaves, and things of that sort. They may know of someone with an interest in young girls or have heard rumors, accusations. We should ask."

"It sounds very unwise to speak with such people," Ahmad objected.

"Was I wrong to assume that you would protect me?" Isabel teased. "Listen, Ahmad, I am also planning to attend Eid al-Fitr at the mosque this evening. I'd like you to come with me. I'd like to get your impressions of the people who attend." She was honestly unsure if her excuse for inviting him was genuine or not; she just wanted him to come with her.

"Yes, it would be an honor to accompany you, Madame."

"I want you to call me Isabel, alright?"

"I am honored, Isabel."

They stopped outside the women's entrance. Isabel turned to look at Ahmad. He was tall and handsome, but young. That made him desirable to her in a way which was extremely sinful. She had no doubt he felt the same way about her. It was almost too flattering. She didn't want so much attention. She didn't want to be the object of his thoughts or desires. She thought, he thinks he knows who I am, but he's wrong. Even I don't know who I am. I play these roles–the youthful coquette, the aloof widow, the Swedish friend, the Muslim aspirant. I don't know that I want to be any of those things; I don't want to be anything but me, she thought. With a troubled expression, she looked up at Ahmad. "See if you can find out about the sort of people I mentioned, the dealers in vices, where they can be found. I have an appointment after prayers, so I will meet you at the mosque this evening at sunset, alright?"

"Yes. I will meet you then."

After prayers, Isabel went to Faiza's madrassa to speak to the girls that Faiza had known. They were all very sad and full of fear, for they had all known Faiza and Sofia as well. "Do you know if either of the girls had any secret friends, or if there was anyone who threatened them or scared them?" She asked. No, no one was aware of such a person. "Is there anything you recall about Sofia that you think now might be related to her disappearance?" No one wanted to talk about Sofia at all; she was already forgotten. A couple of the children began to cry, but Isabel reassured them and got them to promise to look after one another.

Next, Isabel walked slowly through the medina thinking. There were so many souks, so many people shopping. Life just went on. She arrived at Jaloul's shop. Safaa was still in a good mood and helped Isabel choose a beautiful kaftan of light green silk embroidered with gold thread and several genuine white pearls. Isabel didn't haggle too much but still paid Jaloul a fair price. She went home then to spend the afternoon with Omar and Majida, and they prayed together. She asked them to come with her to the feast after sunset, but they declined. It was going to take a long time for the couple to recover. She hoped they would try to have another child.

As sunset approached, Isabel completed her late afternoon prayers and prepared to go out. She changed into her new kaftan and put on a white chiffon scarf as her hijab. Only then did she realized that she had forgotten to prepare something to bring to the celebration. As the sun began to go down, she left the house and walked up to the bakery to see what Hamza had left. His souk was still open, and despite a day of selling fresh bread, Hamza was as usual immaculate. The store, however, was still laden with countless dusty sacks of grains and flour along the walls and atop shelves and tables.

"Asalamu alaikom," Isabel said.

"Wa alaikom salaam," Hamza replied. "You are just in time, almost everything is gone."

"Would it be improper for me to purchase all the loaves you have left now? I wish to bring them to the feast at the mosque." She looked down modestly.

Hamza beamed. "Yes, certainly, you may have all the rest, and then I can close for the day." He began to collect the remaining loaves into a basket for her.

Isabel began to look at the various sacks of grain and flour, many grains she had never even heard of before. "And your wife, is she preparing something special for your celebration this evening?"

Hamza hesitated for a moment. Because she was looking down, Isabel saw that, while Hamza himself was clean, the floor was coated with a thick dusting of old flour. "Yes, that is correct," he replied. Only then did Isabel recall being told that Hamza's wife was disabled. Isabel supposed he was just being polite. She knelt and spread the flour with her hand, and then she noticed the outline of the trapdoor that led to Hamza's cellar. Why wouldn't he keep his flour in the cellar, she wondered? What *did* he keep there?

In that moment Isabel experienced, like a clap of thunder, an insight or vision of divine inception. It was a vision of pure evil. Her heart suddenly leapt into full gallop and her shoulders shook in terror, tears welled into her eyes and she was unable to speak. She turned her head to look at Hamza. As he took in the expression on her face, it was clear he understood at once that she had somehow unearthed his secret. Isabel was suddenly looking into a mask of utter malice.

"You must go downstairs now," he said with icy certainty. He put down the basket of bread and began to come around the counter to seize Isabel.

She scooped a handful of flour from the floor and flung it into his eyes while rising to flee. Hamza's eyes were clouded, but his arms, strengthened by years of kneading bread, flailed in the air in front of him. By sheer chance, he hit Isabel on the side of the head with such force that she flew across the shop and hit the edge of the counter. Blood flowed down her face as she lurched backwards towards the doorway.

Hamza couldn't see, but he could hear where she was. He stomped on the floor with his thick legs as he pursued her. Isabel wiped the blood from her face and saw Hamza coming. She timed and placed her kick to break Hamza's left knee just as he began to raise his right leg. The crack of bones both in his leg and in her foot sounded like a gunshot. Hamza howled in agony. Isabel screamed. Panic still propelled her. She turned over and used her uninjured foot to thrust herself out to the street. Hamza behind her fell to the floor. Isabel raised herself up and, limping in agony, began to run as best she could towards the mosque. The muezzin had just begun the call to prayers.

She arrived at the mosque just as the sun had fully set and a crescent moon was rising into the sky. Women screamed at the sight of her: Her face was a mask of blood, her hijab and light green dress were stained by blood, the scarf falling off her head to reveal her short, chestnut brown hair and striking blue eyes. Her right foot was misshapen, and a small puddle of blood collected beneath her sandal. Suddenly Ahmad was beside her, holding her upright. She was shaking and crying. "It's the baker, Hamza. He kept the girls in his cellar," she gasped. "I saw it, I ... I had a vision." A woman who heard her cried out, another fainted.

Ahmad lowered her to the ground. "I will take care of everything," Ahmad assured her, his anger evident in his cold hard voice. "I will make certain he cannot hurt anyone ever again," he promised.

* * *

Ancient texts were sometimes discovered in surprising places—small remote churches, undisturbed tombs, and even caves that had been undisturbed for centuries. While he was in Egypt, Ren had found the study of ancient Semitic languages such as Aramaic and Hebrew to be useful for conducting research, and after moving from Egypt to work on sites in Tunisia, and as excavations continued at the Salammbô site, Ren implemented a languages program for himself and his students: Experts were brought in to teach some of the ancient languages that had been more commonly used in that part of the world such as Tamazight, Punic, and Numidian. But the ancient languages most commonly found on scrolls and tablets were ancient Greek and Latin, and Ren was fluent in reading and writing both.

It was early in spring when, at Delattre's suggestion, Ren undertook an expedition to visit a number of sites on the island of Malta that were thought to be Punic. In fact, it was largely accepted that Malta had been a Punic colony or trading port long before the city of Carthage was first founded. Unfortunately, the journey to the island involved an overnight trip by steamship to Sicily, several days traveling across the island to another port, and a second day-long journey by steamship to the city of Valletta. The trip was far from interesting, and Ren spent much of the journey drinking large amounts of gin and tonic. When unoccupied, he seemed to take inordinate pleasure in drinking alcohol, and he knew, if it were not for his dedication to his work, he would likely have a serious illness.

Père Delattre had arranged for Ren to be met in Valletta by an elderly Italian priest, the custodian of ancient artefacts at the Jesuit's Collegium. It was still early spring and the days were cool and cloudy; Ren missed his home, but spent two weeks surveying sites that had nothing of interest and drinking a large amount of gin. Indeed, the earliest sites on the island had all been so thoroughly built over by succeeding civilizations that very few traces of the Phoenician culture remained to be found. The elderly priest assured Ren that, in the small village of Żurrieq on the southern coast of Malta, there was a Punic-built lighthouse.

The building had proven so useful to ancient navigators that the Romans had preserved the structure entirely and even expanded it. The elderly priest had been to the site before and had no interest in returning, but he gave Ren the key and sent him to view the foundations which, the priest claimed, were 3,000 years old. If true, that claim meant that the structure would have been a crucial Punic waypoint long before the founding of Carthage itself.

The building Ren found was far less exciting than he was told to expect: A large building in poor condition, mostly rebuilt as a residence in the late middle ages, on top of a Roman-era magistrate's villa, on top of late Carthaginian foundations. Ren estimated that the original building was likely constructed in about 300 BC, based on the stonework he had examined at Carthage. The empty building was dark but dry, and as a light rain began to fall, Ren explored the dark building. Certain rooms, he had been told, contained furniture which had been removed to the museum in Valletta, but much refuse and debris remained. One closet-like storage room on a lower level was so stuffed with papyrus scrolls and vellums, broken wooden furniture, and spare pieces of marble, that it was impossible to even get through the doorway to examine the contents within. The scrolls looked interesting.

After a further week of work utilizing local laborers, Ren was able to safely remove the scrolls which, the old priest assured him, would not have been abandoned unless they were worthless. On the contrary, Ren thought, they wouldn't have been saved unless they were precious.

Of course the scrolls could not legally be removed from Malta, but Ren had them all brought to Valletta and spent

Tamanrasset

weeks combing through them. All of the writing was in Latin, and it appeared that most were records of shipments from Hadrumentum, one of the most important cities in Roman Africa, located on the Mediterranean coast south of Tunis. Ren knew that Hadrumentum had been destroyed by the Vandals in 434 AD, but the scrolls appeared to be documents that had been rescued from the fires. One in particular caught Ren's attention. It was written sometime near the end of the reign of Emperor Nero, about 68 AD. It consisted of a list of soldiers and materiel that had arrived in Hadrumentum from somewhere in the interior of the region: A small cohort of soldiers who requested and were granted transport back to Italia for themselves and 3,387 Roman libra of "ore." And it was explained that these men had previously been assigned by the Emperor (Nero) to oversee a mission sent to dig tunnels in the mountains, a failed mission at which all the laborers had died including its leader, whose name was Lucius Titus Bassus.

This document was a fascinating corroboration of the story about Bassus' search for the lost treasure of Dido, and a strong and exciting indication that gold had in fact been found. The soldiers traveling with the "ore" would have been returning to Rome just after Nero's death as the Roman Empire descended into civil war, and they possibly chose to hold on to their cargo not knowing who would remain in power to receive it. Even more amazing, however, was the soldiers' written request for transport which accompanied the scroll. Submitted by a Roman Legionary, the request stated that Bassus and the deceased laborers had been interred in a cavern at "the quarry for the aqueduct." Ren paused after he read this. There was only one major aqueduct in Tunisia, one hundred-thirty kilometers long from the Zaghouan mountains to Carthage. Did this mean that the place where Bassus searched for Dido's treasure could be located? If there was gold ore found, could there be more? Ren decided to keep his hopes private but to follow up when he returned to Tunisia.

Little was known about the long abandoned aqueduct, but after Ren had returned to the Palais d'Hamilcar, he asked his students to begin studying the Roman structure. When was it built, what were its water sources, and (most importantly) where was the stone quarried? He assigned pairs of students to ride out along the path of the aqueduct to the southwest of Tunis to see what they could find.

After weeks of searches, two students returned from a lengthy search with exciting news: They had found the quarry where the aqueduct's stone was cut. In addition, they found what appeared to be the famous Roman "Temple of Water" built at the site of the mountain spring that was the source of the aqueduct's waters. It was known that the temple was a popular spot for vacationing Roman tourists in their day because of the spring water. Ren was determined to ride out and see it for himself. He selected one of his more dedicated and discrete students, Tom Childers, to accompany him on the three day ride out to the Roman temple. Tom, a recent Oxford graduate, had turned down an opportunity to be one of Petrie's minions in Egypt in order to work at Carthage, so Ren felt a special obligation to bring the young man along.

The temple was situated at Djebel Zaghouan, a lonely mountain some one hundred-twenty kilometers from Carthage. Ren and Tom arrived after dark and made camp just beside the Temple of Water, but at first light its beauty was breathtaking: Built on a wide stone terrace and covered with an enormous shallow pool of clear, sparkling water, the temple was built of fine white limestone. On the south end there was a crescent-shaped Roman portico with an ornate opening that led to a stately chamber. This chamber had been dug into the side of the mountain and was still decorated with magnificent statues of the Roman gods. An overflowing spring in the rear wall of this interior chamber was the source of the water that flowed out the portico to the shallow pool that covered the terrace. The water flowed gently north across the terrace and then flowed into a natural cistern which would have fed the aqueduct.

Ren and Tom spent days exploring the mountain as if they were on holiday: They climbed and hiked around the entire massif, bathed in water collected from the spring, took turns preparing their meals, and spent the cool evenings drinking wine and entertaining each other with mythological tales as the Sun set and the Moon rose. Tom quickly became Ren's favorite student. Still, Ren declined to mention the tales of Bassus or the writings he had seen in Malta. He was still uncertain whether this was the same aqueduct and same place where Bassus had allegedly searched for treasure.

They quickly located the quarry where the stone used to build the aqueduct and the temple had been cut, and they did indeed locate a number of vertical shafts cut deep into the mountain which suggested there had been attempts to mine the mountain for ore—but by whom? Was this really where Bassus had looked for Dido's treasure? Had he mined the mountain's core seeking gold ore? Or were these shafts dug at another time, later or earlier, for an altogether different purpose?

One morning Tom came running excitedly into camp. "Professor, I've found a horizontal shaft," he said, "it looks like the entrance to a mine. I couldn't get into the opening, but I think together we can clear the debris that blocks it."

Ren returned with him at once to examine the find. The perfectly square entrance to the tunnel was obscured by rubble and a dense thicket of trees that had grown up at the base of the ascent, but the shaft into the mountainside was obviously man-made: It was precisely ten pedes wide and ten pedes high (roughly ten feet by ten feet), and it ran absolutely straight and level into the heart of the mountain. After clearing a few stones and chopping down a small tree, Ren and Tom were able to squeeze into the shaft. Inside, they lit their torches and walked in side by side. Dust, sand, and debris littered the smooth floor, but the trees outside had largely protected the tunnel. There were no forks in the path, no rooms, no openings—it was merely a straight, empty shaft. Then the tunnel came to an abrupt end.

"Look, Professor," Tom said, pointing to a crude, blackened etching in the smooth stone wall, more scratched than chiseled: "'Hic Requiescit Bassus, Stultorum Dominus,' Here lies Bassus, Lord of Fools," he recited. "How fascinating. Do you have any idea who this man Bassus was?"

Ren stared at the inscription incredulous. He knew of only one Bassus, but he was still attempting to understand what had happened here. Perhaps Bassus *was* a fool: Had he really found gold ore in this mountain as he had told the emperor? Had he committed suicide or died of an illness, or had he been murdered? Had the Legionaries stolen the gold ore from Bassus and killed the laborers? Ren examined the blunt end of the tunnel. It was far too smooth to merely be the end of an excavation, and indeed it proved to be constructed of stones that had been placed to seal the tunnel. Was this shaft dug merely to entomb Bassus? No Pharaoh of Egypt had ever had such a large, well-constructed tunnel entrance to his tomb. Bassus was back there behind the wall, surely, but he was very probably not alone. As Tom watched, Ren examined every inch of the wall. There was no indication that the floor had been harmed when the stones were pushed into place. It must have been carefully constructed, the joinery appeared perfect. Ren reached up as high as he could and pressed on the stone at the top of the wall. The stone moved.

"Come, let's get this wall down," he said.

Tom leapt forward, and together they pushed the stones starting at the very top. Those stones were quite large and heavy, but with significant effort they together were able to push the stone into the void. The stones below were even thicker, but soon the two men had opened a hole just large enough for them each to pass individually through into the space beyond, where the tunnel continued for only a few more yards before opening upon a large, pitch black cavern.

The darkness in the cavern was absolute, the air was still, and the odor of death remained after more than 1,800 years. The two men stepped forward into the wide space with torches raised high. Bodies lay everywhere. In the sealed dry air of the desert mountain, desicated leathery skin remained on many skeletons. These people could have easily escaped from the cavern unless they were already dead when the shaft was sealed. Some showed signs of knife wounds. These were the laborers who had searched for gold, executed for their failure to find any or perhaps because they had found too much, and Bassus was certain to be among them.

"There is an incident recorded by Audollent," Ren told Tom at last, "that a Roman named Bassus promised to find Dido's lost treasure for the Emperor Nero. Bassus is said to have failed, and the emperor ordered his Legionnairies to execute Bassus and his laborers. This find seems to substantiate that account." But Bassus had previously told the emperor that he *had* found gold ore, and he must have believed there was more, Ren thought. Perhaps the soldiers killed them in order to steal the ore. Had they found it all? Ren and Tom searched the cavern extensively and found trinkets and bones, but there was nothing of value whatsoever and no indication that there ever had been.

The day had gotten late. They returned to their camp and decided to depart in the morning and return to Carthage. The search had been fascinating but not everything Ren had hoped. They had seen a beautiful mountain and an unparalleled Roman temple, but there was no evidence of any treasure. Ren sat admiring the temple as the Sun began to set. The building remained gorgeous after nearly two thousand years, the mineral waters still flowing from the mountain into the shallow pool and spreading evenly over the wide terrace before flowing off the end. The sky turned red, and the sparkling waters of the temple's pool glittered like gold.

Ren was suddenly struck by a thought: He had heard of miners panning for gold, allowing the heavy particles of gold dust suspended in water to sink to the bottom of a pan, separating the gold from other materials. What if the entire temple terrace was built to act like such a pan? Mineral water flowed from the mountain, and any heavy gold particles in the water would sink to the bottom of the pool before the water flowed into the aqueduct. Ren quickly took off his boots, socks and pants. He walked across the edge of the terrace and gingerly stepped into the pool. His foot sank at once into a thick, heavy sludge on the bottom, maybe a foot deep. He reached down and pulled up a handful of the heavy sand-like sludge. The wet sediment in his hand glittered. It was full of gold.

The Sun had almost fully set and the temple glowed, and Ren imagined what would happen if he were to report that they had found a mountain full of gold ore, the treasure of Dido: The temple and eventually the entire mountain would be reduced to rubble in the desperate hunt by scavengers who would come from around the globe; it would all be destroyed for the sake of this gold dust. He could not abide that. Ren rinsed off his hand and watched the heavy gold sludge settle back down to the bottom of the pool. History said that Bassus had not found gold, and Ren would not find it either, he decided. He and Tom set off for Carthage in the morning, wiser perhaps but no richer.

* * *

It was unfortunate that Isabel had not come upon Ahmad privately, he thought, for he would have gone to the bakery and simply executed Hamza at once. Instead, he had stayed with Isabel while a crowd of men and women went to capture the baker and hold him while others went to get the soldiers from the Sultan's palace. Hamza was taken to the dungeon and would be tried by the Sultan's court under Islamic law.

The crimes were easily proven once Isabel identified Hamza as the perpetrator. A capable army officer was ordered to gather evidence, and his staff unearthed the remains of several girls from the soil of Hamza's cellar along with proof that over many years he had kept a series of victims chained to his cellar's wall. Hamza's wife was found in the living space above the bakery, alive but tied to her bed and malnourished nearly to death. He had abused his wife so severely that he had ultimately hobbled her and cut out her tongue in order to keep her from escaping. As for the bakery, there was some evidence that Hamza had even attempted to cremate the remains of his victims in his bread oven. In the end, there being no space left in his cellar and the oven unavailing, he had simply dumped his victims about as far from his bakery as he could carry them. Further confirmation was obtained through physical torture of Hamza and the written testimony of Hamza's wife. It was conclusively proved that he had abducted, raped, and murdered several dozen girls over a period of nearly thirty years.

While the investigation was unfolding over several weeks, Ahmad saw Isabel less frequently than he wished. Following her confrontation with Hamza, rumors about Isabel spread wildly across the city. Many thought that her "vision" had been a sign of her spirituality, a gift of Allah, and that she must be the holiest woman in Fez, perhaps all of Morocco. Others accused her of being a witch and using black magic. Some even claimed she was a djinn, inhabited by an invisible spirit or a demon or an angel in the body of a woman to spread good or evil to mankind. Whenever she was recognized in public, Isabel was surrounded by people who wanted to touch her, kiss her hands, or attack her. She could no longer work in the library at the university or walk the street alone. She had been forced to become a recluse, living with a servant in a small house that she rented in a quiet neighborhood close to the university; she did all her work for al-Kattani there. Few people knew how to find her. But then, the less she was seen in public, the wilder the rumors became.

Ahmad continued his studies under al-Kattani. His work quickly accelerated, and, for the first time in his life, Ahmad felt intellectually challenged. He had a rapport with his mentor and felt that he was beginning to understand what was happening in the world, the struggles between the Western powers and their insufferable claims of dominion over other nations. However, the Hamza prosecution still took up a great deal of Ahmad's attention. He had told Isabel that he would take care of everything, and he was determined to see that everything was properly concluded.

After some weeks of delay, the Sultan's court finally took in all the evidence and, applying the law, found Hamza guilty of the crimes alleged. Further, the court determined that those crimes were "hudud" crimes, crimes against God which are considered the most serious offences under Islamic law. As permitted by the Quran, the court then sentenced Hamza to be crucified in the public market, a sentence that was greeted with cheers by the people of Fez whose daughters had been stolen, abused, and murdered by the monster for decades.

Crossroads of the Nomad

When the Sultan's decision to spare Hamza's life was announced, it sent shockwaves through Fez.

Ahmad had spent little of his life in any place are large as the city of Fez, and he was astounded that the mood of such a huge mass of people could become so palpable. There was shock, madness, rage, despair, and anguish. At the mosques, Ahmad saw people sobbing and praying that the Sultan's eyes would be unclouded and that Allah would make him see the terrible sinfulness of his decision. Others spoke of murdering Hamza in his cell. In the meantime, the torture of Hamza became a daily spectacle unlike any seen in Fez for a generation: In the absence of any judicial punishment, the soldiers who ran the prison simply continued Hamza's torture. Each day he was led to the market square outside the prison and stripped to the waist. Two assistants would hold his arms outstretched while the executioner whipped Hamza's back with switches of thorny acacia, drawing blood with each stroke. Ten strokes were given each day. The number of strokes was limited only out of fear that the weakened baker would die too easily. Crowds would come each day to watch and cheer.

Ahmad received word from al-Kattani asking that they meet one afternoon at a souk not far from Isabel's new residence. However, when he arrived early, Ahmad found that the shop was closed. To pass a few minutes he walked by Isabel's house. He knocked. The servant told him that Madame Pedersen was not at home. Ahmad returned to the souk and arrived just as al-Kattani was opening the doors.

"Asalamu alaikom, and good afternoon, Ahmad," his teacher said. "Come take a look; I have something to show you. Come inside."

They entered a dark cavernous space that had dusty equipment, tables, and chairs.

"What is this place, Sayyid?" Ahmad asked.

Al-Kattani laughed and gestured with both arms: "These are printing presses, Ahmad. And this," he said gesturing to the tables, "are to be the offices of 'Nur al-Fajr,' 'The Light of Dawn.' It is the newspaper I intend to publish that will discuss politics and religious issues in Morocco. I've asked you here because I wonder whether you might be interested in participating."

Ahmad smiled, deeply humbled by the offer. "Yes, I would very much like to assist you, Sayyid, although I know nothing of printing and, to be honest, I still know far less of the politics and religious issues in Morocco than I would like."

"This is an opportunity for you to learn. In fact, I would go so far as to say that this is why the newspaper is needed. Let me explain: I'm sure you've read 'Al Maghrib' and 'es-Saada' and other periodicals like that, haven't you? What about 'Le Réveil du Maroc.'"

"Yes, of course, although I have no interest in what the French have to say about Morocco."

"You're quite right, 'Le Réveil' is a French newspaper, but so is 'es-Saada,' did you know that?"

"It is? But why do the French publish so much in Morocco?"

"They are trying to influence the opinion of the people here. Newspapers have a significant impact on what people believe and what they demand of their leaders, perhaps even which government they have. You're following the situation with the baker, the one who killed those girls, aren't you?"

"Yes, very much so," Ahmad replied discretely.

"Why do you think the Sultan cancelled the crucifixion?"

"I have no idea."

"Many people around Morocco want to know what is happening in that case, so updates are reported regularly in the newspapers. The horrific nature of the crimes caught the attention of foreign journalists who shared the story in France, Great Britain, and even America. However, the story they told depicts Morocco as a brutal and uncivilized country worthy of improvement by civilized Westerners. I've been told it's received a very great deal of attention abroad."

"That's amazing," Ahmad said. It was hard to believe that people in other countries would want to hear about such a terrible thing.

"However, when it came to crucifying the baker, that was something that Westerners with their Judeo-Christian sensibilities could not abide. They objected to the length and painfulness of the execution. They published editorials calling Morocco backwards and arguing that our Sultan is uncivilized. Abd al-Aziz is a young man, and you'll forgive me for saying so but young men tend to be sensitive to negative opinions. The Sultan was too embarrassed to allow the crucifixion of the baker, so he cancelled it."

"He cancelled it because of what was said by foreigners in other countries?"

"That's correct."

"And what will happen to Hamza?" Ahmad demanded.

"The Sultan probably doesn't know yet or it would have been done by now. Or he may simply never decide."

"That's ...," Ahmad had trouble suppressing his anger long enough to speak until, at last, he replied, "that's intolerable."

There was a knock on the door, and Ahmad and al-Kattani turned to see who was joining them. It was Isabel, dressed all in black with a black hijab that almost completely covered her face. She was using a cane to help her walk.

"Asalamu alaikom," she said. She seemed quite nervous and relieved when the doors were shut again.

"Wa alaikom salaam," al-Kattani replied. Ahmad could only look at her: It had been a week since he had last seen Isabel, and the striking blueness of her eyes always took his breath away. Seeing her again, even after a mere few days, was absolutely overwhelming. He wished he could rush to take her into his arms and hold her there safely.

"I have the notes for you that I completed today," Isabel said as she handed some papers to al-Kattani, "and there was a message that you wanted to show me something?" She was still limping but it seemed her injuries from the confrontation with Hamza were healing.

"Yes, that's correct," al-Kattani said. "I was just showing Ahmad where the office of my new newspaper will be."

"Your *newspaper*, Sayyid? Perhaps you are less humble that I was led to believe," Isabel said. "It seems you will have a great deal of work to do to make these machines work again, and won't the Sultan's edict allow his officials to censor what you publish?"

"You seem quite jaded today, Madame," al-Kattani replied.

Crossroads of the Nomad

"I expect you know what you're doing, Sayyid; you always do," Isabel answered. "And how are you, Ahmad?"

"I'm ... I came by to see you just now, but you were out," he said. "Have you been alright?"

"I suppose so, yes, as long as no one recognizes me," she said. "Thank you for asking."

So formal, Ahmad thought. Of course he would ask since she meant so much to him; she hardly need thank him for his interest in her.

"It is helpful that you two already know each other," Al-Kattani interrupted. "I hoped that you would both work for the newspaper with me."

"Have you told Ahmad why you are starting this venture?" Isabel asked pointedly.

"We were getting to that," Al-Kattani said, "and you're correct. He needs to know what this newspaper is for." He turned to Ahmad: "The purpose of 'Nur al-Fajr' is to inform the people of Morocco about who is really running this country, and how and why foreign nations are influencing our government and what they want here, and to provide an editorial voice to the Ulama, the body of religious scholars here in Fez who are the wisest authority on Islam in the Maghreb, and opposing Western involvement in our government. Since you come from a region that is being systematically taken away by French colonists, Ahmad, I assumed you'd agree with our aims."

"You are correct, Sayyid; I'm very grateful you asked me," he said humbly.

After an examination of the printing presses (which did appear to need substantial repairs) and a discussion of which additional people al-Kattani might bring into the newspaper, Ahmad offered to walk Isabel to her home. She accepted, and they set off slowly. Her broken foot had been set and was healing, but she still found it very painful to walk at times. Suddenly a mature woman came up and took Isabel's hand without asking; she pleaded for a blessing for her sick mother. Isabel's expression was more appalled than angry. "Barak Allah fik," she said, "blessings to you." She pulled her hand away and turned to walk away as the woman cried and gave thanks.

Ahmad was stunned. "Does that happen very often?"

"More than I'd like, but at least that woman was friendly. I've been hit and spit on by others. If only that monster could be forgotten, perhaps then I would be left alone" she complained.

"I've been following the legal reports; I intend to make sure that Hamza is finally brought to justice," Ahmad assured Isabel.

"We've stopped him from being able to do it again, Ahmad. I don't have the will any more to care what happens to him. He is in prison, and he'll never be let out. That's enough for me."

"But when I let you know he is dead, then it will really be over," Ahmad replied. "Please, I don't wish to irritate you. I ... I just want to see that you are alright and ask whether there –" Isabel stopped and put her hand on Ahmad's arm to stop him.

"I appreciate it, Ahmad, I sincerely do." She looked at him in a way that was difficult for him to interpret. Was it longing or regret? Or was she chastising him like an errant child? He saw her lips and imagined stepping forward to kiss her. Ahmad was deeply ashamed. "It's so difficult to be here in Fez now," she said. "They won't leave me alone. I need to go away."

Ahmad's expression darkened. "I don't want you to leave," he said firmly.

"I know," she replied with a tender smile. "Listen, I've been invited to the Dar al-Makhzen tomorrow to meet the Sultan's sister. Did you know, that when the Sultan's sister asks you to come for lunch, you are not permitted to decline," she laughed. "Will you come with me? I would very much like to have you accompany me."

Ahmad smiled. "Yes, of course; anything you wish, Isabel."

* * *

There was no doubt in Isabel's mind, as they walked to the royal palace the next day, that Ahmad was completely in love with her. Walking beside her, she could see his face was flushed and he kept stealing glances at her. It could not be, but at the same time she would have admitted, if asked, that she was flattered, for although he was young, she felt Ahmad was more intelligent and had a greater wealth of experience than herself. This made her both want him and, in a way, fear him at the same time. If only he were not so damned young.

They arrived at the Royal Palace and, to Isabel's lifelong astonishment, the great bronze central gate swung open for her as they approached as if she were the Queen of Sheeba. Massive guards in colorful uniforms stepped from the shadows to escort them through the grounds. She and Ahmad were admitted first to an enormous garden, the likes of which Isabel could never have imagined. Not only plants and flowers of unlimited variety, but benches, sculptures

Tamanrasset

and water features dazzled the eyes. There was an opulence she could not fathom.

They were escorted across the grounds to a wing of the palace and brought indoors to a very stately room with large glass windows, a crystal chandelier, and a European-style dining table with chairs; the table was set for two. As they waited, Isabel went to speak quietly with a servant who was attending them and asked that a third place be set at the table for her friend. The servant looked at Isabel with awe, as if he were speaking to an angel. It was the same sort of reverence everyone seemed to give her now. The servant could not have more emphatically agreed to what she asked and quickly left the room to see to her request. In no time, he returned with another man in livery who set a third place at the table. Just at that moment, a gentleman in a western suit entered through another door. He was followed by a mature woman who wore an exquisite kaftan adorned with real jewels and gold and silver thread; she also wore a tiara. She was followed by three large men in uniforms who were armed with scimitar-like swords.

"Greetings and salutations, Madame Pedersen," said the gentleman to Isabel. "May I present you to Princess Lalla Fatima Zohra bint Hassan al-Alaoui, sister to the Sultan Abd al-Aziz bin Hassan al-Alaoui."

The Princess then stepped forward and offered Isabel her hand. "It is an honor to meet you, Madame Pedersen," she said.

Isabel took the offered hand and curtseyed. "I am honored, Your Highness."

"Who have you brought with you?" The gentleman asked, a slight note of irritation in his voice.

"This is my good friend, Ahmad ibn Mostepha al-Haybah, son of Sharif Moulay Mostepha ibn Ali al-Haybah," Isabel said.

Ahmad stepped forward and bowed.

"You are also welcome, Sayyid," the princess said.

"I am honored to be in your presence, Your Highness," Ahmad said.

"Well, I don't think we need you any longer, Fairouz, you may leave us," the princess told the gentleman. He turned and left the room, but the guards remained. "Please come, I see they have set a place for your friend, let us sit. You don't care for wine with your lunch, do you, Madame Pedersen?"

"No, Ma'am."

"Please, you must call me Lalla, I am only a princess, and one of many. I understand that you are a student at the university, is that right? I see our lunch is coming now." They were served an elegant meal of sliced beef and vegetables served on plates. Ahmad had apparently never seen a meal served in that manner, so he watched Isabel carefully and imitated how she ate.

"Please call me Isabel," she said. "Well, I am not a student, no; I merely work for a scholar at the university, reading and writing materials for him. I am a widow; my husband was also a scholar, and we came here from Sweden for his studies at the university."

"I understand and mourn your loss. But I think you are giving yourself less credit than you are perhaps due. I was told you are widely respected for your knowledge of Islam, and that many consider you to be a great Alima. Is that not so?"

"I didn't know that," Isabel replied awkwardly.

The Princess went on: "Even my brother, the Moulay Mohammed who lives a quiet and sequestered life of worship here in the palace, has told me that you are a wise and venerable woman."

"I'm truly astonished, ma'am. Your brother the Moulay Mohammed is revered by so many across all of Morocco. We would be so grateful if he would speak to the faithful at my mosque, but I am told he doesn't like to appear in public."

"Moulay Mohammed is even more revered than my brother the Sultan," the princess replied, "but let us all be grateful that he has no interest in ruling the country. He is beloved, but a religious zealot."

"Oh, no, I didn't mean to suggest that he should do anything like that," Isabel said.

The princess laughed. "As I said, I have many sisters and many brothers, twenty-six in all. Sadly, the fate of such royal families is that half of them think they could do a better job than the other half. We had the incident recently, widely reported unfortunately, involving my brother Omar and his secretary."

"Jilali al-Zerhouni?" Ahmad asked.

"Yes, that's the man," the princess replied. "He was plotting for Omar to replace the Sultan. Now who would give a secretary such an idea or the courage to speak it aloud, I ask you, if not Omar himself? But tell me, the baker who was killing the young girls, how did you find this evil man?"

"It wasn't just me; Ahmad was involved too. The last victim, Faiza Benayoun, she was the daughter of my sponsor here in Fez, the scholar who is guiding my return to Islam. Faiza was a sweet young girl. I knew, when she disappeared, she would not be found alive, and then, when her body was found, to discover that she had been kept alive for days before being murdered, I couldn't bear to imagine to what purpose. I had to make sure it couldn't happen again; girls have been disappearing for years, and everyone just said 'alas, it's the will of Allah.' I couldn't live with that. And there were certain facts that pointed in a specific direction."

"Is it true you had a vision?" The princess asked bluntly.

Isabel was taken aback. "I just ... there was a moment when I suddenly realized that the man in front of me was the one who had committed the crimes. Was it deduction? Intuition? A vision from Allah? I am not wise enough to know which it was."

"That is a fair answer, and I appreciate your humility, Isabel. Whatever the method, you have done my brother and his people a great service. He may not have the good grace to thank you, but I do."

"You're very gracious, Ma'am."

"It is not widely known, but I own a very extensive library of rare books on Islam. Not many women have such an interest, as you might suspect, but it's something from which I've taken intense pleasure over the years. I intend to donate my collection to the university in your name."

"That is a truly gracious gift, thank you," Isabel said emotionally. "You truly honor me, and many will benefit greatly from such a generous gift."

"In any event, it's time for the books to go, and you are most worthy of the honor, Isabel. Did you know, there are no marabouts in Morocco that are women? I had hoped to be the first, but now I'm afraid you will be named before me."

Isabel was uncertain whether this was meant as praise, but it sounded very much like criticism. Surely if the

Princess wished to be named "marabout," a title of enormous respect and mystical power, she could arrange that. Ahmad was even more blunt: "Isabel cannot be a marabout," he said, "because she is not descended from the Prophet or his family."

"Such things are often overlooked or simply claimed without evidence," the Princess replied. "There is a woman marabout in Algeria, I'm told. Her name is Lèlla Zeyneb; she is daughter to Sheik Muhammad al-Qasim, in Ouargla. He raised his daughter to be his successor, and she is said to be exceedingly pious and to have performed miracles of healing. The people call her a marabout. I dare say she has earned it."

"Yes, that may be so," Ahmad agreed, "but Isabel will know whether what she claims is true or false."

"Tell me, Isabel," the princess went on, "you were injured by the criminal, is that right? Have you recovered? Has your medical care been adequate?"

"Oh, yes, I'm fine. I've found it more difficult to deal with the attention thrust on me as a result of, well, of those events."

"Yes, I've heard about that too," the Princess replied ambiguously. "But you have your friend Ahmad to protect you, no?"

"Ahmad is a good friend, but he is a student at the university and quite dedicated to his studies," Isabel answered. She took a quick look at Ahmad and saw he looked disappointed to be called a mere "friend." "To be honest, I am thinking I will have to leave Fez altogether," Isabel announced.

Ahmad looked ill. "I hope that's not so," he said.

Crossroads of the Nomad

The Princess smiled at him. "You are fortunate, Isabel, to have a friend like Ahmad who cares so much for your well-being. I have an idea, and I hope you won't think it too presumptuous of me. As part of your return to the faith, would you allow me to pay for you to travel to Mecca for the Hajj this year?"

Isabel seemed overwhelmed by such generosity. "I am astonished," she said. "I wouldn't even know how to begin to thank you."

"No, no, it is I who am thanking you," the princess insisted.

Ahmad told Isabel: "It is a great privilege to make the Hajj. I will remain here in Fez for you until the fate of the monster Hamza is resolved." Turning to the princess, he asked: "Do you know what the Sultan intends to do with him?"

"Ahmad, that's not her business," Isabel admonished him.

"I'm not asking you to influence the Sultan's decision, Your Highness," Ahmad said. "I'm only asking if you know whether a decision has been made. I'm sure you can understand we are very anxious that the criminal receives a punishment that befits his terrible crimes. Since the crucifixion was called off, many people are concerned that the Sultan will impose no punishment. Some even say that he has bowed to the whims of the Europeans," Ahmad said as gently as possible.

"I don't know," the princess replied flatly, "but I am not troubled by this small delay, nor should you be. The criminal will be punished, you need have no doubt of that."

Tamanrasset

* * *

In the cellars of Chateau Neuf, the plunk of water falling onto stone was like the steady rhythm of a metronome. The walls and floor were moist and a constant indeterminate temperature. There was no way to tell day from night. Bowls of soup with meat or lentils and a bucket of water arrived at variable intervals; waste buckets were emptied once each day. Demoreau no longer knew how many months of his sentence had passed, nor did he particularly care. It was all the same to him—passing the time, waiting, filling moments of his life. There was no objective, no purpose. There would be no reward. There were two factors which kept him from losing his mind during the lengthy period of confinement to which he had been sentenced. The first was his music. Demoreau would not ever discuss the life he led prior to enlisting in the Foreign Legion, but then it had been many years since any fond recollections of his past life had entered his head. However, music played a major role in that life, and he could still remember every note of many compositions. He could perform the music silently in his mind at a moderate Andante as he paced back and forth across his cell, one, two, three, four, five, turn, one, two, three, four, five, turn again. Sometimes he would even hum along. Music had occupied his mind for countless hours over many years—while on days-long marches across the empty wastelands of desert, while stationed for months on end at remote desert forts, and during endless days of imprisonment. Music was in his mind when he went to sleep, when he lay sleeplessly in the middle of the night, and when he awoke in the morning.

The second factor, in the instant case, was Demoreau's firm belief that he had actually done his duty as a Legionnaire because stopping Capitaine Mitterand from killing his wife and Van Hove had been in the best interest of the Legion. So, if, for the sake of appearances or precedent, the Legion wanted Demoreau to spend some time in prison for having struck an officer, then he had no objection. That too was his duty. He had no regrets, and it was merely unfortunate that his jailers at Chateau Neuf didn't know or care to know about the circumstances which had placed him in their cells. And so he spent months like any other errant Legionnaire, expending endless days in a windowless chamber, pacing, with only occasional contact with others.

* * *

Weeks passed, and there was still no word on what would happen to Hamza. Sporadic protests arose when residents of Fez marched to the Palace and cried for justice. These became more frequent after the Ulama issued a fatwa calling for the sentence of crucifixion to be reimposed by the Sultan.

In the meantime, the French-backed papers in Morocco saw an opportunity to weaken the Sultan and render his government easier to manipulate to their advantage. One newspaper pressured the Sultan to adopt a more humane punishment, arguing that crucifixion was a barbaric practice that violated international law. Moroccan merchants, fearing that the ongoing controversy would damage trade, urged the Sultan to find a solution that would appease the international audience. But the other French newspaper decried the weakness of the Sultan and argued that the crimes warranted a painful death. The people were pulled in opposite directions at once. The Sultan was caught in the middle of these arguments, and each day another member of his family (his twenty-six brothers and sisters) would take one side or the other or even advocate for ridiculous sentences like exile or stoning. The government ministers decried the lack of unity and pleaded for patience while the Sultan reached a final decision. It was then reported, true or not, that certain members of the Sultan's government and family had accepted bribes to adopt one position or another. Since the Sultan's family was well known to be struggling financially and the government was paralyzed by debt, these reports were highly plausible.

However, after weeks of divisive arguments and pressure on the government, the sentence of the Sultan was finally announced. A firman was presented to the court bearing the Sultan's own signature. Hamza was sentenced to be entombed until death in a public place so that the citizens of Fez would know that the criminal was dead. The date of the execution was set for the next market day.

Ahmad and most of Fez were relieved that the edict would at least end the dispute. Still, it had severely weakened the Sultan's government. Abd al-Aziz had been shown to be a dilettante who was easily manipulated by his foreign creditors and would bend back and forth like a sapling caught in the winds of public opinion. Al-Kattani had prepared numerous drafts of his newspaper addressing the Sultan's weakness, but the printing presses had not yet been repaired and not a single edition had yet been distributed. Nevertheless, he had kept Ahmad busy, and Ahmad had not had time to see Isabel again.

Crossroads of the Nomad

After the firman was announced, Ahmad went down to the market square adjacent to the military barracks and prison to see what preparations were being made for the execution. Along one side of the square was the thick stone wall of the prison, and a hole had been dug into that wall which was two feet deep, two feet wide and six feet tall. Chains were affixed to the rear wall that would prevent Hamza from sitting or crouching down. Ahmad didn't think Isabel would want to see the execution, but he wanted her to know that the site was being readied. He walked to Isabel's house to tell her. The servant answered the door.

Isabel, Ahmad was told, had already departed for Mecca on her Hajj.

Ahmad was crushed. He had always known that Isabel was not going to end up as his wife, but as long as she was nearby and he could be close to her from time to time, he had at least felt a certain intimacy with her. He was her friend, but she was something more to him—an aspiration, a hope. In her presence he felt a passion that was deep. He did love her. Now he didn't know whether he would ever hear from Isabel again, and he felt crushed.

On the day of the execution, Ahmad joined the thousands that came to celebrate. Hamza was led out for what he thought would be the daily whipping to which he had become accustomed. At sight of the crowds, however, the baker knew at once that his time on earth was over. He struggled and began to cry and beg for mercy. Brought to the niche dug into the side of the fortress, he was pressed against the back wall and chained. The crowd was given time to pelt him with offal and dung. The executioner gave Hamza a last meal of bread and water. In fact, this was merely to keep him alive longer since the crowd demanded a long and painful death.

At last, the masons were let forward and allowed to begin laying courses of stone and mortar, brick upon brick, while Hamza cried and screamed. The final bricks were laid and the living tomb was completed. The throng pressed forward to hear Hamza's muffled screams through the masonry. Night came, and the crowd waited, cheering whenever Hamza began to scream again. A day later, the only sound heard from the tomb was moaning, and that also stopped after a brief time. The crowd cursed Hamza for dying too quickly. Slowly, the business of the market resumed and the crowds disbursed. Ahmad saw enough to know that, although the living entombment had been unfortunately brief, Hamza's life had still ended in crushing agony.

III – The Siege of Taghit

The heavy footsteps in the corridor were untimely. Could another day have passed already? Had one of the other prisoners died? The solid steel door of Demoreau's cell was unlocked and opened, and a guard stood in the bright light of the opening. "Viens avec moi," he ordered then turned and walked off. Demoreau followed, hesitantly stepping barefoot from his cell. They mounted ancient stone steps and climbed to a level illuminated by sunlight. Demoreau straightened his back and took a deep breath. He could smell blossoms and fresh air. He unconsciously used his hands to smooth his hair and the chest of his grey prison uniform and followed the guard down a long hallway to a large room with a high ceiling and French doors that showed a sunny terrace. There were three officers seated in the hall on expensive upholstered armchairs: A Colonel, a Capitaine, and a Sous-Lieutenant. That could not possibly be correct, Demoreau thought: A French Major was in command of Chateau Neuf, and there was no reason whatsoever for a Colonel to visit the prison. The Colonel was a short, narrow man with white hair cut flat on top and a lengthy but unevenly cut mustache of light red hair. Demoreau drew himself up before the officers, coming to attention.

Tamanrasset

The Capitaine complained to the guard of Demoreau's condition: "Bon sang, tu n'aurais pas pu le nettoyer avant de l'amener?"

"Je suis désolé, mon Capitaine," the guard apologized.

"He's here now, let's begin," the Colonel stated in English. Demoreau was known to primarily be an English speaker, and he knew the Colonel would not use English except for his benefit. The Sous-Lieutenant had several documents which he reviewed briefly so as to appear well informed, then he looked up at the prisoner.

"Your name is Jacques Demoreau, is that correct?"

"Oui, mon Lieutenant."

"You struck Capitaine Mitterand?"

"Yes, I did."

"Flemmard," the Capitaine said to Colonel, a mild insult which Demoreau hoped was meant to describe Capitaine Mitterand and not himself.

The Sous-Lieutenant continued: "I see you have about seven months left on your sentence. Afterwards, it's not clear where you will be assigned. You have sixteen months left in your term of enlistment. And ... mon Dieu, is this correct? You are now in your fifth term of enlistment? You're a lifer, then, eh?"

"Yes, Sir, I suppose that's correct," Demoreau mumbled in reply. Not many men re-enlisted that many times, at least not without gaining an officer's commission at some point. Demoreau had a way of earning promotions and demotions in equal measure so that, in the end, they washed out. He would say that he had been a Sergent, "more or less," for over twenty years.

As if hearing Demoreau's thoughts, the Sous-Lieutenant remarked: "You've been struck down to Sergent again, and it says here you're a bit of a drinker. But your record also shows that you've received several commendations and medals, and you've a reputation as an excellent drill instructor. You're not really a bad sort, are you Demoreau?"

Years of service had certainly taught Demoreau the correct answer to a question like that: "No, Sir, definitely not a bad sort at all, Sir." As his mind returned from the darkness of his cell, he was becoming increasingly curious: Who the hell were these men, and what did they want?"

The Colonel asked: "Sergent, would you like to return to your former position and unit following this period of discipline?"

That took Demoreau by surprise. "I, uh, I didn't think that would be possible, Sir," he stammered.

"Let me explain as I see your mind reeling in confusion. I am looking for a competent drill instructor, one that, for whatever reason, is currently unattached, to assist with a private commercial matter. The enterprise will involve travel into hostile terrain, and it may become necessary to handle dangerous or life-threatening situations. If you agree to assist, then I will arrange for your early release from prison, for your conviction to be expunged from your record, and for you to return to your former unit following a brief period of détachment."

Demoreau had never heard of such a thing and was truly taken aback; the offer was unheard of. Had the Colonel really said the words "private commercial matter?" There was only one possible explanation. "Are you asking me to be a spy?" He asked indignantly. A spy, Demoreau believed,

Tamanrasset

was a soldier with no honor whatsoever. A soldier wore a uniform that represented who and what he stood for.

"Oh, good heavens, no," the Colonel replied firmly. "You'll simply be detached from the Legion for a short time. It will make the usual paperwork, chain of command, and so forth, unnecessary. You'll assist with this business affair as a private party, and, afterwards, when you've completed the job, I'll arrange for your reinstatement to the Legion as though you'd never left."

Demoreau looked at the panel a moment. "And if I neglect to return?" He asked.

"You and I both know, Sergent, that if you're not dead, there's only one other place in this wide world for you to be. Or have I misread you entirely? Either way, though, if you finish the job, I honestly don't care." The Colonel said.

"No, you haven't misread," Demoreau admitted. "It all seems quite simple. Is it?"

"Mon Dieu, I certainly hope so," the Colonel said emphatically.

Of course Demoreau agreed.

He was given two weeks leave in Oran to recuperate from his imprisonment, and it made a vast improvement in his physical and mental condition. Oran was a more modern city on the Mediterranean coast swarming with respectable British and German tourists. Consequently, it had few of the old-world conveniences found, for example, in the duskier areas of Algiers or Casablanca. Demoreau remained far more temperate than he generally would have preferred given two weeks of leave. Nevertheless, the weather was fair, he obtained a crisp new uniform and excellent boots, and he ate an ocean of fresh seafood. He was still a

Legionnaire, and, dressed as a Sergent, boarded a train on the appointed date bound westward to Tlemcen, a city on the High Plateau of northwest Algeria only forty kilometers from Morocco. It was in Tlemcen, in what was once the capital of a Moorish kingdom, that the regional headquarters of the Armée d'Afrique was located, and Demoreau was expected to report at the office there of the Colonel, whose name, he had learned, was Lyautey.

The second-class compartment of the train in which Demoreau sat was thoroughly familiar and comfortable, from his point of view. He was closely surrounded by French soldiers, mostly young Frenchmen who had been conscripted. Although few of them had yet been down south to the "Sud Oranais" to places like Taghit or In Salah where the situation between the local tribes and the French remained at a simmering boil, there had been an increasing number of violent attacks in the northwest of Algeria as well, he was told. Moroccan tribesman increasingly raided Algeria for theft and murder. Moreover, the border between northwestern Algeria and the northeastern region of Morocco, which was called the "Oriental," was porous and ill-defined. This led to misunderstandings and accusations and constant attacks on French civilians and property. The Moroccan raiders had no trouble avoiding the French army, for although infantry regiments were constantly moving up and down the border, the criminals sought to avoid all confrontations. There were simply not enough soldiers in all of Algeria to close the border altogether. Nevertheless, those soldiers with whom Demoreau spoke on the train seemed quite pleased with themselves and excited to be in their clean uniforms headed to Tlemcen. Some would undoubtedly be sent to guard the border to the west, but they knew that danger would actively steer clear of them. And, by all accounts, Tlemcen itself remained a quiet city with cheap wine and clean women.

When his train arrived at the station, Demoreau found it was a lengthy walk to his hotel, "Le Charles" on the Places des Victoires, but a couple of friendly French NCO's accompanied him and invited the Sergent out to "explore" the city that evening. He declined, not wishing to be sick when he reported to Colonel Lyautey the next morning. He had been in Tlemcen before, of course, but this was not the time to renew old lapses in judgment.

In the morning, Demoreau, refreshed and sober, walked to the Mechouar Palace. The few remaining useful buildings of that ancient but long-abandoned complex had been converted into offices, barracks, and a hospital for the French Armée d'Afrique. Colorful mosaics and cryptic Arabic writings still adorned the interior walls. Demoreau was directed by one soldier after another through a maze of interconnected rooms, each ornately decorated with colorful ancient tiles and stucco, until he arrived at a large elegantly carved wood-paneled room overlooking a garden of citrus trees in bloom. There, Colonel Lyautey sat on a bare wood chair beside a wide wood table, his legs crossed, while he examined a typed paper that the Sous-Lieutenant, his aide-de-camp, had just handed to him. The Colonel twirled the end of his wide mustache and picked up his pen. He glanced at Demoreau standing silently before him at attention.

"Stand at repos, Sergent,' the Colonel said calmly. "I am pleased to see you looking better than at our last meeting. I am now signing the order of détachment which will allow you to engage in the matter we discussed. When you are finished, you may return here for your reinstatement and orders sending you back to the, what is it," he said examining a file on his desk, "the 6th Mounted Company, 2nd Regiment of the Foreign Legion. Any questions?"

"Have you learned where the Sixth is stationed? Can they even take me as a Sergent?" Demoreau wanted to make sure he would receive everything he had been promised.

"We've determined that the Company is on training patrols near the Tunisia border now; they are still incorporating additional replacements after losing so many Legionnaires in the Sud Oranais. But I can arrange for your Company to be returned to Saïda so you will be able to rejoin them there. Capitaine Roubec is again commanding the Company; you got along well with him, did you not?"

"Yes, Sir," Demoreau replied. "May I know how long you expect this private business to take, Sir?"

"Oh, I dare say a couple of months, Sergent. I don't really know."

"Shall I send you reports, Sir?"

"Absolutely not. I don't care to know anything about it, at least not until you return, nor should you discuss this matter with anyone else. It's private business."

"Yes, mon Colonel; I understand."

"Then that's all there is to it, Sergent. My aide will give you the address where you are to meet the gentlemen in charge; they are expecting you this morning."

Demoreau came to attention and saluted.

The Colonel returned the salute. "Dismissed."

Outside the office, Demoreau was given a slip of paper. "Here you are, monsieur; bonne chance," the aide said flatly.

There was an absence of enthusiasm that made Demoreau wonder what sort of scheme he had agreed to.

As he left the palace and walked to the nearby Place de la Mairie where he was expected, Demoreau felt a lurch in his chest. The uniform he wore was no longer his uniform. He was not actually a soldier anymore. It was in truth a fiction, yes, but he had actually been detached from the Legion and that was not a position that, under ordinary circumstances, he would have accepted. He didn't like it. He liked having a place to belong, and the Legion had been that place for him through many long years. But the less time dwelling on such thoughts the better. He arrived at a large, newly constructed three-story building of offices. Most of the businesses therein were designated on a plaque at the front door: Wineries, solicitors, bankers, and export interests. Demoreau went to the offices of Paixporteur Carrier Int'l. and was shown by a young French clerk to an empty room. He sat at a large table and waited some time. Finally, three expensively dressed middle-aged gentlemen came in together.

"Monsieur Demoreau, a pleasure to meet you, and thank you for coming," said the oldest of the three. He had oily grey hair and a thin mustache; Demoreau took him as either Italian or Spanish. "My name is Adolphe Caroling. These gentlemen are my business colleagues, Édouard Durant and James Bronwin." French and British, Demoreau thought. They all shook hands and sat around the large table.

"It has all been arranged for me to be here at your disposal, Messieurs," Demoreau said, "so, please, I hope someone will tell me what you would like me to actually do."

Durant, a white-haired man in a fine black suit, spoke next: "Let me start off then, and I'll try to keep it quite simple. A little background: We three, through our various commercial enterprises, own a substantial amount of land in western Algeria. Monsieur Bronwin owns virtually the entire coastline between here and the border of Morocco. Monsieur Caroling and I each own vineyards, orchards, and farms. And the three of us together have joint business ventures and other financial arrangements. You do understand that the volume of wine produced in Algeria now vastly surpasses that of France itself, and that our farms and orchards export essential food supplies to France and fourteen other countries."

"I had no idea," Demoreau said.

"Rather a significant business, you might say," Bronwin interjected.

"It is," said Durant, "yes, a very significant business, a business that cannot be interrupted, and naturally a very profitable business in times of peace. But, alas, things are not very peaceful these days, are they?"

"Are they not?" Demoreau asked.

"No, they are not. While our situation here is dire, alas, over in Morocco it is far worse. The Sultan there has little or no control over large areas of his country."

"Like in the Saoura-Zousfana valleys," Demoreau recalled.

"Yes, yes, that's exactly right," Durant replied enthusiastically, as if realizing that Demoreau was possibly not as stupid as he had assumed. "Their ruler has absolutely no control over the barbarians in those regions, nor has he any control along his border with the northwest of Algeria.

The main difference is that in the south the raiders mostly steal from each other, whereas here the raiders are stealing from me, and from Monsieur Bronwin, and from Monsieur Caroling. You understand?"

"Yes, very clear," Demoreau stated, mildly insulted by Durant's tone.

"Alas, it has proven nearly impossible to keep the lawless brigands of Morocco from entering Algeria, and there is absolutely no one in Morocco trying to stop them. Well then, we thought, wouldn't it be lovely if we could locate a friendly Moroccan individual to take charge in the Oriental and put an end to those damned criminals."

Caroling took up the conversation: "Have you heard of Jilali al-Zerhouni?"

"I am not familiar with Monsieur Jilali, no," he replied.

"He formerly held the position of Private secretary to Moulay Omar al-Alaoui, one of the young brothers of the Sultan of Morocco. There were some intrigues at the Royal Palace, we understand, and Jilali was briefly imprisoned. He was released on the condition that he leave Morocco, and he now lives in Oran."

"Well, to be blunt," Durant continued more seriously, "we wish to set Jilali up in the Oriental province of Morocco as a sort of unofficial governor, and he has agreed that if we succeed in doing so then he will put a stop to the Moroccan raiders entering French Algeria."

"That's a very blunt proposition. And how would you propose to set him up as a, as you call it, unofficial governor, if I may ask?" Demoreau inquired with a glimmer of understanding dawning in his mind.

"Well, we've bought guns and ammunition, and we'd like to hire some former soldiers. You'll train them and, as a privately contracted citizen, take them over with Jilali and help him to take control over that region of Morocco."

"I see, so you want to establish a warlord in Morocco who is your puppet, pay his men and equip them with guns, so they will stop anyone stealing from you?"

"Precisely, and where you come in, monsieur, we want you to help him do it. We want you to put together a little army for Jilali and help him to get set up there."

Demoreau laughed. "That's, uh… I mean, … I'm not sure how the Moroccan government will react to our setting up a hostile warlord within their territory," he objected.

"We're perfectly aware that the situation we envision is hostile to the current government," Durant said, "but, since the Sultan has no army or administrative control in that region, he can do nothing about it. Our only options are to either send a man to Morocco who is allied with our interests, or else have the Armée d'Afrique go in and massacre thousands. The French government has already ruled that out. So we are left with no other choice. Now, you're not currently an active-duty soldier, and this isn't an action by the French government. It's a private enterprise with a commercial objective, specifically, to protect Algerian commercial interests. We don't wish to invade Morocco or take Moroccan land or steal anything from the Moroccan people, and we'll install a Moroccan man at the top. We'll pay for what we need. We only want to get that damned region under control."

Demoreau took a deep breath and imagined just walking out and getting on a ferry to Spain. It was obvious to him

Tamanrasset

now why the Colonel had been willing to lend a Sergent of the French Foreign Legion, one who had trained many soldiers, to assist these businessmen with their scheme. If successful, it would achieve what the Armée d'Afrique could not—pacification of a dangerously unsettled region adjacent to French Algeria.

"I suppose we can try," Demoreau said. "But how far do you trust Jilali? If you set him up as a warlord, what will stop him from raiding your lands himself?"

"Of course we want you to let us know if you come to have any doubts about our man," the British man, Bronwin, said, "otherwise, it's not your concern. Jilali, you might say, is leashed by his own ambitions."

"Fine, then," Demoreau replied, "but I want to hire mostly native soldiers here in Algeria, and I'll need a staff, an interpreter, horses, supplies."

Bronwin replied: "Hire whoever you like. Buy whatever you need. We have the money, we have the guns, we have the man. You make an army, take it to Morocco, and help Jilali take control."

"I can do that," Demoreau said. At least, he thought he could try, and then, if he made it out of Morocco alive, he could go back to the Sixth where he belonged.

* * *

The Muezzin was calling the faithful to the prayer, but Isabel was still waiting in a large, breezy tiled hallway. It frustrated her that the French had such little regard for Muslims in a country that they had taken away from Muslims, even those who still lived there. She was surrounded in the hallway by large serious-looking men,

Crossroads of the Nomad

Berber warriors, all waiting as well. She was the only woman, and she pulled her hijab forward to better shade her face.

It had been many months since Isabel left Fez to undertake the Hajj, the pilgrimage to Mecca that was one of the five basic "Pillars of Islam." She had been to the Great Mosque there, but she had not yet returned to Morocco. This was due, in part, to the fact that her fares and expenses had only been paid in one direction. It seemed she should have been more skeptical of the Sultan's sister, for it turned out that she and the Sultan had only wished to be rid of Isabel. But she had no regrets: The pilgrimage had been exceptional. She had travelled by steamship first class across the northern coast of Africa, making stops to see all the major cities along the way, and then sailed down the Red Sea to Jedda. However, after her Hajj was completed, Isabel was left destitute and uncertain where to go. Of course she thought of returning to Fez. She had felt some bond with the community there, but that was before the capture of the baker and before things had changed. The only reasonable option was to take some time before she returned and allow the matter to be forgotten. She decided to travel and learn, but the months since had taken a toll. She had been beaten, robbed, and assaulted but had made it as far back as Tlemcen. Since Isabel could not return to Fez penniless and exhausted, and in debt to the kind widow with whom she was staying in Tlemcen, she decided to extend her stay briefly and had entered a French placement agency to request short-term employment. She had completed a few minor translation jobs, but now Isabel was waiting to interview for a new and longer term position.

Tamanrasset

A Frenchman in a black suit with a large sheaf of papers walked up to her: "Madame Pedersen? Suivez-moi, s'il vous plaît."

He led her to the door of the room where the interviews were taking place and gestured for her to enter. Inside was a bright room with large windows; a number of chairs were arranged in a circle, and three men were seated together: Two appeared to be soldiers of some sort, although their uniforms had no insignia. The other was a man with white hair and a fine black wool suit. All three were looking at her with undisguised curiosity.

"Please have a seat," said the older soldier, an officer of some kind perhaps, a handsome man with graying hair and steel gray eyes. After Isabel sat down, he asked her skeptically: "You understand that you're applying for the post of interpreter in connection with a field operation being conducted by this company. That means we'll be going out to the countryside; there will be none of the conveniences of the city and possibly some danger. Would you like to reconsider your application?"

Isabel smiled. "I wonder whether the countryside is as dangerous for me as it is for you," she said. "As for the conveniences of which you speak, I've had none of them already during many months of travel across Africa."

"You're not Arab or Berber; do you wear the head scarf out of mere fancy? Your French is excellent, but can you speak Arabic?" He asked in a challenging manner.

"Yes, I speak Arabic fluently. I speak also French, English, and Swedish because I am Swedish. I wear the hijab because I am Muslim."

The soldiers stared at her for a moment attempting to comprehend the unusual person seated before them. It seemed to have never occurred to them that a European person could be Muslim, or that a woman from Sweden might wear a hijab. For that matter, Isabel no longer wore a djellaba nor dressed like a Swedish lady: Along with her hijab, she now wore heavy pants, leather boots, and a thick shirt beneath her worn burnoose, the long wool cloak usually worn only by Arab men.

Finally, the older soldier asked an even odder question.

"As a Muslim, do you oppose the terrible violence, murder, and ruthless thefts that are inflicted every day by bandits and thieves upon their fellow Muslims in neglected and unregulated areas?"

"Yes, of course," she replied impatiently.

"Would you answer differently if the violence were being perpetrated by native Muslims against French, Spanish or British citizens?"

"I'm sorry," she laughed. "I don't understand exactly what you mean, but I am opposed to violence no matter who the perpetrator and who the victim."

"Then you object if the police use violence to stop a violent criminal?"

"I have no objection to the use of force to the extent necessary to subdue a man and prevent him from doing further harm," she said, remembering the crack of the baker's kneecap when she rammed her foot into it. "Is this an examination of my morality?" She added testily.

The younger soldier asked: "What are you doing in Tlemcen?"

Tamanrasset

"I've been on a sort of tour of the Sahara. I've just come north through Aïn Séfra and have found myself in need of additional funds."

"You've been to Aïn Séfra? Where else have you traveled?" The older soldier asked her with genuine curiosity.

"I began my journey in Fez, traveled by ship from Tangier to Algiers, Tunis, Tripoli, Cairo, and Jedda. I rode by camel to Mecca on the Hajj. I then crossed the Red Sea to Luxor and rode to Khartoum; from there, I crossed the southern Sahara to reach Timbuktu, and then traveled north, via Aïn Séfra, with a caravan. I've been to many places in between that you would not know; most don't even have a name. I can assure you I would be a most able translator for your company, and I have no need of the conveniences of the city."

"I don't dispute that you are capable, madame. As long as you have no objection to the work we are undertaking which, in essence, involves the establishment of a private security force to maintain peace in certain unregulated areas. You will be most satisfied with the terms we are offering; they are extremely generous inasmuch as we will be traveling to regions that might be considered wild or dangerous, but only for people like me."

"The men outside, they're mercenaries I take it. You're hiring them to do violence or to prevent it?"

"Ideally, we wish to prevent it," the older soldier replied, "but Rome wasn't built in a day."

"And who are you gentlemen—are you the ones I'll be working for?" She asked.

"Yes, this young fellow is Caporal François Mathieu. He's recently completed his period of conscription in the French Army. My name is Jacques Demoreau, formerly of the French Foreign Legion. As you know, our employer is Paixporteur Carrier Int'l., an international partnership of French, British, and Spanish companies."

"And Polish," the white-haired gentleman added.

Isabel felt somewhat dizzy. A part of her just didn't care who these men were: She could do the work, and the pay was generous. Another part of her was concerned whether this position was consistent with her professed faith, since she still couldn't really understand what they were doing or what they needed her to do other than translations. But the employment was real, and perhaps that was all that mattered. She could decide what to do next after the work was completed.

"I think I could be of assistance to you," she said. "I would like the position."

* * *

It was a warm early morning on the coast of Tunisia, and Ren stood alone on the crest of a hill that overlooked Delattre's new excavation. The sun was beginning to rise over the hill behind him, and the slight dew that had accumulated through the night began to steam. The shadows slowly faded. It was Ren's first inspection of the site since returning from his lecture tour, and the work completed in his weeks of absence was astonishing. In the midst of a field of pale green grasses bordered by a ragged line of evergreen oaks lay the partially excavated outline of the interior wall and arena of an enormous Roman amphitheater. It was an absolutely fabulous discovery. A large marble cross had already been erected by the Cardinal at one end of the site to honor the Christian martyrs who had suffered and died there for the sake of their faith. According to Gibbon, it was at this very site that Genseric, king of the Vandals, had the Christian bishops brought out and trampled to death before a cheering crowd of sixty thousand. For the first time, Ren had a distinct impression of Tunis having been, at one time, a major Roman city. As he continued to inspect the work, the army of diggers hired by Delattre began to arrive. Tom Childers was directing the excavations that day. It was a relief that the site had been so remarkable because it would make the rest of the conversation that Ren needed to have with Delattre much easier for both of them.

Ren had previously made short trips to France and England to present the findings from Carthage, to display their most exciting discoveries and lecture on Carthaginian history. Such trips generally resulted in donations that were helping to sustain the excavation site and pay some salaries. However, by comparison, Ren's ten-week lecture tour in America had been an outright miracle.

He first travelled to Cadiz where he boarded a transatlantic steamship to Boston. By chance, Ren met on board fellow archaeologist Bert Hodge Hill, an American from Columbia University who was coming from the excavations at Corinth, the Ancient Greek city-state that, exactly like Carthage, was also sacked by the Romans in 146 BC. Bert was headed to Boston to present recent discoveries at Corinth to the annual meeting of the Archaeological Institute of America. Ren had also been planning to attend that meeting, and he most humbly accepted when Bert made the gracious offer to share his speaking time.

Over the next two weeks at sea, Ren and Bert met every day to play cards, drink gin and tonic, discuss each other's research, and prepare a detailed presentation on how the fates of Corinth and Carthage were both similar and distinct. Since Bert was traveling second class, Ren had all their meals (his and Bert's) brought to Ren's stateroom. By the time they arrived in Boston, they had prepared a groundbreaking address and become fast friends.

Their lecture at the AIA meeting was a resounding success. Ren's tour was immediately transformed from a series of quiet visits at small New England colleges to a major lecture tour of America's most prestigious scientific institutions. His first major presentation on Carthage occurred two weeks later to a packed assembly at the American Museum of Natural History in New York City. Scientists from Princeton, Yale and Columbia were enthralled by Ren's discussion of the funerary urns found in the Temple of Tanit and astonished by the work completed by Ren and Père Delattre to uncover Roman and Byzantine sites in Tunis. This success led to an invitation to stay for a few days at the home of William Henry Osborn, president of the museum.

(Bert didn't go into it but said he had some history with Osborn and begged off on accompanying Ren to Osborn's home in Peekskill; he promised to come visit Ren after he returned to Carthage.)

Ren traveled by train to the village north of New York City where Osborn, son of a famous U.S. Army general and grandson of a Supreme Court Justice, resided in a grand

Dutch mansion overlooking the Hudson River. Osborn claimed to know every scientist in America and all those worth knowing in Europe. He was a generous host with a beautiful wife, and his many adventurous children were spread all around the globe. Osborn was convinced, he told Ren, that the Phoenicians who settled Carthage and founded the empire that controlled the Western Mediterranean for seven hundred years had always remained connected with the Phoenician cities in the Eastern Mediterranean, especially those in the Levant. Ren was a dedicated scientist, but he was caught up in Osborn's enthusiasm and soon became a fast adherent to his novel theories. Osborn was pleased to arrange for Ren to lecture in Washington following lectures in Philadelphia and Baltimore, and Ren's presentation at the Cosmos Club in Washington, D.C. before the gentlemen of the National Geographic Society was a huge success.

Ren's final stop in America was one which held a special significance for him. He boarded a train at Union Station and traveled south to the City of Charleston, on the Atlantic coast in the State of South Carolina, to lecture before the courtly League of Southern American Scientists. The "L.S.A.S." was a society of Southern gentlemen who had been trying to prepare the former American Confederacy for the Twentieth Century. They were still trying. But for Ren, the visit had a more personal meaning: It was in Charleston, thirty-something years earlier, that Renwick Francis Villere had been born.

Ren didn't have any recollections of Charleston. His mother had died there days after his birth. His father had been a merchant who imported finished goods from his family's home country, France, and exported Southern goods like cotton that he purchased from any available source (including from freed African slaves). As a merchant, Ren's father applauded the end of the Civil War and the return of trade, but his pro-Reconstruction stances resulted in attempts on his life, death threats to his family, and arson. He decided to take his money and his children back to France, and there, almost immediately, he died. Ren was left with a trust fund, but, since he was still only able to speak English, his father's estate agents packed him right off to boarding school in England.

In Charleston, the L.S.A.S. adopted Ren as their long-lost son. They listened enraptured to his lecture and, at a dinner in his honor at the Alston House, asked Ren what they could do for him. Ren's visit resulted in the formation of the Franco-American Committee for the Excavation of Carthage, of which Renwick Francis Villere was named "Scientific Director" (and Père Delattre was named only as the Conservator of Christian Antiquities). Fundraising commenced immediately and, thanks to many generous donations, by the time Ren went aboard the transatlantic steamer from New York to Cadiz and eventually returned to Tunisia, expanded excavations at Carthage as well as a generous salary for Ren were fully secured for many years to come.

Having just returned, Ren had not yet communicated any of this news to Père Delattre. In a very obvious way, yes, Ren was aware that he had aggressively supplanted Delattre as chief of the excavations in Carthage (and any place to which the Carthaginian empire may have once extended), but it would also make Ren responsible for managing the Foundation and the people and it would give Delattre the freedom to work on any site he chose with virtually unlimited resources for the rest of his life. It was, anyway, these facts which Ren had chosen to emphasize.

They met, as usual, over their mid-day luncheon with wine in Delattre's office in the seminary building behind the cathedral. Delattre was silent but listened politely to all Ren had to report. He learned of the lectures, of the money, and of the plan to expand the excavations. Ren explained that he would take on the responsibility of the additional hiring and site management; Delattre could have all the diggers and assistants he wanted. It was important, Ren concluded, that they take advantage of this opportunity to purchase land and preserve future excavation sites now, while the money was available, since they could not know whether public excitement for the work in Carthage would persist.

When Ren concluded, Père Delattre took a deep breath and at last replied: "I believe you are afraid you have distressed me with your news, Ren."

"I am afraid it might seem to you as though I'm attempting to discount the tremendous work you have already done."

"I am first and foremost a priest. My legacy as an archaeologist will be in the relics themselves and in the knowledge I leave behind. Your ambitions make you useful to me. Indeed, this is precisely why I hired you to come to Carthage, and your instincts have been infallible. You have done very well for us."

"It is a relief, frankly, to hear you say that," Ren admitted.

Delattre stood to pour them each another glass of wine. "You must also remember that I hired you on behalf of the diocese, and our concession, our permit, at least with regard to excavation rights, is coextensive with the territory of this diocese, which is much of Tunisia. I would like you to make a report to the archbishop personally and emphasize to him our efforts to preserve those sites most relevant to early Christianity. It is very unlikely that the archbishop would wish to express an opinion on the issue of expanding excavations outside of Carthage."

"Of course, that's merely being judicious. Do you have reason to believe the archbishop will object?"

"No, but I must observe again that the matter of the possible child sacrifices at the Salammbô site is problematic: The church doesn't like such things to be brought to light."

"Unlike you, I am a scientist first. I cannot be a party to whitewashing history," Ren objected.

"Oh, I quite agree with you," Delattre continued. "But the less said to the archbishop of such things, the better. I'll go so far as to say, Ren, that your success is certain to provoke a certain amount of envy, of which you will personally be the target. The leads me to the bad news, I'm afraid. You've heard, no doubt, of Paul Gauckler, the Chief Inspector of the Office of Art and Antiquities."

"Yes, of course."

"We've been extremely fortunate that Gauckler has spent the past few years in Algiers dealing with the museum there. However, I've been forewarned that he intends to return to Tunis later this year."

"All I've heard of Gauckler is that he is a difficult fellow, but why is that? In what way? You clearly don't care for him."

"He believes the French government should be in charge of all excavations in Tunisia and Algeria."

"The government?!" Ren howled.

"Gauckler claims to have the authority to decide which sites get excavated and by whom. In the past, he and I have argued about the breadth of the diocese's concession; he would very much like to limit it. However, his power is restrained by the fact that he has no money. He will most certainly be attracted to the funds you have collected, like a moth to the flame. It may anger him if he cannot force you to spend that money as he directs."

"Why, that's outrageous!" Ren protested. "If we buy or lease a site and choose to excavate it or not, it seems to me we are well within our private property rights. I concede the government may wish to protect and preserve certain relics whose irreplaceability and historical significance places them above the realm of mere objects. But to dictate the time, place, and manner of any excavations? It's an outrage!"

"Yes, I agree," Delattre intoned, "but we will have to see what Gauckler does when he returns. I have some acquaintances at the antiquities museum in Algiers who may be able to advise us on dealing with the Chief Inspector. In any case, they have asked for you to come lecture in Algiers when you are available—they've asked twice, actually, and I owe them a reply."

"Algiers? Later in the year, perhaps," Ren offered indifferently.

"In the meantime, it is very well for you that the money is untouchable: The trust fund you've established will give you a basis to tell Gauckler that the expenditures are outside your control."

"That was Osborn's recommendation, for that very reason, and to avoid even the appearance that I am handling the funds for my own personal benefit."

"There is another issue I must mention that has grown out of control in your absence: Your success as a speaker has inadvertently resulted in a very substantial increase in the number of tourists coming to visit our excavation sites. We're at well over a thousand visitors per week now. You simply must hire additional guides to accompany the tour groups, to answer questions and make sure no one falls in a pit, and to watch for signs of theft by overly enthusiastic visitors."

"I'll see to it, of course," Ren agreed. "There's been an absence of qualified English and German-speakers living in Tunis for us to hire, and I've already stretched our current archaeology students thin. I'll write to some colleagues, perhaps some of the professors I've just met in America. They may know of recent graduates who are looking for work abroad."

* * *

Demoreau continued to gaze in surprise at the woman seated before him, and she met his gaze with a wry smile that he understood to mean she was prepared for whatever "travail" he and his colleagues had in mind. That was just the attitude he hoped to find, not knowing for certain himself what complications the company's scheme might provoke. Furthermore, the Madame's professed faith might very well

Tamanrasset

assist them in dealing with people who had customs or ideas that Demoreau and his employers could hardly comprehend. Had she really traveled across the Sahara? Remarkable, he thought.

"Monsieur Durant will discuss the terms of the engagement with you," he said; "I'd like you to begin immediately. You noticed the men out in the hallway waiting. We need to hire a few of them, and I'd like your help if you can stay this afternoon."

Durant suddenly came alive: "Madame Pedersen, would you please come with me to my office so we can discuss the terms and have you sign our employment contract? That would be marvelous. Shall we?" He stood and gestured for her to follow him out through a back door of the interview room.

"We'll wait to continue the interviews until you've come back," Demoreau told her.

After she had exited, Demoreau's young colleague Mathieu turned on him: "That woman is going to be a lot of trouble, if you ask me, Sergent. She's a little independent-minded for my taste. Don't we want someone easier to control?"

"She can help us get what we want. She can handle the locals, keep them quiet. There's going to be some resistance from local leaders; she can help with that too. There'll be men we'd rather pay off than kill. We don't want to be over there and have to eliminate everyone who opposes our man taking over. We need someone who can negotiate, and she's lived with these people."

"You're the boss, Sergent," Mathieu said skeptically, "but I don't trust any of them."

Durant returned with Isabel a few minutes later.

"Listen," Demoreau told her, "we can talk this all out later, but I need to get a few more interviews done. Have a seat here next to me. These fellows coming in are former Tirailleurs, French light infantry. That means they're locals, Chaamba tribesmen, but they've served under French officers and have been honorably discharged so I believe they're dependable. If you have any doubts about whether they'll follow orders, or if they simply seem so hostile that they'll create problems, let me know."

Within minutes, Isabel was running the interviews. Demoreau was pleased with how competently she greeted each of the soldiers in Arabic and spoke to them for several minutes to put them at ease. Some, she told Demoreau, were very polite gentlemen and very good Muslims, a statement which he realized was intended to indicate that they would not be very good mercenaries. Isabel seemed to understand exactly which men would be effective enforcers, which would command respect, and which would obey orders.

By sunset, they had hired ten men. "I can see already that you'll be indispensable to our objectives, Madame," Demoreau told her. "As I've said, I'd like to fill you in on the details; are you able to join me for dinner? I'm at the Charles."

"I must go to prayers," she told him. "I can meet you there afterwards."

Demoreau was patient and feeling upbeat and purposeful: He was putting together a squad of his own chosen men to accomplish a clear objective. This was just the sort of thing France had trained him to do.

Isabel found him that evening seated at a table in the hotel's restaurant with a bottle of water, not wine. She sat and adjusted her scarf so it sat back very slightly on her head. Demoreau stood to greet her: "Good evening, Madame," he said.

"Please call me Isabel, since I believe we still need to have a very honest and forthright conversation about this little project," she replied, sitting.

"As you wish, although my preference is that you call me Sergent Demoreau or just Sergent," he said while joining her at the table.

"It seems we have been hired to create a squad of dangerous mercenaries," She said bitingly. "And what are we going to do with them, Sergent?"

"We're going to take them through Oujda, into the plains of northeast Morocco. There's no one in charge over there and it's become a haven for thieves and bandits. It's causing major troubles on this side of the border, and the company wants someone who will crack down. There's a fellow named Jilali that we intend to set up as a sort of warlord –"

"Sheikh is the word you want to use, not warlord," she corrected him.

"As a sheikh, then, and hire some more men so he has a squad large enough to put a stop to the raiders entering Algeria from Morocco. The fellows we hired today seem like good soldiers, and smart enough that I think they'll be able to do most of the recruitment once we're over there. But I expect there will be some pushback from the local leaders. I'd rather pay people than hurt them, and the company will front the money we need. I'm hoping that you can help us get some of the local leaders over there to see the wisdom of assisting us."

"Who is this man Jilali? You can't mean Jilali al-Zerhouni, do you? Why, he's in prison, in Meknes."

"I think that's the man, yes. He was released and left Morocco; he now lives in Oran. What do you know of him?"

"He demanded that the Sultan abdicate and put forth the Sultan's brother Omar as his replacement. He has a reputation as a grifter, a charlatan, a man who will do anything for money. I suppose that's how the company was able to hire him. If he's going back to Morocco, he'll need a new identity as well as a private army."

"A name is easy enough, and most warlords aren't seen regularly in public places anyway. I've been reading up on that fellow al-Raisuli, the bandit who's in control of the western Rif mountains, and Mostepha al-Haybah who leads the Doui-Menia tribes in the south."

"Yes, I'm aware of those men," Isabel said.

"They both exercise incredible control over their followers. The important thing is that Jilali needs to have a strong inner circle, and then he can be the unseen, anonymous power at its center. And in this case, that inner core of men will in fact all be under contract to our employer. Jilali is scheduled to arrive in Tlemcen in a couple days; you'll have to come with me when I speak to him."

"I'm curious, certainly, but I'm finding this whole affair overly ambitious. Where exactly do you plan to take this private army, Sergent? Through Oujda, but to where?"

"Any decent warlord, or sheikh as you call them, would keep their base up in the mountains. A lot of the raiders and bandits are reportedly coming from the Middle Atlas too. So that's where I expect we'll go."

"I fear that the whole valley, the Plains of Oujda, it is called, as far as the city of Taza, will have to be subdued. The company should be paying me a great deal more."

"I can arrange that," Demoreau offered.

* * *

Jilali al-Zerhouni, as Isabel had feared, turned out to be an extremely wily gentleman who seemed better suited to government intrigues than suppressing bandits in the mountains. He was a tall, thin man with dark skin and sad, drooping eyes that made him look bored, and he listened to Demoreau discuss the preparations with apparent disinterest. He could not bear to listen to Isabel speak at all. At the end of the meeting, he informed Demoreau that, should they fail to establish a secure situation for him in Morocco, he was entitled under his contract to depart with a very substantial bonus payment.

"He's a rogue and not likely to impress anyone by threatening violence," Demoreau said to Isabel after the meeting. "But I wonder whether we could pass him off as religious man, a marabout or saint of some kind. What do you think?"

Isabel hoped the look on her face would express her negative opinion of the suggestion. "I'm not prepared to betray my faith by answering that question."

"But it might reduce the need for Jilali to resort to violence," Demoreau reassured her.

"Sergent, I'm not innocent enough to believe no one will be hurt during this little escapade, but if we could reduce the killings to a mere handful, I'd appreciate it."

"Madame, I'm a soldier, and I've had to kill plenty of people, and I've never lost any sleep over it. Now, we're trying to stop murderers, thieves, and rapists, people you wouldn't want in your mosque. You're not being asked to kill them yourself, and I only want to know if Jilali would be more acceptable as a leader if he was presented as a religious man."

"He certainly doesn't look like a killer, so of course he might be more acceptable as a holy man, if he's able to act like an actual Muslim," Isabel replied angrily.

"And if Jilali actually was a devout Muslim who deserved the reverence and respect we want him to receive, how would he show that?"

Isabel took a deep breath, knowing she would soon be crossing a line and feeling like she had already committed to it: "You said we're riding to Morocco. What if Jilali rode a donkey? He'd ride without harness into each city and town like the prophet Mohammad rode the donkey Ya'four. It would present Jilali as a holy man. And I suppose a man so blessed would be surrounded by strong protectors, men who had 'volunteered' to keep him from harm and who speak of his holiness. He would go to the mosque and pray, and then he would persecute the wicked. He would order the bandits and rogues to desist lest they be declared immoral, unbelievers, or 'Shaytan,' devils. Rather than being the person who orders violence, his overly enthusiastic followers would merely eliminate those men he identifies as evil."

Tamanrasset

"You're going to save a lot of lives, Madame," Demoreau told her.

Additional weeks went into planning, training, readying the weapons, and obtaining a couple of donkeys. A caravan was arranged of various company goods to be transported into Morocco with an innocent-looking "armed guard." It was only seventy kilometers from Tlemcen to the city of Oujda in Morocco, and they had reasonable maps of the roads, cities, and geological features of the Oriental region. But no one could say what would happen once they began to put Jilali forward as the new boss.

The journey across the High Plateau was made in two days. The caravan consisted of many carts driven by company employees, and each of the carts bore olives, wine, cheese, clothing, shoes, rifles, ammunition and, in great secrecy, enough gold to buy a lot of good will; there was no doubt that at least some of the gold was supplied by the French government. Jilali remained hidden in a covered wagon; Isabel rode in another. Demoreau and Mathieu, along with thirty hired soldiers, rode horses and mules. The two donkeys were brought along with a herd of sheep. No one had any interest in stopping or challenging the caravan or the extremely tough-looking men that accompanied it. Late on the first day they stopped outside the village of Lalla-Marnia just on the Algerian side of the border. The next day they continued into Morocco unopposed, reaching the city of Oujda in the mid-morning.

Oujda was a trade center at the eastern end of a long valley between two Middle Atlas mountain ranges. At the other end of the valley was the city of Taza. It was a traditional caravan route, one that had been used for centuries to bring trade goods through the mountains passes to Fez. Demoreau and the others waited outside the ancient city gates of Oujda while Isabel, accompanied by two of the Chaamba mercenaries as her guard, went alone to speak with local leaders at the mosque. She returned after a few hours.

"I've been to the mosque; it's well known among Muslims because Oujda is considered a very religious city," she said. "I spoke to the Imam at length, and, during our conversation, I mentioned that I had been warned about the danger of local criminals and bandits in this area. I can assure you that they are aware there is a problem. There is no sheikh east of Taza in the Plains of Oujda. To the north, in the Rif Mountains, there are many strong tribes, and the Hayaina tribe west of Taza is a large and powerful confederation. These are both strongly protected regions where the tribes are very territorial and well-armed. To the south, there are only loosely affiliated nomadic clans of the Ait Seghrushen and Beni Guil tribes. That is where you are the most likely to find additional recruits. The men committing the crimes, however, I mean the thieves and murderers, they are not tribal men at all; they are exiles from the mountains and criminals who fled Algeria to avoid arrest by the French police. They do not work together. They tend to stay in the villages surrounding Oujda because the people in the city are too hostile."

"Can the local people be convinced that Jilali is a holy man?" Demoreau asked her. "And if so, will they follow his commands?"

"The Ait Seghrushen and Beni Guil tribesmen will be easily convinced. The criminals won't be as easy to fool, but your mercenaries can likely pacify many of the criminals with offers to buy their services. But the others you will need to subdue. Once you've captured them, what will you have Jilali do with them?" She asked.

"We'll take them up to Taza, don't you think?"

"That only postpones the problem."

"Perhaps. Let's bring Jilali around to a few villages first, see how it plays out and allow news of his holiness to percolate up to the larger communities."

In the morning, Jalali was roused from his slumber and dressed in a pure white silk djellaba and an expensive burnoose of white camel hair. He wore a large turban of white with silver thread embedded in it. It was not modest clothing, but neither was he dressed like a dandy. He looked like a prince. His dark skin and sad eyes offset the purity expressed by his clothing. Many hours were spent perfecting his appearance. His "followers" (a squad of twelve large men dressed like Janissaries) surrounded the donkey which Jilali had learned to ride bareback. They made a magnificent sight. The plan was to enter the nearby village of Sidi Moulemya and ride slowly through to see if villagers would demand to know who he was, and, after being told of Jilali's magnificence, wisdom, and miracles, if the people would then demand that he stop to comfort and aid them.

A crowd gathered around Jilali at once and begged for his blessing, calling him "Rakib al-Himar," Rider of the Donkey. Jalali was delighted and relished his new role as holy man and bringer of blessings. After a brief time of Jilali reciting verses from the Quran, Demoreau told him to "ask if there are any evil men among you, murderers and thieves."

"Man hum al'ashrar baynakum? 'arini alqatala walosous!" Jilali proclaimed. A number of men were identified by the crowd, and they were instantly seized by Demoreau's mercenaries. "'Iizalat 'aydihim," Jilali shouted. The mercenaries looked to Demoreau.

Isabel was incredulous. She rushed to Demoreau. "He's told them to cut off these men's hands," she whispered frantically.

"Bring one man up here," Demoreau told his men, and Isabel said in Arabic that it should be done at once. "Have Jilali ask this man, here in the sight of God, to admit if he has done evil deeds."

A scarred, dirty man was dragged before Jilali and questioned. He angrily boasted of the women and riches he had stolen and the men he had killed. The mercenaries looked again to Demoreau, who simply nodded. In a flash, before the entire village, the evil man's hands were chopped off by a soldier using his nimcha, the short scimitar that had only been added to his costume for its decorative effect. The crowd was shocked into silence, but then the cheering began. As the evil man lay on the dirt, likely bleeding to death, Demoreau had three other prisoners removed to a building nearby where they could be guarded and examined away from the crowd. "Rakib al-Himar! Rakib al-Himar!" The crowd cheered and shouted their praise for Jilali. That evening, one of the other prisoners was put to death, but two joined the army of "Rakib al-Himar."

In the morning, they were greeted in another village nearby with acclaim and cheers, as word had already begun to spread. Here, the criminals were not readily found; they had absconded during the night so the show could not be repeated instantly. Demoreau sent Mathieu with a squad of men to go run down and capture a few of the criminals so that, in the villages that followed, a ready victim could be brought forth from the crowd. A fair number were publicly mutilated, since it was the coup de grace that sealed Jilali's moral authority. Over the next three weeks, twenty more villages were given the show. Demoreau and Mathieu became adept at capturing the poorly prepared and ill-equipped bandits that they hunted down in the empty plains; many others ran off to the Rif mountains to become someone else's problem.

As word of Jilali's campaign against evil spread, it also became less necessary to murder or mutilate anyone. His traveling private army rose to eighty-four men, and many more were paid to stay in encampments along the way to enforce the laws and punish thieves and murderers on his behalf. In the meantime, Isabel implemented the "maw'izah hasanah," going into the villages to warn the people about the punishments of Allah and conveying that Rakib al-Himar would allow no further bandits, thieves, murderers, or other criminals in the Plains of Oujda. After a month, Demoreau told her he expected they would soon complete their work and return to Algeria.

As they camped outside the ancient walls of Taza, arrangements were made for Jilali, that is, Rakib al-Himar, to be greeted by crowds the next morning and, at least symbolically, named sheikh by public acclaim. Isabel and Demoreau went to visit the Great Mosque of Taza, and the Imam, a venerable figure with a long white beard and kind eyes, came out to speak with them both. He approached Isabel with a kind of reverence that surprised them both and knelt before her. "Hajjah Pedersen," he said, his voice filled with emotion, "Asalamu alaikom, it is a great honor to have you grace our humble mosque with your presence. I hope you will come in to pray with us."

"I would be most honored," she replied, blushing. It was the most ostentatious display of reverence she had yet received since returning to Morocco. She had hoped that the rumors about her would have abated, but she now saw that the problem hadn't gone away.

The Imam went on: "Your reputation as a woman of faith and vision precedes you. The story of your encounter with Allah has touched the hearts of many. We are truly blessed to have you among us." He turned to Demoreau. "And who is this esteemed gentleman accompanying you?"

"This is Jacques Demoreau," Isabel replied. "He has been a companion and protector on my recent journeys."

The Imam nodded approvingly. "It is a pleasure to meet you. I hope your visit to Taza will be a spiritually enriching experience." He then turned back to Isabel. "Please, allow me to show you around our mosque, Sayyidah. I would be honored to share with you the history and significance of this sacred place."

Isabel replied: "I would be delighted, and there is a matter I wish to discuss with you. I have a gift for you, and a small trinket I would ask that you present to a companion of mine. You've heard of Rakib al-Himar?"

The Imam gasped: "Yes, of course. We are so grateful that Rakib al-Himar has brought peace to our cities and villages. Please let me know what I can do to assist you, Sayyidah," he said as they walked through to the mosque.

The closer they got to Fez, it seemed the more grandiose became Isabel's reputation. She now saw people pointing and openly calling her "Alima" and "Wali." She found it very disturbing and asked that she simply be called "Isabel," but this only convinced people that she was humble and pious.

In the morning, Jilali rode his donkey into Taza through a large crowd, surrounded by his personal guard. People lined the streets and threw rose petals in front of his donkey. Many cried and praised Allah for sending a strong protector. Jilali and his entourage proceeded up a steep road to the top of a cliff where the mosque stood overlooking the city. The sun shone on them as it rose in the east, and the old, bearded Imam, in a ceremonious manner, handed Jilali a short ancient sword which he said had once belonged to Suleiman the Magnificent. (In fact, it was a mere trinket that Isabel had given the Imam for that very purpose.) This, he said, was to thank Rakib al-Himar for bringing peace to the Plains of Oujda. The crowd cheered the man who they believed had rid them of the bandits, thieves, and murderers. Jilali stood before the crowd and assured them he would keep them safe.

"It is my duty to you, my people," he continued. Demoreau and Isabel stood nearby with the Imam, Mathieu, and a handful of their most trusted mercenaries. "But there is so much more we must do to bring our people to the light of Islam and preserve our country," Jilali went on.

"Country is overstating his remit," Isabel commented wryly to Demoreau.

Jilali went on: "Morocco is in peril, weakened by a Sultan who does not honor Allah, who knows nothing of the Prophet, who is not a true representative of the dynasty which has ruled Morocco for centuries. You have done me the honor of calling me 'Rakib al-Himar,' and it is indeed an honor to have this epithet from you. But today, seeing the thousands in this beautiful city who demand justice, I will reveal to you my true name."

"Shit," Demoreau said quietly.

"My name is Mohammed bin Hassan al-Alaoui," Jilali falsely claimed to the crowd. There were gasps, for the name was well known even if its true owner had not been seen in public for many years. "Yes, the late Sultan, Hussan bin Muhammad al-Alaoui, was my father. As I meditated and prayed following my father's death, this country was ruled by a non-Muslim Regent, Ba Ahmad, on behalf of my brother, Abd al-Aziz. Ba Ahmad ran this country and enriched himself with money he borrowed from Christian nations, and my brother has betrayed us by continuing to take that money even now. The dangerous debt which he has imposed on our people has left us in the clutches of the infidel. It has forced me to leave the peace and tranquility of my sequestered life in the Dar al-Makhzen to fight against his evil regime. I come to tell you that I have heard a message from Allah that we must establish a new ruler in Morocco. I shall be your new Sultan and replace my brother. Now we have begun, and you have the honor to join us here in Taza on this blessed day, thanks be to Allah."

The crowd erupted in cheers and acclaim. Jilali raised the short sword into the air. Isabel felt certain someone would notice that it was fake, but the crowd loved the gesture of defiance. "I would like to be paid now," she said with disgust.

Tamanrasset

* * *

Demoreau and Mathieu met with Jilali later that day. They had arranged for Rakib al-Himar to stay at the "High Fortress" which stood nearby the Great Mosque. It was an easily-defended walled enclave that Jilali could use as his base should he decide to remain in Taza, a question Demoreau planned to discuss. Jilali sat upon a large pillow on a dais wearing his expensive white burnoose and large white turban. He seemed quite pleased with himself, but his discussion with Demoreau was heated. Jilali tried to shut down the argument: "So you now see, there is no reason for concern as the people in this region fully support the movement I have begun," he claimed.

Demoreau stood before him. "Your employer is not interested in starting a rebellion in Morocco, and I can assure you they are not going to pay for one. Neither will they pay your inner circle of guards to engage in a rebellion or protect you outside the Oriental region. You may claim what you like, Jilali, but you cannot be made Sultan of Morocco."

"We shall see. Yes, your employer's money is a convenience now, but once I begin collecting taxes we will no longer be dependent on your company and the petty restrictions they seek to impose. Did you not listen to what I said? It is the money of Christians that has weakened Morocco. That means money from your European company as well. Nevertheless, I told your employer that I would prevent all incursions into Algeria, and on that point, I remain committed. Tell them I will do everything in my power to keep criminals from going into Algeria. That is, in the end, all they care about, is it not?"

"That will be for them to decide," Demoreau said. "I can't say what the Sultan will do, either; he might send soldiers up here to arrest you. You have some men and a fortress, but I doubt they will be enough. You've asked for trouble. It was a dumb choice, Jilali. But my work was to get you into this place, and that is now finished. I'll be leaving in the morning. Caporal Mathieu wishes to stay here, against my advice, but I recommend you keep him. He will be an asset to you."

"As long as that's alright with you," Mathieu offered.

"Certainly, thank you for the offer of your service, Caporal," Jilali said. "I don't expect you to agree with my position, Sergent, but withhold your condemnation. You are merely a warrior, a pawn in this game. You have been moved on the board and shall now return to your home in the Foreign Legion or wherever your masters send you. What happens in Morocco is no longer your concern. Farewell."

The sun had just set as Demoreau waited for Isabel outside the Great Mosque; she had gone to pray but he had agreed to wait for her so they could go together to the "Palacio del Rey," a fine Spanish hotel in the city where they would spend the night. The sky to the east was already deepening into a dark purple, and stars were beginning to come out. A warm, dry breeze blew from the south. In the morning, Demoreau would journey back to Tlemcen.

"Thank you for waiting for me," Isabel said as she strode up to him. She still wore her pants, boots, a heavy shirt, and burnoose with her hijab, but she looked calmer and obviously pleased to have had the opportunity to pray at the mosque. For the first time, it struck Demoreau that she was quite pretty, particularly her bright blue eyes. "Shall we walk?" She asked, and they headed down the steep road that led back into the city.

"I'm still leaving in the morning," Demoreau said. "Have you decided when you will go and where?"

"I had been planning to return to Fez, especially as we are so close now, but I now believe it would be wiser for me to return to Algeria for a time. You don't seem to have caught on, but I am fairly well known in Morocco, and my name has now been associated, at least loosely, with the pretender Rakib al-Himar. If I go to Fez, I'm afraid they'll arrest me."

"That's not an irrational fear," Demoreau commiserated. "Ride with me tomorrow, then. There are many people in Algeria who would be grateful for your insights and intelligence, if you were inclined to offer your services, and I don't mean just Paixporteur Carrier Int'l."

"I've found our employer's policies to be somewhat distasteful."

"You seemed to like the aim of preventing bloodshed, didn't you?"

"Is that what we were doing when you had those criminals executed, Sergent?"

"I'm only a blunt tool, but even I know that the aim of warfare is to end the war. That is what I seek to do as a Legionnaire. You could do that too. You could help the French make better decisions about who to negotiate with and who is a threat. At least, I think you should try, because you're obviously good at that sort of thing," Demoreau told her.

"So you will return to your Foreign Legion after all, Sergent?"

"You're teasing, I can tell," he replied with a smile. "But, you know, I've been in the Legion a long time, and I very much doubt that I'm suitable at this time in my life for anything else. It is my home. They expect me to act with honor, and I try to do so. These may be the blinders I choose to wear, but I'm comfortable with that. Even this, this affair in Morocco that I hope we can now put behind us, there has not been a single day when I did not want to pack up and go back."

"But you didn't."

"I did what I agreed to do so that I could."

"They don't take women in the Legion, do they," she quipped.

Demoreau smiled. "I know a clever Colonel who would be very grateful to know you."

"You haven't ever asked me about myself, where I come from or how I came to be in Tlemcen. Is that part of your code as well?"

"Very much so," Demoreau answered. "I wouldn't ask about your background even if I was burning to know. It's your story to tell, not mine, and you can choose what to say and when."

"I want to tell you about my trip back from Mecca," Isabel said, "since you're a soldier who kills people for a living."

The Sergent smiled, "I generally only kill those who are trying to kill me."

"I had finished the Hajj and only then did I discover that I had no means of returning to Fez, which, for one reason and another I had for a time considered to be my home. I wasn't sure I wished to return there right away or perhaps

Tamanrasset

travel, but, regardless, I had no way to pay for passage on a ship to Tangiers. But I had a bit of notoriety because of some things that had happened in Fez, and I had learned much more about scholarly Islam than the typical Muslim, man or woman, and the fact that I had completed the Hajj being Swedish, these were all qualities that I could barter for transport. In other words, Sergent, I became a sort of whore."

"You don't mean you sold —"

"No, not my body. I sold myself, my identity. I became the person of notoriety that others wanted me to be. I became a teacher, a storyteller, a philosopher, and so I paid for passage first across the Red Sea from Jedda to Egypt on a dahabeah, a sort of pleasure ship that sails tourists on the Nile and the Red Sea. On the ship, and then in Luxor and in Khartoum, I became a curiosity to be devoured by the British tourists. They only wanted to hear about the Hajj as a piece of travelogue. They didn't care to know how it felt to walk around the Kaaba in service to Allah; they wanted to know about the exchange rates, if the food was good and the best places to stay. I played that role. But then to travel from Rabat back across the southern edge of Sahara, I was required to be someone else—an Alima, a holy woman, a teacher—as a way of earning my place in one caravan or another, traveling village to village, speaking and teaching like I was an actual marabout, laying on healing hands and blessing people and making prophecies. At one point I became a man just to escape from the obscenely deferential treatment I was being given. I began to dress in a man's clothing—at first all in black with a veil like a Tuareg warrior, but eventually in this more European garb. I spent months traveling to Al-Ubayyid, Nyala, N'Djamena, Niamey, and finally Timbuktu. I won't talk about Timbuktu, but I thought I would just give up and die there. I was rescued by a Black African man who offered me passage to the north. He had a great load of ivory that he intended to take by caravan to Algeria because he had heard that the French would purchase ivory at a ridiculous price. He was not a Muslim, and he needed someone who could speak Arabic and deal with the Muslims for him. It was a crazy plan: It's almost impossible to cross the Sahara unless you know the way, and we did not. He had only a compass and the stars. More than once we lost the path and were lucky to come upon undiscovered and unnamed villages by sheer accident. The trip took months, and when we arrived at Aïn Séfra I got down on my knees and thanked Allah for my salvation. Tlemcen was where I really returned to civilization, and there you gave me the opportunity to play another role. But now I'm not sure who I am, or what I am. What I mean to say is, I truly envy you your certainty, Sergent."

"You seem the most level-headed person I've ever met," Demoreau told her. "I would trust you with my life. In fact, I think I have trusted you with my life during this scheme more than once. But I don't believe you have to limit yourself to the name or title applied to you. You're remarkable just as you are."

She blushed. "Thank you, but at least you know where you belong," she said, "and I still have no idea where I belong."

Later that night, after a pleasant dinner at the hotel and a few glasses of wine, Demoreau walked Isabel to her room.

As they stopped silently outside her door in the oil lamp-lit hallway, she paused. She reached up and, with only mild hesitation, removed the scarf from her head. Her hair had grown out and was a thick, wavy brown color; her blue eyes were raised up to Demoreau's with a look that was piercing and direct. She had a smell that was floral and earthy. She reminded him painfully of the last woman he had kissed, so many, many years before. He put his arms around Isabel and hugged her tightly, and she brought her arms up and wrapped them around him, resting her head on his chest. They held each other for a few minutes, pressed tightly together, before he pulled back from her slowly, not wanting to lose the smell of her, feeling like he should apologize.

"Thank you," he said with a touch of finality.

Isabel smiled gently. "Thank you, Sergent." They looked in each other's eyes a moment. She said: "I'll see you in the morning" then turned and went into her room. Demoreau listened for her to lock her door, then he turned and continued to his own.

* * *

In the major cities of Morocco—Fez, Marrakesh, Meknes, Casablanca, and Tangier—copies of al-Kattani's newspaper "Nur al-Fajr" appeared in cafes and marketplaces. At first, the articles were innocuous, focusing on local events and light national news stories. As time went by, the newspaper occasionally published something more controversial: News of French atrocities in the Zousfana and Saoura valleys, lawlessness in the Oriental region and the Rif mountains, offenses by the Spanish at their ports in the cities of Ceuta and Melilla, French and British actions in other parts of Africa. These reports were not necessarily incorrect, but they painted a picture of threats to Morocco that were possibly unflattering to the Western-oriented Sultan and his government, the Makhzen. The Ulama of Fez was now openly involved in the publication, and as an organization of well-respected Islamic scholars, the Sultan hesitated to place them under arrest.

Now that the printing presses were running, although only weekly, Ahmad spent much of his time at the newspaper's office. He generally worked on his school studies there, but he felt he was learning more from the articles in the paper. He had also prepared an essay he hoped to publish in al-Kattani's newspaper that was intended to open a public discussion about the condition of the country.

Al-Kattani said: "Only if we agree to publish your essay, Ahmad. The Ulama may not think that this is the time to introduce advocacy. There are still some who do not feel it is appropriate to invoke the passions of the people, since the Quran says: 'The true servants of Allah are those who walk with humility and when they are addressed by evil, their response is peace.'"

"Shall I remind you of the story Anas ibn Malik once told? A man said to the Prophet, 'O Messenger of Allah, should I tie my camel or should I leave her untied and trust in Allah to protect her?' The Prophet, peace and blessings be upon him, replied: 'Trust in Allah *and* tie her up.' We may trust in Allah, but I want the people to stand and fight for their country too. I am not interested in peace, Sayyid."

"I won't tell the Ulama you said that," al-Kattani replied seriously. "Fighting is abhorrent to these peaceful city dwellers. Your personal experience is different, Ahmad, because you were raised on the edge of the Great Desert and because of what has happened there with your family and the French."

"It is happening still. My brothers have written to tell me of thefts and murders which are still being perpetrated and permitted by the French. Why should they bring this conflict to my home? I am angry, Sayyid. If they were another tribe, we would be at war with them."

"But they are not a tribe, and neither are we a tribe any longer, I fear. We are a country. Rising or ebbing, who is to say," al-Kattani replied.

"In the Wadi Saoura, my family is strong, my tribe is strong, but here in Fez, it is clear that the sort of connections that bind me to my family and to my tribe are not present, except perhaps with you."

"As Ibn Khaldun predicted, did he not?"

"You speak of Asabiyyah, then? Have we nothing to offer to the people of this country, then, but the scholarly wisdom of the ancients? What, then, are we to do about the frustration, the anger, and the misery that now pervade the mosques and the medinas of Fez? This city was once a fortress of culture and life, but you can sense the despondency and resentment of the people. Have you seen the crowds that stand outside the Dar al-Makhzen? They now stand silently when the Sultan comes out, and I fear any day now they will throw stones at the Sultan, or worse. His indecision regarding Hamza the Baker, his inability to act, deepened that discontent. Yes, it is exactly the decline that Ibn Khaldun spoke of, a society in decay, beset by internal conflicts and the burden of external influences. We are a kingdom in distress; our affliction has been years in the making. Yet we cannot discuss that in the newspaper?"

"The Ulama is not ready, but still I sympathize with your frustration," al-Kattani replied.

"Then let us publish articles about the facts themselves. The Pretender, 'Rakib al-Himar,' in his fortress in Taza, for example, claiming to be the Sultan's brother, embraced by crowds. Or the Sultan's Western lifestyle and incomplete modernization schemes. Morocco's dependence on foreign creditors? Must we permit our kingdom to fade into the sands of history, Sayyid, just another lost empire like Rome? The people must be roused before it is too late."

"Whether they are roused or not, it will not be the Ulama or its newspaper that will be used to incite them," al-Kattani admitted.

The Ulama's concern that Ahmad's essay might inspire violence was well founded for anti-Western sentiment had been rising in the city. An English missionary had recently been attacked and beaten to death in the marketplace. Soldiers rushed to stop the attack, but they were too late. They chased the assailant until he ran into the Great Mosque of Fes. Soldiers surrounded the mosque. The Sultan ordered the soldiers to go in and drag the murderer outside. He was brought to the middle of the street and immediately put to death. The Sultan, it was said, had no tolerance for attacks on his European friends.

Still, Ahmad was stunned when the Ulama steadfastly refused to publish his essay.

Ahmad still met from time to time with his former mentor Omar Benayoun, who was now a member of the Ulama, and after learning of their final decision, Ahmad walked at once through the marketplace and past the bakery (which remained closed) to the Benayoun house to speak with him. The front of the house showed neglect, and a quiet older servant brought Ahmad through the eerily still and silent house to Omar's reading room, a small room with a window, comfortable rugs, and a few chairs around a table.

"Asalamu alaikom," Omar said quietly in greeting.

Ahmad had not seen his former mentor for some time and remarked how much older and thinner he looked. "Wa alaikom salaam. Thank you for seeing me, Sayyid," he said, sitting.

"I will have some tea brought for you," Omar said. He rang a small bell on the table. "I am glad you have come, Ahmad."

"How are you and your wife, Sayyid?"

"Very much the same, I am sorry to say. An unhappy woman is a force no man can quell."

Ahmad nodded. "You have heard from Isabel, perhaps?"

"From Mecca, yes, but not since she left there. She wrote at the time to say she meant to travel and was not certain when she would be returning. But I believe she will come back to Fez eventually."

"She was a good friend to you, Sayyid," Ahmad said. "And you were a good teacher to her. It would be nice for her to return."

"And you have been busy. I've read your essay, of course. I liked it very much. There is much there to invite discussion."

Crossroads of the Nomad

"I am gratified to hear your opinion. Now that you are a member of the Ulama, I assume you also know that my essay was rejected for publication in Nur al-Fajr."

"Not every member of the Ulama is prepared to engage in the sort of discussion you wish to have, and many feared your essay would provoke more violence or even rebellion. Nevertheless, I understand that your essay was read by many members of the Ulama."

"But not by the public, in the newspaper."

"I have friends in the Makhzen with whom I've consulted on many of the issues you identified. I wonder whether your observations about the state of Morocco militate in favor of modernization or against it," Omar said.

"That is the very reason we must begin a civil discussion. I believe it is wrong to equate tribalism with barbarism. There must be advancement. The question is whether Morocco can be modernized without Westernizing it? Presumably, it can be done, but it must be done thoughtfully."

"You should go see what is happening in Algeria," Omar replied. "You must go see for yourself what is being lost and what is being gained in an Islamic country run by a European power. You have personal grounds to hate the French, of course, and I don't mean to suggest that you should abandon your anger over what they have done to your family and your home, but it is only through knowledge that wisdom can be found."

"Are your friends in the Makhzen so eager to be rid of me?" Ahmad sniped.

"They would be glad to see you leave Morocco, Ahmad," Omar replied.

Tamanrasset

"Is that all you can tell me? That I should flee?" He asked angrily.

"The Ulama has decided that the newspaper should be shut down for a time. Muhammad al-Kattani and several others have been advised to go on the Hajj, to get away. You could join them, or you could go to Algeria as I suggested."

Ahmad was stunned. He knew the essay he had written would be controversial and that the Ulama would not protect him, but to refuse publication and be forced to flee was unexpected. If the Sultan would not listen to reason and resist the foreign influences that were weakening his country, then there was only one thing left for Ahmad to do. "Without the newspaper to work on, I have no reason to stay in Fez," he told Omar. "I will go, but I'm going to return to my home in the south. At least there we are fighting the French, and perhaps we will start a war that the Sultan will have to fight. Fortunately, we know where to find the French mercenaries, and we know how to kill them. Thank you, Sayyid, for warning me."

* * *

Ren heard back from numerous friends and colleagues who recommended specific students to study and work at Carthage, and some of those students wrote to Ren themselves. But it was on a hazy hot afternoon when his letters brought the most unexpected result. Ren returned to his office following a trip with Tom Childers up to Utica, a small village that was once a thriving suburb of Carthage, and he was startled upon his return to find a very beautiful although travel-weary woman dressed in expensive traveling clothes seated behind his desk.

"May I assist you, madame?" Ren asked graciously. "My name is Doctor Renwick Villere; I am the director of the excavations and scientific research here at Carthage. You appear to be waiting for me, yes?"

The woman smiled and stood, extended her hand to Ren: "Yes, Doctor Villere, what an honor to meet you. I am Lilian Osborn Beaton. My father is William Osborn."

"Good heavens!" Ren exclaimed as he took Mrs. Beaton's hand. "Why it is my great pleasure to meet you, Mrs. Beaton. I expect your father sent you. How are he and your mother?"

"They're very well, thank you. Yes, father received your letters, and he suggested I drop in; my husband James and I have been in Italy all spring, but he's had to return to New York and I've decided to put off my return to the States."

"It's wonderful of you to visit; you are most welcome. When did you arrive? Where are you staying?"

"I've only just checked in to the St. George this morning," she replied.

"That's simply no good. We have guest suites at the Palais where you must stay. I'm sure your father expects you to be well looked after, and that you'll inspect all the work we are doing. You will allow me to show you everything?"

"It would be an honor, Doctor Villere," Mrs. Beaton said pleasantly.

"Please, then, call me Ren, everyone does, except the students, of course."

"As you wish, Ren; and you must call me Lilian," she replied.

Ren made plans to join Lilian Beaton with two of his best students for dinner at her hotel that evening, and when they

Tamanrasset

arrived, Ren arranged for her belongings to be moved to Ren's mansion, the Palais d'Hamilcar, first thing the following morning. Lilian had refreshed herself, and she met the party in the lounge of the hotel in a magnificent silk evening gown, her hair done up respectably. She was quite lovely, Ren thought.

"Mrs. Beaton, may I present Tom Childers and Edith Murray, both archaeologists from England who are working with us here in Tunisia," Ren said.

"Why it's a pleasure to meet you both," Lilian said.

"The students all live together in our dormitory at the Palais," Ren told her. "Edith and the other women have their own wing, of course."

"You'll love the guest suites, Mrs. Beaton," Edith, a charming young woman from Liverpool, told her enthusiastically; "they're so pretty, and the Palais d'Hamilcar is very comfortable."

Tom, handsome and tanned by days in the Mediterranean sunlight, asked: "Are you and your husband scientists like your father, Mrs. Beaton?"

"Not at all. My husband is a banker, and I suppose I am a painter," she replied.

"I remember now," Ren said, looking at her with refreshed admiration, "your father told me you had a show at the Armory in Manhattan last year, and that your paintings are quite in demand."

"I've been very fortunate," Mrs. Beaton said modestly.

"Shall we go in for our dinner?' Ren asked her. "This hotel has a fine chef, and an excellent wine cellar."

It was a lovely meal, and they each drank a large amount of fine Algerian wine, both Burgundy-style blends from the Coteaux du Zaccar and Monts du Tessalah regions. Even Ren, who was ordinarily a heavy drinker, was impressed with the amount of wine that Lilian Beaton could put away. The students spoke rapturously of Professor Villere, the quality of the work they were being allowed to do, and the importance of the discoveries at Carthage. Ren was extremely proud of his students and deeply gratified by their good opinion of him.

In the morning, Ren collected Lilian and took her on a personal tour by carriage of the necropolis, basilica, amphitheater and, of course, the temple of Tanit, while her effects were moved into the mansion. In the late afternoon, he brought her to the Palais d'Hamilcar where the bougainvillea and prim roses were in full bloom and a cool breeze off the deep blue Mediterranean refreshed the air. He showed her to the guest suites where Lilian had her private rooms and reminded her of the evening schedule: Supper, lectures and discussion, cards, and lights out at 23:00. Ren had a full complement of fourteen students at that time; three were women. There was talk of letting the house next door and making it into the women's dormitory, but Ren liked to have everyone in the same house together.

Lilian enjoyed the evening immensely and fit right in with Ren and the students and Ren's two visiting colleagues from Egypt. It was a wonderful community of scientific-minded people. While the students were playing whist, she asked Ren to step out to the courtyard with her to look at the rising moon.

"Well, Ren, I don't think you need have any concerns about what I might tell my father. I'm very impressed with how you're handling the money he helped to raise. The work being done here is remarkable, and I am deeply impressed by the thoughtful, fair, and egalitarian manner in which you are doing it."

"I am really most appreciative of your good opinion, Lilian," he said. "I knew right off that you would understand what I am trying to do here. It's more than just a place to uncover history; we are trying to learn here how best to understand history. It's important to be in the place and to see it every day."

"In fact, Ren, if you don't mind, I would like to stay here in Tunisia for a while; I may do some paintings, and I'd like to sketch the excavation sites, if you'll allow me."

"You are welcome to stay for as long as you like. Tomorrow, will you perhaps allow me to show you something worthy of your canvas?"

"I should like that very much. Tomorrow, then," she said and returned to her guest rooms for the night.

The next morning, Lilian met Ren in the courtyard of the Palais to walk the two kilometers to the Byrsa Hill. He carried her painting supplies and a spare canvas; she carried a basket with their lunch and two bottles of wine. They passed a number of fascinating sites along their path: The Roman theater, the ruins of the Byzantine basilica, a mosque, the foundations of the palace of Genseric the Vandal, the Cathedral, and the tomb of St. Louis IX, King of France. At last, they reached the top of a high hill overlooking grassy fields that ran down to the Gulf of Tunis. Atop the hill and across the fields were the stumps of ancient building columns and walls made of blackened and disfigured stones.

"What do you think of the view?" Ren asked.

"It's beautiful; the sea is lovely. Do you know what these buildings were?"

"This is the Byrsa Hill," Ren said.

"Tell me about it, while I'm setting up my easel," she said.

"We are standing now in what was once the Temple of Eshmoun, the Phoenician god of healing. He was worshipped across the Carthaginian empire, but, consistent with your father's theory, the only other temple to Eshmoun that we know of is in the Levant, therefore a direct connection between Carthage and the earlier Phoenician civilization in the eastern Mediterranean. These ruins we are standing in today were a temple built in the Seventh or Eighth Century BC, shortly after the founding of Carthage; this would have been the highest place in the city, a place of honor and refuge and, of course, healing.

"Now, if you look out here across the grassy fields towards the Gulf of Tunis, you can see there to the right an unnaturally round body of water on the edge of the sea. That is what remains of the military harbor of Carthage. The rectangular body of water to its right was the commercial harbor. The spit of land there, beyond, had a massive tower that looked out into the gulf to keep watch: The Carthaginians were constantly on guard against the Roman warships that might arrive at any time. Between this hill and the water's edge, all these fields, this was the city of Carthage."

He spread out his arms to encompass the fields the lay between them and the gulf, dotted with blackened stumps of columns and foundation walls, an empty space that suddenly seemed quite full.

"At its zenith, over a million people lived here. It was an exceptionally beautiful city of white buildings constructed on a grid of broad boulevards and narrow cross streets, each building six or seven stories high; there were public squares, gardens, temples, schools, markets. All of that was here, where we are now and all the way down to the shore which was protected against invaders by a massive wall.

"Carthage was once lord of the western Mediterranean. Their infamous general, Hannibal, the one who brought his elephants over the Alps into Italy, killed a million Roman citizens. But, still, Carthage lost that war, and its great empire was reduced to a shadow of its former greatness. In Rome, Carthage continued to be viewed as its most dangerous enemy, so much so that, at the end of every speech he made to the Roman Senate, Cato would demand 'Delenda est Carthago!' – 'Carthage must be destroyed!' The Romans were of a mind to seek vengeance.

"The Roman army was sent at last and landed to the north, up the coast at Utica, and marched around to attack Carthage from the west while Roman ships blockaded the harbors. At that time, the city still had a population of about 400,000 men, women, and children. The city was surrounded and besieged for three years. Thousands starved to death. And these two great powers remained at a stalemate thanks to the perseverance of Carthage's leader, Hasdrubal. That is, until the young Scipio Aemilianus was sent to Carthage to finish the war for once and all.

"In the spring of 146 BC, Scipio launched his final assault on the city. It began, not back at the walls where his army was blocking any escape, but right down there, at the commercial harbor, and Hasdrubal, expecting the attack, set fire to the warehouses to prevent the Romans from holding that ground. But, despite this, a Company of soldiers broke through to the military harbor and captured it. This allowed Scipio to lead an additional four thousand men into the city. There was a delay as the soldiers looted the Temple of Apollo, and Scipio, furious, was unable to stop them. The delay gave the Carthaginians time to withdraw to defensive positions. After finally regrouping, the Romans systematically worked their way through the residential part of the city. They killed everyone they encountered. Scipio set fire to the buildings behind them so there could be no retreat. At times, the Romans were forced to progress by leaping from rooftop to rooftop. It took six days to clear the city of resistance.

"On the last day, Scipio agreed to accept prisoners, and Hasdrubal himself came to surrender to Scipio on the promise of his life and freedom. The only holdouts were nine hundred Roman deserters who fought for Carthage. They had withdrawn here, where we are standing now, to the Temple of Eshmoun, and they set it afire and burnt it down around themselves rather than surrender. Then Hasdrubal's wife came forward, a proud woman, proud of her Carthaginian history and proud of her two small children whom she held tightly in her arms. She stood right here and cursed her husband for surrendering to the Romans, and with their children in her arms she leapt into the fiery temple and burnt herself and the children to death.

"The city remained on fire for seventeen more days while Scipio's soldiers looted and plundered. Only 50,000 Carthaginians remained alive. All were taken prisoner and sold into slavery. The Senate ordered Scipio to destroy whatever remained of Carthage. His soldiers spent a year tearing every building to the ground. It was decreed that no one would ever be allowed to settle on this land again. And, as you see, no one has, and the bricks you see around us, charred and deformed by those fires, are all that remain of Carthage still."

Ren felt a fresh breeze on his face and remembered where he was, and when. He turned to Lilian. She was staring at Ren, a tear running down her cheek. Her face was flushed from the wine, and she looked to him like a delicate rose. He stepped to her and wrapped his arms around her while she cried. He heard her quietly reciting:

> "O Carthage, thy race is done!
> The ruthless flames sweep on
> O'er temple, shrine, and tower;
> And Roman pride and Roman hate,
> With all its universal power,
> Have left thee crushed and desolate."

Ren looked in her face, and Lilian tried to smile to let him know she was alright. "I read that poem in school," she said, "but I never really considered what it meant. To be here now, to see where it happened, all that you've described, it's quite overwhelming. Thank you, Ren."

He looked in her eyes and what he saw surprised him. He released her and stepped back.

She wiped her eyes. "I don't think I can get all of that in one painting, though," she jested.

"Then you must stay and complete all the paintings you wish," Ren smiled at her. "Now let's have our lunch and cast away the shadows of the past."

That night, while the students were playing whist, and after Lilian and Ren had finished a bottle of Champagne, she again asked him to step out to the courtyard with her to look at the moon. This time, she decided to make her intentions clear: "Ren, will you come visit me tonight?" She asked bluntly.

He looked at her in surprise and felt his face flush. She returned his gaze. Her eyes were on fire, and Ren could sense the same hunger he had seen in her expression earlier that day. She was gorgeous and irresistible. "Yes, if you are certain," he whispered.

"Yes," she laughed, "yes, I am very certain, Ren. You are a gentleman to even ask. I'll be waiting for you. Please come as soon as you are able."

Lilian took his hand and brought his fingers to her lips. They were warm and moist as she kissed his fingertips. She released his hand and walked away towards the staircase that led up to the guest suites. Ren watched her go, almost unable to breathe.

* * *

It was a cool evening, and Rosalinda's was particularly crowded. Surrounded by Legionnaires and the thick blue smoke of Turkish cigarettes. Demoreau, reinstated as a Sergent in the French Foreign Legion, was delighted to be back in his old haunt, with his good friends and colleagues, and with his dear Rosa to chastise him. The Sixth had been on training patrols all across the Tell Atlas and had not yet been redeployed to the desert. Hans Mueller was saying to him: "I went up to Oran in July and was told you were no longer at the Chateau Neuf. We had no idea where you were, and then a week ago I was told you would be returning here. May I ask where have you been?"

"Yes, well, there's not much to say about that," Demoreau said cheerfully, hoping that he was not actually blushing although he could feel the blood rush to his face. Since his return, few questions had been asked about where he had been, but, then again, it was the Legion's way to not ask questions. It was probably assumed he had just been in Chateau Neuf the whole time he was away. Yet rumors might spread, and Demoreau hoped that a whitewashed version might get around and forestall further questions.

"I was in Chateau Neuf," he said, "and I was expecting to be paroled when a French officer arrived looking for someone to escort a caravan of French civilians to Morocco. It seemed like they wanted someone in uniform, but also someone expendable, or at least someone who wouldn't be missed if he ran off or was killed. I was told I could come back to the Sixth if I took the job, so I agreed. Perhaps the civilians paid someone for my services. I only knew I wanted to get out of the cell. I waited in Tlemcen while the caravan was put together, and then we had the journey itself. There are a lot of bandits and thieves in that part of Algeria, and many more in Morocco, but we got the caravan to Morocco without any serious trouble. Then I escorted some French civilians back to Tlemcen. Anyway, it all took longer than I think they expected, and I only got back from Morocco a few days ago. I went to report at the regional headquarters of the Armée d'Afrique there in Tlemcen, and they gave me orders to come back to the Sixth as we'd agreed."

"That's a better story than I expected. We were all afraid you had been sent off somewhere worse than Chateau Neuf, perhaps even French Guiana. You did strike the Capitaine."

"I would never let them send me to Devil's Island unless you were going with me, Mueller," Demoreau joked.

"And yet it's quite a surprise to hear that a Legionnaire was loaned out to civilians for private business. Did they pay you anything?"

"The early release was a pretty good compensation, and I'll still draw my pay from the Legion for that time period. Maybe the French government had some interest in those men's business. Who cares. Anyway, I'm back with the Sixth now, and that's pretty much all I could have asked for."

"And just in the nick of time. We're to leave in four days to take the Company back down to Aïn Séfra. No idea yet where we'll be stationed after we get there."

"Are the Bleus ready?"

"They can ride, they can march, they can shoot, and, you know, misery loves company, so I suppose they are true Legionnaires. Most of the veterans are pleased that Capitaine Roubec is back; he has left the planning for this deployment entirely to Lieutenant Hansen. We're going to march south through the Saharan Atlas range before turning west to Aïn Séfra so the men get some experience marching in the desert."

"The Lieutenant knows what he's doing," Demoreau replied. He didn't especially like Hansen, but he did think he was finally maturing into a decent officer. Demoreau had seen plenty of officers set up difficult tasks for their men in order to prepare them for worse challenges ahead. It was better to have an officer who wanted the Legionnaires to be prepared than one who didn't care. The fact that the Company was leaving so soon explained why many of the men were at Rosalinda's that night, and plenty more Legionnaires were probably enjoying the last hours before their departure for the desert. Deployment meant months of intense boredom, months of rotten food and brackish warm water, months in the grueling heat of the desert sun marching in lines, months of rigid corporal discipline, months in the company of dangerous and sometimes unpredictable men, and months of deadly attacks from native tribesmen. Demoreau was eager to go. Certainly, he was disappointed that he couldn't spend more time in Saïda before they departed; his wine consumption had been steady but reasonably controlled since he returned from Morocco. It was still difficult for him to grasp that he had been detached from the Legion, that he had been set free, but that he had still chosen to come back. Perhaps it was true, as Colonel Lyautey had said, that he had nowhere else to go, but Demoreau thought that the reason was that he did not feel he belonged anywhere the way he belonged to the Legion. He was comfortable with the règlement.

Four days later, the 6th Mounted Company departed Saïda on a clear, cool morning in a long column, four across, with Capitaine Roubec, Sous-Lieutenant Cauvain and Sergent-Fourrier Vonheim leading the procession and the first Section. The officers were on horseback, the NCO's and half the Legionnaires on mules; the rest on foot. Behind them, Lieutenant Hansen led the second Section with Sergent Demoreau and their NCO's and their half of the

Legionnaires on mules. More mules carried supplies; sixteen natives tended the animals and served the officers. Two hundred-sixty-eight men, one hundred-forty mules, four horses. For many in the Sixth, it was their first deployment as a Foreign Legionnaire, and they were excited to have completed their training and to be starting off. They had done longer marches during training, but never in such large numbers and never without planning to return to barracks in a day or two at most. It made a deep impression on each of the men to be marching off to an area of active hostilities in such a large formation. It made them proud to be Legionnaires.

Their intentionally indirect march to Aïn Séfra was expected to take a little over two weeks, approximately fifty kilometers each day, a good pace without exhausting the men. As usual, the Legionnaires of a Mounted Company would alternate riding and marching. The first few days were especially easy since they were crossing the relatively level High Plateau in moderate weather and marching on roads through fields of grain and tall grasses before moving on to hard, flat earth. The encampments each evening were lively, with singing and a popular card game called "Cut Fives" played sitting on a square rug unfurled for that purpose.

"Who wants cards?" Demanded Legionnaire Second Class O'Connor, an Irishman with a wicked temper.

"Not I," said Petrov.

"Served," said Dubois.

The cook, Ali ben Khaled, a Turk, drew four. "Nine," he said.

Tamanrasset

"That card was meant for me," cursed Rivoli, the Italian Count who was perpetually down on his luck.

"And five, I had a five," said DeWitt, an ugly Dutchman said with disgust. "If only I had promised to never cut fives! There are times when it is hard, very hard. And look at that beast of an Irishman who plays Charlemagne."

It was true. O'Connor swept the coins into his kepi, rose with dignity, and bowed to the others.

"Until tomorrow, gentlemen."

O'Connor leaving the "table" with all the money created a ruckus that almost came to blows, but Caporal Dormayer intervened before Sergent Demoreau had to get involved. Demoreau was pleased with the morale of the men, and was personally satisfied to be back on the march with his Company. However, sitting in his tent he involuntarily had to listen to the British duo, Mills and Henderson, talking about brothels again. The two were inseparable and frequently continued their in-depth discussion of women they had each bedded.

"Yellow hair, like corn silk, Sylvia was her name," Henderson was saying. "She had an arse like a horse, broad and meaty."

"And just as hairy, I'll wager," Mills replied. "I knew a Sylvie in Marseilles. She worked for a friend of mine, that 'maq' who shared rooms with me there for a time, I told you about him. François was his name, and just as filthy a bugger as that damned American, Lewis. Imagine that bastard being promoted to First Class ahead of us; it makes me spit."

"I wouldn't let him hear you say that," Henderson replied, "although I'd kill the bloody bastard if I could get away with it."

"Somehow François had all sorts of pretty girls come his way," Mills replied, returning to the part of the discussion that kept his attention, "and he kept getting new ones that needed to be checked out, you know what I mean. There was a new girl every few days that needed to be given a tickle."

It was a blessing to womenkind that these two men were being sent deep into the desert, Demoreau concluded. Sous-Lieutenant Cauvain, an Alsatian of short stature, stopped by to speak to them and asked in French if they happened to know his brother who was a solicitor in London and had something to do with the Red Cross Association. Naturally, they did not. Then Legionnaire Bennet, an American from somewhere in the west, a tall fellow built like an ox who had just re-enlisted for another five years, came to Demoreau's tent to fetch him for the Lieutenant: Hansen had prepared another lengthy list of infractions that required punishment. No matter, Demoreau thought, the Lieutenant would forget most of them by the time they reached Aïn Séfra.

After a few days, the terrain changed from grass to just dirt and rock. The column began to descend through the Amour Mountains to the edge of the Sahara. The ground was bare earth or shallow coarse sand, and the mountains had been carved by wind and sand into massive pillars of stone. The canyons were eerie, and the mood of the Legionnaires became more serious. Here there were stones carved by Stone Age humans and ancient stone forts which could only be identified by the remnants of the spires and battlements that remained exposed above the sand. The Legionnaires could look out to the south and see absolutely nothing: The ground became perfectly flat and extended to the horizon. The column proceeded straight into the abyss for a full day before they reached the village of Brézina-El-Abiod just before dark. The village had a decent well, and the Legionnaires refilled their water skins and canteens with the dirty brackish water and watered the mules and horses. In the morning, the Company proceeded west-south-west across the open desert.

The daily temperature quickly climbed, and the march became an ordeal for those men who had never been in the desert before. The air temperature was not so terrible at that time of year, but the dry air and the constant beating of the sun upon their heads sapped the Legionnaires' strength. At night, the men were quieter and returned to their tents earlier.

One morning they awoke at the familiar bugle call to a sharp wind that whipped across the flat landscape, carrying with it grains of sand that stung like needles. Demoreau had already got his Section ready to march on, but they were struggling against the relentless winds, mostly unable to see or breathe. The Capitaine delayed the march, and the Legionnaires were ordered back into their tents. As the day wore on, the wind grew much stronger, and the sandstorm intensified. The sky darkened much earlier than usual, and visibility dwindled to almost nothing. The wind howled all evening, and the sand found its way into tents, eyes, and throats. Finally, as the new day began to dawn, the storm abated as easily as it had evolved. The wind gradually died down, and the sky began to clear. The Legionnaires emerged from their shelters. The desert, once again, lay before them, vast and empty, utterly unchanged.

The next day they arrived at the remains of an ancient forgotten village, it's walls and houses almost entirely covered by sand. Whoever had built the homes had long ago been forced to admit defeat to the forces of the desert. There was a well, but it had filled with sand and the native servants had to spend two hours digging it out. While they were doing so, the Legionnaires who were posted as sentinelles announced the approach of six men riding camels from the south. As they neared, the Legionnaires were astonished: The six riders entering the village ruins were enormous men, dressed in flowing blue-black robes and blue turbans with an indigo veil that covered their faces except for their eyes and the bridge of the nose. They rode massive Mehari camels and bore bone-handled knives and great two-handed scimitars; they were adorned with chains made of silver and amulets of gold. They were Tuareg warriors.

The Tuareg people were rarely seen so far north and west, but they had ranged across the Sahara for millennia, nomads that the Arabs called "Mulatthamin," the veiled ones, and their name provoked fear and dread. Had they come to the abandoned village in large numbers, the Tuareg approaching the Sixth would have been met with stalwart resistance. Instead, Capitaine Roubec, with his Sergents and a translator who spoke the Tuareg's unusual dialect of the Berber language, rode out to meet with the nomads. The six were alone, traveling west to the thriving trading center in Figuig, a city just over the border into Morocco. It was agreed that all would have free access to the well, and neither group would interfere with the other.

Tamanrasset

That night, Demoreau sat beside a small fire with Mueller and a few of the Legionnaires who kept stealing glances at the Tuareg warriors. "Take advantage of this opportunity to take a good look at those men, Legionnaires," the Sergent said. "Everyone in the Maghreb knows to keep clear of the Tuareg, mostly because of what happened to the Flatters Expedition."

"What happened?" An innocent Legionnaire asked.

"There was a French Lieutenant-Colonel named Paul Flatters," Demoreau began, "who was in command of an engineering expedition sent to investigate the possible construction of a railway across the Sahara. His team was ninety-three men; most of them were soldiers. They departed Ouargla in December 1880 and traveled south towards Asiou, in the central Sahara, from which Flatters hoped to reach Sudan. They were less than two months into the expedition, on the 16th of February, when they stopped at a Tuareg village, Bir el-Garama. Flatters left his baggage in camp with half his troops while he and the other officers took the camels to the well. As the camels drank, Flatters and those with him were suddenly surrounded by several hundred Tuareg warriors that, it turned out, had been secretly tracking the expedition for days. Well, the Tuaregs attacked, and Flatters and most of the men with him at the well were slaughtered at once. Ten men made it back to camp and joined the forty-six soldiers who had remained there. They decided to retreat north the way they had come, dividing the food and ammunition and giving the strongest men the skins of water to carry. For weeks, the group struggled, lost in the desert, suffering from hunger and thirst as the Tuareg hunted them down and picked off the stragglers. The survivors, starving and isolated, eventually resorted to cannibalism. After months of wandering lost in the desert, only fifteen made it back alive to Ouargla."

It was not Demoreau's first encounter with the Tuareg and he regarded them as unpredictable and dangerous, but, despite their appearance, these men were simply travelers hoping to do business. As the Tuareg encamped nearby, the soldiers watched them with rapt attention, impressed and daunted by their size and demeanor. Yet at sunrise, when the bugle sounded and the Legionnaires awoke to continue their march, the Tuareg had already departed.

The Company had another two days of desert marching along the edge of the massive sand dunes of the Sahara and were given a chance to climb the dunes to see the waves of sand that ran on into the distance. From the bottom of the sand trough, it was impossible to see which direction you were pointed or where you had come from. The Legionnaires were careful not to get separated. It was well known that the Legion would leave a lost man behind without hesitation.

The next morning they entered a pass into the Ksour Mountains. Excitement grew when they entered the Wadi Tiout and could see the ruins of an enormous castle on a hill off to the west. Near it were the large, white walls of a Foreign Legion blockhouse that overlooked an oasis village. They arrived there before sunset, and the Legionnaires were given leave to swim in the small lake and refresh themselves after their tents were pitched. The desert was behind them, and they gave little thought at that moment to the further dangers ahead.

It was at the oasis village that Legionnaire MacDonald went mad. MacDonald was a belligerent Scot who was believed to have been dismissed from the Royal Scots Dragoon Guards for misconduct; he was a good soldier, but there always seemed to be a lot going on inside his head and he gave the impression he might snap at any time. Demoreau suspected alcohol withdrawal was a major factor in MacDonald's increasingly agitated demeanor during the march through the Sahara. The Scot had a tough time in the desert, and he got more difficult as they got closer to the end of the march. In Tiout, Demoreau had assigned him to water a pack of mules, and the huge Scot viciously dragged the uncooperative animals to the lake. He got frustrated and began, at first, to slap the mules on their hindquarters. By the time he had dragged them to the water, he was punching the mules and had possibly killed one. The other Legionnaires called for help and leapt on MacDonald to try to subdue him, but he fought back like a wild animal. He was finally knocked out and put in chains to be turned over to the PM's.

After a march of seventeen days, the Sixth finally arrived at Aïn Séfra. The small city was a major French trading hub in the Sud Oranais, a walled oasis with a river and large pools of water, well-laid streets with fortified buildings, gardens, parks, and wooded areas, and three large white mosques that could be seen from anywhere. There were already several hundred Armée d'Afrique soldiers and Legionnaires in or around the city, as it was the terminus of the French rail line and jumping off point for French troops traveling north and south.

Beni Ounif was a small border village about one hundred and fifty kilometers to the south; it was nothing more than a stopping point between Aïn Séfra and the

Moroccan town of Figuig, just across the border. The French fortification in Beni Ounif was called Fort St. Louis, and it was regularly attacked by marauding Arab and Berber raiders from Morocco who targeted and looted convoys of French trade goods. That was where the 6th Mounted Company was going to be stationed, Demoreau was told, to replace another Company that had lost more than sixty Legionnaires there in just the past three months.

* * *

The Sun had not yet risen above the ruins of the Mechouar Palace, but at the mosque nearby many Muslim people of the city of Tlemcen were already at their morning prayer. It was a great privilege to be admitted to one of the oldest mosques in Algeria, over eight hundred years old, and an even greater privilege to be allowed to pray before the mihrab there among the great white columns that lined the enormous hall. As the prayers ended, there was a gentle rustling of movement as the faithful rose and exited to the open and airy marble-tiled courtyard of the mosque, still quiet in the twilight of dawn. Isabel retrieved her leather boots and exited a side door beneath the shadow of the towering brick minaret. Covered by her tightly drawn deep brown burnouse, khaki pants, white shirt, and a black hijab, Isabel walked along the great stone wall to the main gate of the palace. The few buildings in the complex that were still usable had been made into offices for the French army, but the pool and gardens of the central courtyard were peaceful and shadowy. She passed an alcove that featured Islamic calligraphy carved into the stucco, and Isabel stopped to read it: "Allah is God, there is no god but He: the King."

Tamanrasset

A quiet voice behind her asked: "Madame Pedersen?"

She turned to find a short, elegantly dressed French officer approaching her. His flat-topped white hair was soldierly, but his crisp, tailored uniform, polished boots, and wide waxed mustache displayed a carefully composed appearance.

"Peace be with you," she said, casting her eyes downward and crossing her arm over her chest as she nodded.

"Peace be with you, Madame. I apologize if I disturbed you; will you come inside?"

"As you wish."

She followed the French colonel to a charming wood-paneled room overlooking an orchard of citrus trees bearing large green fruit. The colonel sat on a bare wood chair beside a wide wooden table, crossed his legs, and twirled the end of his wide mustache. Isabel stood silently before him in a respectful posture.

"I have the greatest respect for your beliefs, my dear, but it would be helpful to me if you would sit and speak to me informally. Would you be so kind?"

"Of course," she said and she sat on the chair beside his. Her demeanor now expressed more of her experience and self-assurance, her hijab more a symbol of her confidence than of her humility. The colonel raised an eyebrow in appreciation of her serene face and brilliant blue eyes.

"You have returned safely from Morocco, and I am pleased to see you are unharmed. Monsieur Jilali, did he make a successful return to his home country?"

"It was successful inasmuch as we delivered him to Morocco with a substantial armory of mercenaries and weapons. However, as I'm certain Sergent Demoreau has already told you," she added, "when we arrived in Taza, Jilali adopted the name Moulay Mohammed al-Alaoui. As you know, Moulay Mohammed is the brother of the Sultan, Abd al-Aziz."

"So Jilali means to play himself off as the brother of the Sultan, but I was under the impression that Moulay Mohammed died some years ago, is that not so?"

"No, sir. Moulay Mohammed is very much alive," she stated. "He is a Wali, a figure of divine wisdom and, you might say, a living saint. He lives in religious seclusion in the royal palace in Fez and has not made a public appearance for several years."

"Then the people of Taza must feel quite privileged that such a man has come to live among them," the colonel replied with a wry expression.

"But, with respect, he's not -"

"Of course I understand your concern," the Colonel reassured her. He smiled gently. "It is no doubt a very great sin to steal the name of a living saint." The colonel stood and walked slowly to the balcony overlooking the citrus trees.

"Apart from the moral consideration, Colonel, a potential usurper, someone who is pretending to be a member of the royal family, is far more likely to provoke a reaction from the Sultan than a random rogue warlord on the other side of the Rif Mountains," she explained. "I'm sure that's not what you intended, is it?"

The Colonel turned and looked at her closely. "I see your point," he said. "However, even if the Sultan wishes to stop Jilali from stealing his brother's name and occupying the Plains of Oujda, I don't believe he can prevent it. The Sultan has almost no functioning army. As for what we intend, all I know is that when Jilali was approached about this affair, he was given an assurance that France would leave him alone to do as he pleases. Was Durant aware of the situation when you saw him?"

"Monsieur Durant was not unhappy with how the company's money had been spent, but, unfortunately, he refuses to understand that appropriating the name of Moulay Mohammed will alienate educated Muslims, the sort of people with whom his company presumably wishes to do business."

"But no one will ever know that Durant or his associates were involved, will they," the Colonel stated.

"You wouldn't be speaking to me so frankly unless you were confident that I would keep my mouth shut, as I'd agreed."

"Well, that is true, but I also don't want you to feel that I have dismissed your concerns. As you've surmised, we could not invade Morocco merely to put an end to the bandits and thieves there, nor, to be frank, would an army have been the correct tool for such a task. This result is not precisely what was planned, and I agree there may be some unfortunate consequences, but, regardless, I simply don't see how it's to be undone at this point."

"You should take time to consider it. In the short term, I believe Jilali's control over the plains will probably pacify the region somewhat and help to prevent incursions into Algeria; if I thought otherwise I would not have remained involved, I assure you," Isabel replied.

"Your involvement, I am told, was essential. Sergent Demoreau tells me that you took charge of the whole affair and it would have come to nothing without your efforts."

"That is surely overstating my contribution. I merely hoped to prevent some unnecessary deaths."

"I'm quite certain you did more than that; the Sargent was quite specific. And did he, the Sergent, meet with your approval? Did he behave himself?"

"Absolutely, Sergent Demoreau was competent, professional, and discrete. He would undoubtedly be of great use to a man like you."

"He was exceedingly complimentary of your contributions. That is why I have asked you here."

"I am not clear what you want from me."

"Surely that's not true," the Colonel said as he sat again beside Isabel. "Well, I'll be more explicit, if you wish: I have been in discussions with the incoming Governor and he intends to give me a new command: I am to be entrusted with the security of the entire Sud Oranais region of French Algeria. It will be my duty, specifically, to create a peaceful and stable environment for the new railway line, but more generally to pacify a border region that has become increasingly chaotic, especially in the south."

"I've been there; I've seen it," she said.

"I'd like to hire you as my interpreter, and, in the spring, when I move my headquarters to Aïn Séfra, I'd like you to come with me."

"Interpreter, like in the Morocco affair," she said.

"Precisely like Morocco."

It meant he wanted more, she thought. He wanted her to help, to speak to the local leaders and convince them to lay down their arms. "Perhaps you presume too much if you think my aims are the same as yours," she replied.

"Peace? Is not peace a noble aim? You don't know my service record, Madame, but I have served for several years both in Indochina and in Madagascar. The lesson I have taken away is that the native people must be looked upon as our partners and collaborators. That is to say, the native people should benefit from the presence of the French, not be persecuted by us, and that means we must respect the native people, their culture, and their religion. I certainly have no objection to the practice of Islam," he said gesturing to her hijab, "nor have I any reason to wish harm to the Algerian people. If you can accept that that is my intention, then I believe you can be of tremendous assistance to me in stopping violence and bloodshed, as a bridge between me and the native people."

"And will this be like the Jilali affair? Or will you invade Morocco this time?"

"Morocco is outside my authority, and I am expressly prohibited by the French government from sending soldiers there. It would destabilize the Sultan."

"Isn't that precisely what Jilali is doing, making Morocco's government less secure in regions where the Makhzen's laws fail to reach?"

"That may loosen the Sultan's grasp, but not his credential. If you wish my opinion, Madame, it is that the balance of power right now among France, Great Britain, and Germany is so delicate that no external power could attempt to unseat the Sultan in Morocco without serious diplomatic repercussions and possibly a European war. My only concern is the security of the Sud Oranais, only in French Algeria, and if my actions in that region inadvertently weaken the Sultan of another country, it is because the Sultan already has no control in certain areas. If he chooses to fall, it is not my responsibility to prevent it."

"I don't necessarily agree with that," she said. She got up and walked to the balcony.

Isabel was stuck now in Algeria and knew she could not likely return to Fez for some time. She would need further employment, and here she was being offered an opportunity to work for one of the top men in the country. Of course, using her small notoriety was inherently prideful and a great sin, but helping to bring peace to an area embroiled in conflict, she thought, wouldn't that, on balance, be virtuous? At the same time, she knew she was rationalizing a poor decision: She was again being asked to play a role. She didn't know what was the proper thing to do, but she could just accept what was being offered. "As for the position, I must pray, and I will let you know," she said.

* * *

The luxurious cotton sheets which Lilian had ordered from Paris were incredibly soft and Ren stretched beneath them, indulging in the gentle friction of the sheets on his bare skin. He had been awakened by rays of the late spring sun shining directly through the windows of Lilian's bedroom. Lilian remained asleep beside him. Ordinarily, Ren would have roused her with a kiss as it was their custom to make love in the morning, but now that the nights were shorter it had become necessary for Ren to return to his rooms earlier.

Tamanrasset

Lilian sighed and turned towards him, and he ran his hand down her back and pulled her close.

"Shall I come painting with you this morning?" He whispered.

"I'll find you this afternoon . . . going to the bazaar with Miss Murray this morning," she whispered.

Ren kissed her forehead and forced himself to leave the bed; her fingernails clutched at his skin just enough to express her regret that he was leaving. Ren wouldn't say so, but he was disappointed that Lilian was occupied that morning. Nevertheless, he had several ongoing excavations to visit and needed to reply to a vast amount of correspondence that he had been neglecting. He threw on his clothes and quickly exited to the service staircase. By going up and crossing over the unoccupied fourth floor, he could climb out onto a terrace and gently drop down to the balcony outside his own bedroom.

Their torrid affair had been going on for months. Both had reason to keep it secret. Ren was doubtful that his relationship with Lilian reflected well upon his character since she was a married woman. He was particularly concerned that Lilian's father might hear of their affair and cut off his funding for the excavations at Carthage. For her part, Lilian had made it clear to Ren that her marriage was one of convenience; she and her wealthy banker husband had never consummated their marriage, but he was willing to pay all her expenses as long as she maintained the fiction that they were happily wedded. Lilian now lived an exorbitant lifestyle that she would not risk losing. Over her months in Tunisia, she had imported cases of champagne, fine French foods, furniture, clothes, perfumes, and jewelry from France, England, and Italy. Such diversions were the only thing that allowed Ren to keep his hands to himself for a while.

Ren, dressed in his usual outfit of trousers, boots, shirt, tie, and field jacket, arrived an hour later at his office in the seminary building behind the Cathedral. Among the letters he had recently received was a notification from Chief Inspector Paul Gauckler of the Colonial Office of Art and Antiquities that he intended to conduct an audit of all the excavations in Carthage, and of every relic and treasure identified and their present disposition, and of the funding for the excavations, and every expenditure of those funds. This outrageous demand had already been referred to the Foundation's attorneys who agreed that Gauckler had no authority with regard to the Foundation or its funding. Ren had no particular cause for concern. Nevertheless, he had assigned a couple of his students to make sure all the paperwork was up to date in case Gauckler sought to find problems where there were none.

After a couple hours of paperwork himself, Ren walked to the Hill of Juno where an excavation was just beginning to reveal the remains of a Roman villa. In one room, they had found an intact mosaic of a hunting party as detailed as any Fifteenth Century tapestry. It depicted a wild boar cornered by a party of hounds and hunters. The hounds, partially protected by leather armor, were driving the boar into a net held by the beaters. The hunters, mounted on horses, brought up the rear. In other rooms they found inscriptions from persons who had lived in the ruins of the villa in much later times; most of those inscriptions were obscene. As Ren arrived, however, the foreman Hassan was excited to lead his employer to a passage that had been discovered leading into the hillside. Steps of a much older design, Punic he presumed, led up to a sealed entrance in the wall beneath a wide chiseled lintel.

"Tomb! Punic Tomb," Hassan shouted joyfully, as hot on the scent as any hound chasing a wild boar. Ren knew people were insanely keen on locating tombs, and Hassan was no exception, for tombs meant gold, jewels, and other small pocketable items that could be stolen from the site. This made him overzealous in identifying them. In the instant case. Hassan was so jealous of his discovery that he would allow no one to assist him in excavating the passage. Ren tried with little success to convince the other diggers of the unlikelihood that Hassan's discovery was, in fact, a tomb, explaining that a Roman villa would not be built on such a site. Nevertheless, all the other diggers had to stop work and gather around to watch, relishing the opportunity to pursue what Ren knew was their favorite activity: Watching other people work.

Hassan continued to bore into the dirt and clay, shoving out the rocks and debris like a mole, disregarding proper excavation techniques or safety, determined only to get "inside the tomb," until only his feet were visible from a narrow hole. Suddenly, muffled shouts or screams emanated from the hole attesting to either catastrophe or triumph. Hassan wiggled his way back out, covered in mud, and holding in his hand a fragment of rotten wood.

"Coffin!" Hassan screamed. Ren's skeptical expression was lost on the excited foreman.

Ren himself scrambled into the hole beneath the massive lintel stone and into the hidden room beyond. To his surprise, it actually was an ancient tomb. Inside was a crumbling box of wood that proved to contain the remains of a Punic citizen from the earliest days of Carthage; however, there were no riches. The only other object in the tomb was a beautiful shard of pottery that lay beside the crumbled skull. Ren wiggled his way out and stood, taking a moment to catch his breath, when suddenly the ancient lintel at the entrance to the tomb, and half the hillside on top of it, collapsed. Ren was fortunate to have survived. Had he been inside the tomb at the time of the collapse, he undoubtedly would have been crushed or suffocated before he could be extracted. He felt his heart racing and stood to catch his breath, but then, acting as though nothing had happened, shared the unfortunate news with Hassan that the tomb had nothing to offer but the small shard of pottery Ren still held in his hand.

Errors in judgment such as this impromptu, careless, and nearly life-ending excavation of the tomb were unusual for Ren. While he had not flinched in the face of near death, he berated himself for having been overly excited about the possibility of a great discovery. There was no question that "buried treasure" inflamed the imagination of the public and thus generated site visits and donations. Yet, for Ren, there was a personal yearning as well, one which he had difficulty expressing because his opinion of himself varied daily: On good days, he would claim the mantle of "noteworthy archaeologist" and "discoverer of amazing artefacts and treasures"; on other days, he might confess that he merely longed for some shred of approval from his colleagues. He would certainly never acknowledge, even to himself, that his binge drinking and night-long rendezvous with Mrs. Beaton might also be having an impact on his work.

Ren dusted himself off and returned to his office for his daily luncheon and bottle of wine with Delattre, as was their custom. While Delattre was not Ren's mentor per se, Ren did respect the aging priest's great accomplishments and the work he had done at Carthage before Ren arrived. Delattre's name would certainly be remembered. However, it was also clear to Ren that Delattre had no interest in archaeology apart from where it intersected with Christianity. It was frustrating for Ren, and he often felt that Delattre was unimpressed by their newer discoveries.

After lunch, Ren returned to the Palais d'Hamilcar in need of some flagrant reassurance and was gratified to find Lilian there in the magnificent front hall where stained glass windows washed the floor and walls with red, orange, and green. She had been preparing to come find him for an afternoon stroll.

"Will you be painting, this afternoon, Mrs. Beaton?" He asked.

"Why, yes, Doctor, I was planning a short walk to the field nearby to work on my painting of the aqueduct," she answered.

"It's a little out of my way, but I could assist you with your equipment."

"That would be so kind of you, as long as you have the time," she said.

"I suppose I need to take a look at that new site over there anyway. Please, allow me," he said taking her easel, blanket, and a chilled bottle of Champagne.

There was no one around, but they played their parts in case someone happened to be listening and to spare the feelings of the servants who undoubtedly knew everything.

It was a warm afternoon with a bright sun. Lilian wore a simple, light silk dress and wide brimmed hat in consideration of the weather. The fabric draped on her in a way that seemed to emphasize rather than detract from her natural beauty. Ren couldn't be certain that she dressed with his arousal in mind, but he could not help but admire her appearance. As they walked the path that led to the fields, she looked at him with a wicked smile. "It's quite stimulating to walk through the wheat field," she said.

Ren blushed. "Stimulating? What do you mean?"

Their path brought them through a dense line of trees, and then they saw before them a wide field of wheat that spread as far side to side as they could see. One hundred yards or so across was another dense line of trees, and between them and the other side of the field, the remains of the ancient Roman stone aqueduct passed through the wheat field. The sun was still high, and it was silent but for a slight whisper of the breeze through the stalks of wheat which, given the early spring, were about three feet high but still quite green.

"Put the easel up here," Lilian said. "We'll come back to it; I just want to get a closer look. Care to come along?"

Ren propped up the easel beside a tree and hung his jacket upon it. "Yes, of course," he said.

"These crops are sure to stain your pants; you better leave them here," she told him.

"Leave my pants?" He asked in surprise.

"You heard me."

Tamanrasset

"What about your dress?"

Lilian looked at Ren provocatively and hiked her dress up until it was gathered about her waist. Ren could see at once that she had worn no drawers at all, not even the open drawers she usually had on. Despite the dense thatch of hair around her sex, she was noticeably swollen. After she let him take a long look, she turned and walked off into the wheat field. "Bring that blanket, too," she shouted over her shoulder.

Ren quickly dragged off his boots, unbuttoned his pants, and pulled off his suspenders. His pants fell to his feet, and he stepped out of them and directly into the wheat. He learned at once what Lilian was doing: The heads of the wheat stalks brushed between his legs as he walked, and it was remarkably arousing. He could barely guess at the sensations Lilian must be experiencing as the soft, firm heads of wheat gently brushed against her. By the time he caught up, he was fully engorged. Lilian reached down to grasp him through his drawers. "You should have left these too," she said. 'Take them off, Ren," she panted huskily.

"You do it," he told her.

Lilian unbuttoned him and pushed his drawers down his legs. As she knelt down to pick them up, she found him waving within an inch of her face and gently kissed him. Standing up she said excitedly: "Let's go over there to the shade of the aqueduct." She took hold of him and gently dragged him across the field, gasping every time the firm head of a wheat stalk touched her in the right place.

In a shady spot beneath the ancient aqueduct, they stomped about to flatten a small area in the wheat, and Ren spread out their blanket. Lilian pulled her dress and camisole over her head, and, naked apart from her socks and sturdy walking shoes, laid down on her side. "Care to take a flyer, Professor?" She asked cheekily as she cupped and held her breast out to him.

He dropped to his knees and pulled his shirt over his head. He gently laid down beside her, and their lips locked in a sensuous kiss. She moaned loudly when he entered her, indulging in the sort of passionate noisemaking that they were forced to stifle in her bedroom at the Palais. And Ren *was* forceful, but he saved himself in time for Lilian to roll on top and reach her own climax seconds before him. Afterwards, they drank the bottle of champagne and made love again.

They returned separately to the Palais to avoid discovery. Lillian had imported many cases of fine French wines which were served liberally with dinner, and then there was more Champagne and brandy. After lectures and cards, when the lights were turned off, Ren returned to Lillian's guest rooms so they could continue through the night.

***

Capitaine Roubec had been unusually observant during his review of the Legionnaires that morning, and as a result more than two dozen men were now engaged in "la course en rond," a punishment in the Legion in which the men found to be derelict were required to run with full packs in a circle within the fort's courtyard until they collapsed from exhaustion. Vonheim and Demoreau, angry that their Legionnaires had been found lacking, were shouting at those running while the rest of the Sixth stood rigidly at attention, broiling in the sunlight. The walls of Fort St. Louis offered

Tamanrasset

no shade to those in the center of the courtyard, and, in the morning, even the shadow of the watch tower and the Tricolore which flew above it, stretched away *outside* the walls.

The Sixth had been at Beni Ounif for months, long enough for the daily routine, the cramped quarters, the terrible food, gritty water, and heat, combined with the constant threat of attack, stray bullets, and the duty to maintain peace in a godforsaken zone between the edge of the barren Sahara and the border of Morocco, to take their toll upon the Legionnaires. Members of the Sixth had been wounded, abducted, tortured, and killed by Moroccan raiders. Four had been imprisoned for gross misconduct. Two had deserted to Morocco, only a few kilometers away, although it was likely they had been captured and put to death there. The Legionnaires at the fort were on edge and exhausted, and minor violations of the règlement were increasing. What, the Legionnaires wondered, had made the Capitaine so eager to impose his unmerciful discipline on the Company on this particular morning? Demoreau and Vonheim were the only two NCO's with whom Capitaine Roubec had shared the information which he had received by courier the previous evening: The Battalion's new commanding officer, General Hubert Lyautey, accompanied by the current Governor-General of French Algeria, Charles Jonnart, were on a tour of the Sud Oranais and would arrive at Fort St. Louis in two days.

After the assembly, Demoreau led ten Legionnaires out on a routine patrol of the fort's extended perimeter. Caporal Dormayer selected the squad. He was learning to speak English and had chosen mostly English speaking

Crossroads of the Nomad

Legionnaires—Lewis, Bennet, Jameson, and Britten, Henderson and Mills, and O'Connor (as well as fellow Alsatians Dupont and Bernard). Since they were delayed that day by the punishment, the sun had climbed high into the sky. It was hot, and the men were angry as they marched out of the fort, but Demoreau could keep the men together.

There wasn't much to the village of Beni Ounif. It was originally just a slight rise in a great empty plain beside the sand dunes with good sight lines along the main road used by caravans to travel between Morocco and Algeria. After the French began building Fort St. Louis, the village attracted more natives who believed it was safer to be close to the French fort. Then a tavern had been opened for the Legionnaires, and a trading shop for civilian and military goods, and a small medina. Demoreau's squad, in a short column two by two, passed through the village silently and continued up the road towards Morocco. They would march a kilometer or so and then make a circuit all around the fort.

Demoreau kept a close eye on the irritating Englishmen Henderson and Mills. They had recently begun showing up at the barracks each evening with bruises and bloodied noses, looking bitter and churlish. Demoreau had a suspicion that both men were being regularly beaten. It was the sort of trouble that would eventually erupt in the barracks one night with an attempted murder; Demoreau had seen it before. Bennet was marching right behind the two Brits, and they were being unusually silent.

Hard, flattened dirt stretched in every direction, but there were dry ravines and channels in the Wadi Zousfana that needed to be checked. The squad reached a sign on the road which purported to represent the border between

Morocco and Algeria; it had been up this time for a week—usually the sign was torn down after only a day or two. From this vantage point, Demoreau could see the town of Figuig some two or three kilometers further up the road into Morocco. All was peaceful, but it was at this spot only a few months earlier that a caravan of merchants transporting French goods had been waylaid, the traders all put to death and their merchandise stolen. Informants said it was the Doui-Menia who had undertaken the raid; it seemed they were no longer interested in working with the French to keep the peace. Demoreau called a halt. He noticed that Lewis sat with Henderson and Mills, and all three sat awkwardly sipping their water in silence. There was a dry ravine a hundred yards away, so Demoreau told Lewis and Dupont to go inspect it, and as soon as Lewis was out of earshot, the two Englishmen noticeably relaxed and began chatting with each other as usual—this time it was something about a woman in Brussels. At the ravine, rifles were fired. Lewis and Dupont had discovered someone and shots were exchanged. The man found was killed or left for dead, for when the two Legionnaires returned to the squad they were unharmed and had nothing to say. When Lewis sat down, Henderson and Mills shut their mouths again.

During his years in the Foreign Legion, Demoreau had seen plenty of strong men abuse their fellow Legionnaires. Henderson and Mills were not strong men and were not the type to do the abusing. Whatever had pushed them to enlist in the Legion, it probably wasn't murder or even assault. They had meant to leave trouble behind them, but now they were the ones being beaten down, beaten and cowed. That was not acceptable to Demoreau. Only a Sergent was entitled to beat down his Legionnaires, and the soldiers themselves were supposed to stick together.

The next two days were a frantic business for the Sixth as they prepared for the arrival of their commanding General and the Governor. Perimeter checks were performed continuously throughout the day while another squad visited every home in the village to inspect the occupants and confiscate their weapons. At night, the number of watchmen on the walls was doubled. Uniforms were washed and boots polished. At last, on the morning of arrival, the Legionnaires were assembled in a condition of near absolute preparedness, standing at attention, on the flat plain before the fort as the Capitaine and his officers watched the road from the gate. Runners had arrived to warn that the approaching dignitaries were close by, accompanied by two Companies of French infantry soldiers from the Armée d'Afrique and a Company of the Méharistes Sahariennes, a fierce group of camel-riding fighters recruited from the Chaamba, the large Arab tribe of the northern Sahara. The massive group finally appeared on the road to the northeast, progressing slowly from Aïn Séfra. Demoreau, standing before his Section with his two Caporals, Mueller and Dormayer, watched carefully as the General arrived with the Governor and their staffs, and the infantry and camel riders took positions surrounding but somewhat removed from the small fort. Demoreau didn't care about Governor Jonnart, the man who administered the entirety of French Algeria, nor his Deputy, Cayard, who accompanied Jonnart and whom Demoreau had met once before. But he was interested to see General Lyautey, the short, narrow man with white hair cut flat on top and a mustache of light red hair, who, when still a Colonel, had made a deal that allowed Sergent Demoreau to return to the Sixth.

Capitaine Roubec introduced his officers to the visiting dignitaries, and then the General agreed to review the assembled Legionnaires. As he approached Demoreau's Section, the Legionnaires all stood at attention, and the Sergent saluted. His eyes met those of General Lyautey, and there was a brief moment of recognition before the General nodded and returned the salute. No words were spoken. And then, as the General passed by, Demoreau saw among the General's entourage a tall woman dressed in pants like a man but wearing a black hijab, whom he immediately recognized. Isabel smiled and nodded to the Sergent as she passed him.

That afternoon, Demoreau was sitting with a few other NCO's in the blockhouse where the Legionnaire's food was prepared; he was enjoying a cup of Le Jus and humming Tchaikovsky's Violin Concerto in D. He wondered where he might be most likely to run into Isabel that afternoon. Then the General's Adjutant came to find him. The Adjutant was about the same age as Demoreau and had served in the French army just as long, but he had been to St. Cyr and was an officer so Demoreau stood up and saluted.

"Capitaine Roubec wishes to speak with you," the Adjutant said.

"Yes, Sir," Demoreau replied.

They stepped out into the sunlight and the Adjutant led the Sergent across the sundrenched courtyard. The blockhouse had few private rooms, but a larger one was used by the Capitaine as his office and sleeping quarters. As they entered, Demoreau saw General Lyautey and two additional officers as well as Deputy Governor Cayard and Capitaine Roubec, and he instantly came to attention.

Roubec made the introduction: "General, this is Sergent Demoreau, one of our most experienced and reliable men. He's personally been to the border point on patrol several times over the past few days."

Cayard spoke first: "Sergent, it is a pleasure to see you again; I recall my visit to Taghit, last year was it, or the year before? You were of substantial assistance during my meeting then."

"You are most generous, Deputy, but it was merely my duty," Demoreau replied.

"Well, I suppose you know that the Governor has expressed a desire to visit the border and view Figuig, and the General and I wish to know your assessment of the risks to his safety?"

"Yes, Sir. Well, I would expect that, in any event, the Governor will require a large force to accompany him to ensure his security. The border point in question," Demoreau said, "which is within view of Figuig, could be watched by any number of raiders, bandits, jihadists, and foreign mercenaries who keep a constant look out for potential targets approaching the border. It is my opinion that the Governor's security force, upon approaching the border, will provoke a violent response. In addition, there are a large number of ravines and gullies around the border point that might already be occupied by thieves and murderers who would be in a position to attack, or at least shoot at, the Governor. We clean them out, those on our side of the border, at least, but they keep coming back."

Cayard asked: "So you believe there is a very significant risk?"

"Yes, Deputy," he replied.

"If you were to send the Sergent out before dawn tomorrow morning," General Lyautey asked the Capitaine, "with enough men, could he take control of those ravines and gullies so that we can be confident they are safely in our hands?"

Roubec replied: "We can certainly send men out there, on our side of the border, to do that, and they'll also be in position to deter any movement in our direction from Figuig or its environs, if that is ultimately necessary."

"I think it's important that Jonnart see the border to understand that there is no line between here and there," the General said. "The threat from Morocco exists in an undefined space." To Demoreau he added: "My people are gathering additional information in Figuig, but I appreciate your observations, Sergent."

"Very good. You're dismissed, Sergent," Roubec told him.

Demoreau noted that Isabel was not with Lyautey, and he guessed that she was the one who had gone to Figuig to gather information. He was glad to see she was working with the General; it gave him confidence that Lyautey was a man who would think before making a rash move. Nevertheless, the affair in Morocco with Jilali suggested that Lyautey was also a man who wanted to get things accomplished at any price.

In the morning, still well before dawn, Demoreau led his patrol out to the border and inspected the nearby ravines and gullies to ensure there were no threats; there were surprisingly none. His Legionnaires occupied a wide scattering of depressions around the border point so as to keep watch, and as the Sun began to rise everything appeared normal and quiet. The Sergent and his men waited, out of sight, their eyes scanning the horizon through the sights of their Lebel rifles. The only sound was of the light breeze shifting the desert sands under the wide blue, cloudless sky. Just across the border into Morocco, the small city lay silent and shrouded in the dim light of dawn.

Demoreau had seen Figuig many times during his service in the Legion, but he had never been there. There was no reason he would ever wish to go. It was just another crumbling desert town filled with the same desperate people, people with whom he shared nothing, people who hated his presence, and people who wanted him dead. Today, at least, provided some novelty. It was unheard of for a French Governor to visit the border. From his palace in Algiers overlooking the Mediterranean, Jonnart could not comprehend the reality of life on the edge of the Sahara. That was why people like Demoreau had to stand guard in places like Beni Ounif, where the line between civilization and chaos was thin and easily crossed.

The Sergent adjusted the faded kepi on his head and looked over his Legionnaires who were crouched low, silent, and motionless, silent shadows in the dawn. They were well-hidden in the ravines that ran along the border, their weapons trained on the road, ready for anything. There was Caporal Mueller, the burly German who shaved his head, Caporal Dormayer, the lanky Alsatian who hated the Germans, Britten, the black-skinned American that the other Americans wouldn't speak to, the irritating Brits Mills and Henderson, the dependable Andreev, Mora, "The Count"

Rivoli, and the rest—men from all corners of the world who had come to the Legion for one reason or another. Demoreau had trained them all, and he knew that these were men he could rely on.

"Remember," he muttered to those nearest him, "we're here to make sure the Governor gets to safely see this border and that's all." He was not one for speeches, but it never hurt to remind his men of their duty. The first rays of sunlight crept up over the sand dunes behind them, and the Legionnaires crouched lower to avoid detection. A faint column of dust rose behind them along the road from Beni Ounif. Demoreau's aging eyes narrowed as he saw the movement: The Governor was coming at the head of a small caravan of soldiers and horses which had started the journey up the road toward them. Jonnart must have left the fort early.

Then came the sound, a distant drumming of hooves, faint at first but growing louder.

"Raiders," Demoreau muttered, his hand instinctively reaching for his rifle. The Legionnaires all tensed, their senses instantly honing in on the threat. Figuig was surely full of nomads, thieves, and bandits who lived outside the law, trading in plunder, smuggling, and violence. But this felt wrong. This wasn't just a handful of raiders. There were too many. It was a full-scale attack.

Demoreau's heart skipped a beat. "Not now, not today," he thought, the discordant notes of Schumann's Liederkreis already flowing past his inner ear.

Jonnart's caravan was still coming up the road when the Arab horsemen rose like a wave from the direction of Figuig, the dust flying up from beneath their mounts' hooves.

Twenty, maybe thirty riders wearing turbans and flowing robes, brandishing rifles and scimitars, came like a storm, fast and fierce, charging straight for the Governor's procession. The sound of the horses' pounding hooves filled the air, mixed with the harsh cries of the riders.

"Take positions!" Demoreau barked, his voice cutting through the clamor. "Mills, Henderson, with me!"

The Sergent's heart hammered in his chest as he led the two men from their cover and up onto the road. The rest of the Legionnaires stood and took their aim. The first shots rang out, echoing in the still morning air, and the Legionnaires opened fire. The Arabs hesitated for a moment, then surged forward, returning fire. It was chaos. The thin line between the two forces, less than a dozen yards, became a haze of dust and smoke and bullets. Demoreau's rifle kicked against his shoulder as he fired, watching as an Arab rider fell from his horse, his body crumpling to the ground.

The real threat came from the leader, a young man who Demoreau recognized immediately: He was the son of the local Sharif, the leader of the Doui-Menia. There were rumors this son had left the region, but now he had returned, a foe Demoreau had fought before. "Mills! Henderson!" He shouted, his voice barely audible over the din of battle. "Go for the leader!"

The two Legionnaires nodded and moved forward with practiced speed, their rifles raised. The sharif's son was mounted, his face fierce and full of anger. The Legionnaires closed the distance, and the young man raised his rifle. Mills and Henderson fired first. Henderson's bullet struck the young man's horse, and the animal broke stride, throwing its rider to the ground.

Tamanrasset

In the confusion, Demoreau spotted the Governor and Lyautey. They were surrounded by soldiers and making their way to the rear of the caravan. Jonnart was shouting, his face pale, his eyes wide with fear. Lyautey was barking orders, trying to keep the men together. Demoreau's blood ran cold. He swore under his breath and waved his men forward. "Cover the Governor!" He ordered.

He and Mills sprinted back towards Jonnart, taking down two more raiders as they passed. They reached the Governor just as the Sharif's son, now on foot, charged at them, his scimitar raised high.

With a roar, Mills lunged forward, his rifle smashing against the young Arab's side. The young man faltered, eyes wide in pain, before the Legionnaire slammed the butt of his rifle into his gut. The Sharif's son crumpled, gasping for air, unable to strike. Demoreau grabbed the Governor's arm, pulling him to safety as the remaining riders fell back, their attack faltering. The Arabs, seeing their leader down, began to retreat, pulling back into Morocco and fleeing for the city.

The battle was over as quickly as it had started. The attackers had failed, but most had escaped, including their leader who had disappeared in the haze. Jonnart and Lyautey were safe. Demoreau wiped the sweat from his brow, breathing heavily. His men moved to secure the area, checking the fallen attackers and making sure none of them would rise again. "Good shot, there, Henderson," he said; Mills received great praise for his defense of Governor Jonnart.

"Well done, Sergent," General Lyautey said, shaking Demoreau's hand. His voice was calm, but Demoreau could see the flicker of anxiety in his eyes.

"They're gone for now, Sir, but we should get the Governor back to the fort."

Jonnart, however, was furious. He stormed up to Lyautey shouting: "Mon Dieu, General, who were those men? Tell me, Sergent, how often does this sort of thing happen? Did they know we were coming?"

"It was just a coincidence, I'm certain," Lyautey told him, but Demoreau wasn't sure he believed that. He hadn't seen a targeted attack like that since Igli.

"I want you to go after them," the Governor demanded.

Lyautey and Demoreau looked at each other: Both wore the same expression of surprise.

Pointing at Figuig, Lyautey replied: "With all due respect, Sir, that's Morocco. Our government has forbidden me from going there."

"I don't care," Jonnart shouted. "I can see the city right there. Damn! Pull up your artillery, then, and bombard them from here. This assault cannot go unanswered!"

Lyautey did not hesitate to comply. "As you command, Governor."

Jonnart returned to the fort with a large contingent of soldiers, and Demoreau gathered his Legionnaires. A couple of the men had been wounded, but none seriously. He sent those men back to the fort, but he had the rest take positions around General Lyautey until the rest of the infantry could be drawn up. Within half an hour, they had brought three French 75's, each with a range of about eight kilometers, forward from Fort St. Louis.

On Lyautey's command, the artillery opened fire on the city of Figuig. The bombardment was not swift, the firing rate was only about one shot every minute or two, but it went

Tamanrasset

on and on. The fixed ammunition used in the 75's sent shells in a high graceful arc over the empty plains of sand to land somewhere in the city. Demoreau could see a spurt of dust and debris as each projectile fell and burst into shards of shrapnel. He had remained at the border with his men, but after the artillery began firing he sent members of his peloton back to the fort to eat and rest. There was no indication that Lyautey intended to send the Legionnaires into Morocco.

Out of the corner of his eye, Demoreau saw General Lyautey approaching and came to attention.

"Sergent," Lyautey said. "I didn't get to finish what I intended to tell you earlier, when we were interrupted by the Governor."

"What was that, Sir?" Demoreau asked.

"Madame Pedersen is there, in Figuig, right now," he said in a grim tone. "She went over to speak with the priest there last night, to assess whether there was any risk of, well, of what happened today, and she has not returned."

Demoreau was shocked. "I can take a peloton there now; we will find her, if you'll give the order."

"I can't, and you may not," Lyautey replied sternly. "But you can pray with me, Sergent, that she returns to us safe and unharmed."

* * *

In Tlemcen, the teachings of Muhammad al-Kattani had gained widespread acceptance, and since Isabel had studied Islam to a great extent through her work for al-Kattani, she was readily welcomed into the community of Muslims there: She attended the mosque and was treated with respect, she was called "Alima" and invited to speak at the madrassa, she prayed five times a day and obeyed all the local customs. Some had heard of the miracles she had performed in Morocco. Because of this, the French government did not trust her, and she had received visits from French officials who wished to send her back to Sweden. This actually improved her reputation in the Muslim community, but the Muslims didn't know that Lyautey, now elevated to General in command of the Sud Oranais Division, was protecting her. She had plenty of time to further her studies while she gathered information and translated Arabic newspapers for him. It was now obvious that the entire Maghreb was being consumed by France, but Lyautey at least claimed to want peace and security, and if she worked to achieve that herself, especially on the edges of the Sahara where violence was endemic, she felt it was acceptable for her to do so. Or not. There was another thought that persisted in her head, that she was neither as good nor as wise as people believed. She was afraid to tell anyone about her work for Lyautey and hoped they wouldn't find out. She did not particularly care if they were misled into thinking better of her than she deserved, but she often felt she was an imposter. At those moments, the practice of Islam sometimes felt to her like an act, just words coming from her mouth, the lines uttered by the character she continued to play; she was no longer sure she believed in any God at all. And when she chose to examine how she felt, the short answer was that she didn't. She felt dulled, and she disingenuously allowed her dullness to be misinterpreted as gravity by others.

Spring arrived and with it the day when General Lyautey and his troops, a large number of soldiers both French and Arab, departed for the southwestern parts of

Algeria. After agonizing over the decision for weeks, Isabel decided to go with them, still uncertain whether it was the right thing to do or merely the best opportunity available. French Governor Jonnart and Deputy Governor Cayard were to meet the General in Macharia so they could review the Sud Oranais regions together. The trip to Aïn Séfra, with many stops along the way, would take nearly a month. They journeyed village to village, and Isabel met with many Mullahs and Imams that she knew from her previous travels. In every village, she prayed at the mosques, she explained what the French were offering to their communities, she arranged meetings between the General, the Governor, his Deputy, and local leaders, she negotiated pacts, and she advised the French soldiers how to behave respectfully. By the time they reached Aïn Séfra, she had, as usual, become indispensable. After resting a few days, it was decided that General Lyautey would continue south. Governor Jonnart insisted on going with him.

Isabel didn't know they would run into Sergent Demoreau, but she was delighted to see him when the expedition reach Beni Ounif. She thought he looked better now that he was back in the Foreign Legion where he belonged, where he was at home. She wanted to speak with him alone, but General Lyautey asked her to find out whether there was any potential danger to the Governor visiting the border. She walked three miles up the road to Morocco to the mosque in Figuig at which she had prayed once before. The Imam remembered her and was delighted to see her again. They had a pleasant conversation outside as the Sun set. The sky behind her was deep blue, turning purple. Then, as she turned to leave, she noticed two men coming together from the mosque, a young man, and an older man. The younger was Ahmad. He appeared more mature to her but still youthful, earnest, and very handsome. He wore a serious expression, but when he recognized her, his face showed his astonishment. He looked around, as if to see if she was alone, and then he came, followed by his companion, across the square to where she stood in shocked surprise.

"Asalamu alaikom, Sayyid," she said, looking down.

"Wa alaikom salaam. What are you doing in Figuig?" Ahmad asked challengingly. "Have you been looking for me?"

"I didn't know you were here," she answered.

Ahmad turned to his companion. "My esteemed father's brother, please allow me to present to you Hajja Isabel Pedersen."

The older gentleman's demeanor changed at once and his eyes sparkled. "Ah, yes, Madame Pedersen, I heard you speak here at the mosque some months ago. It is an honor to meet you. My name is Jamal ibn Ali al-Haybah; Ahmad is my brother's son. You know each other from his time in Fez, I take it?" he asked while holding out his hand to shake like a proper European.

She took his hand gently and shook lightly, uncertain whether she should behave like a Muslim woman before a man who expected her to behave like a European.

"A pleasure to meet you, Monsieur. Yes, Ahmad and I knew each other in Fez," she replied, then she turned to Ahmad. "It's been so long, Ahmad. Are you well? Are you no longer studying at the university or working with Sayyid al-Kattani?"

"I left Fez to return to my family," Ahmad said.

"If you'll forgive me, I must return to my warehouse now to complete my work," Jamal interrupted nervously. "As always, Ahmad, it means a great deal to me that you have come to visit. I hope you will return to your father now to get his decision on the matters we discussed." To Isabel's ear, he sounded less than pleased, perhaps even cold to his nephew. "I wish you safe travels, Madame, blessings of Allah upon you."

"Thank you. Peace be with you," she said.

"And with you." Jamal merely nodded to Ahmad and then departed.

"So, tell me what you are doing here in Figuig?" Ahmad asked Isabel bluntly.

Isabel was at a loss. The one clear and simple explanation was the one she suddenly knew she didn't want to give to Ahmad: There was no doubt in her mind that he would not approve of her work with Lyautey. And for the first time, she felt uncomfortable with him.

"I ... I have been traveling around the Sahara, ever since I completed the Hajj," she lied.

It was obvious that Ahmad knew it was a lie. He looked at her questioningly, but only for a brief moment. Then his face broke into a wide grin. "Allah be praised, it is a miracle that we have met this way. I am so pleased to see you, and there is so much I wish to tell you about Fez and Sayyid al-Kattani. Will you come with me to share a glass of tea? Then I will escort you to your lodging; it is getting dark. You will agree, won't you? It will be most pleasing."

It was her mission to gather information, so she decided to accept his invitation. They walked around the corner and down a few blocks as the evening darkened. There was a well-lit café where they could sit outdoors, and Ahmad ordered tea for them.

"You must have heard that our paper, 'Nur al-Fajr,' was shut down."

"I had no idea," Isabel said. "What happened? Where is Sayyid al-Kattani?"

"Al-Kattani is fine, thanks be to Allah. He and a number of scholars involved with the newspaper went on the Hajj, an excellent excuse for them to leave the country. Al-Kattani is in Egypt now, I believe."

"And the newspaper, what happened?"

"We had no difficulty with the Sultan's censors as long as we published undeniable facts, but, eventually, as we moved towards publishing editorial material, there were concerns as to how the Sultan would respond. The Ulama got nervous."

"I am very relieved that none of you were arrested," she told him. He seemed so different to her, and she had a sense that Ahmad had become stronger, more important.

"There was little cause for concern," Ahmad said dismissively. "The Sultan is quick to anger but his government is slow and inept."

"So I saw myself," she said.

"They did eventually execute the baker, if you didn't know."

"Yes, I did hear that, when I was still in Mecca."

"So you completed the Hajj?"

"Yes, I did," she said with less pride than she intended.

"And you have been traveling since then?"

"I didn't see any need to rush back."

"That was nearly two years ago," Ahmad pointed out.

Isabel did not reply.

"I heard you were in Taza last year," he said coldly.

"That was ...." She said uncertainly.

"Are you working for the French mercenaries that are now across the border?"

She began again to feel quite uncomfortable. What was it in Ahmad that had changed? Or had she always misunderstood him? "Well, I've been traveling with them, yes, but just for my safety," she lied.

"Is it true that the Governor of Algeria is traveling with them as well, or is that only a rumor? It would be so interesting to have him visit Figuig. I believe he would like the city very much, don't you agree?"

"I ... I really, I wouldn't know. What I have been doing – "

Ahmad snorted: "I know very well what you have been doing, Madame," he said derisively. "You have not been behaving as a proper Muslim woman should."

"I don't like you speaking to me that way," she replied sternly.

"It is not for you to tell me how to behave," Ahmad spat back.

His tone unnerved Isabel. She rose suddenly from her seat. "I am glad to have seen you again, Ahmad; I wish you the best," she said and turned to go. Ahmad was instantly beside her. He grasped her arm above the elbow and held her tightly.

"I cannot permit you to leave yet, Madame."

"Let me go, Ahmad, please," she begged.

He shook his head. "There was a time when I found you very desirable, but now, I admit, you disgust me—the way you pretend to worship Allah and honor the Prophet. You know nothing of Islam, or Morocco, or our people, neither you nor the French thieves and mercenaries for whom you work. I wish you had not come here, I truly do, but now I'm afraid you will have to stay with me."

* * *

"I am ashamed that it took me so long to understand what is happening to my homeland," Ahmad told her. He looked at Isabel with disdain. She sat on the rug, up against the wall of his large tent, with ropes binding her hands and feet. He saw she was ashamed and couldn't bring herself to look at him. "Raised as I was in this wasteland between the mountains and the desert, with only a fertile oasis to sustain us, I accepted that our fate was predestined: Does it not say in the Quran, 'Allah has created and balanced all things and has fixed their destinies and guided them'? Are our fates not written in his book of decrees? For centuries, my family has moved between the mountains and the oases where we farm and graze our livestock, as we believed it to be our destiny and our duty to Allah. This year, the French closed the border, and we were prohibited from moving our sheep and camels or accessing our lands, because the French say we have no papers to enter Algeria. We resisted their demands, and two of my brothers were murdered by the mercenaries for crossing the border without permission. Our date palm groves were seized and now belong to a Frenchman who lives in Marseille. My people have been arrested, tortured, killed;

their lands and goods have been stolen; women and girls have been raped and mutilated. It was not like this before the French came to the Wadi Saoura. These are the acts of infidels. Are we not instructed to 'kill the idolaters wherever you find them and take them prisoners, and beleaguer them, and lie in wait for them at every place of ambush'? There are those like my father's brother who would appease the French and seek to profit by them, but I believe that Allah wishes us to resist the occupation and the theft of our homeland by the Westerners. You say you are Muslim, people call you Alima, but now I find you are working for them. You have made me feel very foolish, for I was misled by your pretense."

"I have only tried to stop the bloodshed and ease the path of peace, Ahmad," she objected.

"But you do so by asking my people to obey the Christians, because in your heart you still are one."

"That's not true," she shouted.

"The Quran says to destroy that which weakens Islam. Does not Solomon take his sword and slaughter the horses that distract him from his prayers?"

"That is a false reading of the Quran, Ahmad. The word used does not mean to slash or slay; it's the same word used to describe the rubbing of your face and hands in ablution before prayer. Solomon caressed those horses to show that reverence for the world created by Allah is more important than adhering to hard and fast rules."

"Now you would lecture me on Islam too," he spat back at her, "with watered down interpretations of the Prophet's words to placate the barbarous natives?"

"Your anger has nothing to do with Islam. You are angry at the French for what they have done to you and your family. Please, just let me go."

"Admit you are a pretender, their servant, and perhaps I will spare your life," he said angrily.

It seemed that Isabel at last comprehended her danger, and an anger flowed from her heart that made her flush deep red. She glared at Ahmad with fury and struggled wildly against the ropes that bound her. It startled him: She was like a djinn, and he wondered whether she was truly capable of cursing him. He stood and walked out of the tent. He wasn't sure what to do with her. He was angry and afraid of her, and now he was ashamed that he once loved her. She would have to remain in his tent for the present. It was night, and he walked slowly across the camp to the fire where his followers awaited him. They were good men, strong and brave fighters who were eager to attack.

After the meeting in Taghit with the Deputy Governor which Ahmad attended with his father and uncle, and afterwards while Ahmad was away in Fez, there had been a period of relative peace where the French allowed the native people to do as they wished in the south. However, over time, the contacts between them and the French vendors, French suppliers, French explorers, and French soldiers had created more misunderstandings, tensions, and complaints. The French government had been forced by its own people to take action, and Ahmad returned to the Wadi Saoura from Fez to find the region like a powder keg ready to explode. He also found that his father had grown older and that his people needed Ahmad to take a larger role in the Doui-Menia. He was still deemed a young man though educated

Tamanrasset

by the wisest teachers in Islam and a warrior who had fought bravely with the Sharif, so Ahmad gathered to him a small group of the fiercest fighters who would fight beside him. They began to conduct targeted raids on the French soldiers all along the border with Algeria, from Forthassa to Béni Abbès. They found the French to be highly reactionary, merely dealing with whatever came their way, and it gave Ahmad the first elements of a plan. The men with him in the camp were all from families devoted to the Sharif, families from whom lands had been stolen and brothers lost to the French. They were prepared for war and would undertake any action that Ahmad demanded of them.

After learning from nomads that the French General and Governor were traveling south, Ahmad brought his fighters together near Figuig with a plan to intercept the French leaders. He did not need Isabel to tell him that the French were planning to visit the border for he had many spies in their camp and already knew their intentions. He did not mean to capture or even kill the French dignitaries for nothing would be gained by it. He had another plan.

"In the name of Allah, I again ask each of you to place your life at risk," he said to his men. "Tomorrow, we will kill any of the French mercenaries that hinder our path, but I wish for none of you to be martyred in this battle. Tomorrow is a demonstration meant to open the eyes of those whose opinions are heard by the Christians in Europe, may Allah's curses be upon them. A man whose own life is at risk sees much more clearly than he who sacrifices the lives of others. We want these Frenchmen to confront their deaths, so they will see what is happening here in our lands. We want them to return to their homes to warn others. Kill the soldiers, yes, as many as you can, but the Governor and his servants are to be unharmed."

Ahmad and two dozen of his horsemen soon were hidden on the outskirts of Figuig, watching even as the Legionnaires came to take up positions along the border during the night. Summer was coming on, but the night was still very cold. The horses stamped their feet to keep warm, their breath steaming, but the riders, dressed all in black, appeared only as shadows. As the sun began to rise to the east and the sky became pale grey, the silhouettes of the concealed Legionnaires were difficult to see, but Ahmad had a good sense of their strategy and believed he knew where the soldiers were lying in wait. Then the first rays of the sun began to creep over the fields of sand to the east. Already there was a vast cloud of dust which meant there were many horses coming very slowly up the road from Beni Ounif.

How close would Ahmad and his men need to get to the Governor and his General in order to put them at risk? Not very close, Ahmad assumed. It would shock the Governor enough just to learn that his enemies were waiting for him. That meant the Governor's whereabouts were known and he could be targeted anywhere, at any time. Ahmad could now see the approaching train of horses and wagons with the French Governor. He spurred his horse, and he and his men leapt forward, quickly reaching a full gallop, making as much noise as possible. Their mounts were already raising a cloud of dust as they surged towards the border. The thunderous pounding of the hooves broke the morning silence. Puffs of smoke ahead of them revealed the positions of the Legionnaires—their enemies were already firing their rifles.

Tamanrasset

Ahmad rode alongside the road, breaking left and right irregularly but essentially straight at the French Governor. He was adept at firing his rifle while he rode and shot at the soldiers surrounding the French official. Three Legionnaires leapt into the road before him. They aimed their rifles at Ahmad, but the other riders cut in front of him to divert the aim of the soldiers. The air was full of dust and smoke; it was almost impossible to see. Unthwarted, the Legionnaires kept firing. Ahmad saw soldiers rushing to protect the Governor, pulling him to the rear. Ahmad's horse whinnied in pain and collapsed headfirst onto the roadbed. Ahmad was thrown forward onto the ground. Bruised but unbroken, Ahmad drew his scimitar and charged at the Legionnaire who had shot his horse, hoping to kill the man. A rifle which was swung by another Legionnaire like a club caught Ahmad in his side and he heard an ominous crack. He was thrown off balance and turned to face his attacker, his eyes agape as he found the Legionnaire who had hit him. Then the butt of the Legionnaire's rifle was thrust into Ahmad's gut, and he was knocked again to the ground. His hand grasped the handle of his sword. He spit blood from his mouth, and then struggled to his feet to attack. Out of the smoke and dust a horseman rode up to Ahmad, one of his own men. He took Ahmad's hand and swung him up behind him onto his mount, and with a call to the others, the attackers turned and galloped back into the haze towards Figuig.

* * *

After an exchange of increasingly menacing letters, Paul Gauckler finally came to Tunis. A man about Ren's own age but thin and spidery, Gauckler was a civil engineer by training. He had been raised in Lorraine, and refused to speak any language other than French, it being his opinion as a representative of the French government that anyone wishing to do business with him must speak the official language of France. His letters had been addressed to Ren, Delattre and the archbishop. While Gauckler did not dispute that the diocese had an irrevocable concession to conduct excavations wherever it chose in Tunisia, he still asserted that it was within his power to halt any excavation of which he did not approve.

At the meeting with Ren, Delattre, and a French "avocat," the attorney hired by the Franco-American Carthage Excavation Foundation, Gauckler made it clear that he would be an ongoing nuisance.

"As long as it was only Reverend Père Delattre and a student or two excavating a Christian cemetery and extracting artefacts that went only into the museum attached to the St. Louis Cathedral, I had no concerns," Gauckler said. "But these excavations have grown massively, and it is my duty to ensure that they are being managed in a manner befitting such an important archaeological site. Again I remind you that if I am not satisfied, the work shall not proceed."

"With all due respect, Monsieur Chief Inspector," the avocat interjected, "unless you are able to articulate a sound basis for doubting the professionalism of the work being done—work, I might add, being conducted by trained archaeologists from some of the finest academic institutions in the world—until you can articulate a sound basis for doing so, you have no grounds upon which to interrupt the excavations."

"The same argument was made to me in Algiers, and I give you the same reply: There are always grounds to suspend the work. Was there not a serious collapse at the Hill of Juno recently where several employees, including Monsieur Villere himself, narrowly escaped death? And did this not result in the destruction of a Punic tomb of potentially great significance? That event by itself is cause enough to suspend all work at Carthage."

"I beg your pardon," Ren objected angrily, "but you have misconstrued the thing entirely. I personally inspected the tomb in question and found there was nothing of value inside, and a little back-sliding of the soil after the fact, when neither I nor anyone else was at risk, which could easily be removed if there were any reason to do so, could hardly constitute the sort of overblown catastrophe you are alleging would warrant shutting down the entire site!"

"Monsieur Villere, while I would concede that it is outside of my purview, concerns have also been voiced as to whether your regular excessive drinking is impacting the safety of the worksites."

"That is an outrageous lie," Ren replied angrily.

"Nevertheless, the work must be inspected, and it must be sound, or else I am obligated to shut it down."

"We must also object to your plan to audit the financials of the Foundation," the avocat stated. "This is surely outside your jurisdiction."

"As Chief Inspector, I have the right to examine the financial expenditures relating to these excavations and determine whether there is any fraud being perpetrated."

"Fraud?" Ren exclaimed. "By God, who could even be committing such fraud? No one here in Tunis handles the

Foundation's funds; my only control is to identify the sites at which money is to be spent."

"If you may not spend the money where you choose and may only spend the money where I allow it, then, Monsieur Villere, who is really the one in control?"

"I am a Professor of Archaeology and would appreciate your addressing me by the titles I have earned, either Doctor or Professor," Ren spit back angrily.

"I have been told that you lead a remarkably lavish lifestyle, 'Doctor Villere'," Gauckler replied sarcastically. "From what source is the funding for that, I wonder?"

At that, Ren stood abruptly. His face was red with anger, and had he not been so stunned he would have leapt over the table to pummel Gauckler. Instead, he strode angrily from the room.

After the meeting ended and Gauckler had gone for the day, Delattre found Ren in the workshop where he was cleaning the fragment of pottery from the Punic tomb.

"This is the fragment I brought out from the tomb," Ren said, "a piece of a bowl or urn of yellow clay with red paint on it. Apart from knowing where it is from and when it was made, it looks like mere debris. I wouldn't have bothered to save it, and now I must waste resources and time to ensure it is catalogued and examined by experts."

"We have some time to make certain that the papers are all in order before the Chief Inspector returns; the lawyers will see to it," Delattre told him. "I can't say that you were wrong to be insulted, but I did warn you, did I not?"

"You did, and I apologize to you for my petulance," Ren replied. "I can assure you that I have the utmost confidence in the quality of the work being conducted, and, as I indicated, it is simply not possible that the Foundation's funds are being misspent—they are audited and dispensed by the Foundation itself."

"Oh, I have no concerns whatsoever regarding the excavations or the Foundation, Ren. On the contrary, our sites are in better condition now than they ever were before you came to work with us. On the other hand, the Chief Inspector does appear to hold a certain animosity towards you personally."

"He only wants to be in my position," Ren said.

"Perhaps, but someone has clearly informed him of your increasingly lavish lifestyle."

"I am not the one spending money on Champagne and caviar, I assure you," he replied.

"That is undoubtedly true. Still, it looks very bad. And indeed you have been drinking a great deal more than usual, even for you. And, there's more: I feel it is my duty to advise you that this has become of topic of local gossip and innuendo. May I be forgiven for saying so, Ren, but your relationship with Madame Beaton is possibly less discrete than you believe it to be."

Ren blushed. "I ... I don't know what to say," he stammered.

"There's no need to say anything. I am not your Father Confessor, and it's none of my business, truly. But you needed to be told, and, as a friend, I am telling you."

"Thank you," Ren replied.

"If you chose to put some distance between the two of you, it wouldn't be unwise, and a little distance from the Chief Inspector, for a brief time, would perhaps help as well. I will remind you that the gentlemen at the National

Museum of Antiquities in Algiers have requested, yet again, that you come to lecture there. I am not sure why they are so insistent, but they very much want you to visit."

"I would be remiss to leave the sites here at this crucial time," Ren said.

"Oh, I don't know," Delattre answered. "We agree that everything has been responsibly managed, and, without you here for Gauckler to antagonize, perhaps he can be more quickly mollified. If we can convince him to submit his concerns to us in writing, it would give us time to prepare a written, thoughtful reply when you return. In short, I believe you should go away for a time, a limited time."

"I'll consider it," Ren said quietly.

Ren was deeply embarrassed by Delattre's disclosures, but Lilian, he knew, would be even less pleased to hear that she was the subject of local gossip. It was all Ren could do to get through the afternoon, dinner at the Palais, the lectures, and the cards, without drinking a very large amount of gin. He mentioned twice in Lilian's presence about the invitation to lecture in Algiers, and both times Lilian made a subtle pouty face at him.

Ren eventually escaped to his bedroom so he could freshen up, and from there he climbed to the fourth floor to cross over to the guest wing and Lilian's bedroom. He found her waiting for him in their bed, naked and ready for their evening love-making. Ren undressed and got under the sheets with her. Despite her ardent kisses, he didn't feel it would be proper to delay telling her about Delattre's embarrassing disclosure.

"I have been given some uncomfortable news," he said. "We must speak about it before going any further."

"Why? What is it?" She whispered.

"I have been told, by a friend, that there may be some speculation about our relationship, that we are not, possibly, as innocent as we appear." Even saying those words, which was soft-pedalling the issue even more than Delattre had, made Ren queasy.

Lilian stiffened and pulled back. "Who? Ren, who is saying this? I've told you before, I cannot jeopardize my position no matter how wonderful you are to me."

"I do not know," he admitted. "It was not presented to me as a threat; there was no extortion. It might just be generally known."

"Oh my God," Lilian quietly exclaimed. She got out of bed and stood naked by the window. Ren couldn't resist admiring her good looks, despite the circumstances. She saw him and made a face: "I wish I could be excited to see *you* that way," she said peevishly.

"No one truly knows anything about us for certain," he pointed out.

"I have been looking for a moment to broach some bad news anyway," she said. "I need to return to New York. The Metropolitan Opera's gala is coming up. My husband relies on me to attend with him. I had thought it would only be for a brief time."

"That is still a lengthy excursion," Ren said. "When will you come back?"

"I had intended to return," she asserted, "but, honestly, now I can't say that I will." She saw his deflated expression. "It isn't just for my sake, Ren. If my father found out about us, he could seriously damage your reputation. I've seen him do it to others he's disliked—he's almost ruined your friend

Bert Hill over a matter of no importance whatsoever. You simply can't afford to lose my father's support now, and I must maintain my marriage."

"I would marry you, if you divorced your husband," Ren said.

Lilian laughed. "I apologize for that," she said quickly. "I don't think it's funny–you're sweet, Ren. But, no, I am not going to marry you."

"After these months we've had together, the closeness day in and day out, even considering the inconveniences of the secrecy, I ... I don't want it to end. It seems I've fallen for you, Lilian."

"Let's not make things worse by expressing our feelings now, darling," she said crisply, wrapping a light blanket around herself. "It will only make us both feel rotten. I was married when we met and married I shall be when I leave. I'll make my plans in the morning and depart for New York in the next week, two at most. In the meantime, it might be best if you took that opportunity to go lecture in Algiers."

"Algiers? There is nothing for me in Algiers," he spat back. Ren was crushed. Seeing that Lilian would not return to bed while he was there, he got up to dress, albeit slowly in case she chose to stop him. She did not.

"Never fear," he said finally, "I'll be away tomorrow. We won't be seen together again." He stepped close to her and looked her in the eyes, not threatening to touch her in any way, but yet he sensed her flinch. He took it as a reproach. "Goodbye, Lilian," he said, and left the room.

* * *

Tamanrasset

Isabel remained bound in Ahmad's tent through the night. She was given food and water and was told which direction to pray towards Mecca. She heard horse riders departing the camp before dawn, then return, and then depart again before mid-day. She heard cannon fire throughout the afternoon. Finally, at dusk, an elderly, toothless Berber man came to untie her, and Isabel finally stepped outside.

Hers was the only remaining tent of what had been a small encampment west of Figuig. The older man was the only remaining person. They were alone in a dark canyon, and in the moonlight the minaret of the mosque in the city was visible to the east.

"May I go now?" She asked the old man in Arabic.

He cackled and nodded enthusiastically; perhaps he was unable to speak. He gave Isabel a camel which had been left for her as a message that she should go away. The old man mounted his own camel and rode off to the west towards the mountains of the High Atlas, leaving her alone.

Isabel had spent hours thinking over the things that Ahmad had said to her. She was no closer to knowing whether he was right, whether she was a false Muslim, but she knew in her heart that she was a fraud. She didn't know what she believed or who she was, and she didn't think she could return to Lyautey or Fez or Sweden or anywhere until she knew. She didn't want to speak to any more people or enter any village or town until she knew. She had to figure out what she was doing, and why. And she couldn't know until she healed whatever it was inside her that was so broken. She looked east to Figuig. That was not where she wanted to go. Then she recalled there was a woman, a holy marabout and Sheikha named Lèlla Zeyneb; the Sultan's princess sister had mentioned her. Lèlla Zeyneb was said to be a great healer who lived in the city of Ouargla, far off in the northern part of the Sahara, near Tunisia. She was the person, Isabel thought, who might help her.

Isabel held the reins of the large gentle animal that knelt beside her. She could not bear to think of riding the creature, but leaning back she pulled on the reins and brought the camel to its feet. They would both walk, she decided. They had a long way to go, but the camel was strong and young, and Isabel had nothing left, absolutely nothing, but time.

* * *

The bombardment of Figuig continued until late in the afternoon. Lyautey only called a halt when the Legionnaires spotted two small children with an older man wearing a fine three-piece charcoal gray suit; he was coming out from the city, the General presumed, to negotiate the city's surrender. Governor Jonnart and Deputy Cayard came from Fort St. Louis to join the discussion in a large canvas tent that Lyautey had ordered to be hastily erected. Eager to hear news of Isabel, Demoreau also snuck into the tent.

"My name is Jamal ibn Ali al-Haybah; I am a trader and merchant; Deputy Cayard will hopefully recall that I spoke at the meeting in Taghit he attended some years ago. The residents of Figuig have sent me now to ask that you stop your bombardment. The men who attacked you this morning left the area at mid-day," the Arab man said in perfect French. Demoreau recognized the Arab man—he was the Sharif's brother, the one who had argued with the Sharif at the meeting with Cayard. Demoreau recalled that he was a merchant, and he must be an important figure in Figuig if

Tamanrasset

he was the one sent to negotiate the city's surrender, he thought.

Jamal continued: "We were not aware that those dangerous men were in the city; they were not welcomed. The Quran teaches us that all life is sacred, and those men committed a sin by attacking you. However, it is now you who are attacking the innocent, those in our city. Seven people are dead, and many others have been injured by your cannons. We are a city of families, merchants, and traders. We plead with you to stop."

"How can we know that the horsemen are gone, that what you say is true?" Lyautey demanded.

"If it will stop the cannon, then you may send your soldiers to search the city. They can confirm that what I say is true. Those men left at mid-day."

"You say you speak for the people of your city in this matter," Deputy Cayard said. "Your city is in Morocco, I am told; do you speak for the Sultan Abd al-Aziz?"

"I cannot speak for the Sultan, but many people have come to ask me to seek your mercy. We who live in Figuig have no objection to your soldiers coming to search, provided that you acknowledge that Sultan Abd al-Aziz remains the ultimate ruler there."

Lyautey chuckled and shook his head. Such a condition was ridiculous for it was well known that Sultan Abd al-Aziz held no power in the south except in name.

"That is a difficult concession to request," Jonnart replied gravely, showing Jamal that he was being taken seriously.

"And what would prevent those men from returning to Figuig as soon as our soldiers have departed?" Lyautey demanded. "We must be allowed to keep soldiers in the city to ensure that these criminals do not return."

Jamal looked pained: "Now *you* are asking for a difficult concession," Jamal replied.

"Hardly," Cayard answered. "As you surely know, the Sultan has granted his permission to France to use its soldiers to maintain peace in the Zousfana and Guir valleys. If we were all to agree that Figuig's waters comes from one of those two rivers, well, then, the Sultan has already granted permission for French soldiers to enter. And that permission comes with guarantees from the French government that the principal of Moroccan sovereignty will be maintained."

"What is meant by 'sovereignty'?" Jamal asked.

"The authority of the government of Morocco, the 'Makhzen,' the Sultan, or whoever is in charge in Morocco," Jonnart answered in an unnecessarily ambiguous way.

"I suppose that is agreeable," Jamal said.

The important thing, from Demoreau's point of view, was that he get into Figuig as soon as possible to find Isabel. After the meeting ended, Demoreau approached Jamal discretely before he walked back to the city with the children. "Monsieur, can you tell me if a European woman came to your city yesterday, perhaps to see the Imam?" Demoreau asked.

The Arab man looked at Demoreau with curiosity. "You must mean the Alima, Hajjah Pedersen?"

"Yes, that's who I mean."

"Yes ...," Jamal hesitated and it was clear he was uncertain what to say. "I did see her; she was with the Imam. I didn't speak with her. It was a very great honor to have her

Tamanrasset

come pray with us at our mosque as she did last night. Is there a problem?"

"I expected to see her today, and I am concerned for her well-being if she still remains in Figuig. Do you know if she is in the city?"

The Arab man lowered his eyes. "I ... I last saw her with one of the horsemen," he said nervously.

Demoreau felt the blood rush to his face. "You mean your brother's son, is that right?" He asked accusingly.

"I did see them together, and it did not seem to me that she went with him of her own free choice," Jamal admitted. "However, Ahmad would not do the Alima any harm; she is a revered person in our country, and Ahmad is a fervent believer. But I cannot tell you where she is now or if he took her away with him."

Demoreau had a terrible feeling something had happened to Isabel. As much as he wanted to search for her himself, the Legionnaires had been ordered to return to Fort St. Louis. General Lyautey had arranged for a large number of soldiers to begin a search in Figuig. The Méharistes Sahariennes fighters were to be sent first—they were Berbers and Arabs and less likely to antagonize the local people. French infantry would be sent in gradually to secure the town and create a garrison there. Lyautey had no intention of giving up ground and leaving Figuig now that he had obtained local permission to insert troops there. More troops would be sent down from Tlemcen and from Sidi Bel Abbès, but that would take several weeks. In the meantime, Lyautey's forces were stretched thin.

The search of Figuig and questioning of the local people confirmed what the Sharif's brother had said: The men who attacked the Governor at the border had already fled south from Figuig and were headed towards the town of Bechar, but the Governor insisted that General Lyautey pursue them. The Méharistes Sahariennes and Armée D'Afrique infantry were gathered outside Beni Ounif and prepared for the one hundred kilometer march to the southwest. Demoreau was frustrated for he wanted to help rescue Isabel, who had not been found in Figuig. However, the Sixth was ordered to remain at Fort St. Louis where they had already been stationed for months. The thought of resuming their tedious daily routine when the French Army was moving further into Morocco made the Legionnaires angry. They were eager to fight. While it was understandable that a part of the Company might be kept at the fort, surely one Section could be added to General Lyautey's march to Bechar. Demoreau spoke to Lieutenant Hansen and Sergent Vonheim, and they were also eager to go, so the three men went to Capitaine Roubec's blockhouse on the evening before Lyautey's departure. They were waiting to speak to their commanding officer when Caporal Mueller, in his stocky way, came running up.

"Sergent Demoreau, you must come at once," he said urgently. "Henderson has been beaten to a pulp; Mills has just brought him into the infirmary; he's unconscious and badly hurt."

"What is this all about, Sergent," Hansen demanded angrily.

"I've had suspicions that Mills and Henderson got themselves into something, possibly involving another Legionnaire; it looks like it's come to a head."

"I'll want a full report by morning, Sergent," Hansen said. "I won't stand for this sort of nonsense in my Section. If it's a Legionnaire who has done this, I want a name. Someone is going to the Zephyrs—Mills, Henderson, or whoever else is to blame. I'll have no excuses."

"Yes, Lieutenant," Demoreau confirmed. "Damn bad timing, Mueller, but I'm coming. I leave it to you, Lieutenant, to get the Capitaine to agree with us about Bechar."

Henderson was laying on a cot in the infirmary when Demoreau arrived. The Legionnaire's nose was broken and possibly his jaw, his eyes were blackened, a rib was fractured, and he had lost a couple teeth, but he was awake. Mills sat beside him, also damaged but not as badly.

"Well, gentlemen, it is your duty as a Legionnaire to fight for France, not for Legionnaire Lewis. Henderson, you look like you're not going to be ready for duty for at least a week. The Lieutenant insists that someone go to the Zephyrs for this. Will it be you two, or are you going to start talking?"

Henderson looked at Mills. "Tell him," he mumbled through his broken teeth and swollen lips.

"Lewis has been forcing us to fight for his entertainment," Mills admitted.

"Forcing you how? To fight who?"

"To fight each other, and him, of course. He was a professional boxer in New York, beat a man to death in the ring, they say," Mills explained, "and that's why he enlisted in the Legion. But he loves to box, and he told me and Jimmy here that we had to spar with him or he'd bloody well beat us to death, and I believe him, Sergent. If he finds out I've told you, he'll rip my lungs out."

"You fellows were game to give him a go, though, weren't you," Demoreau said.

"At first, sure; we both hated the cocky bastard and wanted to break his face. But he's good, damn hard to hit and his fists are like lead balls. I've only landed a couple punches on him, and he shakes them off like it's nothing. We wanted to call it quits, but he told us we had to spar with him, that he'd kill us if we complained."

"Well that's it for Lewis, I guess, but if he ever gets out of the Zephyrs, you better watch each other's back. He'll want revenge, and he's capable of killing you both."

It took six men and half the night to subdue Lewis and put him in chains. The Lieutenant ordered that he be locked in the hot box in the fort's courtyard where the prisoner would broil each day until he could be handed off to the prison battalion. There was no question of a court-martial; Lewis admitted his guilt and swore under oath that he'd kill Mills, Henderson, Demoreau and Lieutenant Hansen if he ever got the chance.

By the time this had all been resolved, General Lyautey had taken two Companies and begun the three day march into Morocco towards Bechar. Word came back to Fort St. Louis a few days later that the French had occupied Bechar without a fight. The bandits, thieves and raiders had all fled west to the mountains. Rather than consider whether he was allowed to occupy Bechar, Lyautey renamed the town "Colomb" and reported to the Governor that he had occupied a small town in Algeria that had not previously appeared on their maps. No one in the French government, even those who knew it was a lie, chose to argue with this absurd claim. On the contrary, the General received authorization from the government in Paris to build fortifications anywhere he believed that French soldiers needed a defensive position, even if those positions were across the border in Morocco.

* * *

Only two of Ahmad's men had fallen in the attack at the border; it was impossible to say how many of the French soldiers had been wounded. Regardless, the Governor had panicked and was hurried away from the border, any fantasy of peace with the Doui-Menia tribes shattered. The attackers gathered their belongings and prepared to withdraw to Bechar where the Sharif was waiting to meet them. Ahmad's chest hurt; he had cracked a rib when the Legionnaire clubbed him with the rifle, but there was a long ride ahead of him and they were in Ahmad's home territory, riding on the hamada across wide plains between eroded mountains and through friendly villages in Morocco. Ahmad wanted to reach Bechar as soon as possible so they rode through the night, rested, and continued the next day. They reached Bechar early on the third morning.

    The ksar in Bechar, a castle built in ancient times, was in ruins, but the town had been expanding rapidly block after block in recent years, fed by an oasis which provided water for extensive cultivations. It was on the edge of the Atlas mountains, and many more of the residents were Berbers, some tacitly allied with the Qaid of the High Atlas Madani El Glaoui, but the Muslims, whether Arab, Berber, or Black African, were all allied with Sharif Moulay Mostepha and the Doui-Menia. Ahmad found his father at his riad, waiting for his son.

The Sharif had never fully recovered the full use of his left arm after being wounded by the Legionnaire years earlier, and this had made him seem older and more fragile. "Were you successful, my son?" He asked.

"I believe so, my father. We confirmed that the French governor was there, as we had been informed; I very much doubt he will soon forget his visit to the border."

"They will come, you expect?"

"By repelling our small force at Figuig, the French are certain to believe we are easily eliminated, so, yes, I believe they will pursue us. But, in either case, they are much less likely to wait for reinforcements."

"Then we shall leave Bechar in the morning."

At first light, the Sharif, Ahmad, and his horsemen rode from Bechar and headed west towards the Atlas mountains. The people had been warned that they should expect the French soldiers to arrive within a day or two but to not put up a fight. After riding a few kilometers to the northwest, Ahmad and his men passed out of sight of Bechar. They then stopped and turned south, headed instead for the small oasis town of Kénadsa which was their true destination.

Kénadsa was situated in the midst of a wide hamada, and the enormous ksar there was a city unto itself with high walls and deep wells that were still in good condition. They arrived before mid-day, but even before they arrived in the town, Ahmad and his men came upon the tribes his father had summoned. They had to stop to speak with each tribe and to pass on their instructions. For Ahmad had intentionally led the French into Figuig, and from Figuig to Bechar, and at Bechar they would come to believe that the small group of raiders they were pursuing had fled west to

Tamanrasset

the mountains. In reality, the Sharif had summoned an enormous haraka to Kénadsa, a force of over four thousand fighters (who were accompanied by more than five thousand additional family members), and with these warriors, he and Ahmad would attack the French army and make it fill the sands of the Sahara with blood.

Summer was reaching its peak, and the days and nights were hot. The haraka could not be delayed even though more men were joining every day. With every passing hour they risked losing the advantage of surprise. Word came that the French had come to Bechar as expected, and there had fortunately been no shelling or casualties as there had been in Figuig. Ahmad had risked his reputation, his life, and, potentially, his future on this campaign: It was a huge escalation in the war of resistance commanded by the Sharif, but it was Ahmad's plan.

General Lyautey remained in Bechar, a city he now called "Colomb." The French troops were spread out in the Saoura-Zousfana-Guir river valleys between Aïn Séfra, Beni Ounif, Figuig, Bechar/Colomb, Taghit, Igli, and Beni Abbès, and many soldiers had left to escort the French Governor who was scurrying back to Algiers. At the height of summer, in the middle of August, the haraka began to move: Thousands of warriors, most mounted on horse or camel, all armed with swords, spears, and breech-loading or muzzleloading guns, accompanied by wives, children, and parents, almost ten thousand people in all.

After proceeding in a long train south towards Abadla and away from Bechar, the true military objective of Ahmad's plan was revealed. They would bypass Bechar and head east to besiege the French fort in Taghit. It would not be possible to hide the approach of four thousand warriors and five thousand non-combatants, but Ahmad hoped they would be discovered late enough that his men could cut off any call for aid from other forts, especially from Beni Ounif to the north or Igli to the south where large numbers of Foreign Legionnaires were stationed and eager to fight. The walls of the fort at Taghit were also tall and the haraka had no cannons, but Ahmad did have explosives and he hoped to get men close enough to blast open a hole in the walls or the gates. Whether the attacking warriors could then breach that gap and enter the fort was unknown. The plan, the tactics, the sheer size of the attack, these were all new ground for the Doui-Menia.

They approached Taghit in the dark of night, and Ahmad directed men to surround the town. Hopefully, they could prevent the French forces from sending out runners. Soon, the Sun began to rise over the rugged expanse of sand dunes to the east, casting a golden hue over the village of Taghit. The scent of the dry earth mixed with the scent of the horses, and the murmurs of anxious men filled his ears. The Sharif, mounted on a stately Arabian, stood at the head of the coalition of thousands. As the day began warm and the rays of the Sun began to press down upon them, the Arab and Berber tribesmen moved forward.

"We are many, Ahmad," the Sharif said, his eyes sharp and calculating, "but we must strike quickly and with resolve. The French do not expect us to move with such force, and they will be surprised, but that advantage won't last for long."

Ahmad nodded, his heart filled with anger and the fire of rebellion. These warriors had gathered under the Sharif's banner for one purpose: To drive the French from their stronghold perched on the ridge overlooking the village, a village of Arab and Berber people who wanted nothing from the Western invaders. The fort had become a symbol of foreign power and oppression. Now was time for the Doui-Menia to show that they could strike with the strength of the desert.

The tribesmen began to close the circle, approaching the fort from all directions. It would not be long before they were spotted. Ahmad joined the men entering the village to reach the base of the ridge. He could see the French soldiers standing watch on the walls, their uniforms stark against the rapidly brightening sky. He could hear the occasional shout or the clink of metal as the tribesmen prepared themselves.

"We will surround them," he had told his father, his voice steady, but it would not be as easy as it sounded. "We'll see if they have the courage to defend their outpost."

The Sharif looked at his son with pride. "You have the heart of a lion, my son."

The warriors encircled the fort and dug in, hiding behind rocks and sand dunes and buildings, looking up at the high walls as the Sun rose higher. The French finally saw them coming and decided to not wait for the attack to begin. Shots were fired from the walls, indicating that the soldiers had seen men creeping up the ridge, but Ahmad still needed to get his explosives up to the walls. The battle was developing too quickly. Soon, the warriors and the French soldiers were firing at each other with fierce determination. Waves of bullets flew in both directions. The French cannon were firing, but the attackers were too scattered, too nimble. They were everywhere and nowhere all at once.

From his position atop a building close to the western walls of the fort, Ahmad could see the French commander shouting orders to his men. The French had no choice but to stay inside the fort, hoping that reinforcements would come to their aid.

"Keep the pressure on them, Ahmad," the Sharif ordered. "We cannot give them a moment's respite."

Ahmad nodded, his heart racing. He began to send small groups of warriors towards the gates, testing the French defenses. The first group with sticks of explosives neared the fort, and for a moment, it looked as though the gate might be destroyed and the fort would fall. But then the gates swung open and a French officer in charge of a Company of Tirailleurs burst from the gate with his men, advancing under the cover of fire.

"They're coming out!" Ahmad alerted his men.

The Tirailleurs vastly outnumbered the approaching warriors and killed many of them before retreating back into their gate. There were a vast number of dead men from both sides laying across the approach to the gate. The first set of explosives was lost. More attempts were made throughout the day to bring up more explosives, but the attackers were unable to breach the walls. But, as the Sun set and night spread and the gun fire subsided, the French soldiers remained besieged inside their walls.

"They will have to try to break our lines," Ahmad told the tribal leaders that night, never betraying his doubts. "We cannot let them. You each have an assigned position, and you must hold that place. We must contain the French soldiers as long as we can."

Sunrise the next morning was met with a fierce clash, the sounds of muskets and rifles mingling with the cries of the wounded and, now that the French were making sorties from the fort, the clash of swords and bayonets. Each time, the tribesmen pushed the French back into the fort, but at a great cost. Many warriors fell. There was also a strong possibility that French runners escaped the fort to fetch reinforcements. But by nightfall, the French had again retreated back into their fort and their attempt to break the siege had failed.

On the third day, the fighting intensified. The Sun beat down upon the tribesmen and the soldiers and the air was still; it was so hot that men collapsed from the heat and the remaining sticks of explosive became so unstable they could not be touched. The warriors, tired but determined, pressed on, launching harassing fire at the French position, yet the defenders were resolute. The fort's commander paced the walls unconcerned by the bullets flying in his direction, as if certain something would soon turn the tide. Ahmad stood on the roof nearest in the village, defiant, and shot at the Capitaine, but the range was too far.

That night there were many voicing concern. "The French are not easily broken. They will likely outlast us," the Sharif admitted.

"We must use this time tonight to try to set the fort aflame," Ahmad said. "If we cannot take the fort, then we must make it unusable by anyone. We have archers who can send fire arrows into the fort. Parts of it will burn."

"Some buildings, perhaps, and the gates," the Sharif agreed.

Under the cover of darkness, Ahmad led a daring raid up close to the walls where they could penetrate the French defenses and set fires. It was a risky move, but the French would lose the use of a fort that was on fire; it might even force them out and cripple their ability to fight. The moon was waning and provided little illumination, so Ahmad and his squad of men moved like shadows, silent and swift. They neared the northern end of the fort where the walls were lowest, but there was little cover. A French sentry spotted them, and gunshots rang out. Soon the entire fort was alert. The battle that followed was brutal. The French soldiers, despite their limited numbers, fought with ferocity. Ahmad and his squad provided covering fire for a team of archers that shot fire arrows into the fort. Alarms inside were heard, and more than one large fire illuminated the dark, smokey air. Ahmad was driven back, but not before the fort was irreparably damaged and multiple fires were burning inside the walls.

At sunrise, the fires were still burning inside the fort, and the Sharif expressed his belief that the French would be forced out. He commanded Ahmad to concentrated his forces near the burning gates which were on the verge of collapse, and then, indeed, the gates fell into a burning heap and the French soldiers came out.

"They are making their move!" Ahmad shouted. "Keep the line, keep firing now!"

The warriors surged forward, meeting the French head-on. The clash was chaotic and bullets swarmed through the air, but both sides held their ground. The hand-to-hand combat was brutal and the street ran with blood. The French had badly underestimated the resolve of the tribesmen, but the fort itself continued to frustrate the aims of the Sharif. Yet as the Sun reached mid-day, the Frenchmen seemed to be on the verge of collapse. Their resources were dwindling, and the soldiers only fired when necessary. Smoke was billowing from inside the walls. Ahmad felt they might try the gates again, but then he heard a noise which sank his heart. A bugle sounded in the distance, north of the village, and Ahmad, looking, saw movement: A column of mounted Foreign Legionnaires, dust rising behind them as they rode like djinns towards Taghit. Reinforcements had arrived. The French had been able to summon assistance, and now it was too late to delay them.

The arrival of the Mounted Company from Beni Ounif tipped the scales against the Doui-Menia. The tribesmen had besieged the fort for four days, but the French were now too numerous to defeat. Many had been killed, the fort damaged. Ahmad spread the word among the warriors that they should withdraw into the desert—not together but in small groups difficult to chase, like the windswept sands. Ahmad and his father, along with several hundred men, retreated west towards Morocco to draw off the French soldiers. But there was no pursuit. The French commander needed men to secure the fort and put out the fires.

From a distance off in the desert, the smoking French fort looked like a wounded animal that might never stand again. The Sharif placed a hand on Ahmad's shoulder. "You fought well. And we will fight again. This is only the beginning."

Crossroads of the Nomad

Ahmad looked at his father, anger and determination burning in the young man's chest, and saw that the Sharif looked tired and careworn, his left arm hung limply from his shoulder. "We will, my father. We will retake our lands in time. These men are with us now, and they will not give up."

* * *

The messenger from Taghit had arrived by horseback midday with news of the siege, and the 6th Mounted Company had departed Beni Ounif within the hour, all those on mules and horses proceeding south to Taghit as quickly as possible. It would take them a day and a half to make the journey. The rest of the Company would follow on foot. The Foreign Legion was famous around the world for its ability to maneuver Legionnaires in the toughest conditions imaginable, and even those on foot were expected to march forty to sixty kilometers each day if required. It would take those walking nearly three days to reach Taghit. Demoreau was disappointed that his Section would be the one following on foot, as it meant they were more likely to arrive in Taghit long after the mounted Legionnaires had arrived and the battle had been decided.

Caporal Mueller and Caporal Dormayer had already gotten the Legionnaires into column formation by the time Sergent Demoreau joined the men. All the mules and horses had already departed, and that meant Demoreau would be marching too. These would be a couple of difficult days for him, since he didn't march as much as he had when he was younger. He went to the front of the formation and stood with Legionnaire First Class Andreev and newly-promoted Legionnaire First Class Mills, while the Caporals took up

Tamanrasset

positions at the rear of the column. The bugler had gone with the mounted soldiers, so Demoreau blew his whistle and shouted: "En Avant–Marche!"

They marched with only short breaks for over eight hours before stopping well after dark for a quick supper from their packs. Stale French bread, hard-boiled eggs, and tins of sardines would have to suffice. Demoreau did not let on how sore and tired he felt already, and they would be marching again in a matter of minutes.

Mills, who no longer had Lewis to bully him or Henderson to chat with, apparently decided he would stick close to the Sergent. "It's hard to believe we're going back to Taghit, isn't it, Sergent? How many times has the Sixth been stationed there?"

"I've been in Taghit five or six times, I think." He didn't really want to engage in a conversation with Mills, but it would be mercifully brief since they were departing again so soon. Mills was a fairly good Legionnaire, and Demoreau found it difficult to hold the Englishman's irritating private conduct against him.

"You must know more about Algeria than just about anyone else in the Legion, Sergent. How many times have you been to Algiers?" Mills asked.

"Every Legionnaire goes to Algiers at some point—there's not a vice known to man that can't be indulged there."

"I was disappointed when I came into the country through Oran—I had enlisted in Paris and took the ship from Marseille—and I haven't gotten a chance to visit Algiers yet," Mills shared.

"Hard to believe it hasn't been a higher priority for you," Demoreau replied with light sarcasm. Mills didn't notice.

"I was in Paris for a few months before that, and say what you like about Algiers, there's no place for me that will ever beat Paris—the Louvre, the Pigalle, Moulin Rouge. Ever been?"

Ordinarily, Demoreau would have berated Mills for such a question, but the Sergent was tired and felt it was part of Mills' rehabilitation to engage in conversation with him. "Yeah, I've been to Paris, nice town," he replied.

"There was a woman I knew in Paris, what an amazing woman she was, daughter of that famous conductor, you know who I mean, the one that killed himself."

"What conductor was that?" Demoreau asked.

"Jacquet, Henri Jacquet."

"Jacquet? Henri Jacquet killed himself?"

"Yeah, it was supposed to have been pretty big news when he died, but that was a long time ago, years before I was in Paris. Anyway, he had this daughter named Elise, a very great beauty then; she's a mature woman now. The conductor, Jacquet, was forcing her to marry the son of some wealthy industrialist bloke, but she didn't like him. She had stupidly fallen in love with one of the poor musicians in her father's orchestra. Well, her wealthy betrothed ultimately demanded that the musician fight him in a duel, and by sheer chance the musician killed the bugger. He had to flee the country and never saw the daughter again. But it turned out he was lucky twice, because, after he survived the duel and fled the city, the daughter turned out to be a raving nymphomaniac. Yes, that's right, she told me she's slept with thousands of men *and* women and knows everything there is to know about fucking. It's all she cares about now. Her father was so humiliated by her behavior that he leapt into the Seine during a snowstorm one winter and froze himself to death."

"She's a whore?" Demoreau asked.

"No, no, you don't get it, she doesn't fuck for money. It's said she is addicted to her ecstasy and takes two or three different lovers every day. I had her for two whole days myself, which may be a record, for both of us," he laughed. "But I would have to say, she doesn't fuck for pleasure. She fucks like she's starving for it, with hatred, like she's trying to suck your soul from your body."

"Hasn't anyone tried to restrain her?"

Mills laughed at the Sergent in disbelief: "Why would anyone want to do that?"

Demoreau stood up. He walked to where Caporal Dormayer was resting and told him to get the men ready to continue.

Once they began marching, Demoreau had difficulty staying at the head of the column. He felt exhausted and like his heart would simply stop beating at any moment, yet the march went on and on. Over the next two days, he was barely able to undertake the steps necessary to deliver his Section to Taghit. Thankfully, by the time they arrived, the siege of the fort had been broken and the Doui-Menia had already fled into the desert. For a few days, the Sixth was tasked with helping to restore the fort, but then it was decided to send them back north to Beni Ounif accompanying a caravan of young camels and a Spahi regiment–native cavalry corps that had won great glory fighting for France.

It was the end of summer, and the Company was prepared to depart a couple hours after midnight. The march

Crossroads of the Nomad

would not be as demanding as the one south, and Demoreau would now ride back on a mule, but they expected to march forty kilometers each day. Capitaine Roubec led the column, accompanied by Sous-Lieutenant Cauvain and Sergent-Fourrier Vonheim with his Section; they were followed closely by Lieutenant Hansen, and Sergent Demoreau with his Section. The Spahi riders who were leading the camels brought up the rear. The night had cooled considerably, and it seemed that summer was reaching an end. The sky slowly brightened, and the first rays of the Sun finally broke over the endless sand dunes to the east; to the west, the eroded sandstone ridge line and irregular ground were shadowy and still. The desert was quiet.

By mid-morning, the Legionnaires were tired and looked forward to a longer halt, perhaps with enough time to cook a meal. They had already marched thirty or more kilometers. The young camels had scattered into small groups that had come to a stop on the plain about two hundred yards behind Demoreau's Section. The Spahi rearguard rode back to herd the animals and push them forward. The patrols which Capitaine Roubec now had riding regularly out from the column hadn't reported any threat, so Lieutenant Hansen had the Legionnaires in his Section halt and dismount. They tied their mules together, stacked their arms in tripods (to prevent sand from entering the barrels) and were each handed a small can of sardines.

The Legionnaires heard shots fired, and Caporal Mueller cried out: "Aux armes!" and the Legionnaires rushed to reclaim their rifles. Somewhere off to the rear and west of Demoreau's position, multiple shots were fired; two of the Spahi cavalrymen who were herding the camels appeared to be down and the rest were riding back towards the column of Legionnaires quickly, leaving the young camels behind. Attackers hidden on the ridgeline and in the irregular ground and behind the boulders to the west all opened fire at once. It was an explosion of noise, and bullets swarmed through the air. In the first volley, Capitaine Roubec was shot and fell from his horse. His Sous-Lieutenant was also hit, as well as a dozen or more Legionnaires who fell dead instantly.

A dry creek bed, only about a hundred yards away and unseen by the patrol, contained dozens of Doui-Menia tribesmen. They were all now up and firing upon the Legionnaires gathered in front of them, seeking to kill as many as possible. Within minutes, corpses littered the ground, including almost all of the officers. A number of Legionnaires took it upon themselves to storm the enemy's position and ran right at the firing tribesmen. During this chaos, Lieutenant Hansen was fatally shot and fell from his mule. Demoreau and Vonheim were each attempting to bring the Legionnaires into a defensive position so they could return fire. Vonheim's men were further to the north and had more cover from scrub brush, although it was hardly adequate cover. Vonheim attempted to lead his Section towards a small, newly-built blockhouse some two hundred yards to the northwest, but the tribesmen were in the way. The Sergent-Fourrier ordered a bayonet charge. Bullets flew at his men and many were killed, but they finally were able to reach the enemy and engage them in hand-to-hand combat. The fighting was bloody, but Vonheim broke through and reached the blockhouse to achieve some cover from which they could escape the enemy fire.

The tribesmen attacking Demoreau's men now divided into two groups, one going south to separate the Legionnaires from the camels and the Spahi, the other group hiding in bushes that provided them with cover from the shots fired at them by Vonheim's men to the northwest. Ignoring the bullets, Demoreau led his Legionnaires southwest, taking advantage of the gap that had opened in the line of the tribesmen. He brought his men up onto a ridge from which they had some minimal cover. He decided he would have to send men south towards the camels and mules, to engage the tribesmen there but also to get someone mounted on a horse, mule or camel who could ride back to Taghit for reinforcements.

"Rivoli, O'Connor, Britten, I want you to follow this ridge around and see how close you can get to the Capitaine and Sous-Lieutenant. We need to pull them to safety, and we need to know if the enemy is attempting to flank us," Demoreau ordered. The men began scrambling along the ridge to the north.

The Spahis like wild beasts were charging recklessly at the line of tribesmen, a tactic which stunned the attackers. They had never imagined such insane bravery, and many of them fled in panic rather than face such an enemy.

Wounded men now covered the ground. Vonheim's Section was still under attack but had a strong defensive position. Demoreau's Section was somewhat protected by the ridgeline, and the injured Capitaine and a number of other men had been pulled back behind a hill that protected them from direct fire. The Spahis had bottled up a number of attackers, although some of the enemy had separated a large number of camels from the herd and had fled with them. But the majority of tribesmen were not retreating. It was a standoff, and no one knew for certain whether reinforcements would be coming for either side. The day wore on with bursts of gunfire and attempts to flank each other that got nowhere. Hundreds of bodies, both Legionnaires and tribesmen, lay on the ground.

Demoreau ordered his men to move back, down the ridge to the south. He thought to divide and string out the enemy might weaken them.

"Caporal Mueller, I want you and Dormayer to start moving men back down towards the Spahis and let's try to join up with them as long as we can maintain the cover of the ridgeline," he said.

"Yes, Sergent," Mueller replied, gathering a number of men and scrambling back along the ridge.

"Mills, I want you here with me," Demoreau said.

The Section moved well, and Demoreau and Mills, firing sporadically, kept the tribesmen at bay while the rest of the Section withdrew down the ridge.

The Sun was low in the sky, and no one was certain what would happen after dark. Surely the risk of probing attacks would rise and the night would become a free-for-all of men attacking each other in the dark. Demoreau looked at Mills and considered sending him along the ridge to join the rest of the Section. To the south, a great cloud of dust was rising into the air which suggested that more riders were coming. It could have been more of the enemy, or French reinforcements, or it could be a windstorm that would soon engulf them all in a hazy, darkening oblivion. There was no way to know. Mills looked at Demoreau anxiously. "Are we going to move back, Sergent?" He asked pitiably.

And in that moment, a wave of emotion surged in Demoreau's chest. His face turned white and his heart felt like it had just collapsed. Something inside him died—his sense of hope, of joy, of love. He looked at Mills and was overwhelmed with loathing. Demoreau wished he could atone for his past mistakes, but he could not un-do what had been done. Instead, he lifted his rifle and shot Mills point blank in the head, killing him instantly.

IV – Expedition to Tamanrasset

At the port of Algiers, steamers from around the Mediterranean lined the quay and dozens of small fishing boats rocked up and down at anchor. The docks swarmed with activity as strong-backed workers carried crates of spices, silks, and woven textiles while others loaded wine, olives, and oranges for export. The sharp scent of spices and the cloying whiff of tobacco permeated the air. The Algerian capital, its architecture a haphazard mix of modern and ancient, extended from the port up onto the rolling sun-scorched hills which surrounded the city like a recumbent courtesan. A soft haze lingered over the buildings, caught between the sea breeze and the shimmering heat of the African sun. The P&O steamer from Tunis had docked at its berth, and as Ren stepped onto the gangway he quickly noted the sights and sounds of the city. The French influence was unmistakable, for although the city had been known as El Djazaïr for centuries, Algiers had been a French city since it was taken in 1830. The broad boulevards and grand public buildings gave the city a modern feel, yet they were a sharp contrast to the whitewashed hovels and narrow, labyrinthine streets of the older Arab quarters that had grown over centuries like a cancerous mass on the hills near the port. Lush gardens and public squares shaded by palm trees were populated by soldiers, diplomats, and businessmen who strolled or sipped coffee at French cafés. Only French was spoken in the grand hotels and fashionable restaurants. The buildings of the Place du Gouvernement reflected the grandeur of the Parisian style complete with domed rooftops and stately columns. Wealthy French settlers and merchants, colonial bureaucrats, officers of the Armée d'Afrique, all of whom had spent their lives in and around Algiers, enjoyed the comfort and prosperity assured by a deeply-rooted colonial regime. But Algiers was also a city of mysteries and corruption, absinthe drinkers and hashish smokers, domino players and card sharps and every sort of lewd pastime, Moorish baths, nude female dancers dressed only in jewels and precious amulets, would-be marabouts and poets who pleaded for insurrection in every public square, of slaves, fugitives, vagabonds and squatters, Frenchmen, Spaniards, Arabs, Berbers, Jews, Roma, Chinese, Maltese, Sicilians and Black Africans, together with the refuse of every country adjacent to the Mediterranean.

Ren had reserved rooms at the Hotel de la Régence, a first class in an impressive white building that faced the sea; he was given a luxurious suite on an upper floor with marvelous views of the Jardin d'Essai du Hamma. He ordered bottles of tonic and of gin brought to his room, and he shut the curtains to settle in and drink himself to sleep. It was not heartbreak that had ruined Ren's state of mind, although he missed Lilian, nor was it the threat posed by Inspector Gauckler, whom Ren viewed as a significant annoyance. Perhaps it was being forced away from his work in Carthage and from his colleagues and from his home in the Palais d'Hamilcar, to live an isolated existence in

Algiers. He was used to being a leader of his own little community, the master of his realm, and, now, being forced to leave it, exiled, to be alone in a large city he had never visited before, it made him feel small, stupid, and unimportant. And he thought frequently of Lilian, of her smell and her touch.

Early the next morning, a young Frenchman in a fine suit came to see Ren at the hotel; he represented Ren's patrons in Algiers, the individuals on the board of the renovated National Museum of Antiquities who had requested that Ren come lecture regarding the discoveries at Carthage. Ren was welcomed to Algiers and provided with the location and time of his presentation, and he then spent the day in his rooms at the hotel, mostly in his bathtub. In the early evening, he took a carriage to make his presentation at the Théâtre Municipal near the Port Militaire. To his surprise, he was met by a large crowd of bourgeois French men and women and only a few actual scientists. There were few archaeologists in Algeria, for although there were a number of interesting historical sites close to Algiers, none had undergone the same degree of archaeological investigation as Carthage, much less the popular sites in Egypt and Palestine. However, archaeology had become fashionable and something of a fascination among non-scientists. These were the same sort of individuals who came as tourists to view the excavations at Carthage, and Ren knew exactly what they wanted: He spiced his lecture with anecdotes, myths, and personal reflections, and he was enthusiastically received.

Afterwards, Ren was introduced to a dozen wealthy Frenchmen, leaders in the community who had financed the antiquities museum, the sort of men from whom he usually solicited donations. However, in light of the inquiry being conducted by Gauckler into the Carthage Foundation, Ren had been advised to refrain from soliciting any donations on this trip. In any event, these gentlemen seemed more interested in supporting scientific work in Algeria than in other countries. Ren received an invitation to the house of Madame Arthur, supposedly the most beautiful Arab house in Algiers, for luncheon the next day, and he was assured by one older gentleman that a matter much to his interest would be heard there.

Madame Arthur was a very charming older lady from England known for telling anecdotes about her adventures around the Mediterranean with a great deal of charm. It was known that her house stood in a large garden filled with the most luxuriant flowers and had nothing in it that was not Arab: The open courtyard with its fountain, the banks of flowers, the exquisite furniture and gorgeous hangings, the wonderful collection of weapons and ornaments, all made it seem as though she had rubbed Aladdin's Lamp. "I recently received two lovely Arab women, dressed in beautiful white haiks, long loose robes worn over their lovely kaftans," Madame Arthur recounted: "They came to the door and begged me to allow them to see again the house where they had spent their childhood. I found their recollections to be most interesting. I showed them about and inquired how the house had looked when they were children here, and they both had marvelous memories of specific decorations and furniture. Afterwards, I changed the house according to their descriptions so that it would be not only Arab in a general sense but also in specific detail."

"I must admit that we have succumbed to many western ideas during the renovations of our little palace," Ren told her conversationally. "Of course, we have also had to make it work as a dormitory for the students who have come to Tunisia to work on our excavations, not just as a home for one family."

"Yes, it's just me here," Madame Arthur continued, "no family at all. I shall have to leave the house to the State to become a museum. The exhibits have already been prepared—perhaps I shall be one of them," she jested.

After a fine luncheon with a few glasses of wine, Ren found himself being escorted into a small library. It contained a large number of handsome bound books in English and French, but the furniture and wall hangings were strictly Arab in origin and design. A colored glass window projected colors like a kaleidoscope on the floor and walls. Four men were standing about with their brandy.

"Professor Villere, what a great pleasure it is to have you in Algiers at long last," said an elderly but statesman-like Frenchman.

"It's my honor to have been invited, Monsieur. I recognize these other gentlemen from the theatre last night—a pleasure, gentlemen—but I don't believe we've met," Ren replied.

"No, I don't often go out in the evenings anymore, but I've heard all about your presentation from these gentlemen," he said, gesturing to the others in the room. "My name is Marcel Gallé."

Everyone knew the name Gallé. He was principal shareholder and Director of "Domaine de l'Habra," the largest conglomeration of agricultural interests in Algiers, and the wealthiest man in Algeria, perhaps even the entire French Empire.

"You might say that I am the reason you are here in Algiers today," Gallé said. "I had almost given up on you ever coming, but we are delighted that you are here."

"I must apologize, then, if my failure to visit earlier was an inconvenience to you or gave the wrong impression. You have no idea how busy we have been this year."

"No, no, not at all, Professor," Monsieur Gallé replied graciously. "You met Messieurs Caroling and Durant last night; they are colleagues of mine from the Western areas of Algeria. And this gentleman is the Deputy Governor, Jacques Cayard."

"An honor to meet you, Deputy," Ren said with a respectful nod, "and, with all due respect, Monsieur Gallé, I feel you are the one who orchestrated this little get together today. Am I correct?"

"We've been most eager to speak with you, Professor. Naturally, we have the utmost regard for your work in Tunisia and for your methods of archaeology. In fact, we four are among the principal benefactors who arranged the renovations of the Museum of Antiquities here in Algiers."

"I understand it's a grand museum; I plan to visit tomorrow."

"You'll allow me to notify the Director to expect you; he would be most honored to show you the collection personally. I'm certain you will find it very well organized," Gallé stated with unconcealed sarcasm. "I should explain: You see, we had Paul Gauckler here in Algiers for two long years; he examined and catalogued every item in the museum, despite our best efforts to dislodge him. I understand Inspector

Gauckler is giving you some headaches at Carthage, now, is that right?"

"He is in Tunis now, yes. I can't say yet whether he will create difficulties for us or stay for two years. Of course, we expect his inspections to go quite smoothly."

Gallé smiled. "Yes, we had hoped that as well, but he liked Algiers too much. He took up residence across the street from the museum and came over to putter around the collection day after day. At night, well, we understand he enjoyed all the pleasures Algiers has to offer."

"I'll bear that in mind," Ren replied.

"If Gauckler is in Tunis now, it might be an opportune moment for you to take a leave of absence from your work there, would it not?" Gallé asked in a way that suggested he already knew the answer.

Ren looked at him questioningly. Was Gallé hinting at some knowledge of Ren's issues in Tunis with Gauckler, or with Mrs. Beaton? "Why would I wish to take leave?" He asked pointedly.

"My apologies, I don't mean to suggest anything, although we know from our own experience how difficult Gauckler can be. No, you see, we have a project in mind that I believe might entice you away from Carthage for a time, if you are so inclined, and we've brought you to Algiers primarily to discuss that project in person. We appreciate and value your time, Professor, and I want to assure you that this is a real opportunity with the potential for substantial remuneration and accolades for you."

"An opportunity in the realm of archaeology, I take it?"

"Of course."

"Well, I'm not exactly in the market for a new position, but I'm curious to hear what you have to offer, certainly," Ren replied.

"Monsieur Durant and I, along with Monsieur Caroling and the Deputy Governor, have in mind a specific archaeological expedition, and we believe you would be the ideal person to undertake this project for us, which we would fully fund including generous compensation for your time. You would certainly be free to return to Carthage afterwards."

Ren blushed. He felt honored that these important men would want to hire him, yet, at the same time, the affair seemed quite mysterious.

"But where, specifically, would this archaeological expedition be?" He asked.

"Please take a seat, Doctor; there is quite a bit to discuss, if I have managed to sustain your interest this far. Perhaps you're familiar with the name 'al-Kahina.' She was the last ruler and queen of the Berber people, defeated by Hassan ibn al-Nu'man at the Battle of Tabarka in the year 703."

Ren was well versed in the history exposited by Gallé, but his mention of the Berber queen perhaps revealed something of the group's intentions. "Yes, I am familiar with Queen al-Kahina, Monsieur, and of the legends regarding her immense wealth," he said, "but as far as we know that is all they are—legends."

Gallé nodded. Durant went on: "Inspector Gauckler did a fine job of cataloging our collection here at the museum. Fortunately for us he cannot read Arabic. He discovered certain Arabic writings in the museum's archives, writings from the Seventh Century which he propitiously left for us to decipher. To our immense surprise, the writings are a historical record regarding Queen al-Kahina. They appear to describe her court, her entourage, her travels, her military forces, her properties, and the vast riches of her many palaces. The Arab invaders of that day, as you know, were meticulous record-keepers. The writings go on to state that al-Kahina died on the battlefield at Tabarka but her body was removed by her people for a ceremonial burial. The records seem to identify the location of her tomb, in a general way, more or less. Given the lack of any further known mention of this tomb over the past twelve centuries, regarding its location or its contents, we believe it remains undiscovered and intact."

"You are a serious scientist, Professor Villere," Gallé interjected. "That is why we wish to engage you to locate and catalog the tomb of Queen al-Kahina, so that it can be properly preserved. And we believe there should be a display of its contents at the museum here in Algiers, to honor the Berber people."

"We can't stress that enough," Cayard insisted. "There must be absolutely no question about our motivation."

"Tabarka is in Tunisia," Ren pointed out.

"The tomb is not," Durant said. "In this room, I am the most familiar with the writings since I have looked them over myself. They are in some respects rather mysterious and I have found them difficult to translate. I've written to Paris for assistance with one or two points. However, it is my opinion that they will provide sufficient information upon which an expedition can be undertaken to locate the queen's tomb. It is in the Great Desert; that is all I can impart to you at this time."

"So you don't know where it is, specifically," Ren said.

"Not specifically," Durant admitted, "but once the writings are fully translated, I believe it will be easily found. Its contents can then be secured for the museum. It would only be proper to add that the expedition could be dangerous, as any desert expedition would be. We will of course supply security as well as laborers, provisions, and equipment. We would ask you to provide us with lists of everything else that you would need."

Ren could already imagine being in charge of such a project, of its significance if he was successful. Articles featuring his role as leader of the expedition would be written in newspapers worldwide. He could publish an account of the journey and its discoveries and tour America. He could become rich and famous and could arrange for Gauckler to be sent off to another city. Perhaps Lilian would even choose to return with him to the Palais d'Hamilcar afterwards.

But tombs, as Ren well knew, meant only one thing to most people: Loot. These gentlemen were playing their cards close to the chest and perhaps protested their innocent intentions too much. It would be highly unusual for a tomb to contain a great treasure, but these men might very well expect the tomb to contain Queen al-Kahina's riches as well as her remains. Regardless of the tomb's ultimate value, would they still put the artefacts in the museum? Or did they intend to keep any riches for themselves? Ren's reputation would be ruined if he became the leader of a group of graverobbers who desecrated the tomb of a Berber queen or if he found treasures that remained out of sight in a private collection. He would never work in archaeology again.

"I'll need time to consider your offer," he said.

"Absolutely," Gallé replied. "We are still in the initial stages of planning. Monsieur Durant continues to work on his translation of the writings, and I am undertaking other arrangements for the expedition. However, please bear in mind that this project will be going forward with you or without you; we believe your participation may make the difference between failure and success, Professor."

After the luncheon, Ren was a bit tipsy and decided to walk around the city. He was terribly lonely and missed his Palais and students and Lillian. He was not due at the museum until the next morning, and he had much to think about. The day had heated up and the sky was completely clear, but sunset was not far off as Ren strolled past the gardens, the art museum, and the cathedral along the Rue de la Lyre. It was perhaps impossible to know whether the proposed expedition would be successful and properly conducted; he feared that it could veer out of his control. Unless they killed him, however, it would be difficult for these men to get away with graverobbing without it becoming a public scandal, except they did appear to be very wealthy and powerful. Ren noticed vaguely that the streets on which he was strolling were narrowing and in many places became little more than a gutter as they began climbing, ever climbing up into the hills surrounding Algiers. He found he was entering the kasbah.

The kasbah of Algiers was a place of mystery and dread, delight, and repugnance. The houses thrown up the steep hillside all but touched overhead, with barely enough room

Tamanrasset

for a ray of light to penetrate here and there. The walls looking out upon the street were plain and interrupted only by a rare door, usually one decorated with the hand of Fatma, a palm-shaped symbol of good fortune, surrounded by an arch carved with conventional designs, and protected by a porch overhead decorated with green tiles and supported on wooden props that appeared to be centuries old. Here and there at irregular distances were tiny casements, strongly barred, some not more than a foot wide. The jutting upper stories were often suspended on rough wooden poles, and the structures overall had been covered again and again over the centuries with thick coats of lime whitewash. Little would any passer-by suspect the existence of spacious inner courtyards with their tiles of exquisite colors, their twisted columns, their fountains and their balustraded galleries. The air was hot, balmy, and still. The Sun set, but a bright moon began to illuminate the passageways, with sometimes a smoking oil lamp affixed to the wall. Around the corner came the sound of tom-toms and derboukas from a house whose owner was giving a feast for some family occasion. A door was opened, and a local gentleman in a colorful bisht and turban emerged singing curious Arabic music which flowed like a wild reptile, sleek and elusive. A lover lurked in the shadow below a wall, gazing longingly at the house which sheltered his adored one. In the café maures, native Arabs and Berbers sat on benches within and around the door, smoking their long pipes and listening to a professional raconteur telling tales of love and greed; thick, short coffees were served to them in small porcelain cups. Ren looked back over the steep declivity of the city, over cupolas, minarets, and flat-roofed houses, to the beautiful moonlit bay.

To enter the almost endless maze of narrow and disorganized streets rising through the kasbah, filled as it was with thieves and cutthroats at all hours, was a perilous endeavor even for the natives who knew their way. For an archaeologist to enter at night was either an act of great self-confidence or sheer insanity. More than once Ren had seen men looking at him whom he decided he should evade. In and up he climbed, accompanied by music, singing, and the crying of feral cats disrupting the sultry night as the heavy scents of jasmine and hashish lingered in the air. He was drawn deeper into the heart of the kasbah, through narrow, winding alleys, past snake charmers and fortune tellers who called out to him in French and Arabic, offering everything from jewelry to hashish to dreadful curses. The sounds of clinking glasses and raucous laughter echoed from the shadows. A mix of Arabic, French, Italian and Chinese filled the air, creating a noise that was both foreign and thrilling to his ears.

Outside one dark establishment, he was greeted by a man whose weathered face and dark, hooded eyes looked at him with a mixture of curiosity and amusement. "Welcome, monsieur," the man said, his voice thick with an unidentifiable accent. "You come for a taste of the real Algiers, n'est-ce pas?"

Ren, alone, felt compelled to immerse himself in the offerings of the city. He nodded and was led through a series of twisting corridors, past veiled but otherwise naked women, and into a low-ceilinged room lit only by the flickering glow of a single oil lamp. The air was thick with the scent of hashish and exotic perfumes, and the atmosphere felt heady, as if the very walls were soaked with

Tamanrasset

the stories of the people who had lived and died there over centuries. The room was filled with the almost depleted sounds of a stringed instrument being lazily plucked by a man sitting in the corner, his face hidden by a veil of smoke. The music was slow, sensuous, and haunting—every note tugged at some putrid emotion, making Ren feel both vibrant and unnervingly nauseous.

A tall, voluptuous woman, her skin a dark golden color and her eyes dark with mystery, approached him. She was dressed in a flowing gown of gossamer silk that shimmered with the subtle movement of her naked body beneath. Her lips parted in a knowing smile, and she offered him a drink from a small silver cup. The liquid was dark, harsh. Ren felt a warmth spread through him, a slow burn that loosened his tongue and his limbs. The woman's laugh was soft, her gaze never leaving his as she danced around him, her hips swaying with a hypnotic rhythm. She caressed and aroused him while his vision began to blur, the music melding with her laughter, the flickering lights becoming erratic. Ren lost track of time as the night stretched on, each moment becoming a haze of forgotten faces. He had never felt so unrestrained, so far from the weight of his duties and the decorum of his upbringing. He drank more, his senses growing sharper and then duller by turns, his mind both foggy and electrified. The woman—her name was Samira—led him through the crowd, deeper into the recesses of the house, where the revelry turned darker. There were men gambling, their faces sweating with concentration, women draped naked across divans, eyes heavy with the weight of opium. The air was thick with the tang of sweat and smoke and the sounds of passion. The walls pressed insistently in upon him.

Ren found himself seated at a low table in a small room with Samira beside him. A bowl of fruit was placed before him, though he barely registered its presence as Samira let her dress fall from her shoulders. His mind was lost in the scent of her perfume, the movement of her hands, the press of her naked body against him. He was aware of the heat of the room, the faint rustle of garments, the endless chatter of voices that seemed to dance just out of his reach. He felt as if he were observing his own actions from some far-off place. It wasn't long before Samira's touch turned urgent, her fingers grabbing and tugging at him, her lips whispering words he couldn't quite understand. Another woman joined them, and her tongue was in his mouth.

When the early rays of the Sun crept into the kasbah, Ren stumbled back onto the street, not quite sober, disheveled, and uncertain where he was, his mind full of fleeting images, his desires temporarily sated, his head aching. The sun cast a harsh light on the dismal, filthy streets and the doorways which were the nighttime repository of vagrants, orphans, and diseased souls. Ren made his way back toward the more familiar parts of Algiers, a deep sense of satisfaction in the emptiness he felt.

He returned to the Hotel de la Régence and went to his rooms to have a gin and tonic and bathe, quite certain now that, consequences be damned, he would agree to lead the expedition to find the lost tomb of Queen al-Kahina.

* * *

Ahmad stood outside his father's house overlooking the Guir river, staring at the jagged hills of etched sandstone where the wind whipped the encroaching sands of the Sahara over the dry ground. He was used to the harshness of life and to the constant shadow of encroachment. His father, Sharif Moulay Mostepha ibn Ali al-Haybah, had been a leader his whole life, resisting the advances of the Westerners, bringing the tribes together, spreading the words of the Prophet, and attacking the French mercenaries. Ahmad had learned much at his father's side. But now, the winds were shifting. There was much division among the tribes over whether to continue the haraka, but, more importantly, the Sharif who led them had become deathly ill.

It had begun with the shoulder wound he had received during the attack at Igli years before which had never fully healed. Over time, it had weakened him, making him prone to fevers and fatigue. When Ahmad had returned from Fez, the Sharif pushed ahead in his war against the French. But after the siege at Taghit, he returned to his home in Abadla severely weakened. Ahmad watched as a fever grew within his father's body. The illness continued for several days without change, as if the fever might break at any time. Then, in the quiet before dawn, the Sharif simply died.

The burial of the Sharif was solemn and sad. Beneath a wide cloudless sky, the air was dry and thick with the scent of the desert and the fragrance of the dry brush. It was a morning bathed in pale light, the sun casting long shadows over the rocky terrain as the mourners gathered in the shadow of the jagged sandstone hills. The funeral procession began at the Sharif's home where Ahmad and those family members present had witnessed the Sharif's death. The body was wrapped in a simple white shroud, prepared according to tradition. Made of fine linen, the shroud had been marked with decorative stitching that spoke of a life led with discipline and devotion. Beneath it, the Sharif wore no adornment, to reflect his humility despite his power and importance.

The mourners began to arrive in the early afternoon, moving silently across the rugged landscape. Many came from nearby villages, some traveled through the desert to pay their respects. The men wore dark flowing djellabas, their faces drawn with grief, while the women, covered in traditional niqabs, stayed close to the walls of the courtyard, their heads bowed low. The sound of soft weeping could be heard, but for the most part, the people stood in silent reverence, the weight of their loss heavy in the air.

Ahmad stood at the head of the procession, his posture erect but somber, his face a mask of reserve. Yet, as he looked over the mourners, he felt a considerable pride in his people: They had come and would remember his father. As the body was prepared, the mourners began chanting prayers, their voices blending with the sounds that echoed through the valley. The salat al-janazah, the funeral prayer, was recited by the Imam, his voice steady and filled with remorse. The men stood in lines and lifted their hands to their chests as they prayed for the soul of the departed Sharif.

The coffin, a simple wooden box reinforced with iron, was placed upon the shoulders of the pallbearers. The men lifted it with care, their movements deliberate as they carried the body out of the house. The path to the burial site was narrow, winding through a field of olive trees and dry

Tamanrasset

brush that lined the river's edge, where the land met the foothills of the Atlas. The procession moved in near silence save for the cries of the mourners. As they reached the small hill that overlooked the valley, the mourners stood in a wide circle. The grave had already been dug, its edges still rough, a modest site.

Jamal, the brother of the Sharif, had arrived the previous day from Figuig, and he stood at Ahmad's side, his face composed. Jamal had taken on the burden of arranging the funeral, and as the Sharif's body was lowered into the earth, it was Jamal who recited the final words of prayer, invoking blessings upon the soul of his brother. The mourners stood with heads lowered, hands folded in prayer, as the final rites were performed. A few of the elders who had fought alongside the Sharif in the past tossed handfuls of dirt into the grave, their movements slow and deliberate, their expressions shadowed by grief. The ground was filled as the last of the dirt was heaped onto the grave. The mourners stood in silence for a moment. The heat of the day began to settle in, but it was the weight of the loss that truly lay upon the mourners, as the vast and unchanging desert itself seemed to hold its breath.

Ahmad then stepped forward and lowered himself to his knees, his hands pressing against the earth at the edge of the grave. He whispered a prayer for his father, words of gratitude and respect. His heart was filled with grief, his anger turned to bitterness. He then rose and took a step back, allowing the elders and warriors to do the same.

As the mourners began to depart, some returning to their homes, others staying for a small feast to honor the Sharif, Ahmad remained alone at the edge of the grave for a while longer, his eyes fixed on the horizon. The desert wind whispered around him, carrying with it words of finality. The Sharif was gone. It was now Ahmad's duty to continue the fight that had been his father's and had become his own. He stood motionless, the wind biting at his skin as it carried the scent of dry earth and distant dunes. His eyes followed the meandering Wadi Guir as it cut through the landscape. The silence in the air now seemed deafening. The Sun was still high over the sands but bending to the west. The desert stretched endlessly behind him, indifferent to the loss of a man who had fought to preserve his people.

As news of the Sharif's death spread across the region, people came from all corners of the valley and far beyond to pay their respects—tribal leaders, warriors, farmers, and merchants, all those who had followed the Sharif's call. They came to mourn, but many were also eager to talk about who would take the Sharif's place. Then the first whispers of doubt began to surface. Ahmad was the son of the Sharif, the natural heir to his father's legacy, he had fought beside his father, learned from him, and understood his ways better than anyone, but there were those who said that Ahmad was too young and many did not wish to continue the war that the Sharif had begun.

The Sharif's brother Jamal was known to have a different plan: He was a merchant and trader, a man who lived in the larger town of Figuig and had little interest in war. When the French had recently bombarded the city, he was among those who argued that a speedy capitulation would save both lives and property. He was astute, a diplomat, clever. Unlike his late brother, Jamal had long believed it was acceptable to make concessions to the French in exchange for security and commerce. Over the years, he had developed a relationship with the colonial power, securing trade agreements and exchanging autonomy for stability.

It soon became clear to Ahmad that his father's brother saw an opportunity in the Sharif's death. Jamal had long coveted power, and now, with the tribes questioning whether Ahmad would be the best leader, his father's brother would not let the moment pass. Jamal began to speak of negotiations, of agreements, of a Morocco that would exist peaceably with the French rather than at war against them. It infuriated Ahmad who believed Jamal's vision was a betrayal. To him, peace with the French was against everything his father had believed in.

"Morocco cannot bow to the French," Ahmad said to those who would listen. "Our land, our lives, are not for sale. If we are to preserve our dignity, we must fight. We must take up arms, as my father did, and drive the invaders from our land." But his voice, though filled with passion, betrayed his bitterness.

As the next few days passed, the council of elders convened to give their blessing to the next Sharif. The matter should have been simple, but the currents in the air were murky. Jamal, with his wealth and connections, had already swayed some of the elders to his side. The council remained divided. But then, before Ahmad was even given an opportunity to speak, Jamal was suddenly chosen as the new Sharif. Ahmad, who had spent his life preparing, found himself set aside. It was a blow he could hardly fathom.

Jamal came to speak with Ahmad at the late Sharif's home after the decision was announced. "Asalamu alaikom, my brother's son."

"Wa alaikom salaam," Ahmad replied. He had nothing else to say.

"I accept your anger, Ahmad, but may I come in and speak with you?"

"You are my father's brother and will always be admitted to my house," Ahmad replied. It would be unseemly to argue.

As they sat, Jamal said: "You must be disappointed, Ahmad, and with good reason. I am here because I do not want there to be anger or disagreement between us."

"As the Sharif's son, I should have been his successor. But more than that, I know you will betray our people by discarding the progress we have made against the French. You will betray those who have been martyred in our war against the invaders; you will make their sacrifice worthless."

"You may not believe me, Ahmad, but I did not seek to supplant you. Many of the elders are like me in that they wish to profit from the French, and they are tired of losing their sons to a war that, while laudable, cannot be won. The elders came to me and told me that I was going to be chosen even though I did not ask to be the new Sharif, and if they want to try working with the French –"

"Try again, you mean—we have already tried to work with the French. The elders want to try again? It is madness to expect a different outcome."

"I will tell you what your father would not: You are not ready to be the Sharif, Ahmad. Your single-mindedness

Tamanrasset

would be a great weakness as Sharif. You need to improve your diplomatic skills, and grow up."

"You are the diplomat, not me. If you do not intend to wage war, there is no reason for me to remain in Abadla," Ahmad said bitterly.

"I agree. And for now, I want you to return to Fez, not as a student but as a representative for your people. You understand the government, and I want the Sultan to pay attention to what is happening here. We have gone too long without his support. The French must see that the Sultan can and will stand behind us. And I believe that will only happen if we have alliances with other provincial leaders, alliances that consolidate enough power to force the Sultan's attention. I am asking you now not to think as a warrior but to be a diplomat for your people: Will you go to Fez?"

Ahmad sat stunned. He was being sent away from his people, undoubtedly because Jamal did not want any warriors left to challenge his authority and continue to fight. To be fair, that's just what Ahmad would have done. "If I am to be sent away, then it makes sense for me to return to Fez. I suppose it would be preferable for me to go as our representative, if that is truly what you wish."

"It is."

"Then, as you are now the Sharif and my father's brother, I am bound to do as you ask, at least until the elders see the folly of dealing with the French and choose to continue our fight. But I am very doubtful that the Sultan will ever be convinced to assist us."

* * *

Crossroads of the Nomad

Isabel had traveled slowly for several weeks in a wide arc around the northern Sahara, more or less in the general direction of Ouargla, the city in Algeria where the marabout Lèlla Zeyneb was reported to reside. Isabel still planned to reach Ouargla eventually, but she felt no urgency and had no expectations for what might happen when she got there. Despite having a camel to ride, Isabel chose to walk, and she often walked as few as ten or twelve kilometers each day, sometime leading and sometimes following the camel who carried her food and water. She had no reason to hurry, but she also spent many hours each day in a sort of empty space inside her mind. She sometimes would come to a stop and just stand silently for a while, not thinking of anything at all, and sometimes not even remembering afterwards what she saw or heard.

She entered towns only when it was necessary to purchase supplies, and she spoke to as few people as possible. Unlike her previous journey across the southern Sahara, she no longer traveled with others and did not feel it was proper to accept food, gifts, or lodging. She did not want to be recognized. She still dressed in pants, a shirt and jacket, boots, and also a heavy cloak and scarf, but she no longer strictly covered her face and neck with the hijab. The sun and dust of her journey had darkened her face and hands, and only her bright blue eyes betrayed her foreignness. She was frequently mistaken for a Tuareg, and having no desire to correct such misconceptions, she simply played along. To make the smallest possible impression on those around her, she prayed, but when alone she did not. She had even allowed her appearance to become filthy so that people would avoid her. She was no one at all, and there was no reason for anyone to pay her the slightest attention.

She preferred to walk in the dark. At sunset, she would locate a mountain or campfire in the distance and walk in that direction, sometimes stumbling into a ravine or depression when the Moon was not full. She had bruises and scrapes which she could not recall receiving; a few times she realized she was bleeding but could not recall how she had been injured. In the morning, she often found she had walked off course during the night. Regardless, she would simply lay down, cover her head with her cloak, and sleep on the ground until the sun began to set.

The last few nights, the moon had faded away again, and this made the stars far more visible in the sky, like a thousand thousand eyes winking at her. But starlight barely illuminated the barren plateau on which she walked. She had come to a wide open plain, flat, empty, and dark. She could see almost nothing, only a shadow of her own hand as she passed it in front of her face. There was a slight breeze, grit beneath her feet. She stopped to listen. The silence of the desert was hard to bear. She could hear only the wind whispering quietly as a fine film of sand blew across the hard rocky surface. Otherwise, there was nothing. She felt her solitude.

The wind began to pick up, swirling sand into small eddies that danced around her ankles, and the cold night air seemed to bite through her thick cloak, its chill like teeth piercing her skin. She squinted into the distance and heard nearby a soft sound, like the rustle of cloth in the wind. She turned her head sharply, but she could see nothing. Her heart pounded loudly in her chest.

"Who's there?" she asked, her voice sounding small.

No answer came, but the noise persisted, faint yet unmistakable. Something was moving that she could not see. Isabel reached for the dagger she kept tucked in the folds of her cloak. Her feet moved forward, drawn towards the noise. The wind shifted, and then the air went still, as though holding its breath.

It seemed to her that a man stood nearby, just on the absolute edge of her field of vision. A sudden chill went down her spine, and she gasped.

"Asalamu alaikom," she said nervously.

It seemed as though the wind replied: She heard it whisper back "Wa alaikom salaam." Or that might only have been what she imagined she heard.

Then the same voice said, in a man's voice, clear and deep but barely audible: "Varför är du ensam?" Why are you alone, the voice had asked, in Swedish.

"I don't know," she said, and tears began to well up in her eyes.

"Are you far from your path?" She was asked, the voice a low and subtle growl. It was mere curiosity; she had no sense of any concern for her.

"I don't know where my path is," she replied, wiping her eyes with the sleeve of her dusty cloak.

"Then you stay here?"

"I ... I don't think I can stay, can I?"

There was a deep, quiet rumble like laughter. "You are confused."

She exhaled slowly and closed her eyes.

A chill embraced her, and she could feel its kiss on her cheeks and then on her lips. She could feel the cold sliding into her garments and caressing her. She remembered being touched the same way by her husband, and a great longing rose up in her to be taken into his arms again, to feel his skin against hers, to feel his warmth beside her. Her heart ached with that desire, and tears flowed from her eyes. She fell to her knees, sobbing now, a great agony expressed aloud in her gasps and moans. Her tears fell to the dry barren ground, and she cried until she couldn't focus any longer on what had made her feel so sad. She got down on the ground then, curled up, and wished she could fall asleep.

It was said that the desert was home to ancient powers, invisible spirits that inhabited the wind. Was that gust of air she felt infused with the presence of a creature she could not see? Was it a djinn, a wandering spirit, a being who lived in the space between the real and the imaginary? Whatever it was, she felt its caress, and then as that moment passed she felt alone in a new way, as if she now filled no space at all.

As the sky began to turn grey and the Sun threatened to rise over the horizon, Isabel covered her head and fell asleep.

* * *

Colonel Rabat was still commander of the Mounted Companies of the French Foreign Legion in Saïda, and Sergent Demoreau thought he looked sickly as he sat behind his desk. Rabat's office had a Moorish style enriched with tiles in various hues that made the room, and the people in it, appear green. Furthermore, the commander was clearly uncomfortable answering questions, and Capitaine Joubert (retired) was both quiet and implacable.

"The whole tragic business was entirely unexpected," Colonel Rabat insisted.

"And yet his service record?" Capitaine Joubert prodded.

The Colonel shot an angry look at Demoreau, who was standing at attention at the back of the room. "I concede that, to judge by what is contained in the man's service record alone, his history is far from pristine. Certain events, if viewed by themselves, might suggest that even worse actions could be perpetrated by this man. He has been reduced in rank a few times, yes, but neither those minor demotions nor his brief periods of incarceration should be considered unusual for a man who has served in the Legion as long as Demoreau. There have been a few minor incidents of public intoxication, but, again, what do you expect of a man who has seen and done what this Legionnaire has seen and done, while also fighting with distinction in dozens of skirmishes and battles, as far back as Chott Tigri. He's trained countless Legionnaires over the past two decades. Mon Dieu, there is no doubt whatsoever that Demoreau is a true Legionnaire at heart."

"No doubt until now," Capitaine Joubert added.

Colonel Rabat slapped his thick hand onto the desk. "These events occurred in the heat of battle, after all of the officers present had been gravely wounded. There may be rumors, hearsay, yes, but there is no proof that what happened was deliberate. In any case, I predict the whole incident will prove impossible to unravel. And, to be blunt, any result will be worth far less than the effort will cost."

Tamanrasset

It was generally understood that Sergent Demoreau had likely shot Legionnaire First Class Henry Mills in the head and killed him. However, there were also rumors that the shooting was intentional, in other words, that the Sergent had murdered Mills. Demoreau refused to comment on the incident, and he had even declined to speak when questioned about the event by his superior officers. Since then, the Sergent had been confined to barracks. However, Colonel Rabat had not been eager to continue an investigation of a matter which could blow back upon himself as commander of the Mounted Companies. Indeed, it now seemed he had cause for concern, for it was unusual, perhaps even alarming, that the austere Capitaine Joubert had been sent from the Governor's office to investigate what should have been an internal Foreign Legion matter. Granted, there had been a distinct lack of follow-up since Demoreau and the Sixth had returned to Saïda.

Throughout Algeria, news of the siege at Taghit and the following battle at El Moungar were discussed endlessly at dinners and in cafés, as all battles are, and it was generally viewed as a victory for France despite the considerable number of casualties. But, in the socialist French-Algerian newspaper "La Kabylie Française," the death of Legionnaire Mills had become the topic of repeated editorials condemning the Foreign Legion's cavalier attitude towards the loss of life: Were the Legionnaires no more to France than expendable mercenaries who could murder each other in cold blood? The conservative newspaper owned by Marcel Gallé, the wealthy landowner with the largest winery and olive oil production facilities in Algeria, had, not surprisingly, argued that Legionnaire Mills' death was a necessary sacrifice, no more or less tragic than the hundreds of other deaths each year which preserved and expanded French rule in Algeria. But, based on the few details that were reported publicly, it seemed questions would continue to be asked regarding how Legionnaire Mills came to be dead. Joubert informed Colonel Rabat that he had been instructed by the Governor's office to find out what had happened.

"Is Sergent Demoreau a member of an important family," Colonel Rabat asked, "or does someone on the Governor's staff hold a vendetta against the Sergent? Or is the Governor just attempting to use the death of Legionnaire Mills for political purposes? Do you even know why you have been sent?"

"My assignment remains the same, regardless: To determine whether Sergent Demoreau played any role in what might be outright murder."

"You go too far, Capitaine. Anyone might speculate, but an unfortunate death on the battlefield is far from murder. I want your report to state clearly that Sergent Demoreau has always been a dependable Legionnaire," the Colonel persisted, making it clear that he was more concerned about how the affair might reflect on the Foreign Legion and himself than how it would impact Demoreau. "As for whether the Sergent has any family or political connections, there is no mention of anything of the sort in his record. As you know, our tradition in the Foreign Legion is to not ask the Legionnaires about their pasts or the circumstances of their enlistment. Nevertheless, you may do as you wish; you shall have our complete cooperation."

"Then you allow me to question the Sergent?"

Tamanrasset

"Certainly, although I caution you that, so far, Sergent Demoreau has offered no statement regarding the death of Legionnaire Mills. Isn't that correct, Sergent?"

"Oui, mon Colonel," Demoreau replied.

The Colonel rose from his desk. "Please use my office to question the Sergent, Capitaine; he is not currently allowed out of barracks."

After Colonel Rabat left the office, the Capitaine told Demoreau to stand at ease. "You have heard who I am and my mission, Sergent Demoreau; perhaps you know better than I do why I have been sent here. Do you still decline to make any statement regarding the death of Legionnaire Mills?"

"I do, Sir," Demoreau stated.

"Mills' service record contains your recommendation only a few days before his death that he be promoted to Legionnaire First Class, for actions taken in defense of the Governor at the border, is that right?"

"Oui, mon Capitaine," Demoreau replied.

"Then you make it necessary for me to speak with the other members of your Company. Perhaps you could tell me what they will say and save me some time."

Demoreau smiled weakly to indicate that he appreciated the humor, but at the same time he looked simply exhausted. "I have no idea what they will say, Sir."

Joubert looked at Demoreau as he stood passively. "Are you, Sergent, insane?"

Demoreau considered for a moment—there was always a possibility he had been struck with le cafard. But that wasn't it. "No," was his simple reply.

"Then what do you expect will happen to you? Do you believe you will eventually return to duty, or will you be sent to the guillotine? What do you deserve?"

Demoreau sighed and shook his head in disapproval of the question, but his face showed no emotion at all; he looked empty. He stared at the colored window glass and tried to keep his mind utterly silent.

"Very well," the Capitaine concluded. "You may not care what happens to you, but the matter will lead where it may. You are dismissed."

Demoreau came to attention and saluted and then retired to his quarters.

* * *

Ren contacted Delattre to check on the Carthage excavations only to learn that Inspector Gauckler was continuing to indulge in an excessive examination of every penny spent, every piece of paper filed, every relic unearthed, every treasure displayed, and every hole excavated, down to the smallest grain of soil sifted. He had thus far failed to identify any serious issues, but it also appeared that he intended to remain in Carthage for the foreseeable future. This had the additional and unfortunate effect of driving away most of the students: Except for Tom Childers, the Palais d'Hamilcar was empty, and without the students or Lilian and with Gauckler breathing down his neck, Ren had little interest in returning. He decided to just remain in Algiers to push his new project along. Unfortunately, he was becoming increasingly frustrated with the slow pace of preparations for the expedition to the tomb of Queen al-Kahina. Durant was having difficulty with the translation of the ancient Arabic scrolls, and his partners were hesitant to spend

Tamanrasset

money on the expedition until a path to the exact location of the tomb was obtained. Their translation problems were compounded by the extreme secrecy of the project and the unwillingness of Durant and Gallé to show the ancient Arabic writings to anyone else.

As Ren waited in Algiers, weeks passed. Left with too much time, he sought out ways to engage his active mind. At first, he read all the accounts and memoirs of travel in the Sahara that he could find. The earliest modern account was from James Richardson, a British explorer who first visited the Sahara in 1845. Then Ren visited every museum, mosque, and local Roman and Punic site. He next began to visit the casino each evening to gamble and the theatre to watch the beautiful actresses. He became a connoisseur of the excellent Algerian wines, often drinking far more than he should. His excessive desires also led him each night to less public venues in the kasbah. Eventually, he discovered there that he had an insatiable appetite for women. He had never felt such visceral desires nor such a deep and constant need to indulge.

Ren would find himself each night taking the same now-familiar steps to the kasbah. There, he would ingest exotic herbs and powders and spend hours in the Moorish baths doing things to women, or having things done to him, which it later sickened him to recall. The next day he would always swear to get to bed early, to drink nothing but water, to rise with the Sun, but then, each night, he would again succumb, unable to rebuff his desires. On nights when he remained so sore from abuse that he could not bear to be touched any longer, he would smoke hashish, or opium, or some other concoction that had no name, often with others in a dark and humid room, with women who undressed and begged him to induce their hysteria with his hands or mouth.

In time, Ren developed a passionate self-loathing due to his failure to keep his urges under control. He knew that there was something wrong with him, a mania that arose from his moral failings, although there was also possibly an illness he had inherited: He didn't recall his father suffering from dipsomania, but it had been hinted to him by an aunt, when he was still but a child, that his mother had suffered from a delicate moral condition. That was before Ren was born, before his mother and father died, before he was sent off to school in England. Now his family was dead. He missed them. He missed his work and his students. He missed the Palais. He missed Lilian. He missed the way she made him feel. She had made him feel that he deserved her kindness. He didn't suppose that he deserved it anymore.

***

Isabel arrived in Ouargla covered in rags and dust, dehydrated, starving, her body exhausted and her spirit crushed. The city lay at the center of a forest of palm trees, and from a distance, only two minarets rose high enough to indicate the position of the city center. Isabel led her camel through the groves of trees and entered the low, whitewashed gateway into the city. As she walked up the sand-covered main road toward the busy marketplace, having completed the one and only thing she felt any need or desire to do, which was to reach Ouargla alive, her strength finally gave out. She sank slowly to her knees, then sat. Her camel could smell water and she released him so he could wander off to drink, but Isabel had no desire to move. She felt no hunger or thirst, she wanted nothing. She would have remained in the street until she expired, but when a

Tamanrasset

passerby saw that she was European, the French Gendarmes were alerted. She was carried to the Magistrate's office and placed on a bench while the doctor was summoned. She was unable to speak having suffered throat and lung damage from the desert, and she was placed in the care of a local midwife.

Over the next few days, Isabel remained silent, but the midwife gave her a rug and a blanket in her warm house. The midwife was an old Berber woman, quite hardy, who adhered to the old traditions. She fed her patient broth and camel's milk. She kept amulets, animal carvings, and tablets inscribed with symbols of the Sun and Moon. She never seemed to pray. Isabel could only smile at her and nod to express her gratitude, and, even when her voice began to return after a few days, she and the midwife didn't speak the same languages. There were many French and Arab speakers in Ouargla, but the midwife spoke only a Berber dialect that Isabel didn't understand.

As she strengthened, Isabel began to feel guilty for accepting the midwife's hospitality. Her wayward camel had been claimed by a local man, but the Gendarmes had forced the man to pay Isabel for it. She gave the proceeds to the midwife. After two weeks, Isabel was able to speak again and conveyed to the midwife that she wished to see Lèlla Zeyneb. That was a name the midwife recognized. She would not believe that the sacred marabout might come to her humble home, but she let Isabel know nevertheless, through signs and expressions, that she would let Lèlla Zeyneb know that Isabel was there.

But, quite unexpectedly, Lèlla Zeyneb did come. She was a mature woman of fifty, the daughter of a powerful sheik and heir to his Islamic school. As a woman, Lèlla Zeyneb had faced opposition to becoming her father's heir when he died, from both distant family relations and French administrators, but she was a shrewd woman who ably consolidated her power. Even then, her succession would have been challenged but for the tales of the miracles she had wrought, the faithful she had healed, and the children she had rescued. Now she was the Sheikha and called a living saint, a marabout, and revered by everyone in the city.

As she entered the small dark room where Isabel still lay recuperating, Lèlla Zeyneb wore her customary Bou Saâda garments, Berber garments made of a heavy white cloth. Her face was deeply tanned and wrinkled since she traveled widely throughout the province, but her large black eyes gazed gently at Isabel, full of wisdom. She found Isabel still weak but very much alive, her skin still sunburned but her icy blue eyes burning with cold flames.

The Sheikha looked hard at the frail young woman and was disturbed by what she saw. "You have seen a djinn," she said accusingly.

"I ... I think so, yes," Isabel croaked.

"Did it speak to you?"

Isabel lowered her eyes and nodded. The midwife, standing at the door, recognized the words she had just heard spoken. She passed her hand over her face and spit on the floor. Djinns were known to be dangerous and unpredictable.

"I know who you are," she said to Isabel. "I will have you brought to my house. We have a great deal to discuss once you have recovered. You are welcome to stay with me as long as you wish." The Sheikha spoke to the midwife for several minutes in the Berber language. She turned back to Isabel at last: "Gida thanks you for the payment you made, but she does not wish to keep the money from the theft of your camel. She will return that to you before you leave. She says you have been a good patient, and she has made many devotions to her gods to plead for your recovery."

"Tell her, please, that I am very grateful to her," Isabel whispered.

Isabel soon found herself resting in a larger house in a bright room with a fireplace. Servants brought her food and helped her to wash. Lèlla Zeyneb left on a brief journey to several nearby villages and was gone for a week. During that time, Isabel continued to recover from her illness, but she remained quiet and in her mind continued to wonder what she would say about her journey and why she had come.

At last a day arrived when she was feeling somewhat recovered and the revered Sheikha had many questions. They sat together in her glass-covered courtyard on that cool day basking in the Sun's warmth and sipping strong coffees.

"We are all relieved that you are recovering, Madame," the Sheikha said. "Even here in Ouargla, there have been many stories told of the Swedish woman whose sky blue eyes have received visions from Allah, who has studied at al-Quaraouiyin and become an Alima and has undertaken the Hajj. I am pleased to know you and to welcome you here to Ouargla. I believe Allah brought you here, and it has been my pleasure and a privilege for my servants to care for you. But now, I must ask you, why have you come?"

"I don't have an intelligent answer to that question, even though I knew you would ask it. I first learned of your work here in Ouargla several years ago during a conversation with Princess Lalla Fatima Zahra, sister of the Sultan of

Morocco. I had always thought I would like to meet you. Most of what I know about Islam, I have learned from men, but I've found that women's experience and understanding of Islam is different and is more meaningful to me. But, perhaps more importantly, you have learned that Muslim women need not only obey. Here in Ouargla, you are the Sheikha, the one who is obeyed, and I admit I found that ... inspirational."

"It is said that you have traveled across the Sahara. Do you know of the Tuareg people?"

"I have met several Tuareg men and women, yes."

"They are a matrilineal society, are they not?"

"Yes; although the women are not warriors, they are given a special status in their culture."

"Many of the Muslim people in this part of the Maghreb are Berbers, and while traditional Berber culture is not matriarchal, in many respects it has much more in common with the Tuareg culture than with the Arab. Perhaps the most famous Berber ruler of all time was Queen al-Kahina. That is not to say that I myself encountered no resistance when I sought to become the Sheikha as my father wished, but neither was my ascension dismissed out of hand. Of course, I was also not married, and it would have been my duty to obey my husband if I had been married, would it not?"

"I was married; my husband died several years ago, but I would have to say that, between the two of us, I was the decision-maker in our marriage."

"But that was a Swedish marriage, was it not? Regardless, it would be easy to pass it off as good fortune for you, but perhaps not, perhaps it is written that you are one that others will follow."

"I've heard that before, and I don't wish to become a leader."

The Sheikha laughed. "But you already have followers, many more than I do: There are people across Morocco, across the Maghreb, and as far as Mecca, who believe you are a living saint. It is hardly to be wondered at that the servants in this house worship you. There are stories to explain that you were born in the Sahara but kidnapped as an infant, stories which claim that you are a direct descendant of the Prophet and a marabout."

Isabel looked at her dumbfounded. "That's ... not true. If you want to know what I think, it is all just an excuse to keep me at arm's length."

"How do you mean?"

"I think people don't know what to make of me, so they invent reasons why I am different from them, making me unapproachable."

"But you know who you are?"

"That's another problem altogether."

"Regardless, if you did not come here to learn from me about Islam, which you clearly do not need, or how to become a Sheikha, which you say you do not want, why then have you come?"

"Well ... I hoped, maybe, that you could tell me that," Isabel replied.

"You crossed the Sahara to come here on a whim, just to please yourself, because you wished to undertake the journey?"

Isabel shook her head. "No, no, my desires, my pleasure, my happiness, these concepts hold little interest for me anymore. How did we come to believe that being 'happy' is all life has to offer? I came because I felt compelled to come. I traveled here almost in a dream, unconsciously. I needed to lose myself, and it almost killed me."

"So perhaps I should be asking not why you have come, but who is it that has arrived. Who is this person named Isabel Pedersen?"

"No one," she whispered, "or someone who is dead, the person I was before I came to the Maghreb."

"Tut, tut," the Sheikha admonished her. "You are here, speaking to me. Who are you?"

"Not that person; I don't know anymore."

"Hmm. Then it seems that you will have to discover who you are; I cannot tell you that."

Isabel blushed. "I suppose you are correct."

"It will take time for you to see, but you are still young, and the young are never as complex as they believe themselves to be. Will you stay here with me? I will help you if I can."

"As long as I am welcome. I have no obligations elsewhere."

The Sheikha thought a moment. "I shall not call you 'Isabel Pedersen' any longer since you say that person no longer exists. I believe you should have a new name. I shall call you Hajjah Bella min Alsahra,' if you agree. You and I together can discover who that person is."

Tamanrasset

"Yes, I want that," she replied. She liked the idea of abandoning the debris of her life and fashioning a new person, a real person.

"However, you bear the mark of the djinn, Bella, and it is among many marks that cannot be removed."

"That is true."

"Do not let those scars alone define you. You are also a woman, a scholar, a traveler who has crossed the Sahara. You have heard the voice of Allah. You have circled the Kaaba. You have punished the wicked and brought peace to the Plains of Oujda. You are all these things, and more yet that you do not know."

She began to cry. "Thank you," she affirmed.

"I am told you have not prayed since you arrived at my house. It would honor me, truly, if you would pray with me today. Are you willing to do that?"

"I will pray with you, of course, while I am staying in your house."

"Will you come with me to the mosque? I would like you to see how your presence has influenced the faithful here in Ouargla."

"Yes, I will come," she replied.

For the first time in weeks, the woman now known as "Hajjah Bella" dressed for the outdoors and stepped out to the street that ended at the Sheikha's door. The afternoon was fading and the muezzin was calling those nearby to prayer. The two women walked slowly, and many other people came to join them. They reached the mosque and entered the door for women, and the people there were eager to get a glimpse of the Sheikha and her guest.

Crossroads of the Nomad

After they had prayed, many women and men came to speak with the Sheikha, but many more came specifically to meet Bella, to seek her acquaintance and to express their relief that she was recovering from her illness. She shook each man's hand in hers in the Western manner, and she kissed each woman on both cheeks. The Sheikha was laughing at something, and suddenly Bella felt a burden lift from her chest. She smiled. It didn't matter what she believed, she was just so grateful to be alive. These people were kind and she felt their good wishes for her. Bella felt like she could live again, but it would take time. She wanted to be certain of her feelings and be the person she was, not the person others wanted her to be.

* * *

The same day that Ahmad returned to Fez, the newspapers reported that French General Lyautey had sent soldiers to the town of Ras El-Ain, south of Oujda, thirty-five kilometers inside the border of Morocco. The soldiers established a French military post, and, as he had with Bechar, Lyautey renamed the town in order to gloss over political difficulties. He called it "Berguent." The Sheik in Ras El-Ain, outraged by the blunt invasion, proclaimed a jihad against the French. The Sultan met with the French ambassador and subsequently denounced any call for a holy war.

It was the first hot day in Fez that spring but the city remained as it had for centuries, the same labyrinth of narrow streets and bustling marketplaces and ancient traditions filled with the shouting of local Berbers and Arabs and the call of the muezzin, the smells of spices and herbs

Tamanrasset

and leather curing in vats at the tannery, the rush of people dressed in colorful kaftans or white jellabas, the laughter of children and the wails of those struggling to survive. In the central marketplace, embedded in the wall of the prison, stood a small stone structure, a tomb, which was passed each day by countless residents, a constant warning of the evil that men can do.

Ahmad still felt like an outcast. He had been passed over by his people, and his father's brother, who had been made Sharif, had sent Ahmad back to Fez. His village, Abadla, was no longer his home. In Fez, he saw enormous changes that were happening in Morocco: There were now French diplomats and French bureaucrats and French businessmen welcomed into the holy city. Ahmad had read that a new friendship agreement had been signed between France and Great Britain. As he expected, that meant that vast numbers of British diplomats and businessmen began coming to Morocco as well. Many people were uneasy with the changes. Yet letters from his family praising the new Sharif steadily wore away at Ahmad's anger. Feeling empty and purposeless, Ahmad eventually chose to do what he could to serve his kinsmen as their representative, and in time he came to know many of the officials in the Sultan's government.

Muhammad al-Kattani also returned to Fez and reopened his newspaper. The scholars of the Ulama in Fez had the support of the most religious people in Morocco, and it was believed that the Sultan could no longer get away with closing down the Ulama's printing presses. Unfortunately, Ahmad's new role as a representative left him with little time to reassert Moroccan sovereignty or to write for al-

Kattani's newspaper. Ahmad felt useful, but the important things that he believed should be happening in his homeland were no longer happening, and he no longer felt like he would even be welcome there.

When summer arrived, a new crisis rocked the Sultan: A Greek-American living in Tangier and his stepson were kidnapped by a charismatic warlord in the Rif mountains, Ahmed al-Raisuli. Al-Raisuli expected a cash ransom from Sultan Abd al-Aziz but also demanded the authority to control six of Morocco's wealthiest districts, a condition the Sultan had to reject out of hand. However, it seemed the United States President, Theodore Roosevelt, could not stomach a rogue Moroccan warlord targeting Americans, and so he forced the Sultan to capitulate to the warlord's demands by threatening to use American naval gunships to bombard the city of Tangier. Even the British and French understood that forcing the Sultan to yield to al-Raisuli's ridiculous demands was a catastrophic humiliation (not to mention that the country needed all of its tax revenue to pay the enormous loans the Sultan had secured from European banks). Despite editorials in the French-owned newspapers applauding the Sultan for his handling of the crisis, many traders and merchants, prominent landowners, and religious leaders, began to voice reservations about the Sultan's actions. He urgently needed to reassert and consolidate his power.

In an almost unprecedented step, Sultan Abd al-Aziz called for a "Shura," an assembly at which he would obtain a consensus on the direction of the country and assure that he had the support of the major (native) powers in Morocco. Ahmad was invited to attend as representative of the Wadi

Tamanrasset

Saoura and Wadi Guir, and important men came from many other provinces and cities in Morocco, leaders from the important trading port cities of Agadir, Casablanca, Rabat, and Tangier, as well as members of the powerful Glaoui family from the High Atlas. There were only two men not invited: Ahmed al-Raisuli, the rogue warlord who had caused the crisis with the Sultan's sovereignty, and the Pretender, Jilali al-Zerhouni, known as Rakib al-Himar, who was still in Taza claiming to be the brother of the Sultan. Indeed, there were rumors that the Sultan had sent soldiers to arrest Jilali and that the soldiers had been outmaneuvered and roundly defeated by the Pretender's small European-trained and European-supplied army.

The Shura was scheduled to take place at the Kasbah of Moulay Ismail, an imperial fortress constructed within the city of Meknes, a day's ride west of Fez. It was easily reached by all those invited. Ahmad was eager to see the imperial castle which, at one time, was larger than the city of Meknes itself and still represented the power and glory of the Alaoui dynasty that had ruled Morocco since 1631. No one who came to the Shura missed the Sultan's intended meaning: He was the ruler of Morocco by divine right, and he would remain its ruler no matter what.

Ahmad was amazed by the extensive high walls of the fortress. Constructed with a heavy lime content in an aggregate of crushed stone, clay, sand, and straw, the amazingly thick walls were impenetrable. Ahmad rode around the fortress to the dazzling main gate. It was decorated with ten thousand colorful tiles and colored plaster, with huge iron-reinforced doors which spanned the Moorish "keyhole" archway, open but guarded by many soldiers in elegant livery, yet another extravagant and excessive display by the Sultan.

Ahmad was admitted to the palace and directed to his private rooms. The dinner that evening would begin the meetings that would take place over the coming days. He dressed in a fine new thobe, a long loose-fitting robe of rich brocade fabric, beneath a fine wool bisht, an outer robe, both crafted for just such formal occasions. However, before Ahmad could reach the main hall, a servant came up to him in the hallway: "The Qaid of the High Atlas would like to speak with you before the meetings begin. If you have a moment now, would you accompany me to his rooms?"

Ahmad followed, his curiosity piqued—he had never met any members of the Glaoui family, but he had been quite critical in the past of their allegiance to the Sultan. Was that what the Qaid wished to discuss? Ahmad followed to another part of the fortress where the halls were bigger, brighter, and even more opulent, each archway decorated with an ornate profile of lobes and points and the walls engraved with Islamic art, often with Arabic writings from the Quran. Ahmad was admitted to a large room with a terrace that overlooked a garden in full bloom; it was much nicer than his own rooms—that didn't surprise him—but it was also an extremely traditional Moroccan room with camel-hair rugs and pillows to sit upon. However, he was not introduced to the Qaid, Madani El Glaoui, but to the Qaid's younger brother, T'hami El Glaoui.

"Thank you for coming to speak with me," said the young Berber chieftain. He was only a couple years older than Ahmad himself, a remarkably intelligent-looking man with

Tamanrasset

a thin frame and gentle face. But why had the Glaoui family sent T'hami El Glaoui instead of his brother, the Qaid?

"It is an honor to meet you," Ahmad said, as he was gestured to take a seat. "I naturally expected the Sultan to invite the Glaoui to attend this Shura but I am pleased to see a young man like myself who understands how Morocco is being threatened. Will your brother also be attending?"

T'hami smiled to acknowledge the compliment but his expression remained serious, and his eyes narrowed at mention of his brother. "Then you have not heard," he said. "I am here representing the Qaid. My brother has recently found himself out of favor with Abd al-Aziz and will not be attending."

"No, I hadn't heard that," Ahmad replied gravely, "but neither am I surprised to learn that the Sultan's childish behavior has deprived him of a valued and experienced advisor. All the same, it is well that *you* are here, as the Shura would have no legitimacy without the involvement of the Glaoui."

"Or the inclusion of your family, the Haybah. I must take this opportunity to express my deep regret at the passing of your father. The death of Sharif Moulay Mostepha is a terrible loss for our people."

"You are most gracious, thank you," Ahmad replied.

"You might have already heard, but I must tell you there was no small relief within the Makhzen when your father's brother was named as the new Sharif of the Doui-Menia rather than you: Abd al-Aziz has promised the French that he will quell resistance to their presence in the Wadi Saoura and Touat regions, and it had been feared that you would have chosen to continue the war against the Westerners."

"Yes, indeed I would have. I believe it is our duty to combat the foreign invasion of our lands," Ahmad said coolly. "Is that what you wished to discuss with me? We've had little cooperation from the tribes in the High Atlas in our battles against the invaders thus far."

"No, I asked you to come because you have spoken openly against the Sultan, have you not?" T'hami asked bluntly.

"I have objected to a number of policies implemented by the Sultan and to his response to the crisis that grips our country. In that regard, I am hardly alone."

"A measured response to my question, but your denunciation of the Sultan remains a matter of record. At least, I have seen the unpublished essay that you wrote. Apart from your denunciation of my own family, I found it very provocative."

"Thank you."

"You are correct that the Glaoui profited greatly from our close relationship with the Sultan's father, Moulay Hassan, and then with the Sultan's Regent, Ba Ahmed. My brother Madani chose to continue to support Abd al-Aziz since he came into his majority, but there are concerns, particularly with his acceptance of the French incursions on our eastern borders and his profligacy, and he is perhaps too fascinated with Western ideas and innovations."

"I am glad to know your opinion, but why do you tell me this now?" Ahmad asked.

"There are others, if one of them were to become Sultan in place of Abd al-Aziz, who might more aggressively oppose the French and seek to restore control over Morocco. My brother still wishes to support Abd al-Aziz, but I believe his mind could be changed. Is this information of interest to you?"

"Were it in your brother's power to bend the Sultan's will towards the greater preservation of Morocco, to change the Makhzen's policies, I would be pleased for him to do so. But as a topic of mere idle conversation, if the Sultan were to name a successor, is there anyone in particular that you believe your brother would favor?"

"No, not my brother, but for my own part, I believe the Khalifa of Marrakesh is the most likely person to receive the support of the majority of tribes were he to succeed Abd al-Aziz to the throne."

"The Khalifa? You mean the Sultan's brother Abd al-Hafid?"

"Yes."

"I do not know him, but I will make it my business to learn." Ahmad replied, "for I fear that with each passing day, Abd al-Aziz becomes more a puppet of the French."

After a few days of mild, polite discussion, the Shura concluded and a bland statement was issued in support of the Sultan. The entire event did nothing to improve the situation. Ahmad returned to Fez and met with Muhammad al-Kattani, who had pointedly not been invited to the Shura.

"I met T'hami of the Glaoui family in Meknes," Ahmad told him. "Do you know why his brother the Qaid Madani El Glaoui has fallen out of favor with the Sultan?"

Al-Kattani snorted in disgust: "While you were in the south, Abd al-Aziz had Madani El Glaoui lead his warriors and a regiment of the Sultan's army against the Pretender in Taza, Rakib al-Himar, the one who continues to pose as the Sultan's brother Mohammed. The Pretender, it seems, has friends in French Algeria who have supplied him with weapons, mercenaries and even a European military advisor. These were enough that Madani's forces were held off and forced to retreat. The Sultan was furious and claimed that Madani El Glaoui had failed him intentionally. So, the Qaid is no longer welcome at court and has been staying in his fortress at Telouet in the Atlas mountains. He refused to come at the Sultan's call."

"No wonder he was not at the Shura; he sent his young brother T'hami instead. You and I have spoken many times of the need to remove Abd al-Aziz, but have you any thoughts about who would replace him?" Ahmad asked.

"The Sultan could only be replaced by another member of the Alaoui family, I presume. Abd al-Aziz has more than a dozen brothers, and he is not even the eldest."

"T'hami suggested that Madani could be convinced to support Abd al-Hafid."

Al-Kattani laughed. "Madani will support whoever it profits the Glaoui to support, and right now that is Abd al-Aziz; I don't expect that to change. The Glaoui probably do business with the Khalifa of Marrakesh since it is the city closest to their fortress in the High Atlas, but that is a far cry from supporting him as a replacement of the Sultan, despite what T'hami may say."

"Would Madani obey the rulings of the Ulama if they put forward someone other than Abd al-Aziz to be Sultan?"

"That is hard to predict. The Glaoui are proud of their Berber heritage, it likely outweighs even their outward show of devotion to Allah. Certainly, the Berber people have been in the Maghreb far longer than the Mohammedans, for thousands of years, in fact. Abd al-Hafid's mother, of all the wives of the late Sultan Hassan, was reportedly descended of an ancient Berber lineage, perhaps even descended from their great queen, so perhaps that gives him a special advantage in the eyes of the Glaoui."

"Surely the Ulama of Fez is the one to decide who should be Sultan, if Abd al-Aziz is removed," Ahmad argued.

"The reality of Morocco is that the northern regions, and that includes all the royal cities and the ports, are geographically separated from the southern regions by the Atlas mountains, and the mountains are controlled by the Glaoui. To speak plainly, Ahmad, nothing can happen in Morocco unless Madani El Glaoui agrees to let it happen, and if he does not support replacing the Sultan, then it will not happen."

* * *

Demoreau's fate was still undecided, and he could see that Capitaine Joubert was becoming increasingly frustrated. In the midst of the Capitaine's investigation, the Foreign Legion suddenly decided to charge Demoreau with "homicide involontaire," or manslaughter, and conduct a court martial. The Legion commanders evidently concluded that, as long as the Governor's office was watching, there could be no slow-walking or covering up the matter, nor could they simply give Demoreau the benefit of the doubt: He would have to be charged, and the chips would fall where they may.

Many of the facts elicited at the Sergent's trial were undisputed: Testimony regarding the physical condition of the corpse of Legionnaire Mills when he was found immediately after the battle indicated that he had been shot in the head by a rifle at close range, just a few feet to judge from the powder burns he had sustained. Neither was there any possibility that Mills shot himself. Demoreau was the only other person present when Mills was killed, and the Sergent was equipped with a rifle at that time. Moreover, when questioned, the Sergent did not dispute that he was the one who shot Mills in the head. But, it could have been an accidental shooting; some believed that the Sergent's silence was due to his overwhelming feelings of guilt for having caused a Legionnaire's accidental death, while others made the incredible accusation that Sergent Demoreau had smuggled alcohol into the desert so he could secretly get drunk while the battle was taking place. It was unfortunate that there was no evidence as to whether Demoreau had or had not a motive to murder Mills. Many theories were put forward, from a love affair gone wrong to gambling debts. Capitaine Joubert had questioned every member of the Sixth and had not been able to deduce any motive that Demoreau might have had to kill Mills.

For weeks, Demoreau sat alone in the barracks, in the private room allotted to him as a Senior NCO. He had gotten quite good at thinking of nothing and feeling less. He still did not know why Capitaine Joubert had been sent to Saïda by the Governor, but there were a few possibilities: Obviously, Governor Jonnart might just be grateful to Demoreau for helping to shield him at the border near Beni Ounif, but that was just Demoreau doing his job. Perhaps Lyautey, Durant, or someone else from Paixporteur Carrier Int'l. wanted to make sure he kept quiet about Jilali. Possibly the Governor had a political interest because of the newspaper accounts. In the main, Demoreau could only think of individuals who might want him exonerated, although he couldn't be sure that Capitaine Mitterand was not involved somehow to seek revenge. Demoreau himself had no ambitions—he knew he had murdered Mills in cold blood, and he would willingly do it again. He had no mercy for his own conduct, and he expected none from the Legion. The motive was ultimately immaterial. It would take a great many words, an embarrassment of language, to express something so simple and small as Jacques Demoreau's motive for murdering Mills. Demoreau himself would think less of anyone who needed it explained: It should simply be enough to say that Mills had destroyed the one remnant of compassion left in the Sergent's old heart, his memory of a woman he had once loved. Still, the murder had been a betrayal of the Foreign Legion, and therefore the Sergent knew he could not remain. He had waited to see whether they would choose to bring a court martial against him, but if they did not then he would go en pompe and become a mercenary, for although there had once been a flickering vestige of compassion left in his heart, that too was now dead. He felt nothing. Capitaine Joubert was waiting to see whether the Sergent would be saved or hung out to dry by the Legion, but to Demoreau the answer hardly mattered.

At last the final day of the court martial arrived, and the verdict was to be announced. Demoreau was escorted by the PM's to the hall where the hearings were conducted. The officer appointed to argue on his behalf was not yet present, neither were the prosecutors nor the judges, but it was not uncommon for them to meet in Colonel Rabat's office beforehand and come into the hall afterwards. Demoreau sat at a plain wood table to wait. It was a long time before the prosecutors entered the room and went to their table. They looked quite angry. Demoreau's advocate came in next; he looked angry as well and would not speak to the Sergent. Then the three senior officers who were judges on the court martial entered. Everyone stood at attention while the judges took their seats behind a wide table. They also looked angry, particularly Colonel Rabat. Demoreau noticed that while they were all getting seated, Capitaine Joubert came in the back of the room and stood by the door checking his pocket watch as if patiently waiting his turn.

"Sergent Demoreau," Rabat stated in his loud bombastic voice, "have you anything to say before this tribunal announces its judgment regarding the charges brought against you?"

"No, mon Colonel," he replied stoically.

"Very well. After hearing all the evidence presented and weighing the credibility of those who have testified, this panel has reached a decision on the charges brought against Sergent Jacques Demoreau. Sergent, you are found guilty of homicide involontaire in the accidental death of Legionnaire Henry Mills, and you are sentenced to a term of ten years of imprisonment. However, after the consideration of certain additional factors, this panel further orders that you be immediately released en liberté conditionnelle into the custody of Capitaine Joubert to serve at the Capitaine's discretion. If he determines, for any reason or at any time, that you are no longer of service, then the remainder of your term of punishment shall be spent in a penal facility in the Overseas Department of French Guiana."

Demoreau turned and glared at Joubert who grimaced in a manner that expressed a certain fatalism, as if to say,

Tamanrasset

as the Muslims believe, that Demoreau's fate was already written. Demoreau could only shake his head in disbelief—he had no interest in doing whatever it was Joubert wanted.

"I didn't want this," Demoreau said angrily once he and Joubert were left alone together in the hearing room.

"You could have told them that you killed that Legionnaire in cold blood," Joubert retorted, "but you were prepared to let the situation run its course. You must have known the worst they would do is imprison you; you fully expected to get away with murder, no? Well, now you have."

Demoreau turned away, ashamed because what Joubert said was probably true.

"You served France admirably for twenty-five years, Monsieur, but your time in the Foreign Legion is over. That was a certain consequence of your own deliberate actions, not mine. Now you'll need to decide whether to undertake the work being offered to you, or else get sent to French Guiana. The correct response seems obvious."

"The last time I agreed to participate in some clandestine affair, I was not pleased with how it ended."

"Yes, I know a little about that," Joubert said with a laugh. "Look here, this is not at all like that affair in Morocco, not at all, I guarantee it," Joubert said with a wink. "Now, wouldn't you like to come have a glass of wine with me to celebrate?"

Demoreau turned to look at the door through which Colonel Rabat had departed. He could go right through that door and tell the Colonel that he preferred to spend ten years in a prison deep in the infested swamps of French Guiana where he would almost certainly die of yellow fever or dysentery. The thought made Demoreau shake his head in disbelief: He certainly wasn't going to be that stupid. Joubert was correct that Demoreau was now out of the Foreign Legion. He had thought he would stay in the Legion until he died in battle. He had no one to blame but himself.

"Yeah, let's go then," he said.

* * *

Ren awoke late one afternoon in his room at the Hotel de la Régence sore and exhausted and so disgusted that he knew he must leave Algiers at once. Durant and his partners still knew only that the tomb was in the vicinity of Tamanrasset, a Tuareg city that had grown up around a crossroads in the Hoggar mountains deep in the heart of the Sahara. Ren had read that Richardson had traveled to the village of Ghadames by traveling alone through the desert, some eight hundred kilometers south of Tunis, in 1845; he was warmly greeted by the locals who had not yet learned to mistrust Europeans. Ren wondered what sort of reception he would receive from the Tuaregs at Tamanrasset now.

He leapt from his bed. The expedition was stalled while he awaited additional information from the writings which were allegedly necessary to pinpoint the precise location of al-Kahina's tomb, but that information was now twelve hundred years old. What use could it be? Ren couldn't believe it was worth waiting any longer. There could be no substitute for going to Tamanrasset himself and doing his best to identify the burial edifice. Like Richardson, Ren would just travel south into the Sahara and see what could be found. Yes, Tamanrasset was easily two thousand kilometers from Algiers. The journey would take months,

Tamanrasset

and Ren would have to make many stops along the way just as Richardson had. But it was time to begin.

"You're insane," Durant told him, when Ren marched into the trustee's house that evening to announce that he planned to depart on the expedition the very next morning.

"We're wasting time," Ren insisted. "Your discovery in the museum's scrolls about this tomb is a secret now, but it cannot be kept secret much longer. Once word gets out there will be a rush of people going to search for the Queen's tomb. You have no idea how the very word 'tomb' motivates people; well, perhaps you do. Anyway, we don't need to plan every detail of the expedition. I shall take what servants we have, ask a few junior colleagues to catch up, and whoever else you have ready; we'll take only the camels and supplies required, and not make ourselves a target for the bandits and Tuareg warriors (although I will need to take some silver and gold to buy supplies and pay baksheesh along the way). And I must take a copy of the writings from the museum—photographs, I think. This is the way archaeology is done, sir. I must go there and look for the tomb myself; I'll know where to look once I see the terrain. There is a far greater risk in this endless delay."

Ren had calculated that the risk of losing the tomb to others might motivate Gallé to launch the expedition, and he was correct to a point. His persistence (and possibly rumors of his unfortunate nightly behavior) convinced the partners that Ren should be sent the very next day to Garanda, a city in the foothills of Tell Atlas southeast of Algiers which was the center of Gallé's agricultural empire, and from which the expedition would commence, for it was where the others hired by Gallé for the expedition were assembling. Ren made it through a sleepless last night at the Hotel de la Régence without succumbing to his almost unquenchable desires, but his dependance on alcohol and opiates and women manifested itself in cold sweats and intense nausea.

Dressed as usual in his field uniform of khaki trousers, boots, shirt, tie and field jacket, Ren took a hired carriage to the Gare de l'Agha. Unfortunately, his first-class compartment on the train was small and crowded with loud, heavily perspiring officers of the French army. In his delicate condition, Ren was forced to lean out the window to vomit. With a bang and a sudden severe jolt that threw Ren off his feet, the train began its journey. At first, they proceeded quite slowly through the suburbs of Algiers past comfortable French homes on comfortable tracts adjacent to well laid streets, but soon the train carried on through farmlands full of fruit trees and hay growing in the rich coastal soil. Here and there were habitable dwellings and the ruins of past civilizations: The remains of a Byzantine villa, an ancient Greco-Punic structure, the half-columns of a ruined Roman temple, and the dome of an Islamic marabout's tomb. Houses appeared further and further apart. After a few hours, they began to climb into the Tell Atlas range and through valleys full of olive trees and grape vines. At last the train came abruptly onto a verdant plain and came to a stop on the edge of a busy city just after the sun had set.

Gallé's people had been telegraphed to expect Ren, so he was met at the station by two well-dressed Frenchmen. They brought him straight to the Hotel des Colonies where Ren was escorted to a fine suite. He soon discovered, after a fine dinner had been sent up by the hotel with only one bottle of wine, that his employers had arranged for him to be locked into his room. In the morning, Ren had no opportunity to view the town which had been built atop the ruins of a Roman outpost, since he was scheduled to meet with other members of his expedition at a luncheon that day. Horses were brought to the hotel so Ren and the two Frenchmen could make the lengthy ride to Gallé's residence and renowned horse breeding facility outside the city.

It should have come as no surprise that Gallé had constructed an authentic French chateau in the middle of a field of wheat in Africa, but Ren's first sight of the building was still disorienting. Combined with his persistent aches of withdrawal and the jostling of his horse, Ren arrived unsettled and feeling somewhat sick. As he dismounted beside the stables, he saw a tall, grey-haired, soldierly man in a safari jacket and well-worn boots approaching.

There was something familiar about him, Ren thought, and then, unexpectedly, he felt the blood rush to his face, and his heart began to pound.

He looked again.

Yes, he was certain. Ren knew the man.

Jacques Demoreau stopped a dozen feet away and looked back at Ren with an expression of both curiosity and astonishment.

Ren spoke first: "By God, Jack, is it really you?"

Demoreau, now visibly confused, took a step closer. "Ren?"

Ren stepped quickly to the older man and threw his arms around him tightly. Demoreau gradually reciprocated the embrace.

"Ren, I ... I didn't know you were in Africa," he stammered.

"I didn't know you were alive!" Ren retorted joyfully as he held Demoreau by his forearms, face to face. "Yet here you are, Jack, alive and well, my dear brother! Do you recognize me?"

"Yes, Ren, of course, you look, somehow, just the same."

"How I've hoped over the years that you were still alive somewhere, all those years, and you turn up here, Jack, in Africa," Ren exclaimed. "And you're working for Gallé, I take it, as am I now, I suppose. Didn't they tell you who was coming?"

"Only that the professor leading the expedition would be arriving today, that's all I was told, not your name."

"How very clever of them; I wonder if they knew. Dear Jack, have you been here in Africa all these years?"

"You were always the clever one, Ren, and here you are a professor, a scientist, of all things." It did not pass Ren's notice that his brother did not answer his question. "I always knew you'd do fine, especially with all the money Father left in trust for you, well, I wouldn't have been of any use to you."

"Not just my money, but yours as well, brother. The French government pronounced you dead and gave me your accounts. You'll have it all back, of course," he said quickly. He wanted to add the he would rather have had a brother than the money but held his tongue, thinking it too confrontational a remark.

"That's not important, Ren, really. It's just astonishing that you're here. And I'm told we're going on a hell of an expedition together. Now I'll really have to make sure we make it back alive. Come inside and let me introduce you around to some of the men who are going with us."

"Certainly," Ren agreed.

But he found he couldn't move. It was all too much: His feelings of disorientation and withdrawal combined with the strangeness of running into a brother he hadn't seen in thirty years. There was a sense of sadness, disappointment in himself, but also astonishment at having run into the long-lost brother whom he had believed dead for decades. Yet it seemed to mean much more to him than to Jack. And there was no explanation from Jack as to why he had never contacted his younger brother.

Ren stood stock still, struggling to absorb his feelings. Only one thing mattered for now, he thought: He should keep his mouth shut and let Jack speak when he was ready.

"Listen, though," Demoreau added, "you need to know that around here I go by the name 'Jacques Demain.' You can call me 'Jack,' of course, if that's what you prefer, but, look, we can talk it all through some other time, if you really want to hear it, I guess."

"'Demain' means 'tomorrow,' in French, doesn't it?" Ren asked triumphantly. "What a lark, Jack! I remember every time Father asked you to do something, you'd always yell 'tomorrow!'" Ren shook Jack's hand. "'Jack Tomorrow,' I used to call you, isn't that right? I can't believe you're here," Ren said, tears now forming in his eyes. "I missed you, Jack."

"It's alright, Ren. Hell, I guess we'll be spending the next few months together," he replied soothingly. "We've all the time in the world to catch up."

Ren wiped his eyes. "Yes, yes, as you say, Jack, sure thing. Come on, though, you wanted to introduce me to the other fellows, and we've got to get this journey begun."

* * *

Jack Winston Villere, once known to his brother Ren as Jack Tomorrow, formerly known to the French Foreign Legion as Jacques Demoreau, now known as Jacques Demain, was dumbfounded to have stumbled upon the little brother whom he had left behind many decades before, and whom he had not seen since little Ren was shipped off to boarding school in England. And to find him here, of all places, in the middle of Algeria, well, that was virtually an omen. He knew he should be pleased, but in fact Jack was extremely uneasy. Did Ren know why Jack fled Paris all those years ago? Did he know that Jack had been in the Foreign Legion or that he had been court martialed following a conviction for manslaughter? And while Ren didn't immediately ask why Jack had remained out of touch for thirty years, the question was sure to be asked eventually. Jack had no idea what he would say. His life, his current life, began when he was expelled from the French Foreign Legion. Joubert had eventually come clean: While he was indeed a retired Capitaine of the Armée d'Afrique, he currently worked for Marcel Gallé as his chief of security. On Durant's recommendation, Jack had been targeted as a potential employee with deep desert experience who would be able to lead security details in the most remote corners of the Gallé commercial empire. Jack naturally acknowledged it was his own fault that he had been court martialed, and Joubert, satisfied that the incident was concluded and Jack was not insane, had evidently influenced the outcome of the case by ensuring that an asset like Jack wasn't wasted in prison. Gallé had obtained the Governor's permission to take Jack "en liberté conditionnelle" after ensuring that he was convicted of manslaughter rather than murder. For several weeks, Jack had been at Gallé's estate adjusting to being out of the military and to being in something that often felt very much the same. The only difference was that, in the Foreign Legion, he used to jest, he couldn't be called a mercenary because the French didn't pay him. Now he was a genuine mercenary, and that would have been hard to bear were it not for the fact that he no longer cared.

"If you have any concerns, see anything, you'll speak to your captain first," Ren was saying to the assembled team—two dozen of the hardest and strongest of Gallé's employees, mostly former Chaamba Tirailleurs who had been brought together for the expedition into the Sahara. Jack had also hired former Legionnaires Hans Mueller and Fedir Andreev, both of whom had declined to re-enlist at the end of their five year terms in the Foreign Legion. Jack would lead the security team, but his little brother was the expedition's chief. "I intend to maintain a tight chain of command once we enter the desert," Ren continued, "but I don't want any of you to feel that you mayn't speak to me; my ears will remain open at all times. In that vein, have you any questions for me now or concerns you want to raise?"

"Do you know yet where we're going?" Asked a young, brown-skinned man with a very severe facial scar.

"There's nothing to add to what you probably already know, but bear in mind that I have surveyed precisely this sort of archaeological site. Rest assured we will not be flailing about in the mountains for weeks on end–days, possibly, but not weeks," he jested. The men were smiling, and Jack was relieved that Ren had shown he would be an apt leader for the expedition, even if he looked like he'd just been drinking all night. Jack knew nothing of Ren and hadn't seen him since he was a boy of seven or eight. He suddenly recalled that as a child he had held Ren responsible for the death of their mother and realized only now, as an adult, that blaming his brother for being born was hardly fair.

Ren seemed extremely eager to get the expedition begun, but there were others coming to join them, including an archaeologist named Bert Hill coming from Greece and another named Tom Childers coming from Tunis with a structural engineer and surveyor, a photographer, and journalists from the National Geographic. A few skilled laborers had been assembled, and more laborers would be hired as needed. They did not know exactly what they would find when they reached Tamanrasset. Jack had passed once through the Hoggar mountains, where the tomb was expected to be found, many years earlier, but the situation there was likely quite different now.

That evening as the setting Sun turned the sky red and orange, Jack ran into Ren outside. He was standing on the stone walkway and staring at the young green wheat. Jack felt he should say something.

"You, uh, you've done well, Ren," Jack said.

Ren turned to him, a somewhat vacant look in his eyes like he had been thinking of something far away. But then he shook his head and came back to the present. "I went back to Charleston, a couple of years ago," he said.

"Did you?" Jack said, surprised. "Did you remember any of it? You were only six or seven when we moved to France."

"No, I remembered almost nothing of the town; it's changed so much since we were boys. Our house was gone, torn down for something new. I visited Mother's grave. But there were folks who remembered Father and us. I think some of them were even sorry we had been forced to leave after the war."

"I can't imagine going back after what they did to Father," Jack said.

"You loved him more than I ever could. Even as a boy I could tell he hated me. I used to think he dragged us to France and died as his way of getting even with me."

"He was never a strong man, really," Jack said. "He was just a merchant trying to make a decent wage. The war ruined him."

"You're older, so I guess you knew him better than I did. Besides, it was you, not him, that I looked up to and admired as a boy."

Jack took that as a rebuke. "Look, Ren, I'm sorry I never got in touch."

"Of course I knew that you left Paris all those years ago, Jack, once I was old enough to come looking for you, but you had already been gone for years and years. I never heard from you. I just assumed you were dead. I could have been a good brother to you, Jack."

"I ... was never someone that it would have done you any good to know."

"Don't say that. You're my brother, that's all that ever mattered to me. But the past, it's just water under the bridge now. I don't care to rehash thirty years of our lives; no more do you, I'm sure. Can we just move on?"

"If you can, yes," Jack said. "I'm glad you're here, brother. I'm glad you've come."

"As am I. I hope this expedition will prove to be good for both of us." Ren turned to take a last look at the wheat. "Good night, Jack," he said and walked alone back to the chateau.

Ren and Jack remained busy, and it was a relief to Jack that Ren wasn't overly eager to talk through every detail of their lives. They both continued to do their work, and within two days the decision on their route was made. The team assembled the following morning at the train station.

Biskra was still the most southerly point in the French rail system at that time, and they would reach it that day before sundown. The train passed slowly through the high plains, through long valleys, hour after hour through lush agricultural regions of Algeria with nothing to see but crops and grey mountain ranges in the distance and a few small lakes. Jack kept busy on the train with the men in his security detail as he discussed his past experiences with the Tuareg warriors. At last the train came into the station of Biskra. The Armée d'Afrique had a large fortress there and that meant the city also had two magnificent hotels to accommodate the French officers. The Royal Hotel was first class. Biskra also had a casino, the Dar-Diaf, with a theatre and a boisterous concert-room. Patrons there were entertained by local musicians and the Ouled Naïl dancing girls, the most alluring young tribal women painted and dressed only in scarves, chains and jewels, whose abdominal gyrations and hip quivering were said to drive men insane

Tamanrasset

with desire. Jack visited with Hans Mueller, but Ren chose to stay at the hotel.

In the morning, they learned that the Compagnie de l'Est Algérien was extending the train tracks south to Touggourt, and this made the route south much more secure. Their journey to Touggourt also gave some indication of the sort of route that lay ahead: Grassy plains gave way to dry, hardpacked tan-colored soil across a plain that was flat as far as the eye could see, interrupted only by dusty oasis villages–Stile, El Meghaïer, and Djamaa–although each was bustling with French soldiers and railway workers. The expedition camped near soldiers and tourists each night at whichever oasis came along. They made the trip to Touggourt in six days.

While far more isolated and ascetic than the Royal in Biskra, the Hotel de l'Oasis in Touggourt was still comfortable. A large oasis there sustained an enormous grove of nearly two hundred thousand date palm trees. Jack was able to secure the purchase of a small caravan of camels from an Arab trader in the marketplace, but the local French authorities recommended that they purchase supplies for the desert excursion at the next village to the south, one which was well-known as the point from which caravans regularly embarked across the northern Sahara to Libya and Egypt in the east.

They set off again on a journey of a mere one hundred and forty kilometers, accompanying a caravan of serious-minded but friendly Arab traders who were on their way to Egypt. The blue sky each day seemed impossibly wide, and the Sun beat down on them. Ren remained busy with Bert Hill and Tom Childers poring over maps that had huge white spaces of unexplored desert. At night, the Moon rose enormous and fat, a point of purity in the night, while a cascade of stars blanketed the sky. Everyone was excited. They arrived in Ouargla at the end of the eighth day.

Jack had been given a letter of introduction to a French merchant who had rooms available to let. The situation was quite acceptable, and they took a house with good ventilation and well-appointed with fine furniture that had, incredibly, been manufactured in China. Jack and Ren began at once to investigate the purchase of the supplies necessary for the expedition. From Ouargla, a direct path to Tamanrasset would likely take several weeks to traverse, but there was no established direct route. There was an oasis village many kilometers to the southwest of Ouargla called El Menia, and from there the expedition could journey to In Salah, but from there they would need to take an extremely long and dangerous path through the desert to the Hoggar mountains in order to reach Tamanrasset. This less direct path would take at least two months.

* * *

Ren was still trying to comprehend how his brother had materialized out of thin air. Renwick Villere had still been a small child when his family had moved to France, and despite his efforts, he had had difficulty with the language. He had felt isolated in a foreign land with only his brother to speak to until Ren was sent to England. It was not until long after he was grown that he had begun to wonder why his brother Jack had never been in touch. When Ren received notice from his trustees in Paris that Jack was to be declared dead, he finally went to France to make inquiries. Sadly, it took no time at all to learn that Jack had fled the country and why. There was nothing to be done. But here suddenly was his brother, back from the dead, and not demonstrably happy to see his younger sibling. Jack seemed an unnaturally calm, quiet, and observant man, and Ren understood that Jack did not want to be pressed about the past.

But of course Ren had no hesitance to show Jack the leather-bound package he had brought from Algiers which contained dozens of photographs, each picture depicting a single scroll of papyrus which contained ancient Arabic writings about Queen al-Kahina, the writings found by Gauckler in the archives of the museum in Algiers. The translations of the writings were still incomplete: Durant had said there were passages regarding the Queen's tomb that he could not read in part because of legibility and in part because the language had changed significantly during the twelve hundred years since the scrolls were written. He could not recognize many of the words and was certain that they were no longer in use, a vestige possibly of the pre-Arabic language spoken in more easterly regions such as Arabia and Persia, he thought. On Jack's advice, Ren asked the French authorities in Ouargla whether anyone in the town could look at the photographs of the Arabic scrolls for him. Unlikely, he was told, as more residents could read French than Arabic. The Imam could probably only read the Quran.

While Jack went to the marketplace to ask if anyone had traveled recently to El Menia, In Salah or the Hoggar mountains, Ren visited the mosque and conversed with the Imam in French. The Imam was an elderly man who appeared to have been sun-blinded; he was barely literate and could not make out any of the words in the one photograph of the scrolls that Ren had brought to show him. The Imam claimed that the Sheikha could read, but she traveled frequently and was probably away. He was hesitant to say more but agreed to escort Ren to her house.

The day had already become unbearably hot as Ren guided the nearly-blind Imam through an endless maze of identical alleyways baking in sunlight, turning here or there as directed, through archways and tunnels, turning at last down a wide alley that came to an abrupt end at a massive oak door. The door was the width of the entire street, about eight feet, and the height of one's shoulder. They approached reverently, and the old Imam knocked lightly for, he said, the Sheikha would not wish it to be known that she had been visited by a Westerner. A servant admitted them to a courtyard of which the ornate walls were spotlessly whitewashed, the floor was of green tiles and the roof was of glass. They were led into a cool, windowless reception room the length of one side of the house. It had low divans set around the walls leaving but a long narrow aisle from the entrance arch to the end of the room. Rising on a tier at the end opposite the arch was a higher, broader divan whose luxurious upholstering was made of the richest native silk. About the room, above the divans, were hung many silver ornaments and oil lamps and silver sprinklers filled with rosewater.

Two little girls giggled at Ren as they brought in a samovar, a cone of sugar, and a slim silver box containing tea biscuits. They poured a tea made in the native fashion which was brewed with large quantities of sugar and flavored with mint. Ren was reminded of the home of Madame Arthur in Algiers, the reconstruction of what had once been a grand Arabic residence. Here, however, he was in the genuine place where actual natives lived in the authentic manner. He felt strangely ill at ease, like a tourist. The Imam was chattering in some Berber dialect with the little girls and with a young Black African man who was also a servant; Ren could not understand what they were saying. Then a young woman entered the room, but this did not appear to be the Sheikha either: She was dressed in an inexpensive kaftan and wore a scarf that covered her head and neck, but her skin was pale and she had blue eyes like a Tuareg. She spoke to the Imam in Arabic for a few minutes, then she turned to Ren, and in perfect French, said to him:

"It is not clear to the Imam what you are requesting from the Sheikha, Monsieur, but she is away for a few days; I expect her to return at the end of the week. I am called Hajjah Bella. Perhaps I might be of assistance to you."

"Good morning, Madame. My name is Renwick Villere; I am a professor of archaeology associated with the National Museum of Antiquities in Algiers. My colleagues and I are preparing an expedition into the Sahara on behalf of the museum's trustees, and I am hoping to find someone here in town to look at certain scrolls I have brought with me, photographs of them at any rate. They are written in ancient Arabic, and I hoped to make one last effort to see if they can be translated."

"If you bring me the scrolls, I will assist you," the woman replied. "I have done such translations for the masters at al-Quaraouiyin."

"You mean at the university, in Fez?"

"Yes."

"Well, I, yes, I can bring photographs of the scrolls. Are you a student, or perhaps conducting research of your own?" He felt that the question was impertinent as soon as he spoke it; it was none of his concern what she was doing in Ouargla, but he was worried that perhaps somehow she was searching for the Queen's tomb as well.

"No, I am here merely as a guest of the Sheikha," she replied with a mild grimace. "I am studying with her."

"My apologies, Madame; I didn't mean to encroach upon private matters. I would be enormously grateful for your assistance; may I return tomorrow with the photographs?"

"Yes, tomorrow would be fine," she replied. She spoke to the male servant who had listened to her conversation in French without comprehension, then nodded farewell to Ren, and strode from the room.

From the Imam, Ren learned that the locals held "Hajjah Bella" in the highest regard, and many viewed her as a living saint or miracle worker. It was said that she was European but had been born in Africa, that she had emerged from the desert like a spirit and could fly like a hawk, that she could cure leprosy with a touch, that she had spoken to djinns, that she knew the Sultan of Morocco personally, and that she had heard the voice of Allah. There was such a great adoration of her that Ren lost all his suspicions. Furthermore, if she had really trained at al-Quaraouiyin, she might indeed be able to read the scrolls.

He returned to the Sheikha's house with his leather case the next morning and was led to a small separate room with a large glass window that let in the blazing sunlight, the

Tamanrasset

better for reading, he assumed. The young woman was seated at a wide wooden table and rose when Ren was shown in by the servant.

"Good morning, Madame, and thank you again for agreeing to assist me," he said striding forward and extending his hand. She rose and shook his hand firmly. She was now wearing khaki pants with a white shirt and boots, along with a white scarf to loosely cover her head, but Ren could now see that she was a young European woman, very pretty although with a somewhat gaunt and haunted look.

"It's no trouble at all," she replied, having put aside, it seemed, her coldness from the previous day. "In fact, I don't often get the opportunity to read these days, so this is really a pleasure for me. But may I ask, before you bring out the photographs, what you believe the scrolls contain and why you did not get them translated before you came to Ouargla?"

"With all due respect, Madame, you raise another issue that I must first address with you, one of secrecy. You see, I am an academic, conducting archaeological research for a reputable public institution. I am not a tomb raider, but there are others who would use the information I will impart to you for their personal enrichment, specifically through grave robbing and theft. As you are a scholar who I believe will understand the necessity of preserving our antiquity, I must ask you to keep this entire matter secret until such time as our research is published and our findings, if any, are displayed in the museum. You will be generously compensated for your time and for your discretion. Of course, if you don't agree or simply cannot read the scrolls, then there's no harm done anyway."

"You scare me, Professor," she teased him. "No, you need have no concerns; I certainly understand and agree with your request."

"Very well," he replied. "Then I will tell you right out that we are seeking the lost tomb of the Berber's great queen."

She gasped in surprise: "Do you mean al-Kahina?"

Ren was impressed that she knew whom he meant: "The very one, yes. Certain uncatalogued ancient writings were found quite by accident in the museum's archives in Algiers. The trustees of the museum began to translate them, and soon understood that they contain an account written contemporaneously by an unnamed Arab historian regarding the death of Queen al-Kahina. It was known only that the Queen had died in battle and her remains had disappeared. This Arab account describes how she was removed from the battlefield and taken to a secure location in the desert where she was entombed until the day she would be reborn, as the ancient Berbers believed."

"Ibn Khaldun wrote that she was beheaded, and her head was sent back to the Caliph in Damascus as proof that she had been killed," Bella replied.

Ren was taken aback. "I was not aware of Khaldun's account," he explained. "But ... I would judge that ... his report was written at least five hundred years after the fact, so I suppose it must be discounted on that basis. What we found in the museum is a contemporaneous account, and as you know the Arabs have always been very particular about recordkeeping. Furthermore, I might speculate that, at the time of her death, the Caliph would have been embarrassed that al-Kahina was secretly buried with all her worldly possessions, so it is hardly surprising that an alternative story was circulated publicly."

"That is very sound reasoning. And what is the difficulty with the scrolls that you were unable to have them translated in Algiers?"

"The museum's trustees were rightfully concerned that the information could be misused, so they kept the scrolls quite secret, perhaps too much so, and they are not as competent at translating the writing as I might have wished. I myself cannot read Arabic and only speak a little."

"I will look at them; you honor me with your trust," she said.

Ren opened his leather case which contained dozens of large photographs, each depicting another page of the scrolls, and Isabel began looking them over quite quickly, as if she were reading nothing more difficult than a copy of *Le Figaro*.

"These first pages summarize the Queen's history and provide details of the battle at Tabarka, as you said," she observed. "This page is just a list of all the Arab tribes which took part in the battle, the Kabyle, the Zenata, the Glawa, and so forth. Then here we find the first mention of her death and removal from the battlefield for burial by her followers. They were Berbers who had rejected Islam and practiced the old religion. It speaks of a sacred place in the mountains."

"Yes, and the location in the mountains is identified in a particular way, I believe."

"There is something about the location of the Sun in the sky, at the summer solstice, I believe."

"Yes, exactly," Ren said. "These passages have been analyzed by astronomical experts in Paris, and the account, in essence, places the location of the tomb below the Tropic of Cancer in a specific area of the Hoggar mountains. Unfortunately, the Earth's orbit is now understood to have a slight wobble, thus making it impossible to identify the exact location of the tomb with those data alone and, in any event, the Hoggar mountains have never been mapped."

"This passage here references the nearby villages, but I'd assume they no longer exist. Here is a description of the tomb," the young woman said, referring to one photograph. "It mentions a pyramidical mound."

"Does it describe the exterior of the mound in any greater detail?"

"There are long passages, and it will take time to decipher them. I see a reference to pillars. There is much more."

"It will still be a challenge to locate. And the contents of the tomb? I believe it says something about the hopes of her people."

She laughed. "No. You see, many of these are not even Arabic words. Here, for example," she pointed at a bit of writing that, to Ren, was nothing but a black swirl, "it's an Arabic transliteration of a Berber word for something, a thing for which there was no Arabic word at the time or perhaps because the account was conveyed orally to this recorder in Berber words, it was simply written phonetically. That's why your trustees couldn't read it, I'm certain."

"What does it say?"

"It translates as green gemstone, like an emerald, I assume. 'The emeralds of her ancestors,' it says."

"My God!" Ren exclaimed. Queen al-Kahina's tomb might well contain one of the great undiscovered treasures of the Maghreb: the Emeralds of the Garamantes!

* * *

Jack was aware that Ren had met with a local scholar but had no reason to ask the fellow's name. Had he been told that the scholar was a European woman, he would have known at once who it was, but it was not until Ren asked for his opinion on bringing a woman along on the expedition that he came to suspect that the scholar in question was, of course, Isabel.

"I want to come with you to talk to her about it," he said.

"Yes, if you wish," Ren replied.

As soon as he entered the sun-drenched reading room, Jack recognized her at once, and she him.

"Sergent!" She shouted joyfully and rushed over to hug Jack. He was so surprised that he actually smiled.

"What a pleasure to find you again," Jack told her as Ren looked on astonished.

"It must be written that we are bound together in some way, is it not?" Bella said, "and how do you come to know Doctor Villere?"

"Why, to be honest with you, he is my brother," Jack said, laying a hand on Ren's shoulder, "although I don't use the name Villere anymore. These days I am called Jacques Demain, or just Jack to you. You don't need to call me 'Sergent' anymore."

"You're brothers! Well, then it must be that all our fates are predestined. And I, who was known as Isabel Pedersen, have a new name as well. I now go simply by the name Hajjah Bella min Alsahra, or just Bella."

"A pleasure to meet you both," Ren said. "And may I please ask that you call me Ren; I am Doctor Villere only to my students."

"Come and sit with me, my friends," Bella insisted. "If I have learned anything from my friend Jack, it's that there is a great deal we should not say, and perhaps even more that we should not ask, but I must know how you come to be involved in this expedition, Jack. Please do tell me."

"I work for an associate of Durant's now," Jack said, "the man who is the money behind this expedition. It is entirely a coincidence that Ren was brought on to lead it; we had not seen each other for many years. But I must tell you how relieved I am to find you here, Bella. I am sorry that the last time I saw you, I was not able to be of more assistance to you."

"You didn't do anything wrong, Jack, but thank you nonetheless," she told him.

"The General and I were worried when you didn't return. You weren't harmed?"

"Only my pride," she answered. "No, I decided not to go back, but I appreciate that you were concerned for me. It was my mistake to not come bid you all farewell."

"It's astonishing that you know each other," Ren said. "It does seem like kismet. Thanks to Bella, we now have a much better sense of where to look for the Queen's tomb, and I have a much better idea of what we might find there. You cannot guess how important this expedition has become: I believe we are seeking one of the great, legendary treasures of the African continent. And, Bella, Jack and I have come specifically to ask you to join us, if you're able."

Jack laughed, "she's definitely able," he said smiling, knowing full well that Bella was capable. But Bella took on a serious expression and looked hard at Ren and then at Jack, and he could see she was uncertain.

"In Islam we use the expression 'mashallah;' it means 'Allah has willed it'," she said finally. "I believe it is not a coincidence that we are met here in Ouargla. Allah has put us here together for a reason. I do not know truly whether I wish to join you, but I am certain Allah wants me to join you. Yes, I will come on your expedition, but what our true purpose may be, we have yet to discover."

Just then they could hear the muezzin begin the call for prayers at the mosque nearby, and a chill ran down Jack's back. Their journey would take them across the Tropic of Cancer, deep into the desert lands controlled by ruthless Tuareg warriors. They would need to reach Tamanrasset by mid-summer to use the astronomical data in the ancient Arabic writings and then hopefully locate the undiscovered tomb itself. The expedition would have to begin at once.

***

Ahmad often sat in the library at al-Quaraouiyin to read the latest newspapers and to speak with his mentors Muhammad al-Kattani and Omar Benayoun. The Ulama's new weekly newspaper now often included editorials critical of the Sultan's government, and Omar Benayoun, who had once been considered a reformer, had become the most conservative member of the Ulama in Fez. That panel of scholars, in the minds of many, had replaced the Sultan as the chief defender of Islam in Morocco. The light of the oil lamps in the university's library cast long shadows on the stone floors as Ahmad stared at the printed pages, but his thoughts were elsewhere.

As a representative of his homeland, Ahmad had become a fixture in Fez and was well-known to government officials and foreign diplomats alike, but he often felt he was playing a role out of obligation rather than any personal desire. This was not the duty he was raised to fulfill, but he would perform it each day as well as he could. It was on one such day that he received an invitation to an event being hosted by a French businessman, a wealthy landowner with large farms across French Algeria who likely wanted to smooth the flow of commerce from his producers there to the marketplaces of Morocco and Europe. The thought of mingling with Westerners filled Ahmad with a quiet dread, but such opportunities helped his family and others from the Wadi Saoura.

The evening event was at a fine riad near the Sultan's palace in the heart of Fez. It was an immense spectacle, a dazzling display of naked wealth. As Ahmad approached the entrance, the warm evening air carried the scents of nearby gardens. He was met by a parade of servants dressed in flowing robe-like costumes, their faces masked. They guided guests to the inner chambers where the sound of a lute echoed softly in the background, and the rhythmic clink of silver cutlery and the quiet hum of conversation filled the air. The central courtyard had been transformed to look like an oasis, not the places that Ahmad knew well from actual experience but a rich man's gaudy imitation. The surrounding columns were decorated to look like date palms with torches flickering between them casting a warm golden glow over the lush greenery and hanging ivy. Tapestries embroidered with the royal colors of green and gold hung from the walls. Low tables were scattered across the floor, draped in rich silk cloths, each holding trays of pastries, figs, and glasses of wine or mint tea.

The other guests were a mix of well-dressed diplomats, wealthy traders, and local businessmen. French, Spanish, and British diplomats mingled in their evening attire—dark suits, starched collars, and waistcoats—all bearing some insignia of their respective countries. Officials from the Sultan's Makhzen wore long, embroidered caftans, fez hats, and gold jewelry intended to impart their importance as they exchanged pleasantries with the Westerners. The atmosphere was calm but tense, as if the international crowd was aware of a delicate balance of power in the room.

Ahmad spent an hour speaking with French and British men interested in doing business in the southern regions. All wanted assurances that the violence there had been suppressed. Meanwhile, at the far end of the courtyard, on a platform draped in rich velvet, stood the white-haired host, the French landowner from Algeria. He greeted each guest with care. However, the guest in the greatest demand was a German businessman named Heinrich Richter von Falkenhayn. It was a name Ahmad had heard before, and it was evident that Herr Richter's presence in the room was discomfiting to the French and British diplomats who were uncertain whether to speak with him or, if so, how friendly they should be. In recent years it had become clear that Imperial Germany wanted to invest in Africa, and with the advent of the new special relationship between France and

Great Britain, the Germans were now afraid they were going to be shut out completely. Ahmad knew that Herr Richter had been touring Morocco in order to cultivate potential trading partners, although he had not visited south of the Atlas mountains. Ahmad was determined to speak with him.

Ahmad approached the German and bowed respectfully. "Peace be unto you, Herr Richter. If I may, my name is Ahmad ibn Mostepha al-Haybah; I am from the Wadi Guir and Wadi Saoura regions of Morocco and represent the merchants and traders there."

Richter bowed as well. "An honor to make your acquaintance, mein Herr. Yes, I hoped to meet someone from your provinces here tonight for there has been little opportunity on my travels to visit."

"I understand that the journey over the mountains is difficult, and yet there are many in our region eager to do business with foreign interests."

"Are they not the captive business partners of the French already? France lays claim to much of the territory you say you represent."

"It is regrettably true that French soldiers maintain order in specific regions of Morocco with the Sultan's consent, inasmuch as the Sultan is idle and a poor judge of character, but it would be incorrect to say that the territory belongs to France or that the French have an exclusive monopoly on trade there."

Richter smiled. "I have not heard your countrymen speak so bluntly of your sovereign, yet it is not surprising to those of us who have watched France creep like an infection deeper and deeper into your lands. It is an infection, don't you agree?"

"That is a conversation for another occasion, I believe, one with more privacy," Ahmad replied. "But I am at your disposal any time, Herr Richter, if you would also permit me, as is my duty, to share with you some information regarding the many commodities offered in my distant provinces. May I call upon you?"

Richter nodded. "As you wish, I am at the Hotel Cavilla."

Ahmad nodded as others came also seeking a word with the German.

The next morning, Ahmad arrived at the hotel and Herr Richter allowed him to speak at length about the Wadi Guir and Wadi Saoura, the Tafilalt and the Touat, all regions which, thanks to a string of oases that stretched for hundreds of kilometers, produced a large amount of dates, wheat, and silage, as well as goats, camels, leather goods, and metalworks.

"But as I suggested yesterday," Richter interrupted, "would not the French authorities in your region object to the locals engaging in business with German interests?"

"I don't agree that France is entitled to take any position regarding the persons with whom Moroccans choose to do business," Ahmad replied. "But if you have some concerns in that regard, perhaps Germany should express its support of Moroccan sovereignty, using the exact terms with which France in the past has professed its own position. That would make it clear to all that German businesses are here on an equal footing with the French and British and Spanish."

"Except that the British and Spanish have expressly agreed not to interfere with France's actions in Morocco," Richter said.

Ahmad had read in the newspapers that France had recently entered into new agreements with both Spain and Britain, but he didn't know they had anything to do with Morocco. "What do you mean?" He asked.

"In the case of Spain, as you know the Spanish have occupied certain port cities for many generations, but they have now agreed to allow France jurisdiction over the rest of Morocco, provided that she preserves Spain's existing interests; with regard to Great Britain, their agreements state which countries in Africa each will control while promising to preserve each other's trade rights, and the British have given Morocco to the French."

"But this is not something to which the Sultan has agreed."

"Why, it is well known that Abd al-Aziz is a puppet of the French; he must acquiesce to their demands since France sustains the Sultan's government. Our German diplomats are incensed, for the French and British behave as though they are entitled to keep the whole world just between themselves. By contrast, we in Germany also prefer Morocco to remain a stable, independent nation, as you claim it to be."

"And what will Germany do to support us?"

"That, I'm afraid, I do not know, but I would be surprised if it is not already under discussion."

Although Ahmad's meeting with Herr Richter was ultimately less fruitful than he had hoped, an answer to his question came sooner than either could have possibly expected, and with unintended consequences.

That spring the German Kaiser, Wilhelm II, while sailing in the Mediterranean, elected to come ashore at

Tangier. He met with representatives of the Sultan and toured the city. Before departing, the Kaiser gave a speech to his countrymen in which he declared his support for the independent sovereignty of Morocco. No one could report exactly what the Kaiser said and accounts differed wildly, but the speech was received as an ultimatum in France and Britain to keep out of Morocco and that led to talk of war. To temper the situation, Germany's Chancellor called for an international conference to discuss Morocco's future. It seemed unlikely that Germany could halt French colonial expansion, but a conference was hoped to enhanced Germany's prestige.

At Algeciras, the Spanish port across the bay from Gibraltar, representatives from France, Spain and Britain stood in lockstep regarding Morocco. An agreement was reached, to which Germany was humiliatingly forced to consent: It left the preservation of Morocco entirely in the hands of France. The French were authorized to regulate Morocco's police and customs, prevent the smuggling of arms, and create a new State Bank of Morocco that would issue banknotes backed by gold. The new bank would impose strict caps on spending by the Sultan's government and be overseen by bankers from Germany, Britain, France, and Spain. New laws would establish the right of Europeans to own land in Morocco, and new taxes were to be levied towards public works. The Sultan of Morocco retained control only of a small police force in certain port cities, a force composed of Moroccan Muslims who would be overseen and paid by French and Spanish officers. A new Inspector-General would be Swiss.

The Sultan's delegates found the agreement so abhorrent that they refused to sign, but Sultan Abd al-Aziz ratified it anyway. Across Morocco, there were immediate calls for his removal.

* * *

The Sun had only just begun to lighten the night sky, the Moon had set, and the stars had already faded. The days were blistering hot, but the nights were still frigid. Ren was wrapped tightly in a new bisht, a wool cloak worn over his usual expeditionary outfit, as he joined others walking from Ouargla out to Gara Krima, the deep well that was the last place for caravans to water their camels and refill their skins before entering the desert. At one moment, Ren was walking down an ordinary, unpaved street between silent tan-colored riads, and the next he had stepped out onto hard-packed fine rocks and sand on a well-worn path to the well. Alone in the distance stood the flat-topped mesa upon which the well of Gara Krima was located. Others who were also departing Ouargla that day were walking with him, all Arab or Berber or Black African men who were silently steeling themselves for the great ordeal ahead. Unlike those men, whose caravans would be heading east towards Libya and Egypt, Ren's expedition would head south, straight into the deep desert.

Bella had slept in a tent near the well, and Jack and his soldiers had slept in other tents beside hers. Jack was already awake and checking on the final preparations when Ren arrived, still long before sunrise. "We're all ready to go," Jack told him. Tom and Bert were having a last-minute lesson on how to ride a camel from the expedition's guide, a tall dark-skinned man that Bella had hired for them. His

Tamanrasset

name was Ayrad, the son of a Black African man and a Tuareg woman; he was also a Muslim, as were most of the soldiers on Jack's security team, and they were all zealously devoted to Bella. Bella laughed with them and helped Tom up when he landed with his face in the sand. Poor Bert, in his already well-worn expedition outfit, had a camel spit on his chest.

Meanwhile, former Legionnaires Hans Mueller and Fedir Andreev were working with the expedition's staff of laborers and attendants to make sure all the supplies and equipment were properly packed. There would be no chance to re-supply (other than the water they would take from local wells) until they reached El Menia in about two weeks, and they were uncertain what reception or supplies they would find there.

"Let's take a look," Ren said, and he and Jack walked towards the mesa's edge which stood high above the desert floor. At that height, they could see for perhaps fifty kilometers and easily discern whether there were any encampments or movement on the hard plain. As they walked together, Bella joined them. She was dressed in pants like the men, but her worn bisht, patched and stained, looked like she had owned it for many years. "Good morning, Madame," Ren said to her. She smiled and nodded to him as they came to a stop on the edge of the cliff. There was a gentle breeze, but the enormous, barren plain of sand before them was still and silent. Ren was excited but also aware that he had never been tested in the desert the way his companions had been. He and Jack had carried on as if there had been no thirty year gap in their relationship, as if Jack had never run off to join the French army in Africa, or more likely the Foreign Legion since he had been wanted by the police in Paris and could not have enlisted under his real name. And as for Bella, the fact that she knew Jack in some unspoken professional role testified to her own history of adventure and courage. What Ren had was educated good sense and determination, and despite his lack of practical desert experience, he was eager to go.

As they stood looking out at the desert, Bella turned to Ren: "I dreamt last night that we three were standing like Ali Baba at the entrance to the den of forty thieves, looking through a doorway cut into the mountain, into a huge chamber filled with jewels piled in great heaps and bags and bags of gold and silver coins and bales of silk and wool. Will that dream come true?"

Ren laughed. "No, there won't be a room full of treasure; I have never heard of, much less seen, any such hoard even when there are artefacts of gold or pieces of jewelry. Anyway, each piece must be photographed and catalogued in situ before we even think of touching them, and, I mean, that's assuming we find the queen's tomb in the first place."

"I was hoping it would be more like 'King Solomon's mines'," Jack complained.

"You ought to hope that no one has been in the tomb since the queen was left there. All too often sites like hers have already been looted, and for her tomb to remain untouched after twelve hundred years is more good luck than we should hope for. But it will still be an archaeological marvel, and the relics I hope to recover for the museum will be priceless nonetheless." It would be fine to let the others know that the tomb might contain modest treasures, but Ren believed that to even name the Emeralds of the

Garamantes aloud would place the expedition at a new level of scrutiny and risk. He had decided not to mention the gemstones by name, even though he suspected that Bella had guessed. Nevertheless, Ren thought ruefully about his work with Flinders Petrie in Egypt, specifically, the barren pharaonic tombs they had excavated there. Nearly every tomb he entered had already been plundered. It was not something he would tell the others, but it did temper his optimism somewhat.

"Let's just try not to die on the way there," Bella said.

"Or coming back," Jack added.

Within the hour, just as the Sun rose over the distant horizon far to the east, they set off. Ren and Bella led with Ayrad, followed by Bert and Tom, then the official photographer, the two journalists who had just arrived from the National Geographic, a French surveyor-engineer and a German cartographer, then Jack with Hans and Fedir and their native Chaamba soldiers, all French-speaking former Tirailleurs, followed by a crowd of Berber and Black African porters, attendants, cooks, wranglers and laborers, all told fifty-seven people and seventy animals, camels and mules.

They rode on, hour by hour, and the air soon became quite hot. It would be a short day of travel, but they would begin the next day's journey much earlier in the morning. They quickly came across a small oasis—only a few date palms remained beside a dry well. There, the desiccated carcass of a camel lay at the base of one of the palms, the animal's mouth clamped around the trunk of the tree. It had died of dehydration while desperately seeking to suckle moisture from the fibrous wood.

"The native men will take that as a bad omen," Bella said to Ren. She leaned over and spat on the ground. Their guide Ayrad, dressed all in black with his face veiled, uncovered his mouth to do the same, then he spoke to Bella in Arabic for several minutes. She told Ren: "He says that the next few days we will see the remains of a great many animals, animals who strayed too far from the wells and got lost or abandoned by caravans coming up from the south who did not bring sufficient water." Indeed, they soon came across the whitened bones of an entire herd of large Mehari camels, dozens of animals that had all died together in a group. The members of the expedition were silent as they passed through the boneyard, no doubt thinking of how they would eventually appear themselves if they were to die in the deep desert.

The expedition stopped that day after eight hours of travel, and a camp was quickly set up with tents so everyone could stay out of the sun for the afternoon. Rest came first, then Bella joined the Muslim members of the crew to pray in the late afternoon; Jack believed that encouraging the men to follow the dictates of their religion with her would foster their sense of duty and protectiveness over the group.

A small dinner followed at dusk. The warm water from the skins had an unusual taste, not to mention sandy grit and salt, but it helped to wash down the first day's meal of dried camel meat, unleavened bread, and dates. After an additional rest period, the expedition set off again and traveled with small rest stops until the middle of the next morning. Jack encouraged Ayrad to set a fast pace for their marches, and they made excellent progress on the first full march across the hamada.

Tamanrasset

Three days later, they made an unexpected find. It was nearly dawn, and the members of the expedition were looking forward to stopping for a brief meal at sunrise. Ren sat upon his camel quietly dozing off and on, although he had been warned repeatedly that he could slip off his camel and be lost at night. Suddenly, out of the gloom, he dreamt that a great archway rose up before him. It was really three archways, a huge central one and two smaller ones on each side, separated by immense unadorned pillars. They were certainly not Roman or Greek, Ren thought, but they even looked pre-Phoenician. Then he awoke fully, for the archway was not a dream, but a huge reality looming from the darkness right in front of them. Ayrad came up next to Ren: "Not here," he said cryptically.

"Well of course it's here," Ren replied testily. "We can both see it. Bella, you see the archway as well, don't you?"

Ayrad spoke quickly to her, and then she explained: "The arch, it is not supposed to be here. He believes we have gotten off the proper track for he has never seen this before and does not know where we are."

"We had better stop, then," Ren concluded. "Besides, I want to ask Bert what he thinks about this architecture."

"The archway looks early Egyptian to me," Bert pronounced. "The columns are fluted and the archway is slightly corbelled, the walls are stepped inwards as they rise to the horizontal stone that is laid across the top."

However, even more amazing was that, beyond the archway, there were ruins of an entire abandoned city, and none of those on the expedition had ever heard of it before. Ren decided they had better stop to take a good look, so camp was set up while he, Bert, Tom, and Jack spread out to look around. Undoubtedly, the city had been constructed around an oasis, but it had been abandoned and then devoured by sand and wind. Well-preserved streets intersected at regular intervals, but only the foundations of the buildings remained intact. Here and there an especially large building suggested a temple or public edifice of some communal purpose, or possibly a "palace" like that of the Pharaoh Akhenaten in Amarna.

Over a breakfast of bread, dates and nuts, Ren said to Bert and Tom, "I can't shake the opinion that this city must predate any known Egyptian civilizations. The layout, the materials—it just doesn't line up with what we'd see in the early dynastic period of Egypt."

"I agree," Bert replied. "At first, I thought it might be a minor Egyptian outpost, but there's no way that's right. Look at the construction techniques: The stonework is crude compared to what the Egyptians were doing even in the Old Kingdom. It's much more in line with earlier, pre-Egyptian cultures. This site definitely existed before the emergence of pharaonic Egypt."

"The pottery fragments I've found seem to match the Egyptian tradition," Tom pointed out, "although I admit the absence of hieroglyphic writing. No Egyptian scripts here."

"May I show you this," Bert said excitedly as he uncovered a flint axe head sitting in his wicker basket: "I found it quite nearby, and it appears to be made from local stone. Now, my first thought was that the absence of a better quality material from the Nile Valley indicates a civilization largely isolated from or even pre-dating pharaonic culture. But then it occurred to me that this chipping technique is not merely pre-pharaonic but absolutely ancient. Why, this axe head could easily be 200,000 or even 300,000 years old!"

"I agree, these are exactly the sort of marks I would expect to see on arrowheads found in Neolithic sites near Tunis," Ren said.

"That's consistent with my impressions of the city itself," Tom added. "I mean, the architecture was the first thing that struck me as suspiciously old: Mudbrick for large walls, simple dwellings? It's a lot closer to what we'd expect to see in Neolithic African settlements than anything found in early Egyptian cities. Not to mention the absence of large, monumental tombs or mortuary temples—the Egyptians were already constructing them by the time they started building their major cities, but here there's nothing of the sort."

"Absolutely," Ren said. "This could be one of the first truly ancient prehistoric civilizations in the Sahara, lost to time and buried beneath centuries of desert sands. It's fascinating."

"Will we have time to work here for a while?" Tom asked.

"Unfortunately no, not if we mean to stick to our schedule," Ren said sadly, "and I'm afraid we must stay on schedule, though I'm not prepared to go into all the reasons at this time. But we will hopefully return. I'll speak to Ayrad and make certain we have a good gauge of our location recorded on our maps."

But Ayrad, in fact, had no idea where they were. Somehow during the night, the expedition had veered off course and had begun to travel easterly, perhaps by overcompensating for the movement of the stars from east to west. Ren and Jack were extremely angry with their guide and threatened to leave him behind. By simple good fortune, however, their French surveyor had been playing around with a sextant, trying to determine whether it would be equally useful for calculating a celestial position in the desert as it was indispensable at sea, and he announced that they were still a significant distance from their intended destination. The rest of the day was spent at the mysterious city, which Bella suggested they call "Iram, because of the pillars."

"I'm not familiar with that. What does that mean?" Tom asked her.

"It's from the Quran," she said:

> Did you not see how Allah dealt with the people of Iram, they of the lofty pillars unmatched in any other land, who carved their homes from the rocks of the stone valley like the temples of the Pharaoh? They transgressed throughout the land, spreading much corruption, so Allah unleashed on them a scourge of punishment, for He is truly vigilant.

"Ah, yes, very apt," Tom smiled at her approvingly.

"Yes, that's perfect, thank you," Ren said.

Ren spent the morning running about the vacant city taking notes with Bert and Tom, but by noon the sun was high and the heat was unbearable. After an afternoon of rest, a decision was made to depart early in the evening to make up for the day they had already lost. The expedition set off again shortly before the Sun set and headed west-south-west, attempting to return to their intended path somewhat below their current latitude. Ren actually managed to fall asleep and slip from his camel that night, but he was not the only person to be struggling with the schedule. Were he to speak openly, however, Ren would have admitted that he also still retained a certain weakness, or perhaps an anxiety, because of the enormous absence he felt. Yet, overall, he did feel much better. He had brought together a new team, he had reunited with his brother, and he had made an extraordinary new colleague in Bella. With Tom and Bert, and all the staff and soldiers who were still smiling and excited, Ren felt exceedingly proud of his little crew.

By mid-morning, they could see their next destination a few kilometers off in the distance: Hassi-Inifel, a French fort that was home to a Company of the Méharistes Sahariennes, the native mounted infantry commanded by French officers.

***

As they approached the fort of Hassi-Inifel, the expedition crossed a plain of pale pink sand upon which regularly-spaced stone markers had been placed. Jack immediately realized that they had entered an enormous cemetery with more markers than he could count, and he didn't care for it. During his years in the Foreign Legion, he had known commanders who made a show of their lost comrades in this manner as a sort of threat to the living. Now, indeed, this was a desolate fort, one situated in the middle of the desert, a way-station between pivotal locations like Ouargla and In Salah, places that might call for reinforcements, but, while Hassi-Inifel itself was built to last, the native soldiers in it were considered expendable. No relief was likely to come for them if the Tuaregs rose up from the desert and attacked, so the message of the enormous cemetery was that the men would either defend the fort to the last man or end up in the ground with their comrades.

The expedition came to a halt a hundred meters or so from the fort, and Ren and Jack left their camels to walk up to the massive wood gate. The high stone walls of the fort had loopholes from which the defenders could shoot, but in many respects the fort looked to Jack more like a prison: It was designed to keep men in as well as keep them out. There was no way to drop over the high outer walls, no exit but the barred gate.

"Who are you, and what is your business?" A soldier inquired from the battlement above.

"My name is Doctor Renwick Villere. I am an archaeologist leading a scientific expedition on behalf of the Museum of Antiquities in Algiers. We are journeying to a potential excavation site, and I'm afraid we got a bit off course," he said.

"You have a small army," the soldier complained.

"Of course we have a security staff to provide us with some measure of protection in the desert, to fend off potential bandits and whatnot, but the rest are laborers for the journey and the excavation. My colleague here is Jacques Demain; he works for Marcel Gallé, of whom I am certain you have heard. Monsieur Demain is in charge of our security."

Jack nodded to the soldier. "Who is your commanding officer?" He asked.

"Our Commandant is Capitaine Jean de Saint-Avit."

Tamanrasset

"Will you ask your commander if we may water our camels and fill our water skins at your well?" Jack asked. "We don't mean to overstay our welcome."

From the fort there was silence.

"What do you think is going on?" Ren asked Jack quietly.

"They may be getting the Commandant," he replied, but ordinarily the Capitaine would have come to the wall already or the gates would have simply been opened as it was the French custom to allow desert travelers, at least European ones, access to their wells.

After waiting a few more minutes, Jack began to get uneasy. There were only two men up on the fort's battlement, and they were difficult to see. Jack wasn't certain, but he thought they might not have been in uniform. But there was also no indication that the fort had been attacked, and there was nothing outside to suggest there was anything amiss.

"Perhaps you could ask the Commandant to send an officer out to speak with us; we need to go check on our camp," Jack shouted up. He took Ren's arm and whispered: "We should make a graceful retreat."

As Jack and Ren began walking together back to the rest of the expedition, Hans came over to meet them.

"I don't have a good feeling about this fort," Jack said. "It's possible that the French officers have been murdered. I believe the men we were speaking to were native soldiers, but they looked out of uniform. Hans, did you ever hear of Jean de Saint-Avit? They say he is the commandant of the fort."

"Oh, yes, yes, I know of Saint-Avit. He is a ... well, I came across the man once in Oran, when we were both off-duty.

He had gotten into an altercation with some locals there. He is a very violent and prejudiced man. It is no surprise that his superiors have sent him to the middle of the desert. But you think he is dead?"

"It's easy to imagine him trapped inside with a Company of native soldiers, and how that might turn out for him," Jack said. "There's no way we can get inside those walls if they don't allow it, even if we had artillery, which of course we don't."

"But can we make it to the next oasis without stopping?" Ren asked.

Suddenly there was the sound of a sharp report. Jack turned back to the fort and saw a puff of smoke from the battlement. He shook his head.

"Now the bastards are firing at us," he said, unsurprised.

"They what? They're shooting at us!?" Ren shouted.

"We better withdraw to a safe distance," Jack replied calmly. "We can't stay here."

"Can we reach the next well?" Hans asked.

"We need to go whether we can reach the well or not," Jack said.

Two more shots were fired before they returned to the main body of the expedition, and Ren and Hans quickly got the group moving again while Jack took a rifle and fired off a few shots at the gate to let the soldiers know they should not come out. As the group got moving, Jack and Hans waited to see if anyone from the fort would pursue them, but after a while it seemed the expedition was in the clear.

"How is it coming along with your brother?" Hans asked suddenly.

Jacked eyed him skeptically for a moment.

"I have a brother in Cologne," Hans said. "I have not spoken to him for seven or eight years."

"I'm sure he'd like to hear from you," Jack said.

"Your brother is no fool, Jack. He must know most everything by now," Hans said. "except possibly why you shot Mills. I have my own suspicions about that, but …," he shrugged, "the less said, I know. Still, if you hadn't shot him, I would have."

Jack laughed. "You're a trustworthy friend, Hans."

Ayrad knew of another well to the west, and Ren made the decision that they would go there immediately. The day became extremely hot, and the march went on through the afternoon. The sun beat down on their heads, and at the same time the glare was reflected up from the sand into their faces. The smell of the camels became nauseating. The water in their skins became almost undrinkably hot, which raised the question of what was going on with the blood in their veins. Jack pushed them as quickly as he could, afraid that the native soldiers from the French fort might still pursue them, but the heat dragged everyone down into a stupor; he, Bella, and Ayrad were the only ones seemingly unaffected.

The Sun began to descend towards the western horizon. Its rays shone right in their faces. Ahead of them was a low ridge and, according to Ayrad, a steep-sided ravine. They reached the edge of the ravine just as the Sun reached the horizon and the sky before them was fiery red. In front of them, they found a split in the ground, twenty or thirty meters wide, that extended north to south as far as they could see in each direction. The darkening ravine looked to be about ten meters deep.

"We must get down into the ravine," Ayrad had Bella translate for him. "You cannot see the entrance to Aïn Taïba from here."

"Entrance?" Jack inquired.

"There is a cave in which a spring may be found and a pool of fresh water. I do not know if the cave is to the north or south of where we are standing."

Jack said: "The Sun is down, so we have that relief. How long is this ravine, and how far is the cave from the north end?"

"I'd guess it's about ten kilometers long. I have only entered from the north end. The cave is two or three kilometers south of the north end; there is a large opening in the eastern wall at the floor of the ravine."

"We may as well send the camels north along the edge to where they can get down into the ravine," Jack said. "Some of the people can climb down here with ropes and locate the cave."

It was another couple of hours until the entire expedition arrived at the pool of water, after what had become a twenty-eight hour march. Everyone was exhausted, and a few of the laborers had become ill from the heat and sun. Bella met with Ren and Jack that evening to ask that the expedition be allowed to rest for a day, since the cave was cool and shaded and water was plentiful. Both agreed.

* * *

Following a few uneventful days of fast night marches, the expedition arrived one morning at El Goléa, a large town with an abandoned ancient fortress perched high upon a ridge and a body of standing water known as the Lac de

Hassi El Gara. For Bella, who spoke frequently with all the porters, laborers and soldiers on the expedition, the town was much like the places they had grown up, and they were grateful for the opportunity to pray at the mosque.

Bella and many of the expedition's members went together to the mosque to pray at mid-day. Walking down the narrow streets of the sandy, khaki-colored village towards the minaret from which the muezzin called the faithful to prayer, Bella looked like a saint in a fresh, white abaya and hijab surrounded by the tall, strong young men of the expedition. People stared and whispered for some had heard of Hajjah Bella and were amazed that she had come to El Goléa. People who might otherwise have prayed at home came to the mosque that day despite the mid-day heat, and the small interior soon became crowded with people who wanted to see her.

Afterwards, she stepped outside to talk with the Imam, a tall man with large brown eyes. She approached him with her eyes cast down, while those who accompanied her from the expedition stood patiently in the shade of the building watching. "As-salaamu alaykum, Imam Tahtawi," she said.

"Wa alaikom salaam," he replied, "we are most honored to have you attend our mosque, Sayyidah. Fruitful indeed are the believers, but especially those who humble themselves in prayer."

"Glory be to Allah. I apologize if my presence was disruptive."

"Nothing happens without the permission of Allah. Many people came to pray today that I have not seen in many months, so on balance your presence was a blessing."

"I am traveling with a scientific expedition, Sayyid. We are crossing the desert, and many of those involved are good Muslims. May I ask, on their behalf, for your blessing for our journey?"

"I am honored you would come to me for a blessing, as it is said that you are a powerful marabout. Of course, I will say a dua for your journey."

"Thank you, Sayyid; with your blessing, I know we will be kept safe from harm."

There were two reasons why she wanted the Imam's blessing. The first, very simply, was that it would mean a great deal to her and to the members of the expedition and give them hope for a safe and successful journey. The other reason was that many of the town's residents, already convinced that Bella was a powerful marabout and possibly even a djinn, would come to her at their camp to ask for her blessing (or, in some cases, to ask that she curse someone with whom they were feuding). By asking the Imam for his blessing, she hoped that people would see him as the one with power rather than her. Her tactic was somewhat successful. As she and the members of the expedition walked back to their camp on the edge of town, only two people stopped her. In the past she had tried to explain that she had no magical power and refused payments, but increasingly she felt this only disappointed those who sought hope and inspiration. It was not her responsibility to change their beliefs and many of their requests came with a payment of food that would benefit her companions, so she often indulged a few requests and had become adept at a quick flick of her fingers or arms to provide the blessing or curse requested.

When they returned to the camp she went directly to Ren's tent and challenged him to a round of backgammon.

Later that evening Jack came to look over the maps with them. Bella thought how much they looked alike, although Ren was a bit younger and perhaps a little less gray than Jack. But who were they really, she wondered? From her time with Jack in Morocco (and the information provided by General Lyautey), she was aware of Jack's many years in the desert serving in the Foreign Legion, yet his past remained unknown. It was quite surprising to her that he had left the service and put the name of Sergent Demoreau behind him. The soldiers on their expedition had already guessed that Jack was a former non-commissioned officer and an American, thus he had certainly been a Legionnaire. What Bella also knew was that nothing could rattle Jack; even his mild drinking seemed more a reaction to boredom than apprehension. He drank when he wasn't worried or busy or in danger. But he was also the steadier one. Ren ran hot or cold, either ablaze with excitement or inertly watching and listening in quiet contemplation. He too, she could tell, had been worn down, and while he would readily discuss his work or education at great length, his personal life remained unspoken. Perhaps, in the end, there was no more to him than what you saw. Not that she was any better, she admitted. She never spoke of her dead husband or what had happened in Fez, or in Timbuktu, or in Figuig with Ahmad. Perhaps one of the reasons she liked Ren and Jack was that they didn't pry into the dark recesses of her life. They were eager to support each other. They knew their responsibilities, and they treated the others with respect. She sat to look over the maps with them, curious about the direction they had come and where they were going; there was a long journey still ahead, but she felt it was right for her to continue with these two men with whom she felt such a bond.

It was a relief when they departed the next morning before daybreak. By sunrise they were back in the deep desert, on hard, rocky terrain, flat and barren as far as the eye could see. The sky to the east turned yellow, and then the Sun slowly rose over the horizon. Several days later, and with several more days before they would reach In Salah, the expedition entered a great field of wind-blown sand dunes. The soft, light sand had been blown into huge, shifting crests reaching two or even three hundred meters in height. It would be insanity to climb over such crests, so the expedition's progress slowed to a crawl as it made its way back and forth through the deep valleys of sand.

It was not generally too awkward for Bella to be the only woman on the expedition, but there were times when she wished for a bit more privacy. They had camped one day on a wide plain between two enormous dunes of sand to rest for the afternoon; unlike her last desert passage, Bella now had a tarpaulin tent just for herself which the porters erected each time they stopped. After a light supper, as the Sun set below the western horizon and the temperatures fell to a pleasant warmth, she decided to go for a brief walk in the dunes, careful not to lose her direction back to the camp. Eventually, she began to climb to the top of a crest of sand. The fine particles cascaded away from her feet with each step up, but she still made enough headway to eventually reach the summit. Far to the west the sunset still illuminated the sky low on the horizon, and a mild breeze blew fresh air on her face. She removed her hijab to let the wind blow through her brown hair which had grown long and wavy. She shrugged off her cloak and unbuttoned the front of her white, collared shirt. The breeze crept through her clothes, and she recalled the time in the desert when she felt the cold wind caress her. There were moments, she thought, when she still longed to be touched. And that thought led to another, that perhaps she would someday like to be married again and have children and live a quiet life.

The next morning, the expedition made it out of the sand dunes and Ayrad led them to the well of Hassi Berkan. Here, they found something they did not expect. A small, one-room stone building had been constructed, although it looked abandoned. As the camels were being watered and the skins were being refilled, Jack and Bella went to the small building and, to their surprise, the door suddenly swung open and standing before them was an emaciated, white-skinned man dressed in rags with a long, straggly beard. He was hollow-eyed and filthy and looked quite shocked to have been disturbed.

"I apologize for interrupting you," Jack said. "We're a scientific expedition and mean you no harm. We've only stopped to replenish our water. Is this your well? May we be of any assistance to you?"

"Are you Christians?" The man demanded to know.

"Uh, yes," Jack said.

"What about them?" The man asked, pointing at the rest of the men.

"I believe most of them are Muslim," Jack said turning to Bella, "isn't that right, Madame?"

"Yes," she said firmly. "I take it you're an evangelist?"

"Infidels! They must all profess faith in our savior," he croaked at them.

"Well, I don't think we have time for that," Jack said. "Besides, it's none of my concern who they worship, there are so many gods to choose from."

"That's blasphemy," the man said angrily. He turned and reached to the back of his little cave-like hermitage to take hold of a ridiculously long and rusted sword. When Jack saw it, he pulled the door of the building shut and held it by the loop of rope on the front. They could hear the hermit slashing pitifully at the back of the door.

"I don't wish to lock him in there," Jack said, "but we can't have him attacking our fellows."

"I will talk to him; I can calm him down," Bella said. "Here, let me hold the door, Jack; he is not strong enough to get it open." She stepped to the door and took the rope handle.

"Demons!" The hermit shouted.

"Listen, old man," she replied, "I need you to explain something for me. Who was it that said: 'Take care to be silent. Empty your mind. Attend to your meditation in the fear of God. If you do this, you will not fear the attacks of the demons'?"

"Saint Onuphrius!" Was shouted back at her, and the slashing at the door stopped.

"Who was he?" She asked.

"One of the Desert Fathers, of course, from the Third Century," the hermit said. "Shall I tell you about him?"

"Yes, please," Bella said.

"Give us a holler if he gets out," Jack whispered, and he went back to the camels leaving Bella to manage the hermit.

She spent the morning listening to the old man talk about the Desert Fathers, the early Christian ascetics who lived alone in remote places, whom he was emulating. Still, she could see that the old fellow stood on the edge of death— he rarely ate, and his food mostly came from the generous donations of passing caravans or, when necessary, creatures he found dead near the well, and he spent weeks entirely alone inside his small man-made cave, meditating and praying, and either broiling in the heat of the Sun or freezing. He said he had been there for more years than he could recall.

After the expedition rested and drank their fill of water and replenished their skins, they departed, right after midnight. They had several more days before reaching In Salah, and, before they arrived, two of the laborers went mad and ran off into the desert.

* * *

In Salah was a paradise after their days in the desert: An oasis town with an ample water supply, the town was verdant and peaceful. It stood at the end of the long line of oases that stretched from the Atlas mountains in Morocco south through the Wadi Guir and the Wadi Saoura. Many still believed that In Salah and the entire Touat region belonged to Morocco, but it was also on the southern edge of territory deemed to be under French control ever since General Cauchemez's operations in the region (when Jack had been in the Sixth) several years earlier. There remained a large force of the French army stationed there. Camp

Bugeaud was garrisoned by the Compagnie Méhariste Tidikelt, a camel-riding Company of three hundred native Chaamba troops and French officers.

The expedition had traveled about half of its intended journey, but the remaining weeks would be far more difficult. Ren decided to give everyone a few days to recover before the final and most dangerous journey would be undertaken. He and Bella had not spoken about the ancient Arabic scrolls containing the description of the tomb since they had last conferred in Ouargla, but he asked her to visit his tent the first evening in In Salah to discuss the writings again. They were sitting on folding chairs beside a large lantern that harshly illuminated the tarpaulin room, the photographs of the scrolls spread on a wool rug on the floor between them.

"In Tunis, at my home there," he told her, "there were about a dozen archaeology students, men and women, who lived in the Palais with me—Tom was one of them, as you know. We had a lecture each evening and discussed the work done at the active excavation sites that day. I admit that I miss the intellectual stimulation of that community."

"I understand what you mean," she replied looking down at the photos.

"I'm very pleased that you've come on our excursion," he said. He looked at her as she looked down. They had been lucky to meet Bella, and Ren enjoyed speaking with her. He was not attracted to her specifically but her hair reminded him of Lilian and that gave him an occasional pang of desire. It surprised him how often his darkest longings kept resurfacing, and he was steadily coming to terms with the knowledge that he might never completely recover: There was a part of him that would always need to be locked away. He was disappointed in himself to feel so weak and distracted.

"Tell me about the scrolls," he said, to break his mind away from his thoughts. "What more have you been able to translate?"

"I've read through the entire set now," she replied. "The history has been a particular pleasure. The scrolls are a complete biography of al-Kahina, her birth, her defeat of Hasan ibn al-Nu'man and her reign as Queen of the Berbers. There's also a description of the Battle of Carthage and her conquest of the Byzantine emperor in, well, it would be ...."

"698 AD in the Gregorian calendar," Ren said.

"Yes, and there were only a few pages that described the queen's death and burial."

"You've mentioned that pillars surround the tomb, I believe, the exterior description. Is there more to its location?"

"Only a story, a proverb, I suppose, about the animals nearby, an elephant and a lion; it's allegorical, probably relating to the character of the queen, although I suppose there could have been actual animals about. The astronomical location has already been transcribed from the scrolls for you. The geographical location speaks of mountains and river valleys, but it is vague and hard to imagine that information is usable today. I'll write it all down in English for you."

"I can't yet imagine it nor have I any idea what the landscape will look like. Ayrad has not been to the Tuareg homeland for many years, so while I trust that his information in genuine, I don't know that it is still current. Have you been to the Hoggar mountains yourself?"

"No, I haven't: You know the French have no control there. The Tuareg people are not farmers, shepherds, or merchants as in the north and west: They are a race of nomadic warriors. It will not be at all like the lands we have traveled through so far."

"Be that as it may, there are only four weeks remaining until mid-summer, and we must arrive in time to use the astronomical locators to guide us."

"I will ask at the mosques to see if anyone has traveled south recently; I know Ayrad is asking at the marketplace."

It turned out that Jack was the source of the newest information.

"A Company of Legionnaires came up from Tamanrasset a month ago," he told Ren, Ayrad and Bella the next afternoon over dinner in Ren's tent. "It's not good news: A Foreign Legion outpost in Arak had been overrun by a party of four hundred Tuareg warriors. The attackers might remain in the area. They've avoided Tamanrasset itself because the city is, by default, the Tuareg capital, and I'm told that peace is maintained in Tamanrasset by a Tuareg 'king' under penalty of death—even French Legionnaires have passed through the city unharmed. But we have to go through hostile territory around Tamanrasset to get there."

"And we don't know precisely where the tomb is located. Ayrad, you have told us that your mother was a Tuareg woman," Ren said. "Would you not be able to intercede with the Tuareg to assure them that our expedition is purely scientific in nature? Why should we view the enemies of the

French nation as our enemies; can we not embrace them as allies in our cause?"

With Bella translating, he replied: "I could not persuade the Tuareg that your intentions are innocent, nor would you be the first to attempt to do so. You are entering their territory without their permission to locate the tomb of a queen and take everything away."

"To the best museum in their country, in Algiers," Ren insisted. He was getting frustrated.

"Regardless, we have only enough men to defend ourselves against a few bandits or a small attack," Jack said. "We can't fight off four hundred Tuareg warriors, Ren."

"Well, what about the damned French army, then?" Ren asked. "Surely it's their responsibility to keep the route to Tamanrasset open. I know that the telegraph lines can't be kept intact in this damned desert, but I'm certain that if we were able to inform Gallé, he would have the Governor order the army to accompany us. Who the hell is in charge down here?"

The current commander of the French forces in the Touat region was Colonel Robert Huré, a tall, thin, bald, and menacing man, but a realist. Ren and Jack found him at Camp Bugeaud, a compound of office buildings, barracks, and palisades with an adjacent parade ground inside a walled area of the town. Colonel Huré had a small, modest office to demonstrate that he was a serious man. There being little else to do in In Salah, he listened politely as Ren explained:

"Colonel, thank you for taking the time to meet with me and my chief of security, Captain Jacques Demain. My name is Doctor Renwick Villere; I am the Director of the French scientific mission at Carthage under the direction of the Archbishop of Algiers. I took leave this year from my position at Carthage to organize and lead a truly extraordinary and groundbreaking scientific expedition on behalf of the National Museum of Antiquities in Algiers. Now, to be clear, the museum's principal founder, a man with whom you are undoubtedly familiar, Monsieur Marcel Gallé, perhaps the wealthiest man in Algeria if not the entire French Empire, is the individual who selected me personally for this expedition, on behalf of the museum's titular Director, Governor Jonnart himself. And at their request, we have journeyed all the way from Algiers, and we must reach Tamanrasset in less than twenty-four days. We have learned of the situation at Arak and come to ask about the Tuareg warriors. Specifically, we want to know, what can be done to make our route through French Algeria somewhat safer? Will the French Army accompany us to Tamanrasset?"

"Doctor Villere, let me be clear: If I were ordered to do so, I would find the Tuareg warriors that attacked Arak and execute every last one, but the French government will not permit me to do so. There is a new policy in the air, one of pacification. We are to become friends with the Tuareg now." The Colonel's voice dripped with sarcasm.

"To adapt the American President's sage advice," Jack replied, "if you intend to speak softly, be certain you carry a big stick. The French Armée d'Afrique is a very big stick, and its presence allows the government to speak of pacification. In that regard, we believe that the participation of your soldiers in our scientific expedition would both deter any attack on us and set an example for a peaceful military presence in the province."

The Colonel laughed: "On the contrary, the Tuareg are eager to draw us into a battle on their home territory, Captain. If my soldiers were to accompany your expedition, we would draw the Tuareg warriors towards you like moths to a fire."

"Then don't send them with us. Send them somewhere we won't be and draw the Tuareg away from our small party," Ren suggested.

The Colonel shook his head. "The camel corps is headed out tomorrow on its regular patrol and reconnaissance. What I can do is tell you where they are going, and you can go any other damned place you please."

Back at his tent, Ren told Jack he was worried: "Is that the best we can hope for, that if we keep away from the French forces the Tuareg might not notice us? For my own part, I would accept the risk, but I cannot lead an expedition into the face of four hundred hostile warriors while we are already dealing with the desert itself."

"I don't believe anyone who joined this expedition expected it to be free from danger, Ren," Jack assured him. "We all know about the Flatter's Expedition, and many others like it. Surveyors, businessmen, scientists have all entered the Sahara for good, rational, even moral reasons, only to be attacked and slain. That is the nature of this place, and everyone on this expedition came knowing that, even Bella. She, and I and Bert and Tom, and Hans and Fedir, and all the rest of the men, we all knew what risks would be involved, and we are all here because we want to help achieve something."

Ren looked at his brother skeptically. "This is your job, Jack. You were paid to be here, like all the men."

"No, Ren. My job is to decide when your quest needs to be called off. So far I've decided we can keep going. But otherwise I'm following your lead, and when you're ready to go find the queen's tomb, we'll go."

'And the Tuareg warriors, what about them?"

"Colonel Huré is right that they will pursue the camel corps, and because of our visit with him we now know which direction not to go. But all we can do is send out our own scouts: Four hundred camel-riding Tuareg should not be too difficult to avoid."

"Alright, then, Captain Demain—we go tomorrow."

Jack laughed, "and thanks for the promotion, by the way."

Colonel Huré's camel corps were going south and then west; it would patrol through the many villages that made up the Touat region. Jack decided the expedition could take the most direct route towards Tamanrasset, south-east and maybe just a little further off the direct track easterly. That would take them away from the camel corps and still allow them to curve around towards Arak, where they had to go: Even if unsafe, Ayrad only knew one path to enter the Hoggar mountains. The journey to Arak, on camel, mostly at night, could be done in little more than a week. From there, they expected another ten or more days to reach the vicinity of the tomb.

* * *

The passage became increasingly difficult. The heat was horrendous. The expedition set off each day just as the sun fell to the horizon. The air cooled slightly at night but only long after sunset, and they were forced to halt each day shortly after sunrise. No campfires were permitted so as to avoid detection by the Tuareg. The camels were pushed to maintain a quick pace. Their water supply was adequate. Bella had been overly careful to conserve her personal supply. As days passed, she could feel her tongue begin to thicken and swell, while her skin became slack from dehydration. She rode easily now on her camel, and spent the long hours of night following Ren and Jack who were being guided by Ayrad and the stars. She spent the hours reciting verses of the Bible and the Quran in her head.

Five days out from In Salah, the sandstorm hit. The afternoon had passed silently and Bella, like the others, had remained in her tent preparing to depart that evening; she ate only a few dates, nuts, and hardened goat cheese for her supper along with a cup of water and a salt tablet. It was only when eating that she noticed the ruffling of her tent walls and gentle whistle of the wind. She stepped outside and the sky was already red like fire. The wind sharply increased, and sand pelted her. She ran over to Jack's tent. Ren was there just finishing a meal with Jack; they often ate together now. "It's going to be bad, I think," she said. "Jack, you better take a look."

He stepped to the tent flap and pulled it aside to look. "We'll have to call off the march tonight. Even if we could ride in this, the camels won't be able to follow each other and we won't be able to see the stars. We could get separated, lost, or even wander right into the Tuareg camp."

"If that's what you recommend, then spread the word, Jack," Ren said. "Everyone will remain in their tents, and we'll depart when you say we can."

Crossroads of the Nomad

Bella went back to her small, dark tent and shut and tied the flap tightly as the wind picked up. Sand spattered on the light tarpaulin of her tent walls. Before they departed In Salah, she had been offered a small oil lantern but had turned it down since they expected to be traveling at night. Now she regretted not having a light. The hot wind began to howl and scream, and it felt like her tent was flying through the storm with her inside it. The wind continued after the sun fully set and the sky became black and filled with dust. It was a long, restless night.

In the morning, the wind was unabated. Bella could only tell that the sun had risen because she thought she could again see her hand in front of her face, but the gloom persisted and the storm seemed to worsen. Two of the laborers' tents blew away, and those men now huddled together under a spare tarp.

The bellows and groans of the camels were alarming, for it was obvious that the poor animals, even evolved as they were for life in such an environment, were suffering. Bella took her turn going out to tend them and assure the creatures that their people were still there. A spare date or piece of dried apple helped to calm them. As night began to fall again, however, everyone became concerned. The storm had continued throughout the day and even worsened as night fell. Now everyone would be forced to spend another twelve hours in complete darkness with only the sound of the wind to ease their isolation. They were all thinking the same thing—bad sandstorms in the Sahara could last for days, and their supplies were limited.

Bella returned to her tent that evening after checking in with Jack. She laid down on her blanket, the wind now a roar in the pitch black. This was the second night they had been trapped on an open plain of hard desert rock, sand blowing hard enough to rip the skin from any exposed flesh. The dust in her tent choked her lungs and stung her eyes. It was impossible not to feel that they were being warned away, told to leave, threatened. She unrolled her prayer rug and knelt facing what she believed to be the direction of Mecca. What had they done, she wondered, to deserve such torment? Why had Allah chosen to punish them? Wasn't there anything she could do to ease their suffering? Then another voice seemed to laugh at her, as if to deprecate her tenacity and renewed purposefulness. It was a voice she recognized, the voice of the djinn. She rose and quickly wrapped her scarf around her head and neck, covering her mouth and nose. Through a small hole in the flap of her tent, she thought she could see Ren's tent. His lantern seemed to be lit, and perhaps Jack had even joined him. On unsteady feet, bracing herself against the savage winds, Bella stepped out into the storm. The wind whipped her scarf across her eyes and she was spun like a top, pushed across the empty space between tents. She looked for the lantern, and headed towards a light. Suddenly she tripped over a tent's guy ropes and ended up with her face in the sand, her mouth full of grit. She spit it out but then choked on the dust forced by the wind into her lungs as she lurched towards the light.

    The lantern that had seemed to guide her floated in the wind and then slowly rose into the sky and evaporated into nothing, an illusion, and the voice of the djinn laughed and mocked her, that she was alone, that she didn't belong, that she was nothing, that she was nothing more than an assemblage of ashes that the desert would eventually reduce to its individual particles and send flying across the distant barren reaches of an empty world. Lost, fumbling in the dark, uncertain which direction to go, she was in no condition to argue. She was no one, she had done nothing, and she would become nothing. The sand blowing across her bare face and hands was biting at her skin, tearing her away, reducing her body to dust. She could barely see or breathe, and in time her skin, her flesh, and her bones would be lost. Her life would be over. She knew that the universe was almost empty; it was full of vast vacant spaces with here and there a smattering of inert matter. But she also knew these things: By whatever trick of fate, she could move, she could think, and she would not die alone. She pushed with all the strength against the wind and sand and forced herself to her feet. Bent nearly double she pushed forward towards what she hoped was their camp. If she was wrong, her body would disappear before morning, and she would become a djinn herself, just the voice of a spirit in the wind. Without seeing or even knowing where she was going, she walked directly into the side of a tent. She pushed herself along until she reached the front and knelt at the flap. Raising it just enough to squeeze below it, she made it into the tent and forced herself to her feet. There before her eyes Tom Childers sat upon his cot, and he appeared at first frightened and then shocked that someone had come through the storm. He leapt from his cot and took Bella in his arms just as she collapsed. She wrapped her arms around him. "Thank you, thank you," she coughed, spitting out sand and dust. She laughed at the absurdity of life and held on to him. He laughed too then, and she kissed him, and she could not recall anything ever feeling so good. They spent the night reassuring each other while the world shuddered and groaned around them.

By morning, the storm had begun to slacken, and it was light enough to see the other tents. Jack thought they might be able to leave by nightfall if the wind continued to abate. As the Sun set that day, the wind lessened enough to allow the tents to be struck and the expedition made ready to ride. As the sky to the east turned a dark, angry purple, stars began to appear in the sky for the first time in days. But they were still two nights' ride from Arak.

* * *

The fortifications at Arak could be seen from a great distance across the wide open plains of the Sahara for they sat upon the crest of a ridge that overlooked the small village there at the base of the foothills that led up into the rocky Hoggar mountains. The expedition was still a few kilometers away as the sun began to rise after two days of intense riding, but even from that distance the fort was visibly breached, deserted, and blackened by fire. Jack halted the camels while he and Fedir rode forward alone to reconnoiter.

"We are not expecting to run into any of those Tuareg men, are we?" Fedir asked.

"They're not the kind to lie in wait, so, no, I'm not expecting trouble in the village, but they could be nearby, close enough to see a party as large as ours if we just rode in together. Let's hope they've headed up to the Touat in pursuit of Huré's camel corps."

As they neared the small village, however, they found that no one remained in the area—both the fort and the village had been deserted. Not only had all the Legionnaires been killed, but the few Berbers and Black Africans who lived in the village had been run off as well. The houses were empty, and inside the fort—really just a small outpost—the desiccated remains of a dozen soldiers lay scattered in the dust, all ravaged by vultures. The most unfortunate discovery was a dead mule that the Tuareg had pushed into the village's well, so the well water was undrinkable. The delay from the sandstorm had already left the expedition with little remaining water.

"We're probably better off in the village taking advantage of the shelter there," Jack told Ren when he and Fedir returned to the expedition. "We'll enter the village in ones and twos, not as a group, and slowly. I doubt anyone will want to go into the fort. The well has been spoiled, so we're on short rations until we reach the next water."

"Yes, as you say," Ren agreed. "Send a few of your soldiers in first, Jack, and have them keep everyone else out of the fort."

That day they slept in houses which, while still hot, provided much better protection from the heat of the Sun. But they were thirsty, and Ayrad could not recall how many days it would take them to reach the next well.

"It could be a day or two, or maybe longer," he told Jack and Ren uncertainly that afternoon. "There could be new wells along the route to Tamanrasset or all the wells could be defiled like this one."

"Jack, do we have enough water?" Ren asked.

"At this point, we're better off going forward than back," he said. "We'll either get to a well, or we won't. We'll let people know that they need to stick to a minimum of water,

Tamanrasset

less than a pint each day probably, although for some it could be even less."

That night the expedition entered the Hoggar mountains. Unlike any mountains that they had seen before, these were the remains of an ancient volcanic dome that had been worn away over billions of years. Great chasms had been etched by the sand and wind between the remaining pillars of grey stone. Many of the chasms were full of rocks and made for difficult terrain. Although Ayrad took the expedition along the trail that the Tuareg had used for centuries, it was almost impossible to travel in the dark. Fortunately, they were no longer on the open plains, and there were many places for the expedition to stop where they could not be seen. As days passed, the entire expedition suffered for the lack of water. Jack developed a terrible headache and his back hurt which he thought might mean trouble with his kidneys. Everyone looked worn, their skin peeling, and their lips chapped and bleeding.

The expedition had stopped for the day to rest in a sort of hollow or dell, a rocky open space cut by the wind through the mountain with a narrow opening at each end; Jack always ensured they had a path to retreat if they encountered anyone hostile. He was sitting with Bella and Ayrad at mid-day eating some dried fruits when he noticed that the Sun was right above them, and their shadows slowly compressed until, at last, they completely disappeared. He realized with some excitement that it meant they had passed the Tropic of Cancer, the latitude at which the Sun stood directly overhead. He got up to tell Ren and crossed the hollow.

"Have you noticed where we are?" Ren said. He was holding a walking stick perpendicular to the ground, and it cast no shadow.

"I was just coming to tell you. We must be getting close to Tamanrasset."

"We'll need to get into a position tonight where we have an unobstructed view of the horizon; we ..." Ren trailed off. He was looking intently with an expression of shock toward the opening of the hollow behind Jack.

Jack swung around, his hand rapidly drawing his sidearm and taking aim at whatever was coming. Standing at the narrow opening, looking them over with evident surprise, was an enormous Barbary lion. His shoulders bulged with muscles, and his huge mane ruffled as he shook his head. His shaggy paws were large enough to take off a man's head, and the pupils of his round amber eyes narrowed as he took in the scene before him. Jack had never seen a lion before, and he had been told in the past that the Barbary lions were extinct. He held his fire since the lion might be the last of his species. Anyway, it would take several well-placed shots from his pistol to even stop such a goliath if it chose to attack. Everyone at once stopped talking while the animal observed them.

The noble giant seemed to be examining the intruders in his domain as if trying to decide how he felt about it and, perhaps, whether he was hungry. The oppressive heat and glare of the sunlight had likely rendered him as uncomfortable and stupefied as his potential prey, but, as the crowd of people watched motionless, he took a few steps forward as if they were not even there. He clearly had no fear of the thin, nervous, and exhausted primates that were spread across his path, just as his ancestors might have a million years before. As he walked past one by one, he looked them over briefly, not in fear but out of mere curiosity. As he neared Jack, the magnificent animal, easily three or four times Jack's weight and length, stopped and looked him in the eye. What Jack saw there unnerved him, for the lion seemed to view him not as prey nor as predator in his domain, but almost as a colleague, as if the lion was saying to him: "This damned heat, it's not easy to do a job like ours under these conditions, is it? I can see you've done well taking care of your pride. You're fortunate to still have yours. My people are gone now; I'm the last."

The lion shook his mane to swat away the flies about his head, then looked at Jack one last time and continued walking past the people until he reached the end of the hollow and disappeared into the twisting gorge beyond.

"Magnificent!" Ren exclaimed boyishly. "We must try to get a photograph of him," he said and rushed off to speak with the expedition's photographer.

Jack had another thought: "Hans, take a couple of men and follow that animal carefully. He may lead us to water nearby." Hans instantly jumped up and tagged a couple of the native soldiers to follow him as they ran off in the direction of the great animal.

As he holstered his sidearm, Jack looked around the hollow at the people relieved to have been spared by the lion, laughing away their fear, taking a meager sip of their dwindling water. He had not thought of them before as "his" people, but he supposed now that Hans, Fedir, Ayrad, Bert, Tom and the rest of the men, the natives and the Westerners alike, were his people now. Jack had not felt like he belonged anywhere since he had been discharged from the Foreign Legion, but in that hollow with those men at that moment he felt that he belonged with them. And even more so with Ren, his rediscovered brother, and with Bella, he cared deeply what happened to them. Perhaps, after all, he was not as dead inside as he believed.

* * *

The lion did not lead them to water, but that evening as the Sun was setting the camels became excited—they had the ability to smell water and were given free rein to follow their noses. The expedition climbed along a trail towards the top of a wide valley and, just before they reached the top, the camels turned into a wide, low-ceiling cave. A large pool of shallow water spread across the floor. The camels drank voraciously, being able to consume up to 30 gallons of water in a few minutes, but a spring at the back of the cave replenished the pool so that water skins and flasks could be refilled and everyone could slowly drink away their severe dehydration.

Ren sat on the smooth rocks with his bare feet in the pool, drinking slowly to prevent cramps, chatting with Jack and Bert, and looking about the cavernous space. He saw Bella standing inches from the back wall silent and motionless, and he went over to see if she was unwell.

"You've remembered to drink slowly, I hope," he said to her. She had uncovered her head again, and her chestnut brown hair lay loosely around her shoulders. She turned her head to look at Ren, and her piercing blue eyes fairly twinkled with excitement.

"You've got to look at this," she said.

As Ren approached, he could see that the wall was covered with ancient cave paintings. Although crude, these red and yellow ochres combined with charcoals and gypsum created a wonderous tapestry over an enormous area of the wall. There were drawings of many people, often in small groups like families, coming together to form communities, to gather edibles, to collect water, to protect against predators, and to hunt for meat. A menagerie of wild animals—monkeys, lions, gazelles, zebras, giraffes, and alligators, among many others—testified to a world that was once abundant and rich with life, back when the Sahara was not yet a barren desert but rather the first homeland of Mankind.

An elephant caught Ren's eye because it wasn't quite an elephant: "Look, take a look at this one," he said to Bella. "The twisted tusks and shaggy coat, I don't believe it's an elephant at all; it looks more like a mastodon. That would make these paintings tens of thousands of years old."

She put her arm around Ren and stood with him admiring the intricate drawings. Jack came over to join them. In his years in Africa he had seen many cave paintings but none so intricate or of such an enormous scale. He pointed at a trio of people standing together.

"There we are, on the expedition," he said as he stood beside them.

"They're looking at us and wondering whether we're ever going to find this damned tomb," Ren said.

Bella laughed. "Of course you will, Ren. We're close now, aren't we?"

"I think so, yes, another day or two and we'll be in the right area," he said. He actually felt pretty certain about their location and their proximity to the tomb. "Thank you, both of you, for sticking with me this whole way."

"I'll keep my fingers crossed until we find the tomb intact," Jack said.

The next evening they reached the precise point from which the position of the stars were written down on almost the same day of the year some twelve hundred years earlier by an Arab who sought to record the location of the tomb of the Berber Queen al-Kahina. Ren had been told that the wobbly orbit of the Earth meant that the exact location of the tomb could not be found with those coordinates alone, but it remained the place from which their search would begin.

Ren asked the entire expedition to join him for a meeting that night. They were encamped in a field of giant volcanic boulders, surround by a plain of rock spires and buttes jutting from the ground like giants. Although just a few kilometers from the Tuareg capital of Tamanrasset, they were well hidden from view and had a full Moon and torches so all could see and listen to the discussion.

"We are close to reaching our objective," Ren began, "the great Berber construction we hope to find and excavate. We know it was described as a pyramidical mound. It is located in the southern stretch of a mountain range among three peaks each seven thousand feet high, above the junction of two riverbeds. If you look around us, there are mountain ranges, including one that heads north, so we are here on the southern end. Are there seven thousand foot peaks? We really can't tell. We do not have the time to make those calculations, and, frankly, I don't believe they did so twelve hundred years ago. But there are several very tall peaks nearby. And as for the riverbeds, well, the rivers probably don't exist anymore. If any of you have any ideas, I want to hear them now, because tomorrow we'll begin sending out small search parties in different directions to look for the burial mound."

Bert Hill was sitting in the crowd with some of the soldiers; he had been playing cards with them quite often. "I was thinking," he said, "well, I thought, maybe, we should try asking some of the people that live here, in Tamanrasset?"

"Are you going to walk into the Tuareg capital and ask them for us, Bert?" Tom asked.

"He has a point," Jack interjected. "Tamanrasset is a peaceful city, and we don't all need to go. Some of our Chaamba soldiers can certainly go safely. We haven't seen or heard anything of the Tuareg warriors and hopefully they're still off in the Touat region. Even if they're not, I'd prefer that we run into them in the city than out here."

"If there's a mosque, I'll go," Bella offered, and several of the devoted Berber soldiers immediately offered to accompany her. "Ayrad, you want to come with us, don't you? This is your homeland."

"Yes, I wish to come, thank you," he said.

"I will go as well," Ren said. "It is my duty to you all that have come so far to ensure that I put forth every effort. But I will be the only white man to go. Jack, you and the others must stay here until we return."

"I don't like that decision, Ren," Jack said.

"You can come with us part of the way, Captain, but I sincerely doubt a couple solitary travelers, one a Muslim woman, will be harmed, especially when we're accompanied by a few of our excellent soldiers."

The silence in the morning was deafening as Ren, Bella, Ayrad, and three of the expedition's largest Chaamba soldiers mounted their camels to ride into Tamanrasset. In the distance, the towering, jagged peaks of the Hoggar mountains resembled the battlements of an ancient fortress, and the spires and buttes that rose out of the plains before them had been eroded into frightening shapes like ancient monsters frozen in time. It was an alien land, lifeless, gloomy, and sad. It took only an hour to reach the outskirts of the small oasis city where their path was obstructed by a small Tuareg encampment.

"We are here as scientists first," Ren reminded his people. "We want to befriend these fellows, not antagonize them."

As they neared the camp, several of the tall, majestic Tuareg men, dressed in blue-black robes and black turbans, their faces veiled with a "litham," such was their custom, stepped into their path. They were naturally wary of strangers, with good reason, and would not seek to initiate a conversation. Ren drew his small party to a halt and dismounted so that he could speak to the imposing nomads.

Ayrad could speak some of the Tuareg's local dialect, and two of the Tuareg men spoke some Arabic and one, whose name was Akhou ag Biska, even spoke English. This made communication with the small clan easier than expected. After a brief greeting and introduction, the Tuareg men, whose stature even exceeded that of Ren's accompanying Berber tribesmen, became quite hospitable. They invited the men to share tea, which Ren felt they had no choice but to accept. As the men sat in a large tent with the Tuareg (Bella was shown to the women's tent), Ren could still sense a certain malignity behind the veils of the Tuareg men, and he half expected that they would rise up and slaughter his little group on the spot. Yet the Tuareg had been called "Knights of the Desert," and Ren believed that if he spoke with the respect which these men deserved, they would honor the ancient guest-host obligations. The warriors were surprisingly curious about Ren's expedition and understood that he was a sort of historian seeking clues from an ancient civilization. He was fairly circumspect about the possibility of buried treasure, and the Tuareg men seemed unconcerned about the potential exploration of an ancient Berber ruin. After an hour or so, Ren explained that his men wished to visit the mosque in the city for mid-day prayers and that the woman who accompanied them was an Alima. These Tuareg men were not Muslim themselves, but they honored those who were. Two of the Tuareg men agreed to accompany the group to the mosque, and so Ren's group again mounted their camels to enter the city.

Tamanrasset was an ancient city nestled among the black volcanic ridges of the Hoggar Mountains, an oasis settlement that over millennia had become the beating heart of the Sahara, or at least one of the handful of such places. It was home to a fluctuating population of nomads whose tents appeared and vanished with the seasons, a people that came to rest, to water their camels, to meet kin, and then scatter across the sands. Caravans drifted in from the north and south, great lines of camels groaning under their burdens of salt or dates, yet nothing much was sold or bought in Tamanrasset. It was not a marketplace for such goods but a waypoint, pulsating with life as caravans came and went on their way across the desert. It was a place of murmured news and fleeting footprints, always inhabited, yet never quite settled. Street by street, Ren saw dozens of Tuareg men, tall and imposing in their blue-black robes and veils, but here were also Berbers, Arabs and many more Black Africans than Ren had seen in Algiers or Tunis. There were also Tuareg women, some with dark skin and some with skin that was almost white. Tuareg women did not wear a veil and were treated with great deference. It turned out that Ren's chaperones were indispensable at assuring those they met along the way to the mosque that the white man was harmless. Indeed, after Bella and the Muslim men were left at the mosque, just as the muezzin began the midday call to prayer, the two Tuareg men with Ren asked if he would like to meet the "King" of the Hoggar.

"I would be most humbled to meet such an important man, my friends," he told them. "Of course, we would do nothing in this region without his knowledge, so I would be most grateful for your introduction. Do you believe he will be willing to speak to me?"

"We shall bring you to Amenukal Amanstan and see," Akhou ag Biska said.

"Your English is quite good, by the way; where did you learn?" Ren asked.

"I spent many years in Egypt and came to know Englishmen there."

"Why, so did I," Ren said. "I did my practical training there among the ruins of Ancient Egypt."

"You are English?"

"I'm an American."

His guides stopped and looked at Ren curiously and spoke to each other in their private dialect for several minutes.

"We have neither of us ever met an American before," Akhou ag Biska told him. "We are not certain whether the Americans are our allies or our enemies. The Amenukal will tell us."

"Well, for my part, I hope to be considered friend, not foe," Ren answered.

The dry heat of the day was oppressive, and Ren was grateful when they arrived at a modest building—not the home of the Tuareg "Amenukal" but merely his meeting place, for the Tuareg lived only in tents being a society that prided itself on being nomadic. Ren waited while the Tuareg men went inside, but he was only delayed a moment: It seemed that Amenukal Amanstan was delighted to meet an American archaeologist.

The close room was cool and poorly lit, and the king was a gigantic man, easily seven feet in height, dressed in the finest cloth and a magnificent blue turban. He wore seven bands across his chest decorated with gold and silver and carried two sheathed knives and an enormous two-handed scimitar. Ren bowed respectfully as the king approached.

"It is a great honor to meet you, Your Majesty," he intoned. This was immediately translated by Ren's chaperone inasmuch as the king did not speak English or French.

"We have not seen any Americans here before. I have been told you are a historian, is that right?"

"Not exactly, your majesty. I am a scientist who studies ancient civilizations by uncovering the clues they have left behind."

This was translated, and Ren recognized several words added by the translator which were the names of famous Egyptian excavations.

"I understand now," the king replied at last. "I am told you search for an ancient Berber pyramid. It will be full of great golden riches, will it not?"

Ren smiled when this was translated for him.

"It is a universal belief that such structures always contain treasures and are often sought after for that reason, but the truth is that such riches don't exist. Nevertheless, I can assure you that if any relics are removed, I am obligated to delivered them to the museum in Algiers which has sent me here."

The king, it seemed, was unfamiliar with the concept of a museum. After this was clarified, he said: "I know the locations of many treasures scattered throughout the mountains. I know the location of Berber treasure. You may inspect it if that is your pleasure, but you must not remove any items from our territory without my permission."

Ren was surprised at this turn of events. Most of the land, including that which contained the tomb he sought to excavate, belonged to France. He had been given a concession by the French government to excavate with the specific requirement that all relics be properly conserved for study and potential public displayed. Clearly such legalities were irrelevant to the self-proclaimed King of the Hoggar.

"There may be many items in such an edifice, Your Majesty," Ren said, "which are not treasure—bones, pottery, stones, paintings, sculptures, scrolls and tablets. Sometimes there are also gold or silver trinkets, but the primary value of such items is in their historical significance which can only be appreciated when they are studied and placed in view of the public. As precious metals, they are often next to worthless. This is all to say, Your Majesty, that I have no intention of taking anything that has meaningful 'value' from the mountains, and that which we will take only has value when displayed in the museum in Algiers."

The king looked quite cross with Ren. "Nothing gold or silver may leave these mountains without my consent," he stated adamantly and spoke again to the Tuareg at length.

The translating Tuareg finally told Ren: "I, Akhou ag Biska, am required to accompany you on your search and ensure that you follow the commands of the Amenukal." He didn't sound pleased. "Furthermore, I am told that the structure you seek lies to the south."

At that point, the king dismissed Ren and left the room. There was little more Ren could do at that moment, but he knew he needed to have a frank discussion with his new Tuareg companion. They returned to the mosque to meet with Bella and the Berber soldiers.

"I've had a fascinating conversation with the Imam, Ren," Bella told him excitedly.

"We'll have to discuss it when we get back to camp," Ren said, pointedly winking and cast glances at their new Tuareg companion. "Our friend Akhou ag Biska here has been commanded by his king to join our expedition; he has some specific thoughts about where we should be looking."

"Ah, yes, I look forward to going over it all when we get back," she said knowingly.

After they had traveled about a kilometer from the city, Ren stopped and climbed down from his camel. He rummaged about in his saddle bags for a moment, then he pulled out a pistol and pointed it directly at the Tuareg.

"I'll ask you to climb down and walk with me now," he said. "There are a few additional facts which I didn't mention to your king that I'd like to share with you."

Akhou ag Biska was furious. He threatened to ride off, but one of the Berber soldiers slipped down and grabbed the Tuareg camel's reins. The Tuareg obviously felt that Ren and his people were so far beneath him that he could not be forced to do anything they asked. Ren fired his pistol into the sand. The Tuareg camel was dragged down to its knees and Akhou ag Biska begrudgingly slid off.

"Your weapons, please," Ren said. "I only mean to talk, so let's agree there will be no more violence, all right?"

Akhou ag Biska handed over his knives and a short scimitar but neglected to agree.

"I have three soldiers with me here. You may be Tuareg, but these are Chaamba warriors, veterans of the French army, with rifles and swords. When we return to our camp, you'll find that we have many more soldiers there, not to mention laborers and scientists. Now listen to what I have to say: I am charged with recovering any artefacts we find for the museum, and that is what I will do; your king has no say in the matter. I am restraining you simply so you cannot interfere, but I have no desire to see you harmed. And when we release you, if you wish, you may tell the king that you were our prisoner, although I may not release you until we are far from Tamanrasset. Do you understand?"

"Yes," the man said, disgusted.

Tamanrasset

"And your king tells us that the Berber ruins are to the south. Rather vague, I think."

"It's not south," Bella interjected. "I know where it is, and it's not south."

"How fascinating. I did assume the king would try to mislead us. I think he simply wanted us to go off in that direction," Ren said. "You'll tell me all about it as soon as this gentleman is firmly bound and made ready for our return to camp."

The three Berber soldiers bound the Tuareg while Ren spoke to Bella confidentially.

"What did you find out?" He asked.

"I had a lovely conversation with the Imam, and I asked him about the pyramidical mound, and the four pillars, and all of that. It turns out that most everyone raised in Tamanrasset knows where it is, even though they don't know what it is. And you won't believe this part: These giant spires of rock that we see all over the plains, the eroded rocks, well, it seems there are two mounds that overlook the site: Of those two, one is shaped like an elephant and one is shaped like a lion, so the tomb is actually being observed by a lion and an elephant just as the scrolls say. But it's not to the south, it's about twenty kilometers north of the city."

Ren laughed and shook his head in disbelief, then hugged Bella as she laughed with him.

"That's the best news I've had today. What a miracle worker you are, truly, my dear. I suppose I shouldn't have come to the city; I should have let you come to the mosque by yourself and sort it all out. Now we have to take Monsieur Akhou ag Biska as our prisoner and hope that no one comes to look for him. We'll do what we must. Let's hurry back and get everyone moving before the day is out."

The very next day, the expedition found the site of the tomb of Queen al-Kahina. The pyramidical burial site, which was visible from a great distance, had been worn down by time, and the four stone spires mentioned in the scrolls now lay on the ground beside the mound, but two enormous rock formations, one decidedly in the shape of an elephant and the other of an enormous recumbent lioness looking back over her shoulder, stood guard over the Queen's tomb. Its discovery sent a thrill through every man and woman on the expedition. A mass of stone crowned the hill, a fallen structure of some kind, perhaps a temple or entryway, made from the distinctive stone of the Hoggar mountains. Somewhere beneath lay the burial chamber of Queen al-Kahina, where she lay perhaps with the precious Emeralds of the Garamantes that had since become legend across the Maghreb.

As soon as their camp was set, Ren had Ayrad go to a nearby village of Black Africans to hire more men to work as laborers on the excavation, to supplement the men that had traveled with them from Ouargla. About twenty-five respectable individuals took up the opportunity. Jack established regular patrols to preserve the security of the camp and keep watch for the approach of any Tuareg warriors. A few of his soldiers were also stationed around the burial mound to prevent idle thievery. The photographer began work at once documenting the discovery, and the National Geographic journalists explored and asked questions as the surveyor began to create a detailed scale drawing of the mound. Ren, Bert, Tom, and Bella approached the edifice to decide how to stage the excavations, awed that such a magnificent and enduring monument could have been constructed in the heart of the Sahara.

The formidable blocks of square-cut stone, a meter or so in length and height, which made up the exterior walls of the pyramidical mound were piled up to a height of twenty meters. To their surprise, a great many of these blocks bore inscriptions, thousands in all, some ancient and some very recent. Many of the inscriptions were confessions of love engraved by Tuareg tribesmen, suggesting that the edifice had a more modern usage, perhaps one imbued with powerful magic. A structure, perhaps a temple, built atop the mound had collapsed long before, and its debris lay on and around the mound itself.

Having decided to start a passage into the center of the mound, exterior stones were brought away, which revealed, just within the exterior wall, an interior arrangement of rooms. The exterior wall at its base was perhaps six or seven meters thick, while at the top the wall was merely one to two meters in depth. In the process, they located a sculpted entrance engraved with ancient writing which Bella went to work transcribing, but it seemed to be an ancient Berber dialect.

The doorway at the entrance had been sealed for more than a thousand years by a massive stone slab held in place by intricately carved pillars of black volcanic stone. Behind the doorway, a passageway led to a large central room. As the work went forward, it became evident that the building they were excavating was much more than a tomb. At some point after the mound had been constructed for the great

Berber queen, it became a sacred temple or place of worship. Many of the laborers, especially the men from the neighboring village, were convinced that the building had become the resting place of the spirits of evil giants and were afraid of what ills such desecration might bring about. However, the excavation, surveys, sifting and identification of relics progressed over several days. The work was laborious, and Ren was an exacting and meticulous excavation director. It was also his duty to review all the items which, through careful examination, were recovered from the dust and debris. Yet there was also a decided sense of urgency, as if they all knew their time was limited, that the Tuareg could come at any moment, that their food and water could run out or that a sandstorm or flash flood, as occasionally occurred in those mountains, would wipe out their camp. Perhaps the djinns or even the gods themselves resented the disturbance of this ancient shrine.

A stockroom was next uncovered in which a great store of dates, millet, seed, and other vegetable matter were discovered, as well as tools and pieces of glass and stone. It was in the next room, after the first bones were uncovered, not those of al-Kahina but perhaps a Berber nobleman or elevated servant, that the laborers began to raise objections. However, when the workers were shown the diminutive size of the bones found, they were greatly assuaged since "it was known" that djinns were giants and their bones would be proportionately massive in scale. Yet trouble returned when, on the fifth day of excavation, clouds suddenly formed above the distant peaks and, within minutes, massive raindrops fell from the sky. This rare event further convinced the laborers that the gods disfavored the desecration of the burial mound. The local men disappeared, having returned swiftly to their homes, and those who had accompanied the expedition from Ouargla, now convinced that the locals were correct, huddled in their tents in fear. It was only through the intervention of Bella and her ability to confidently assure the men of their value in the eyes of the almighty Allah, to pray with them and to lead a rational discussion of a quotation about the weather from the Quran, that the laborers put aside their fears and returned to the dig.

On the seventh day, a new room was opened, and the discoveries there made Ren, Bert and Tom ecstatic: Burial jars, dozens of them, and on each of them could be plainly seen, engraved or painted, a crescent moon and sun–the same symbols of the goddess Tanit that Ren had found upon the jars in her temple in Carthage. Here was convincing evidence that trans-Saharan Berber culture had adopted or indeed evolved from that of the Punic civilization which had spanned the Maghreb. This discovery alone would secure Ren's professional reputation and furnish him with material for years of lectures and books. He felt a new sense of confidence in the expedition. He had already justified the tremendous effort and cost involved with the discoveries they had already made. He set Bert Hill at once to examining the relics already catalogued to determine whether there was further evidence that Carthaginian culture had spread into the heart of the Sahara.

They came at last one morning to a room which contained only a large leather floor covering, painted and engraved with intricately carved designs which seemed to represent some ancient mystical powers. It was obvious that this room was set aside for a special purpose, for the floor covering, which spanned from wall to wall, was not intended to be trod upon: This was a room not meant to be entered once sealed. After photographing and examining the leather object at length, it was carefully removed, and beneath it lay a burial stone, an enormous slab of native rock three meters by four carved with many mystical symbols. Ren was certain this was the royal tomb. He halted all other work and had the laborers together remove the heavy slab. Hours of labor lifting out the massive slab revealed beneath a shaft that went deep down into the very floor of the Sahara. The shaft had been backfilled with stone and debris which required the efforts of the entire camp for one full day to clear, but excitement was growing and everyone wanted to know what would be found.

In a cloud of dust, the workers, almost unable to see or breathe, took the debris outside bucket by bucket. Larger stones had to be hoisted out. There was a strange fear in Ren's heart that there would be little remaining at the bottom of the shaft, perhaps only a scrap of cloth or leather, or nothing at all, and he could sense the tension among the laborers who hoped their toils would soon be at an end and there would be treasure to share.

Tom and Bert took turns with Ren climbing down into the shaft to check on the progress of the clearing and see whether anything had been found. By midnight, doubt crept again into Ren's heart—perhaps this was the shaft of a deep well or served some other meaningless purpose, despite his instincts to the contrary. His spirits nearly collapsed when late in the day Bert proclaimed that there was no point in going on, that the search was useless. The laborers lost their enthusiasm and a rumor spread that they would all be abandoned in the terrible shaft at the center of the ancient edifice as a sacrifice to the evil spirits of the temple. Ren sent them to rest until dawn so as to prevent a total collapse and abandonment of the project.

Ren stayed and worked alone through the night. Then, having reached the very bottom of the shaft sometime still before dawn, choked on dust and weakened by his lack of food, Ren came upon another leather covering. Covered in grime and sweat, his oil lantern smoking lazily by his side, he knelt to gently wipe away the dust that lay upon the large patch of leather, barely able to catch his breath, his heart racing with excitement. Beneath was a hollow space. He pulled the leather away and found an opening: It was only large enough for one thin man at a time to lower himself into the room below. A lantern held above his head, Ren wriggled into the void and dropped a few feet to the cluttered floor. His lantern illuminated a small room less than three meters by four and its ceiling less than two meters high. But here there were objects, dozens of objects, and, encased in taut strips of leather, the remains of a person, undoubtedly Queen al-Kahina herself.

Ren sat as best he could among the objects left for the Queen's benefit in her afterlife, and he cried for joy and to relieve the fear and tension he had felt for days. When his tears subsided, he looked around at the magnificent objects—carved ivory and amethyst, polished pieces of glass, beads of cornelian and bands of silver, chests of myrrh and other precious resins, a small cache of salt, peppercorns, and dozens of other objects whose value to science was incalculable but whose practical value was nil. Having taken a quick inventory in his head, Ren turned to the remains of the Queen. She was wrapped in painted leather with traces of gold leaf. All that now remained of her were bones, and this had left the leather gaping and loose enough that Ren could see, beneath the leather straps, the gold jewelry she wore in death. Upon her ribs were nine interconnected necklaces of gold, and embedded within in each necklace were dozens of crystals—enormous, beautiful crystals. But they weren't emeralds. They were diamonds. Green diamonds. The priceless heirlooms of the Berber queen.

Ren caught his breath and slowly reached into the folds of leather to touch the precious jewels. Everything else could be handled by Bert and Tom, but he would take care of the Queen's remains himself. After a time, he stood and returned to the opening in the ceiling of the room. Pulling himself up, he re-entered the shaft. He was too tired to climb to the top, so he sat to drink from his waterskin and wait for the first laborers to arrive for the day.

Hearing the stirrings of the foreman and first laborers of the day, Ren climbed to the top of the shaft on the loose arrangement of ropes and ladders. With great fatigue, he told the laborers to return to their work in the other rooms, for, he said, he had reached the bottom of the shaft, and there was no more to be done. He took a deep draft from his waterskin and wiped the grime from his face. Soon Jack came by, and Ren asked his brother to place guards at the top of the shaft to prevent anyone from going down while he went to his tent to clean up. By the time Ren returned later that morning with Tom, the entire camp had begun to suspect that something significant had been found. Bella even heard some of the laborers say that gold had been discovered, and soon there was not a man at the site who

Tamanrasset

was not under the impression that the burial chamber contained a huge treasure hoard. That afternoon, Ren climbed from the shaft only to find an assembly of men waiting there, looking at him and trying to get a glimpse of the loot he was supposedly bringing from below. Ren always paused to allow those around him to satisfy themselves that his hands and pockets were empty. Still, rumors spread like wildfire.

"What was a scientific expedition is now changing very quickly," Jack warned Ren when they met in his tent with Bella and Tom late that afternoon. "Everyone seems to believe that gold has been found. Several of the laborers, especially those we hired from the village, are convinced they can kill us and take anything of value. While I do trust our Chaamba soldiers, there may even be one or two desperate to do something rash if the reward is high enough. Word will also soon spread to Tamanrasset, and the Tuareg may come with a large force to seize the treasure. How quickly can we wrap up the excavation and leave?"

"Now look, Jack," Ren replied emphatically, "there are many important artefacts here, and our duty is to preserve the site, not run from it. But let me be clear–there is no golden treasure."

"Even if we were to leave, where could we go?" Bella asked. "We can't return to Tamanrasset; we'd have to retreat to In Salah, and that is a long journey. Would we be safe in the open spaces of the desert?"

"We could return to the cave with the spring of fresh water. Neither the local laborers nor the Tuareg must know of it since we were the first visitors there in a thousand years or more," Tom said. "If we stay hidden for a few days, perhaps our pursuers would lose interest in the chase."

Bella disagreed: "Even if we could make our way back to the cave," she said, "we are running low on food; we can't feed this entire crew for days on end while we wait for the Tuareg to lose interest in gold, or at least what they believe to be gold. And anyway," she added, "we would be bringing our trouble with us since there are evidently members of our crew that aren't trusted.' She turned to Jack. "You can't mean to abandon the soldiers and laborers we brought with us all the way from Ouargla to just fend for themselves, do you?"

"We can't run away, for it wouldn't do us any good," Ren said. "We shall have to come clean, let everyone see the artefacts, and trust to those who have journeyed all this way with us. The local laborers must be watched by your men, Jack. And I will invite the Tuareg king to come see the 'treasure.' I have an idea on how to manage that. The bottom line is that we have no other choice. It is the only way we can possibly return to In Salah."

Ren and Jack went to the tent where Akhou ag Biska was still being held against his will, locked with iron chains to the tent pole.

"You have not been treated too poorly, I hope," Ren said with a sideways glance at Jack.

"No," the Tuareg replied icily.

"Look, I'm sorry this was necessary. We're going to let you go now. I want you to go back to Tamanrasset and tell your king that he is welcome to come look at the relics we've uncovered; we've only just found the burial chamber this morning."

"You will release me?"

"Yes, we release you now, Akhou ag Biska, and I'll show you the burial chamber before you go. It's untouched. We will finish our work here while you speak to Amenukal Amanstan, and you are welcome to bring him here or whoever he likes. Jack, unlock him now."

"Are you sure about this, Ren?" Jack asked.

"Yes, certain. And give this man back his knives and sword; we're not thieves. Akhou ag Biska, may I take you to see the chamber yourself before you depart? Then you may report what you have seen."

"Yes, I will look."

Ren took Akhou ag Biska to the pyramidical mound and showed him all around, telling him the history of the Queen and her tomb, finally taking the Tuareg down the burial shaft, preceding him into the hole which he only entered very warily, and showing him the burial chamber itself. All of the items scattered about the tomb remained in their exact places since they had not yet all been photographed and catalogued. Ren asked Tom, who was taking copious notes and making sketches, and Bella, who was helping him, to leave for a few minutes, and they both climbed out.

Akhou ag Biska examined all the trinkets, beads and crystals, the chests of myrrh and peppercorns, and the thin bands of silver. Nothing seemed to be out of place, for the room was quite full of objects. At last he approached the remains of the queen. He looked down at the leather-bound bones a long time, knelt and looked closely, but there was nothing to see but the bones themselves.

"Akhou ag Biska, I don't wish to make a big deal about your imprisonment in our camp here, and for the good of your own reputation I'm sure you don't wish to either. Can we agree, you and I, that you chose to stay with us here in our camp of your own free will these past few days, and that you were never our prisoner? Not to mention that our mutual silence will help prevent things from escalating unnecessarily, especially when you hear what I have to offer."

The Tuareg looked at Ren with malice, and for a moment Ren felt certain that Akhou ag Biska would kill him on the spot. But then he said: "Go on."

"Even if I wanted to, it is simply not possible for us to take everything back with us to Algiers. Therefore, I would like you to convey to Amenukal Amanstan my sincere desire that, with our assistance, he establish a museum for antiquities in Tamanrasset. It will show his people that he is a generous and thoughtful ruler of your confederation, for Amenukal may place many valuable items on exhibit there for his people to see and learn about their history. In that sense, he would possess a great many of these sacred items, for the benefit of his people and also with my approval and express agreement as the representative in situ of the French government."

Akhou ag Biska looked at Ren silently for a full minute.

"I will convey this message," he said.

After they had climbed back up to daylight, Ren shook off the dust. "Now, as you can see, there are quite a lot of us here, and a small but formidable force of soldiers. We're not looking to cause trouble and we don't want any. I know, on your beautiful camels, your people would quickly catch up if we tried to run off, and anyway our work here is not done

Tamanrasset

yet, so we will be here when you and your king return. Let's get your camel for you."

Akhou ag Biska mounted his camel and rode off towards Tamanrasset. Ren prayed he had done the right thing.

* * *

Jack brought all his soldiers into camp and set up a defensive perimeter while Hans oversaw preparations to depart swiftly in case there was an attack from which they could flee. Bella met with the laborers, including all those from the village, and brought them in small groups to see the burial chamber and look at the items found there. There was still skepticism about the lack of gold, but her effort swayed many and likely forestalled a full-fledged insurrection. Ren tried to hurry along Tom's cataloguing of the artefacts.

As Jack expected, Amenukal Amanstan arrived the next day with more than forty Tuareg warriors prepared for battle, but they found no one interested in fighting. Ren insisted that they be greeted respectfully and invited into the camp. A gazelle was purchased from the village, and it was roasted to provide a generous meal for the visitors. Tours were arranged of the entire tomb including the burial chamber which had still been untouched. Akhou ag Biska, had returned with the king but said little. Jack's Chaamba warriors, whom he had instructed to treat the Tuaregs as brothers, challenged the Tuareg warriors to traditional games and contests, and Bella asked the Tuareg men whether any of them had inscribed the name of their wife on the pyramid, then showed them where others had done so.

At a grand dinner in a large tent quickly made ready for the event, Ren sat with the king. "Your Majesty, there is a matter on which I beg your earnest consideration," Ren said, addressing Amenukal Amanstan. "You see, in Egypt where I did my early field work, the grand tombs of the Pharaohs in the great pyramids often are found to contain a large number of remarkable artefacts which must be protected and preserved for scientific examination and public exhibition. Egypt has enacted strict laws and customs which restrict and control the opening of ancient burial chambers and dictate what happens to their contents. Yet the French have unfortunately enacted no such specific laws in Algeria. Now, this is of course not the tomb of a Pharaoh, nevertheless, as a scientist, I must do my duty as I have learned it to protect the antiquities located at this site. So far, I have required that nothing from the burial chamber itself be touched or removed until every single item has been catalogued and photographed. But it would be a great relief for me, your majesty, if you, as the highest authority in the Hoggar, would issue an order requiring that these magnificent relics be appropriately recorded and preserved. And, once that is done, we can do as you commanded at our last meeting and see about transferring a great many of the items to your new museum in Tamanrasset for further study and display."

The king laughed scornfully: "So, you would give me these things, and yet they will not be mine."

Ren distractedly swatted at a fly and ignored the king's statement as he said: "I also wish to know whether the remains of Queen al-Kahina should be transferred to the museum. If you prefer, I am prepared to leave her remains here: Given the effort involved in uncovering her burial chamber, I sincerely doubt anyone will ever attempt to do so again once we refill the shaft and return the tomb stone to its proper place."

Just then, Tom came running up. "We've found another silver bracelet, Doctor Villere. That makes seven in total now."

"Magnificent, Tom. Well done. We'll be along shortly. Would you care to visit the burial chamber yourself, Your Majesty?"

It was at that moment, as he saw the king's furious expression, that Ren believed he had miscalculated. "I am not a genie, Your Majesty. I cannot make a treasure appear from thin air. If there were some treasure here and you wanted to take it, I am certain that after some bloodshed and violence, you could. There is far more than we can take with us back to Algiers, so I mean to leave the vast majority of relics with you for a museum, as I've said. If you still feel it is your desire or duty when all is said and done to take the baubles, I cannot stop you."

Once this statement had been translated, Amenukal Amanstan took a deep breath. "I will see the tomb now," he replied with disgust.

In the end, the king was too large to get through the opening at the bottom of the shaft into the burial chamber. He leant through the opening and looked and very carefully considered the value of every item he could see. Of course, Akhou ag Biska and others had already told the king exactly what was in the chamber and that there was no gold at all and only a few worthless silver bands. Seven of them, he had heard.

Once they left the tomb, the king called for his camel to be brought and turned to Ren: "Leave us what you choose," he said. Then he mounted his camel, and he and most of his entourage departed. Several of the Tuareg remained because they were enjoying themselves. One who had heard of Hajjah Bella swore an oath to protect her life and followed her around like an Ottoman Sultan's Janissary.

As the sun set that day, the items in the queen's burial chamber were brought up and the laborers were set to work refilling the shaft and returning the tomb stone to its place on top. The queen's remains would be left in place. Ren had decided that it was more important to show his respect for her people than to further disturb her final rest.

Ren found Tom in the artefact tent examining several items that had been found outside the tomb that day.

"Turned out to be a pretty good day, Professor," Tom said.

"Yes, better than we had any reason to expect," Ren admitted. "You played your part quite well, Tom. But I suppose we'll have to really set up a museum in Tamanrasset now; I hadn't planned on that, but it's not such a terrible idea. We have the money to buy a building, and it shouldn't be difficult to set up a modest exhibit. I wonder, Tom, whether you would have any interest in remaining in Tamanrasset for a while, to arrange it."

"Me, sir? Not Bert? By the way, Professor, I haven't seen Bert all day."

"Oh, yes, Bert's fine. It seems a better fit for you, Tom; you've developed such a keen interest in these artefacts, and it would be a tremendous opportunity for you to create the museum from scratch. You'll probably have the whole thing wrapped up in a month. We can leave a few laborers and soldiers with you; I'll ask Jack if Fedir or Hans could stay on. And I want to make a very generous donation to Akhou ag Biska; perhaps he could help you out with local matters and then guide you up to In Salah when you're finished here."

"I would be most honored, Professor. Yes, and thank you for this opportunity," Tom said hesitantly.

"Are you uncertain?" Ren asked.

"No, sir, not for myself. But I wouldn't ask anyone to stay except of their own desire. That's quite important to me, you see."

"Yes, of course. I'll leave it to you to arrange it, then," Ren said. "Ask whomever you wish."

Ren went on to make plans for the expedition's departure. He and Jack were conferring that evening about departing for In Salah in two days' time when Bella stopped in.

"We had quite a close call, there, didn't we," she said.

"We did," Jack replied. "You handled it very well, Ren. It certainly helped that there was nothing worth killing us for."

"Still, I will feel better when we have gotten back at least as far as In Salah," Ren replied. To Bella he explained: "Jack and I are making plans for our return journey now, the day after tomorrow, probably."

"Must we leave so quickly?" She asked. "We still haven't found the gemstones. Shouldn't we continue looking?"

"Well, as to that, I have a confession to make to you both. You see, that first morning when I entered the burial chamber, it was still a couple hours before dawn, and I was quite alone, so I had time to look over all the artefacts very carefully. There were certain items that I, well ... I removed them."

"Removed? How? What did you take?" Jack asked.

"I removed a set of gold necklaces from the skeletal remains of Queen al-Kahina. Each one of those necklaces was studded with more than two dozen massive green diamonds. Diamonds, they turned out to be, not emeralds, as the legends say. I placed the whole kit into my waterskin that morning and smuggled it out from the chamber as if it was still half full; I even took a sip from the skin in front of witnesses."

"Ren, are you saying there was a treasure after all?" Bella asked.

"Not just a treasure, my dear, but perhaps the most valuable collection of jewels in the whole Maghreb. The only way I could think to protect them was to act as though they didn't exist."

"But where are they now? Do you still have them?" Jack pressed.

"No. I was afraid I would be searched or that my belongings would be stolen, so I gave them to Bert Hill at once and had him leave the camp."

With everything that had happened, and with several members of the expedition staying in Tamanrasset and several leaving for In Salah, it had not occurred to anyone to wonder about the whereabouts of Bert Hill.

"But where is he now?" Jack asked.

"Well," Ren admitted, "I honestly thought he would have returned to the camp by now. We must get the artefacts to the museum in Algiers as soon as possible. Gallé will spare no expense to protect them once we've brought them there."

Ren could tell from Jack's expression that he wondered whether Gallé was as honest a man as Ren believed. But the more pressing question that evening was "Where the hell is Bert Hill?" A thorough search of the camp was conducted, but there were no signs of Bert. At Ren's tent, Jack was preparing to send search parties out to the perimeter of the camp and to search around the massive "lion" and "elephant" when Tom came running up with Bella close behind.

"I didn't know you were looking for Bert, Professor; Bella just told me and I had totally forgotten," Tom said breathlessly. "I hope I haven't caused any trouble."

"Of course not," Ren assured him. "But what did you forget?"

"This," he said handing Ren a sealed letter.

Ren almost fainted as he took the letter, his head in a swoon. He ripped it open. His eyes flew over the page, and an icy chill ran down his spine. Looking at Jack with an ashen expression, he said: "Bert's stolen them.

V – The Ruin of Casablanca

The people of Morocco were stunned by the agreement made by the Western nations at Algeciras, an agreement decreeing European control over their country that was ratified by their own Sultan. Abd al-Aziz was now a puppet of the European bankers, and anti-Western sentiment was rampant in every city and town across the country. Demonstrations were held in marketplaces every day, and there were more violent attacks on Westerners. Nowhere were these tensions more heightened than in Marrakesh, the royal city governed for the Sultan by his brother, Abd al-Hafid.

Pierre Mauchamp was a French medical doctor who had come to Marrakesh to open a dispensary and care for children. Rumors spread about the city that he was spying for the French government and pushing harmful "Christian" beliefs. These accusations were heightened when a flagpole was erected on Mauchamp's roof, as the residents of Marrakesh believed that the pole was part of a wireless telegraphy device that was being used to send reports to the French government. An angry crowd gathered outside the doctor's home. When he stepped outside to speak with them, he was pelted with stones and killed.

The Mauchamp murder made headlines around the world. Fueled by propaganda coming from the French newspapers in Morocco, French citizens demanded retribution for the "unprovoked and indefensible attack from the barbarous natives of Morocco." General Lyautey, this time on orders from the government in Paris, marched the Armée d'Afrique across the Algerian border and entered the Moroccan city of Oujda, occupying it without a gunshot. Territory that France flatly acknowledged was part of Morocco was now being taken into French possession.

Many Moroccans now called for the removal of Sultan Abd al-Aziz. Certain provinces of Morocco were already openly autonomous and others now simply ignored the Sultan's orders, but to hold the country together and resist the French invasion, a strong national leader was needed. The conservative Ulama in Fez privately discussed the selection of a new Sultan who would commit to protecting Islam in Morocco, but there was no consensus on whom they would advance. Al-Kattani, who had studied Islamic law in several Arab lands and Constantinople, drafted articles for his newspaper advocating for policy changes, but he had stopped short of calling for the removal of the Sultan, a step that would have resulted in his arrest. Ahmad had spoken with other provincial representatives who, again and again, agreed that Abd al-Aziz had failed their country.

That summer, Ahmad joined Omar Benayoun and Muhammad al-Kattani on a secret visit to the Royal Palace in Marrakech. They were admitted through a small, private back door of the palace, a door made of blue-painted iron surrounded by blue mosaic tiles, which led into a labyrinth of dark hallways and shaded rooms. It was widely believed that the French were watching Abd al-Hafid very closely, wary of his political aspirations: Even if he had not specifically instigated the attack on Doctor Mauchamp, he had long espoused anti-Western sentiments and loudly complained about his brother's European ways.

The four men were seated in a small, windowless room of the palace, a room with solid walls to keep their conversation confidential, in the guarded inner apartment of the former Grand Wizier's favorite concubine. The air was thick with a murky haze from the solitary oil lamp. The Sultan's brother, Abd al-Hafid, the Khalifa of Marrakesh, sat on a low divan in the nearly empty chamber. A few years older than his brother, he had a longer beard than the Sultan and a calm, seemingly more intelligent expression. He dressed all in white, and was reputed to be a very pious man, one ready to fight for his country and his faith. The flickering lamplight cast long shadows on the walls.

Since the murder of his daughter, Omar Benayoun had become a religious conservative. He was now a leader in the Ulama while remaining a scholar at the university, and he still held Abd al-Aziz in contempt for his wavering on the execution of the monster Hamza. Omar's hatred for the Sultan was deeply personal. Nevertheless, he spoke to the Khalifa calmly and explained the difficult reality they all faced: "Morocco is at a crossroads. Your brother has proven incapable of preserving this country as it faces discontent among its people and an invasion of Christian foreigners. The Ulama is prepared to issue its blessing to a new Sultan who embodies the true faith of Islam and the civic traditions of our people, a person that we are all able to unify around. A few such persons have been suggested, and of course you are among them, but there is no consensus yet. There was great surprise when you were passed over for the throne, being the elder son of the late Sultan Hassan. I believe it would come as welcome news for the people of Morocco to hear that you are willing to take on that responsibility now."

Ahmad had grown up hearing such statements from his father, and about how important it was for the country to be led by a Sultan who not only honored the traditions of the Makhzen but also the dictates of Islam, the very basis to their laws and civil society. Sharif Moulay Mostepha al-Haybah had also been a man who could take his people to war, and Ahmad was uncertain whether the Khalifa had the courage to lead men into battle.

Muhammad al-Kattani was now well-known throughout the Maghreb as a statesman and scholar whose newspaper roused the passions of the faithful. When he spoke, his voice was sharp and full of conviction: "The people are demanding change, Your Highness," he said. "We've made their demands clear to the Makhzen, the specific reforms that are needed, reforms that will push the Europeans out and restore Morocco to its rightful status in the Maghreb. Yet nothing changes, and the French and the European bankers and businessmen block reforms at every turn."

Ahmad interjected: "But reform isn't just about good policies. It's about power and the courage to exercise that power. A man who wishes to rule Morocco must be prepared to fight for it. He must be prepared to exercise power to wage war against those who would take our lands and our wealth and impose their religion upon us."

Abd al-Hafid listened carefully, his intense expression betrayed his keen desires. But Ahmad knew the Khalifa was no fool, not one to be taken in by three lone men no matter their credentials. When he replied, there was an almost reluctant tone to his words: "While I am in the sincerest sympathy with your concerns," Abd al-Hafid said, "one does not simply seize the throne of Morocco by having the support of a few salty intellectuals or an unruly mob. To rule Morocco, I would need much more than that: An army, weapons, money, and, most importantly, allies. Is that what you are offering me? For I will not make a move unless success is certain."

Ahmad, sitting across from the Khalifa, straightened his back. This was the part he had expected, the reality that couldn't be avoided. He had seen the influence of powerful families firsthand, his own family included. In the south, it wasn't just about religion or intellectual ideas. It was about control of the land, the trade, the allegiances, about who had guns and could gather a haraka. Having traveled throughout the country, Ahmad knew that there were many who simply wanted to profit off the French regardless of the cost to their people or of what would be lost.

Omar Benayoun said, almost as though he were reading Ahmad's mind, "Madani El Glaoui's support is essential. The Atlas mountains are a gateway between north and south, and therefore the Glaoui family's power reaches much farther than to the simple tribes of the mountains. Furthermore, Madani El Glaoui can summon an army; he remains, at least in name, commander of the Sultan's armies. Nothing will change without him."

Madani El Glaoui wasn't just the Qaid of the High Atlas, he was a man whose alliances could shift the entire balance of power. He was no longer an avid supporter of Abd al-Aziz, but convincing him to side with Abd al-Hafid was another matter entirely. Madani El Glaoui was pragmatic, a man

Tamanrasset

driven by power, and, at the moment, power in Morocco was tied to the French.

Abd al-Hafid looked down, lost in thought, before he spoke again, his voice cautious but clear. "I agree. I would certainly need Madani El Glaoui's support."

"Madani El Glaoui will not support you just for the sake of your throne, Your Highness," Ahmad replied. "He seeks power for himself. He will only align the Glaoui with those who offer him more influence, more control. He has never supported a ruler unless it directly benefits him." Indeed, the Glaoui had sided with Sultan Hassan, and then the Regent, and then Abd al-Aziz. "Perhaps, you could offer him something that would elevate his position even further: A role in the new government. The Glaoui family controls the Atlas, but would you offer Madani El Glaoui greater influence in the Makhzen, perhaps even the position of Grand Wizier?"

Abd al-Hafid's eyes narrowed. "That is a possibility," he murmured, "but if such an offer appeared desperate, I would be made into a puppet myself. If we approach the Glaoui at all, Madani will understand at once that his support is crucial, but he must not come to believe that he is indispensable. You must pave this road if you wish me to walk it."

As the conversation continued, uncertainty hung in the air. In the end, it was Omar Benayoun who said that "it seems we are at an impasse. It is premature for us to approach Madani El Glaoui on your behalf, Your Highness. Before we do, we must have in place an alliance that makes your ascension inevitable. That will take time."

Ahmad agreed: Nothing would move forward until their allies were committed and Abd al-Hafid's victory was demanded by all. Then, perhaps, Madani El Glaoui would join them.

* * *

There was no time to lose if they had any hope of finding Bert.

"Where could he have possibly gone?" Ren asked. "We must find him, Jack. I must get those artefacts back. My reputation, my career are at stake. I'll be expelled from the professional societies and probably lose my position at Carthage if anyone finds out I've lost them."

"Bert wouldn't dare go to Tamanrasset," Jack said, "so that means he must be headed back to In Salah. From there he would have a comparatively safe journey through the Touat region; he may be planning to go north to Oran, but my guess is he will go to Morocco."

"Not back to Algiers?"

"Gallé would have a hundred men out looking for him. Bert might be able to disappear in Morocco. It won't be easy for him to sell the damned things."

"But can you catch him up, Jack? My God, we must recover them," Ren pleaded.

"I'll get them back for you, Ren: I'll take a couple men and leave within the hour," he said. As a Legionnaire, Jack had ridden a camel as far as eighty-six kilometers in a single day, so there was no doubt in his mind that he could eventually catch up to Bert Hill, but Bert had a significant head start and could very well get lost in the desert and amble about in a very un-straight line making him easy to miss. Jack felt he must do everything he possibly could to recover the jewels. "Look, I want you to follow along as soon as possible," he told Ren. "I can probably get ahead of Bert, but I need you all out looking for him. Bring as many men as you can, spread out. Keep your eyes open, look for any sign of a fire at night. I'll have Hans go with you; he'll know what to do."

"Yes, we can depart tomorrow evening since Tom will be staying to set up the new museum in Tamanrasset. You can close up the excavation, can't you, Tom?"

"Of course, whatever you need, Professor," he answered.

"And, Bella, you'll come with us tomorrow?"

She looked uncertain and cast a sideways glance at Tom. "I thought I might help Tom setting up the museum," she told them hesitantly, "but I can see that this is an emergency. Yes, Ren, I'll go with you."

"I have every confidence in Tom's ability to set the thing up," Ren said.

"As do I," she said.

Ren looked at his brother, and Jack could feel his panic. "Listen, Ren, I swear to you I'll do everything I can," he said. "We're going to make this right."

But Bert Hill proved to be a difficult man to find. Whether it was fear that drove him or some disguised skills that rendered him invisible to detection, or perhaps just blind luck, Jack found no signs of him as he traveled northwest from Tamanrasset with two of the Chaamba soldiers. They reached In Salah in only eleven days, and there was no doubt in Jack's mind that they must have arrived several days before Bert could have possibly gotten there. Yet, no one in the oasis town had seen the American archaeologist. Jack waited, and waited. He sent his soldiers to search in the surrounding desert. He pleaded with Colonel Huré at Camp Bugeaud to send out search parties. The Colonel's camel cavalry was still searching for the Tuareg warriors who remained at large in the desert—it turned out that Ren's expedition had avoided being caught by the Tuareg warriors and slaughtered near Arak by only a couple days. Jack spun a story about Bert being the son of an American Congressman and insisted that he be found at any price. The Colonel wasn't moved, but, as a small concession, he ordered his patrols to keep an eye out for a missing archaeologist. After a few days, Jack began to wonder whether Bert might have gone a different way: Perhaps he had gone to Tamanrasset after all, or perhaps he had died in the desert or been captured. Ren was sure to be traveling back with the main caravan of laborers and attendants and was likely more than a week still from In Salah, but Jack nevertheless prepared to head back towards Tamanrasset to meet up with his brother so they could scour the desert. Indecision stalled him two more days until the Colonel unexpectedly reported that Bert had been seen. Would he arrive at In Salah soon? Not at all, the Colonel told him. Bert had somehow bypassed In Salah altogether and had traveled another three hundred kilometers northwest to Timimoun, another oasis village under French control.

Jack was baffled: Bert must have hired one of the expedition's Chaamba soldiers and used his help to pass through the desert undetected. Jack knew that Bert had been regularly playing cards with the soldiers, and perhaps one fellow owed him money or for some payment was willing to accompany Bert. With such assistance, he would be much harder to catch, and he was traveling damn fast, obviously hoping to shake any pursuit. Jack left word for Ren at In Salah and left immediately for Timimoun. Even at his quick pace, he and the Chaamba soldiers would have trouble catching up. But they still followed doggedly, arriving only a few days behind Bert in Timimoun, and in Béni Abbès, in Igli, in Taghit, and in Colomb-Bechar, and arriving only a few hours after Bert had reportedly departed there.

Colomb-Bechar had changed since Lyautey had taken over the town. French infantry and Foreign Legionnaires were now permanently garrisoned in the town, although it was still generally considered to be in Moroccan territory. Nevertheless, the French government had extended the train line there from Aïn Séfra. Jack was able to confirm that Bert had not taken the train north, so it seemed he wasn't headed towards Oran. Bert must be going west to Morocco.

Telegraph lines were difficult to maintain in an area with insurgents who would constantly cut the wires, but the French had been experimenting with an optical telegraph—a line of manned towers spaced close enough to allow the passage of signals by means of lights or flags. From Colomb-Bechar the line was fairly reliable, so Jack took advantage to send a succinct message to Gallé with an explanation of the crisis at hand:

> ARTEFACTS STOLEN BY BERT HILL
> RECOVER AT ALL COSTS
> HEADING MOROCCO

Jack wasn't sure how Gallé would take the term "artefact" so he sent a somewhat more detailed letter by rail in which he made it clear that the "artefacts" stolen were of extraordinary value and that no expense should be spared to find Bert Hill.

While it was unclear which way Bert had gone from Colomb-Bechar, even assuming he had gone towards Morocco as Jack presumed, then he would eventually have to get over the Atlas mountains somewhere and that was not so simple. There were many possible paths, some more dangerous than others, and Jack himself had never been through the Atlas. Then a telegram arrived from Gallé instructing Jack to follow Bert to Morocco at once. Luckily, the Chaamba soldiers with Jack found a dependable guide to lead them, and with Jack in disguise as an Arab they were led over the mountains.

Jack also left instructions for Ren to travel north to Oran; Ren could travel to Morocco by ship and meet anywhere on the coast, but Jack was fairly sure he knew where Bert was headed.

By the time Jack reached the village of Boudenib in the foothills of the Atlas mountains, he was hot on Bert's trail. There had been sightings of the white-skinned American and his Berber guide, and Jack now felt certain that they were traveling to the one place where Bert might be able to sell the stolen green diamonds. There was only one place in all of Morocco so lawless that literally anything could be bought or sold in its medina—Casablanca. Jack and his companions pursued, climbing high up through isolated stone passes across the barren mountains, then down into the more fertile lands to the north, trading their camels for horses, and following Bert's path until, after days and days of travel, they finally tracked him to Casablanca.

Tamanrasset

There were many cities in Morocco, but none so reviled as Casablanca. Known as al-Dar al-Bayda to the Berber population who had lived there for two thousand years, it had been a port for Phoenicians, Romans, and Arabs. Then the Spanish had come, but it was the Portuguese who colonized it and called it "Casa Branca" and allowed the city to become a haven for pirates, criminals, and fugitives. It remained a place where human lives were traded with the same frequency as stolen or illicit goods.

Casablanca was a city of wide arches, deep shaded arcades and whitewashed walls, a city whose residents were crammed into small townhouses that filled the city's filthy kasbah: Moorish buildings crowded the narrow, twisting streets as the desert sun held the city in its burning embrace. Every day, shots were fired, sirens and whistles shattered the calm, refuges and street urchins hid in doorways and veiled women ran for shelter. Under the agreement signed at Algeciras, the French were now paying a French company to enlarge the port: La Compagnie Marocaine was the target of intense local rage after the company built a railway to the quarry on the northeast edge of the city straight through an ancient, hallowed necropolis. The fact remained that the people of Casablanca did not want a port or a railroad and most emphatically did not want the French, Spanish, or British.

Jack sent his men to search through the city and ask for news of Bert from the local populace. To avoid becoming a target of the locals' wrath himself, Jack traded his military-like clothes for a simple, inexpensive suit and explained, when asked, that he was an American—the first time he had identified himself as a United States citizen in nearly thirty years. He took rooms in the main European-style hotel on the main square, the Continental, and he spread a lot of money around to ensure that he had a lot of goodwill in the city.

If Bert had any brains, which he had indeed proven himself to possess, he would be extremely careful about the persons to whom he offered the green diamonds for sale, holding out not only for an excellent price but also for a trustworthy and highly confidential purchaser. The question was whether he could avoid being caught before a payment and transfer were made so he could also make an escape. But Casablanca was the perfect sort of town to stay hidden out of sight for weeks. Jack visited the kasbah to make inquiries among the less reputable French and Spanish dealers of illegal and stolen goods.

"There are always rumors in Casablanca that special items might be coming up for sale–artefacts, gold, even slaves," he was told. "If it's gemstones you're after, there is always something worth buying. Where can I find you?"

"I'm at the Continental," he told them.

"But if I may give you a piece of advice, my friend, be careful who you speak to. You are not the only one asking about 'interesting gemstones' for sale."

When Jack returned to the hotel that evening, he found Édouard Durant waiting for him with a bottle of wine at the café on the square. Jack turned from the door of his hotel and crossed to the café, coming to a stop directly in front of the French businessman. "Come, Monsieur, and take a seat,' Durant said. "We have much to talk about. How are we to address you these days?"

"Just tell me what you want, Durant."

"It's been a long time since we first met in Tlemcen, n'est ce pas? You've proven far more useful than any of us expected. I was certain you'd just go back to the Foreign Legion and disappear."

"I don't mean to be rude but it's been a long day already," Jack said, refusing a glass of wine. "So Gallé got my letter and sent you, is that it?"

"Well, I'm aware of the letter you sent to Monsieur Gallé, yes. And you remain on the trail of the American, Bert Hill? He has been quite adept at avoiding capture, or has the thief now been found?"

"He's employed an assistant to guide him and keep him out of sight, but he's here in Casablanca, laying low."

"Then I have no doubt you will find him."

"Searching for thieves and stolen items isn't my usual repertoire, but I've asked around. Listen, were you sent here by Gallé with instructions for me or not?"

"Not precisely, no. What if I were to tell you, with absolute certainty, that Gallé has no intention of putting the ...." He stopped to look around, "... stolen items into the museum in Algiers."

"Aren't you on the museum's board of directors?"

"That's how I know. Gallé has blocked a motion to hire additional men here to assist you, but I have learned that he has sent his own people to seek for Bert Hill himself."

Jack looked at Durant blankly for a moment. "I believe I am still employed by Monsieur Gallé as well," he said.

"Then you will condone the blatant theft of these precious artefacts simply because you are paid? Why, if so, you should work for me," Durant said. "I know you are a man of many resources, Monsieur, and I would guarantee you a substantial finder's fee if you were able to secure the artefacts for me."

"Secure them, *for you*," Jack repeated.

Durant twisted in his seat. "For the museum, if you prefer," he said petulantly.

"I'm sure you have your own people looking," Jack observed.

"They don't know what they're looking for, exactly."

"And I haven't seen the items with my own eyes. I only know what I've been told."

"That's more than the rest of us," Durant answered. "Your letter to Gallé was vague. Intentionally, I'm sure. But you made it quite clear that these items are priceless. We can all use our imaginations, n'est-ce pas le cas?"

"I can't say how much more effort I can put into finding them," he said. "I've just come over a thousand kilometers; I might need a little rest."

Durant looked cross. "You'll let me know, then, when you're ready to continue the search."

"Oh, yes, I'll let you know first," Jack said as he stood up and walked back to the hotel.

A telegram from Joubert was waiting for him:

UPDATE REQUIRED
REPLY IMMEDIATELY

Jack balled up the telegram and threw it in the wastepaper basket.

* * *

Omar, al-Kattani and others were quietly visiting different areas of the country to shore up support for Abd al-Hafid. For most, there was no doubt whatsoever that Abd al-Aziz had to be removed. Ahmad had gone first to the Tadla region and had found the leaders of both the Beni Zemmour tribe and the Ouardigha confederacy were receptive to the message of reformation. These tribes controlled rich farmlands in the Plains of Marrakesh and were happy to sell their grain to whomever paid the highest price, but they were also Muslims and had no love for the Europeans. They had heard that Abd al-Aziz had become a Christian. If Abd al-Hafid were to be named by the Ulama of Fez as the Sultan's successor, they told Ahmad, he would be most welcome.

Ahmad rode next to speak with the Chaouia, a confederation of powerful tribes that occupied the lands around Casablanca; they ruled autonomously, without interference from the Sultan. Such areas of virtual anarchy were not unusual in Morocco, but the Chaouia region was known particularly for its lawlessness and the tribal leaders had little or no concern who was the Sultan of Morocco. However, the French had recently taken over the customs house at the port in Casablanca and had begun collecting customs duties there on Chaouia grains and wool (products that were mostly sold to the British). The tribesmen raged against the French and tensions were high. So while they did not especially care who was Sultan, the tribes would support anyone who promised to remove the French from Casablanca.

Hajj Hamou was the long-time leader of the Ouled Hariz and an imposing figure in his long robes with a weathered face that reflected the hardships of the Chaouia region. He invited Ahmad to accompany him into the city to watch the protests and demonstrations that the tribesmen had planned. Ahmad joined a long line of grim, heavily armed men making their way into town. The kasbah, which was ordinarily languid, had become a raging hornet's nest, and everyone expected violence after the tribes spread out through the city. Ahmad first went with Hajj Hamou to see the Qaid of Casablanca, Abu Bakr, an overly calm, politic man appointed by Abd al-Aziz.

It quickly became clear that the Qaid had no conception of the anger across the city or the danger posed to him personally. He was waiting to meet Hajj Hamou and Ahmad in a dimly lit room of his house near the port. The air was thick with tobacco smoke, and Ahmad, who had never seen the ocean before that day, could see waves crashing against the rocks through the open window. The rough, pastoral appearance of Hajj Hamou seemed out of place in the Qaid's refined, Westernized home. Abu Bakr was dressed in fine robes and sat obstinately behind an ornate wooden desk, his gaze steady.

Hajj Hamou bowed slightly: "Asalamu alaikom, Qaid Abu Bakr. I have brought with me Ahmad al-Haybah of the Doui-Menia."

"Wa alaikom salaam. Yes, I am most appreciative of the wise counsel I have heard from the Sharif of the Doui-Menia. He is your father's brother, is that correct?"

Ahmad bristled, for if Abu Bakr knew that Ahmad was the son of the late Sharif, then he was really just pointing out that Ahmad had been passed over as the Sharif's successor.

Hajj Hamou understood the subtext and replied promptly: "He has come to ask our opinion of the recent actions of our Sultan, Abd al-Aziz. Alas, my words are heavy in my heart, more so because the men of the Chaouia expect me to bring them peace when I cannot."

"Hajj Hamou, you are most welcome here as always," Abu Bakr said. "Ahmad of the Doui-Menia, I suspect you have come a very long way to hear what you already know. But, please, take a seat. Speak your mind. What is it that troubles the Chaouia and the Doui-Menia?"

Hajj Hamou sat with a deliberate slowness: "We are indeed troubled. The people of the Chaouia, as well as those in the surrounding regions, have suffered under the weight of foreign interference. It is time for us to reclaim what is ours."

Abu Bakr said nothing. "Go on," he said patiently.

"The strength of this nation is in its tribes," Ahmad said. "Our connections, our familial ties and our tribal affiliations are, on their most basic level, the bedrock of our society. It is these connections and affiliations which give us both strength and flexibility. We do not need more commerce or better transportation or greater affluence to honor Allah in the best way possible. Yet the French are attempting to sell us their Christian society with their competitive worldview. Yes, they have been favored with many blessings—great ships, great wealth, a thousand wonderful things most useful to people who live such hasty, restless lives. But they have no value to each other unless they can profit by it. Now, I see, you have done very well, Qaid. Your home is beautiful, and the view of the ocean, I could look at that for hours. But you are not making Casablanca any better by allowing the French to do what they wish here."

"We have demands," Hajj Hamou said, "and I will state them clearly for you. The French officers must be removed from the customs house. They have no place in our lands, no right to interfere with our affairs. The customs house was never meant to be the tool of a foreign power."

"But the customs house is vital to the trade and flow of goods in and out of Casablanca. The French have ensured that it runs smoothly and efficiently, though I know their presence stirs anger. Removal of the French officers is a matter that cannot be taken lightly."

"By what authority are the French collecting duties on our products? Let us run our own affairs, as we have done for centuries without their interference."

"But they are spending the duties collected to expand our port."

"The port does not need to be expanded. When did we become merely a nation of merchants and traders? All construction at the docks must be halted. Enlarging the port serves only one purpose—it merely expands the reach of the foreign invaders and bring legitimacy to their claims."

Abu Bakr raised his hand as if to stop a rising storm. "The port expansion is critical for our advancement. The French intend to increase trade which will benefit all the people of Casablanca. But I hear your concerns. The encroachment upon sacred lands, the toll it takes on the dignity of our people—these are matters I do not take lightly."

Ahmad replied angrily, "the prosperity of a few should not come at the cost of our nation. What are we without power or control? What good is wealth if the wealth of the land and the people is lost?"

"You speak with great sincerity," Abu Bakr replied, an observation without approval. "I hear your words. What else do you demand, Hajj Hamou?"

"This new railroad that runs through the heart of our ancient necropolis, desecrating what should remain untouched, this cannot stand. The railroad must be removed. It is sacred ground, and that must be respected."

Abu Bakr's eyes narrowed and his hands gripped the edge of the desk. His voice was now tinged with derision: "The dead are gone, and the stones of the ancient necropolis have no significance to anyone, but the railroad is at the very heart of our progress. The French say it will bind our country together, bring wealth and opportunity to all."

"Then you reject our demands, Qaid?"

Abu Bakr paused. Looking away, his fingers drumming lightly on the desk, the Qaid backtracked. "I will not make this decision in haste. I must weigh the consequences carefully."

"It is not the French we must fear," Hajj Hamou replied. "It is the loss of the soul of our people. We are watching you, and our patience grows thin. I speak not only for the Chaouia, but for all in this land. Do not ignore our voice."

"I cannot promise that all will be as you wish. But I do promise that your words have been heard."

"Then you think on them, Qaid. The Chaouia will wait, but not for long. The winds of change are even now sweeping across Morocco."

Abu Bakr turned back to look at Ahmad and Hajj Hamou. "We shall see where those winds take us. Return in two days, and I will tell you what I believe can be done."

Hajj Hamou rose and nodded respectfully before turning to leave. He tried to catch Ahmad's eye, but Ahmad was looking at the Qaid.

"It is said that the Sultan's army is small but mighty," Ahmad said to the Qaid. "In fact, I have been told that the finest fighters in his army are those from the Chaouia region."

"Yes, that is so," the Qaid replied.

"It is unfortunate that the Sultan did not send soldiers to help you protect the French, but then, I suppose, you could not be certain on which side they would fight. I hope, for the sake of the people in this town, that you will not have to find out."

Ahmad stood and walked out of the room, Hajj Hamou beside him, as Abu Bakr remained seated.

* * *

Shots were fired outside the hotel, and Jack saw a squad of French soldiers running for the port. They carried no weapons, and Jack surmised that they had been on leave, had been attacked, and were beating a retreat. There was no doubt that things in the city were heating up. For one thing, there were more people than ever in the kasbah. Jack intended to check in with the illicit traders there, but he had begun to feel decidedly unwelcome. And then he had also received a summons, a message from the French Consul to be at his office that morning.

Jack had seen nothing more of Durant and had heard nothing more from Joubert, but he was also no closer to finding Bert Hill. There were rumors, but Jack couldn't be sure he hadn't been the one himself to set them off. Nevertheless, when the only thing approximating the force of law in a place like Casablanca required you to be at a certain governmental office at a certain hour, well, it was at least considerate, if not wise, to show up. Yet even the short walk to the consulate had become risky. Large tribesmen from the countryside had flooded the streets. Jack got to the consulate the shortest way he could.

The number of foreigners—French, British, Spanish, Italians, and Germans—packed into the French consulate was impressive. Anti-Western violence had been on the rise the past few days and was reaching a fever pitch. Many people simply wanted the safety of a government building and had come to do nothing more than sit, hour after hour. In the Consul's small offices, however, all was quiet. A pretty French receptionist greeted Jack with a lascivious smile and went to see if the Consul was ready for him. Jack was shown right in.

Standing by the window looking down upon the crowded street below stood Deputy Governor Cayard.

"I'm not surprised they sent you," Jack said.

"You've made quite a trip, Monsieur, in search of something that everyone seems to want, although no one seems to know what it is."

"Are you here on behalf of Gallé, Durant, the Antiquities Museum, or your damn own self like the rest of them? I can't say that I'm enjoying this carousel—the horses all look the same."

Crossroads of the Nomad

"There are those who believe that anything of such apparent value has the potential to cause great harm. You were once a soldier of France. Of course we all know that men like you come to the Foreign Legion for private reasons, but you, sir, you stayed because you were proud of your service. France needs you again."

"I have no doubt France wants something. That's a far cry from saying it wants something I would be proud to provide."

"But you are in her debt. The Governor allowed Joubert to interfere in your case because of your service to him at Figuig, and he wanted to repay you. We all understood that you probably had good reason to murder that Legionnaire, but had Joubert not received permission to influence the outcome, you would surely have had a rendezvous with Madame Guillotine."

"In my book, if the Governor paid a debt to me, that doesn't leave me further indebted to him, but I suspect doing a favor for Gallé was closer to the Governor's true intent. But what does France want with more treasure anyway? Isn't the Louvre full of the stuff already?"

"It isn't about treasure, though. Did you know that the Moroccan Sultan has also sent people to Casablanca to recover these supposed artefacts? Whatever these items are, Monsieur, news of them has already spread widely, and they have captured the imagination of a good many people. That gives them a tremendous power, a power to control and to influence, and we both know there is no power in the Maghreb that France does not want."

Jack laughed. "Well, I don't know where the artefacts are now, and your luck is as good as mine—you go find them.

Only I wouldn't go outside asking around right now: It looks like a little riot is brewing. You might get shot, or worse."

"Have you no love for France anymore, Monsieur?"

"I have no love for France or anything else, Deputy. And I'll tell you, at this point, I wouldn't be surprised if Bert Hill dropped the damn things in the latrine and made a run for it. But for the moment, I think he's still here, in Casablanca. I feel certain of it. But he won't be here for long."

"Then you intend to recover these artefacts and simply give them to Doctor Villere? Why do you believe *he* is trustworthy?"

Jack laughed. "I don't much care whether he is trustworthy or not. I'm a man of my word, and I've told Doctor Villere that I will get those items for him. The items themselves mean nothing to me. They're an inconvenience."

"And if Doctor Villere was no longer in a position to accept the items from you?"

"Well, as it turns out, Deputy, Ren and I have known each other a long, long time, and I dare say I owe him a little something. So if your statement was meant as a threat, you should reconsider whether you want make an enemy of a man like me."

"No, no, not at all," Cayard backtracked. "But you'll find the items?"

"You'll know if I do," Jack said. He winked and walked out.

* * *

Late that afternoon, the Chaouia tribesmen set fire to a warehouse by the docks, and the entire city was soon covered with a cloud of smoke and light ash. All the ships quickly left port; only one arrived that evening—a third-rate ferry from Tangier carrying Moroccan natives. As the passengers disembarked, tribesmen stood on the dock to block any Europeans from entering the city. One exception was made, for it was considered ill-advised to obstruct the path of Hajjah Bella. She herself was naturally allowed entry into the city since it was well known that she was really a djinn who had taken the form of a woman. No, the one exception was made for her white-skinned manservant (white-skinned though dressed like an Arab) who was also allowed entry: She said he was an American, and no one knew of any reason to kill an American since they had never seen one before.

Ren had no objection to playing Bella's manservant if he could get off the boat and get to the hotel where Jack was staying. It had taken weeks for him and Bella to travel by camel from Tamanrasset to Colomb-Bechar then up to Oran by train. It was in Oran that they first heard from Jack of the unrest in Casablanca, and they quickly made plans to head there. However, all the usual ferries had been temporarily halted, and only the third class ship for locals was scheduled to depart from Tangier. But, needs must, Ren insisted, and so they took the third class. Bella had no objection—indeed, she had been a good sport during the entire journey from Tamanrasset and Ren suspected her interventions had probably saved his life a dozen times. It was all he could do to remain calm on the ferry. "Tell me," she asked him, "these necklaces, and the jewels you've described, I know they are valuable, but can you really be blamed if they are stolen?"

Ren laughed. "I told you about my trouble in Tunisia and about the antiquities inspector. It's like having a wicked stepparent or schoolmaster who takes advantage of every misstep to beat you. The irony is that, in Oran, I received a telegram from Delattre saying that Gauckler has finally been recalled to Paris. He couldn't find one damn thing wrong with our work in Carthage, and I'm wanted back as soon as possible. But if word gets out that I've allowed Bert Hill to run off with these necklaces, I shall not be welcome anywhere again. It's a small world, the world of archaeology. We all know each other, and we're very harsh critics of each other's work. I must recover the necklaces and tender them to the museum. After that, I don't care what happens to them."

As they passed through the streets of Casablanca, Bella asked for directions to Jack's hotel. Night was falling, and suddenly to the north there was a single, loud explosion. The level of excitement throughout the city dramatically increased; a certain frenzy or hysteria took hold. People were rushing through the narrow alleys and small squares. Sporadic shots were fired, and women were screaming. Smoke and falling ash from the warehouse fire continued to cloud the streets. The flames had spread to two more buildings near the warehouse.

By the time Ren and Bella arrived at Jack's hotel, there were French soldiers surrounding the building who would only let authorized persons enter. It was necessary for Jack to come down to gain their admittance.

"I can't believe they've let you off the ship," Jack said worriedly. "For Christ's sake, come inside before you're shot."

"A pleasure to see you, as well, brother," Ren said. "As always, I couldn't have gotten here if not for our dear friend Bella. Have you found Bert? Any news?"

"News?" Jack said derisively. "Why, you heard that explosion, didn't you? The local tribesmen blocked the train tracks and murdered the work crew on board it earlier today. That was the sound of the train engine being dynamited. The whole city is in chaos, and no one knows who is in charge. We're told the mayor refused to kick out the French authorities and was forced to flee for his life. I'm sure Bert is stuck here with us now; there's no way he can get out of the city. I'm surprised he hasn't shown up either here at the hotel or at the consulate—they're the only two buildings in town that the French are guarding, though I'm told more soldiers are on the way."

"But that's the very reason the Chaouia tribes have taken over the city," Bella explained. "This is not Algeria or Tunisia. The French have no right to be here. If the tribes want them to leave, then they must leave."

"I'm afraid neither the French nor any of the other European nations give a damn what the Chaouia want," Jack said.

"Then they shouldn't be surprised when the people revolt."

"It's far too dangerous to go out at night, even for you, Bella," Ren said.

"Come upstairs and we'll have some supper brought to the room," Jack added." Tomorrow perhaps we can get back out to look for Bert."

In fact, Jack's Chaamba soldiers sent him word that they expected to soon learn where Bert Hill was hiding: They had

Tamanrasset

run across their friend at the medina—the very soldier that Bert had hired to guide him from Tamanrasset. The fellow wouldn't say where Bert was hiding, but the soldiers were following him and believed he would eventually lead them to Bert's location.

* * *

After days of smoke and ash, the fires at the port finally burned out. Several warehouses and most of the new construction by the French contractor had been destroyed. While the fires had burned, the city had devolved into chaos. Thousands of the Chaouia tribesmen had taken control of the streets, and armed men had rioted in every part of town. Both European and native homes had been looted and burned. Men found on the street had been beaten and murdered, and women caught in public had been raped. Some captured Westerners had been taken to the docks for deportation, others put to death. Those in the Continental hotel and at the French consulate, both guarded by French soldiers, prayed they would be allowed to escape. But then the Sun came out again and in the quiet of early morning the violence briefly subsided. For a moment, many of the tribesmen, like demons, slank back into their dens to rest until nightfall when their rampage could resume, although some still roamed the streets through the day making it unwise to venture out.

Two French warships arrived that morning, the Linois-class cruiser Galilée which had been dispatched from Tangier and the cruiser Du Chayla which arrived from Toulon. Both were anchored just outside the port, and many more troops from each ship were being ferried ashore, reportedly to evacuate the Westerners from the city. More ships were expected to arrive and many more soldiers. There was a growing expectation that there would be a major battle between the French army and the Chaouia tribesmen.

Jack, Ren, and Bella had stayed in the hotel for three days, and the men had insisted, much to Bella's chagrin, that she have the bedroom in Jack's suite while the two men took turns sleeping on the chaise lounge in the parlor. She appreciated having a private space to pray, but she felt so accustomed to these two men that it made her smile when she listened to them in the next room playing cards at night like children as she fell asleep. Their meals were sent to the room, and Jack went down to the lobby to speak to their fellow guests and learn whether the city was yet under any semblance of control. Whatever he learned, he always told Bella and Ren that the hotel was well guarded by French soldiers and there was no indication of peril. She didn't believe him.

On the second morning, as the shooting in the city temporarily subsided, a large crowd began to slowly gather in front of the hotel. The hotel's manager, a tall Frenchman with a thin mustache and oddly muscular hands, knocked on the door to Jack's rooms and was admitted to the crowded parlor.

"We are of course delighted to have you here, Monsieur Demain, and your associate. Monsieur," he said acknowledging Ren. "Yet, as you are aware, the city is in a state of general upheaval, which, unfortunately, makes it necessary for me to speak to your–ahem–guest," he went on. "La mademoiselle?" There was more than a hint of disapproval in his terse statement; it was not even a request.

"I will have to check if she is available. May I convey the matter you wish to discuss with her?" Jack answered.

"Under the circumstances," the Manager replied as he gestured vaguely to the window, "I have no objection to your permitting the young woman to stay in your rooms, Monsieur, but her visit at the Continental has enflamed certain tensions (or created a certain level of risk, you might say) that we expect she will be so good as to ameliorate."

"Can you possibly be any clearer," Jack replied, but Ren understood. He crossed to the bedroom door and knocked.

"Bella, my dear, are you able to come speak with the hotel's Manager?" The pocket door to the bedroom slid open, and Bella stood in the doorway, dressed in her white robes but with her head uncovered and her brown hair cascading over her shoulders. "There is some concern about your presence in the hotel, it seems," he told her.

The Manager at first seemed somewhat taken aback. Perhaps he had not realized that she was a European woman.

"Yes, I heard what you were saying," she told them.

"I apologize, Madame," the Manager explained, "but it seems there are a number of people outside the hotel, local people, who are demanding that we 'release' you. They are under the misapprehension that the Hotel Continental is holding you here against your will."

"Oh, I'm so sorry to hear it," she gasped.

"Moreover, the Lieutenant in command of the French soldiers guarding the hotel is afraid that these misinformed individuals might try to storm the hotel in order to attempt a rescue. I have come to express our sincere desire that you will come down and speak to the crowd and assure them that you are here of your own free choice," and then he turned to Jack, "if that is indeed the case."

"Of course it is," Jack replied testily.

"Yes, yes, I will come down at once," Bella replied. "But tell me, please, the al-Adārisah mosque is quite close—would it be safe, do you think, for me to walk there? It's almost midday."

"I really cannot say, Madame. The mosque you mention is merely four blocks from our front door," the Manager replied. "It's rather quiet outside at the moment, but I do not know what reception you will receive."

"I do," she answered almost despairingly.

"I'll go with you," Jack offered.

"No. Thank you, Jack, but I need to be seen alone, not in company of a white-skinned guardian," she said.

After three days of hiding, Bella realized she would have to make an appearance, something which she had been hoping to avoid. It seemed her notoriety was even greater in Morocco and nowhere more so than in the cities, and she began to wonder whether she would ever be able to live a quiet, simple life again. She could always throw off the hijab and dress like a European woman, change her name, pray privately at home, and at times she even imagined being married to Tom Childers. It was a heartwarming fantasy, but in the instant moment she simply put on her scarf and Jack and Ren accompanied her to the lobby.

"You'll be alright, won't you?" Ren asked.

"It's only four blocks, Ren," she chided him.

The crowd in the square outside the hotel was too large to be silent or still. There was a general flow of movement and a rumble of angry voices which was naturally threatening to the thin line of French soldiers who were attempting to prevent any entry to the hotel. Yet the crowd did become disturbingly still and watched silently as Bella stepped out of the hotel right before mid-day. She walked down the steps and the soldiers allowed her through the line where she was immediately surrounded by men and women who had come out of concern for her well-being. Bella smiled and nodded respectfully to the men and laid her hand on the arm of any woman who came near. She assured them she was well and that those in the hotel were just trying to stay out of harm's way, just as they were themselves. When asked when the violence would end, she tried to sound optimistic. It seemed that the residents of the city were equally terrified of the Chaouia tribesmen who were running riot, killing, stealing, and attacking women. She invited everyone near to come with her to the mosque for prayers, and even considering the shortness of the distance, a large crowd soon gathered around her as they walked through the narrow streets to the mosque. Everyone said that, at sundown, the city would lapse into chaos again, and there was talk that the hotel and the French consulate might not be safe much longer.

As she knelt in the mosque and meditated silently before the prayers began, Bella again felt surrounded by a community of people whose attention was piercingly focused upon her. She had come to rely on the kindness and generosity of these people, but, at the same time, the attention made her feel removed from them. She was not allowed to just be another member of the community: She was different and was treated differently. They wanted her to be more; they wanted her to be an oddity, a djinn. They wanted her to have power, they wanted her blessing, and they expected she would somehow save them. Now that she was in Casablanca, more so than any other place she had been, the fear with which these people lived was both palpable and contagious. She was afraid for them, and she was afraid for this city, and she was afraid for her friends. She had grown attached to Ren and Jack. She felt a great bond with them—joining the expedition had been a good choice for her. She hadn't had to play a role or be a specific person for Ren and Jack. She had just been herself, and they took her happily at face value and respected her and maybe even cherished her a little. She felt that they loved her. She would go anywhere with them and help them do whatever they sought to achieve, and she felt, in her heart, that they would be proud to be given the opportunity to help her too. And maybe she could include Tom Childers in their little tribe, and Hans Mueller, who had brought her and the expedition back from Tamanrasset, and while she had never become very close to Bert Hill, he had never struck her as a bad person, really. And she realized she missed the simplicity and clarity of the desert; it was so much easier to be herself there.

She stood and brought her hands up to begin the prayer. The room was very crowded, probably more so than usual. It might have something to do with her presence, but it was surely also because of the lull in the violence and the fear in the city's residents. She couldn't help but glance at the people around her, many elderly men and women, children, young women who looked battered and were having difficulty holding back their tears. These people were fragile, and they had only each other. When the prayers concluded, she begged them to return to their homes. Most came to wish her well and seek her blessing, and one older man came to spit at her—it was the usual sort of thing. She tried to give everyone a smile and a blessing.

Then, as the crowd dispersed and she was almost alone in the mosque, she saw him: Ahmad was there, looking at her, an expression on his face that was pained and difficult to interpret. Bella's heart raced nervously, uncertain what he would do to her this time or what he might want. He came to her quickly and, before she could even speak, he dropped to his knees before her.

"I know I owe you an apology," he said earnestly. "I treated you very badly and I was wrong to criticize you. I was terribly angry, angry with my people, with the state of my lands and my country, and I was wrong to take that out on you. I pray to Allah each day for forgiveness, and I beg your forgiveness, too, Isabel. It is written that our lives shall be intertwined, and as my life has become more complicated, I think of you often and I am inspired by your journey. I only wish I could have better followed your example."

"My journey? I have been abandoned, lost, homeless, battered, cast out, cast aside, and placed on a pedestal. It all happened to me; I didn't ask for any of it," she said bitterly. "And I don't forgive you, Ahmad. You treated me like a hostage."

"I ordered that you were to be released as soon as we departed. I left a camel and supplies for you. I had al-Kattani write to all his contacts across the Maghreb to ask that they keep watch for you. Didn't it occur to you that Lèlla Zeyneb

Crossroads of the Nomad

took you in very readily in Ouargla? That's because we asked her to look out for you."

"I didn't realize that," she said.

"There is another reason I mistreated you. I, also, will admit ... I did love you very much when I first met you in Fez. I felt betrayed and was jealous that you were working with the French. It was childish anger, and I am very ashamed."

"Good, fine, then you have atoned. You can go on with your life without me now. I don't wish to be involved."

"Of course, I don't expect you to be." He stood up, and she turned away. "Anyway, thank you for letting me tell you that I am sorry."

She hesitated, still angry. "What are you doing in Casablanca, Ahmad?" She demanded. "Are you somehow involved in this chaos, this violence that has injured and frightened these people?"

"No, I am not. In fact, for all the good it will do, I went to the Chaouia leaders and pleaded with them to rein in their tribesmen, but they have no control over these men. Yes, there are many innocent people at risk in the city, but there is also a great deal of anger at what the French are doing here. To answer your question, I came to Casablanca for another reason entirely: I am working with Sayyid al-Kattani and Omar Benayoun to develop support for replacing Sultan Abd al-Aziz with his brother, Abd al-Hafid. I came here to meet with the Chaouia leaders for that reason."

"So you would have me believe you are now a politician?"

"I suppose I am. It is the only thing I can do."

Tamanrasset

"I know that Abd al-Aziz is widely distrusted but I can't understand why you believe that Abd al-Hafid would be any better."

"At least he purports to be a better man, and I believe he might be made to be better with the right guidance and political pressure. Regardless, he is the best of very few possible candidates to take the throne once Abd al-Aziz is removed, and we are past the point now where that can be debated: He must go."

"And do you believe the tribes, working together, can replace the Sultan without resorting to violence?"

"We have been working to sway enough tribal leaders to convince Madani El Glaoui that he must support the change: Not only is he the only one strong enough to remove Abd al-Aziz, but his warriors also make up a substantial portion of the Sultan's armed forces. There will be no fighting if Abd al-Aziz has no army to fight. But we don't believe the Glaoui will consider changing their alliance yet; they have backed Abd al-Aziz for many years."

She nodded. Bella recalled her visit to the palace in Fez, and the memory brought back the time she had lived with Omar and Majida and Faiza. Everything had changed since then. The French and British were now everywhere. Perhaps it would be unfair to say the changes were all the fault of the Sultan, but it was reasonable for Morocco to want a Sultan who would better protect his people.

"How are Omar and Majida?" She asked.

"Unfortunately, Majida does not leave the house, and I have not seen her for several years. Omar says she is well. He has become a strict religionist and is now a leader of the Ulama in Fez."

"While we were traveling through Aïn Séfra, I also heard that your father passed away. I am sorry for your loss. Allah yarhamho, may Allah have mercy."

"Thank you for your kindness."

"Do you think, if Abd al-Hafid does become Sultan, then he will make you Sharif of the Doui-Menia?"

"No, my father's brother is Sharif now, not me. I cannot take that title away from him."

"But if the Doui-Menia will not fight, can Abd al-Hafid still resist the French?"

"If Morocco were to fight a war against France, then it would lose that war, and our position would be much worse. They would claim we are a conquered nation. But, as I have said before, there will be battles, and unfortunately that means there will be losses. But the only way France will ever leave Morocco is if the cost of being here is greater than the profits it can wring from our land and our labor. But even worse than what the French are doing, in my opinion, is the expectation they are spreading among our own people that if we exploit our fellow Moroccans, then we too can attain the Western standard of luxury and idolatry. It grieves me to see the minds of our people oppressed by such desires, for it is a betrayal of our culture and of Islam. We are people of the desert. We are a great people because of where we come from and where we live, perhaps not in ways that Europeans would call great, that is true, but we are a people bound to each other, nonetheless. We will certainly not remain great by abandoning what we are in order to become what the French or British or Germans would like us to be."

Bella nodded. "You've grown, Ahmad. I am glad you spoke to me today."

Tamanrasset

Ahmad smiled at her. "And have you been well?"

"I have been, yes, I have been very well, I think."

"I am told you came to Casablanca with an American archaeologist. Would he have any interest in seeing the necropolis that the French destroyed with their railroad?"

She smiled: "I will ask."

At that moment, there was an explosion, not the rolling thunderclap of a detonation but a deep *boom* followed by an intense reverberating echo and the shrill whine of a shell fired from a cannon. It was impossible to breathe while waiting for the aftermath of that distinctive sound. And then it came, a huge explosion in another part of town but not far away.

"Oh, what is happening?" Bella asked worriedly. Ahmad blanched. They ran together to the door of the mosque. The smoke of the explosion was still rising over the kasbah. Just then another shell was fired, and the whine of the missile seemed longer this time as they waited to see where it would fall. Then again came the crash and boom of an explosion in the kasbah.

"The French warships are shelling the city!" Ahmad shouted. "We must go; we cannot stay in Casablanca any longer!"

"I have to go back to the Continental," she gasped as another shell exploded, this one in another part of town. They ran from the mosque into the street. There was shooting, many guns involved in a battle nearby. Ahmad took Bella's arm and helped her around the corner to where it was quieter.

"They won't be shelling the European hotel," he told her, "but we must leave quickly."

Crossroads of the Nomad

"I know, but I need to go back to the hotel first. Please, I'll follow you," she said.

He took her hand and they ran down the street and made a couple turns before arriving back at the central square. The Continental was across from them, but the plaza was in chaos: People were being hustled out of the hotel and down to the port. French soldiers were brutally beating away locals who were either attempting to attack or merely seeking refuge, it was hard to tell which.

"I don't know if we could even get you into the hotel," Bella said, "but I know for certain you cannot go into this square, Ahmad. Let me try to reach my friends."

"Do you believe they have not already fled from the hotel?"

"Believe it or not, I'm sure they haven't. For an archaeologist, Ren is pretty fearless, and his brother Jack used to be a Legionnaire."

"Very well, but I insist on waiting here until I know you are safe."

Bella quickly removed her hijab and looked at him with gratitude; she recalled, after seeing his surprised expression, that he had not seen her uncovered since the day she collapsed into his arms in the mosque in Fez. "I will come back in a moment, then," she told him. "If I don't return quickly, just assume I can't get away." She smiled at Ahmad and touched his cheek with her hand, then she turned and walked into the square.

The area before the hotel remained crowded, but her pale face and blue eyes marked Bella instantly as someone the French soldiers would protect, not attack. She was escorted through the cordon, and she explained to a French

Tamanrasset

officer her need to locate her friends in the hotel. She ran into Ren and Jack immediately for they were in the crowded, chaotic lobby where a French official was ordering everyone to join the others going to the ships. Jack was arguing with the man as Ren saw her and rushed over.

"Thank God you've returned," he said. "We've got him. We know where Bert is hiding. He may not be there much longer. We must go at once, but this official is insisting we go to the port."

"Jack," she shouted to get his attention. He looked her way. "We've got to go now!"

The French official reached out to grab Jack's jacket; Jack swung and knocked the smug fellow to the ground.

"We're leaving now for certain," he said as took Bella and Ren by the arm and rushed them out the door.

In front of the hotel, local people were spread on the ground—they had been beaten, and Bella saw blood. Some had been shot. The French soldiers still maintained a tight cordon around the hotel's entrance. The shelling continued with explosions around the city. The ground shook, and many additional buildings had caught on fire; a heated gun battle between the French soldiers and the Chaouia tribesmen could be heard taking place at the entrance to the kasbah nearby.

"Come with me," Bella shouted. She led them across the square where, to her relief, Ahmad remained, and she wrapped her arms around him protectively. Both Ren and Jack were taken aback, but Ren was the first to step forward and extend his hand.

"A pleasure to meet you, Sir. My name is Renwick Villere. You are a good friend of Bella's, I take it. This is my brother, Jack."

Ahmad was clearly surprised. "I believe we know each other," Ahmad said to Jack and nodded. "My name is Ahmad al-Haybah. Not to waste time, gentlemen, but may I ask why you have not already gone to the port? The French gunships are leveling the city, and you would be safer on board the French ships."

"We have an urgent engagement and must get to the Tnaker district as quickly as possible," Ren explained.

"How do you know Bella?" Jack demanded.

"Bella, that's the name by which Faiza addressed you, isn't it?" Ahmad asked her, then he turned to Jack. "I have known Bella for several years, my friend: She used to live with my mentor at the university, in Fez. I do recognize you, Sergent, but I see you are not in uniform. If you are no longer a soldier of France, then I will only say that I have no argument with you, and if it will be of any assistance to Bella, I will help you any way I can. I owe her that," Ahmad said.

Jack looked at him a moment as if undecided, but then he nodded. "I don't work for France anymore, and I'll go along with whatever Bella says."

"Can you show us the way to the Tnaker district, Ahmad?" Bella asked.

"Yes, but let us go quickly for it seems the fighting is getting much worse. Follow me, please," he said.

Getting through the city was not a simple matter. Ahmad led them a far distance out of the way to avoid the kasbah and the ports. Because they were walking away from the more European areas of the city, the risk of being shelled by the French gunships increased. Bombs were raining down in some areas. They passed buildings on fire and others that had exploded, but Ahmad was a careful guide and kept them from harm, twice fending off local tribesmen who would have murdered them. Then they entered the Tnaker district, an impoverished worker's area full of simple wood shacks. One of the Chaamba soldiers was waiting for Jack on the main road and led them a short way to a small, dirty hovel where the other soldier was standing guard.

"He is dying," the soldier told Jack in French and pointed to the house. Ren took a deep breath and went in first, Bella followed close behind him, then Jack and Ahmad.

Bert was alone in a small dimly lit room that smelled of death. He lay on a mat covered by a thin, dirty bedsheet. He was unable to stand. He looked terrible, perhaps a blood infection, and would likely not live out the day.

"I knew you'd find me, Renwick," he said cheerfully.

"Oh, Bert," Ren replied fatalistically.

"I am so deeply sorry, Ren. It was a stupid thing to do, I know it. Your brother should get the credit for running me down–I was stung by a damned scorpion in the desert and couldn't stop anywhere long enough to seek treatment or recover. Now my leg is dead, and I'll be next."

"I wish we could help you, Bert, but first I need more than an apology. I need my waterskin. I need the artefacts. Where are they?"

Weakly, Bert objected: "You don't know their value, Ren."

"I know what they are worth to me, Bert: My good name and reputation, which you have tried to ruin."

Bert made a face and shook his head. "You think only of yourself. If you had acted properly in the first place, they never would have been removed from the tomb. They are not just 'artefacts,' Ren, any more than they are buried treasure. They are heirlooms, the heritage of a great people. I never intended to sell them. I admit I hoped I would be given some sort of finder's reward, but I took them only to find their proper owner."

"What owner? Queen al Kahina has been dead for twelve hundred years. Where are they, Bert? I'll make sure they are treated with respect."

"No, you wouldn't, Ren. You believe they are merely scraps of history, but they have meaning, they have always *belonged* to someone. They aren't ours to possess. You," he said pointing suddenly at Ahmad. "Who is the leader of the Berber people in the Maghreb?"

Ahmad was surprised to be singled out for the question and he had no convenient answer: "No one is the leader of the Berber people," he said. "The Sultan of Morocco is Arab; the Governor of Algeria is French. Of course there are many Berber tribes across the Maghreb, some more powerful than others. The most powerful Berber tribe in Morocco is undoubtedly the Glaoui."

"The Glaoui?" Bella gasped.

"Yes, that's right," Ahmad said.

"Alhamdulillah, praise be to Allah," she whispered.

"Where are they, Bert?" Ren insisted.

Bert could hold out no longer. He pointed to the side of the shack, and then collapsed into his bedsheet, unable to rise again. Sitting by the side of the shack in plain sight was the waterskin. Ren rushed over and took it in his hands.

Tamanrasset

Pulling the cork plug, he upended the skin, and the necklaces ran out like water onto the rush mat: Nine intricately crafted and interconnected gold necklaces with gold and silver beads and dozens of green diamonds; several of the green diamonds were over twenty carats apiece, and there were hundreds of carats in total.

Ren and Bert were the only ones in the shack who had seen the necklaces before. The others were stunned into silence, and in that moment the sound of the French bombardment of the city could be heard clearly and felt through the shaking of the ground and the dust that fell from the ceiling of the shack. The screams of the dying, the smell of smoke and burning flesh, and the roar of the guns sent shivers down their backs.

"Wow!" Jack said finally. "Those are ... they are much more than I imagined."

"These are the Emeralds of the Garamantes," Ren said, "subject of legends and myths, and, I suppose, they are the sacred heirlooms of the Berber people."

"They're beautiful, Ren," Bella said. "But, listen, I have an idea. You may not like it."

Ren looked at her, and he had a tear in his eye. "Go on, my dear. The world is going to Hell around us, but we have time. Tell us your idea."

"Well, they belong to the Berber people, that's what Bert is trying to say. They don't belong to Gallé or France or the Sultan or to us. They should be put on display, certainly, but they're too important to just be given to a museum. They should be returned to the Berber people. And, I think, my proposal, is that we bring them to Madani El Glaoui. And you can ask his permission to put them on display, for his people."

Ren laughed. "The archaeological society would never forgive me."

Ahmad interjected: "Bella, do you mean to suggest that you would give these," pointing to the necklaces, "to Madani El Glaoui?"

"No, not me, Ahmad. You would give them, although with certain conditions," she answered.

"I think I see now why the Sultan and the French government have also been seeking these items," Jack said. "Someone could buy a lot of influence with these jewels. Is that what you're suggesting, Bella?"

"Madani El Glaoui cannot be bought," she assured him, "but these could have a tremendous influence upon him, and Ahmad needs that. He has been working with my friends here in Morocco to replace the Sultan with his brother, the Khalifa of Marrakesh, so that Morocco can remain what it is and what it has been for centuries."

"I begin to understand," Jack said, "but, to be honest, I don't have to understand. If that is what you want, Bella, and if it's acceptable to Ren, then I'll go along with it."

"That is a very difficult thing to ask, Bella," Ren said. "But ... Bert is right. They could mean a great deal to me, for my name and reputation, but they don't belong to me. I'll go along with your plan as long as this fellow Madani El Glaoui agrees that they will be displayed to the public, and, frankly, because you are the one asking and we owe it to you. What do you think, Ahmad al-Haybah: Can you save Morocco with these priceless heirlooms?"

Tamanrasset

"They will not fail to move Madani El Glaoui, for I know he is proud of his Berber family and his heritage, and I believe he will understand that he is to be the custodian for his people of such trophies. Will you come with me to share their history?" Ahmad asked.

"We'll all come," Jack said, "if you can get us out of this damn city before we're all blown up or shot."

Ren insisted they wait for night to fall before leaving the shack. He sat with Bert until his friend passed away; there was nothing else they could do for him. Around them, parts of the Tnaker district were in flames. Shells continued to fall on the city, and many more French troops were coming ashore. It would turn out to be an invasion. By morning, the Tnaker district had burnt to the ground and the rest of the city had been reduced to ash and rubble. Many thousands were killed by the bombardment. Over the next few weeks, French and Spanish troops hunted down and killed countless more Chaouia tribesmen across the region.

* * *

After their escape from Casablanca, Ahmad led Bella, the two American brothers and the two Chaamba soldiers to a farmhouse outside the city where he arranged for them to spend the night. Jack offered Ahmad the service of the two Chaamba soldiers to deliver messages, and the two men set off at once for Fez to locate Omar Benayoun and Muhammad al-Kattani and arrange for them to come to Marrakesh. Ren purchased horses, and, over the next few days, Ahmad led Bella, Jack, and Ren to Marrakesh.

Their route was quiet and peaceful, primarily during daylight with a break during the heat of the afternoon. They passed through a vast green land of rolling hills and picturesque valleys, the most fertile region of the country, where the rich red soil produced olives, figs, dates, persimmons, lemons, and oranges in vast quantities. At intervals, wide expanses were filled simply with wildflowers—iris, mimosa, lily, wild poppies, and daisies— spreading color atop areas of verdant green. For the most part, they rode in silence, listening to the muffled thud of the horses' hoofs on the soft grasses. It was a striking contrast to the clamor and strife they'd left behind, almost as though they were riding off into a dream.

Small towns and villages had ample supplies to purchase as they journeyed, and the markets were easily navigated. Ahmad and Jack went into the towns to do the shopping so Bella did not have to deal with local crowds, but she visited a couple mosques along the way when she didn't want to pray only with Ahmad. Ren was busy cleaning the "Emeralds," sizing and grading each stone and sketching the necklaces before they left his possession again.

It was on the fourth evening, after Ahmad had collected their water and Ren had cared for the horses and Jack had prepared a supper of roast lamb and kouss-kouss with fresh herbs, that they sat together beside a small fire, sitting in silence yet at the same time as something more than just friends. Bella told them a story:

"After I completed the Hajj, as I've mentioned before, I had no money, and I was in Jedda wondering where to go. I probably would have come back immediately to Fez then, but I had no means to pay for my passage. There were a lot of Europeans visiting Jedda (since they're not allowed in Mecca itself), and I struck upon employment lecturing to

French and British tourists. Probably I was just the sort of oddity they expected to find in a distant, exotic country, like an attraction recommended in their *Baedeker's*. Naturally, I was asked many questions about myself and about Islam. I often shared passages from the Quran. I liked to mention the beginning of this verse from the Surah Al-Hujurat:

> 'O People, you were created from male and female and divided into tribes that you might know one another.'

There are many explanations for this verse, and that's only a short part of it, but I like the idea about knowing each other's tribes; I believe it's about how we, in our little groups, while we're of course bound to one another, we still have a duty to know or learn from others, for we remain, ultimately, part of the world we all share. At least, that was what I told the tourists."

"The word 'tribe' has been used since antiquity," Ren said, "yet since Roman times it has generally had a pejorative meaning, to refer to the barbarians or uncivilized people, or in other words, the un-Roman. I sense that the word has another meaning in Islam, is that correct?"

"Tribes are the foundation of Arab society and have been throughout our history," Ahmad replied. "Ibn Khaldun wrote that tribes are the most basic and elemental units of civilization, but I admit he defined the word rather loosely, as an organization of people who share kinship or solidarity or the like."

"And is your tribe only your kin, or does your tribe include others?" Jack asked.

"My family is the Ouled Abadla. The tribe to which my family belongs, as you know, is the Doui-Menia. That tribe is made of five families who share a common ancestry, but others by alliance and intermarriage have also been brought into the tribe. Are you and your brother members of a tribe?"

"We're orphans," Ren said.

"I shall invite you both to join the Doui-Menia then," Ahmad said jokingly.

Jack laughed. "There's some chance that if I were arrested by the French right now, I would be sent to Devil's Island, so let's not make things any worse by having me join an organization which is the sworn enemy of France."

"I like to imagine that we are own little tribe," Bella told her friends.

"How do you mean?" Ahmad asked.

"I feel like I've known each of you my whole life, the parts that matter," she said. "I don't think there are any other people, besides you three, that I would stop everything to help, that I would protect with my life, that I would honor any request. I ... I only hope, and I know it is a serious thing to ask, that you would make that same commitment to me and even to each other, for my sake. Whatever you call this, this group, I shall call you my tribe."

"We are, my dear," Ren said. "You have made us so."

"I agree," Jack said.

"As do I," Ahmad added.

In Marrakesh, they stayed in a riad to await the arrival of Muhammad al-Kattani and Omar Benayoun. Anti-Western sentiment in the city remained high and had worsened since the French invasion of Casablanca, so Ren

Tamanrasset

and Jack remained indoors. When Omar and al-Kattani arrived, they were very moved to see Bella again and went to pray with her at the mosque. Then Ahmad, al-Kattani and Omar went to the palace and were admitted again through the discrete blue door to meet with Abd al-Hafid.

When the meeting concluded, Abd al-Hafid issued a proclamation that placed Marrakesh under his sole control and rejected his brother's authority as Sultan. Omar sent a message to the Ulama in Fez to set their plan in motion.

Ahmad, Ren, Bella and Jack, with Abd al-Hafid, Muhammad al-Kattani and Omar Benayoun, all traveled together up to the Atlas mountains to the fortress of the Glaoui family, the "Telouet Kasbah." It was a massive building with high walls, recently re-constructed, still being expanded and refined, with dozens of rooms and gardens all meticulously crafted and decorated. While the mountain village which it overlooked was quite busy, few people actually lived inside the fortress, and parts of the building, while beautiful and lushly decorated, were almost unused.

They were admitted politely at the enormous formal entrance, a colonnaded room with a glass ceiling, decorated with nearly a million colorful tiles and engraved bronze doors. T'hami El Glaoui came to greet them, and he and Ahmad and Omar went off with him to speak privately for a few minutes. Over the next day, there were further discussions, some between Madani El Glaoui and Abd al-Hafid, between Madani and Muhammad al-Kattani and Hajjah Bella, and between T'hami El Glaoui, Ren, and Jack. Agreements were made, actions were pledged, allegiances were sworn.

Madani El Glaoui, moved to tears and pledging his eternal gratitude to Ahmad, accepted custody of the Emeralds of the Garamantes and agreed that they would be placed on permanent display at a new Museum of Antiquities to be established under Ren's direction in Tangier (not Algiers), a compromise that Ren deemed acceptable. Madani also pledged to support Abd al-Hafid and agreed to recall his soldiers who comprised a significant portion of the Sultan's army. These warriors were ordered to assemble in Marrakesh in support of Abd al-Hafid. Upon receiving word from Omar of these successful meetings, the Ulama in Fez proclaimed Sultan Abd al-Aziz dead and issued a Bay'ah in favor of Abd al-Hafid naming him as the new ruler of Morocco.

Sultan Abd al-Aziz was stunned by the news. Having lost virtually his entire army, he fled to Rabat to seek the protection of the French government, but this merely hardened Moroccan opinion against him. With the help of Madani El Glaoui and his army, Abd al-Aziz's depleted forces were defeated at a brief battle near Marrakesh and he was forced to abdicate, opening the path for Abd al-Hafid to at last become the Sultan of Morocco.

Epilogue

Our departure from Cairo has been delayed so that we might attend the afternoon lecture at the Shepheard Hotel by the eminent visiting scholar, Professor Renwick Villere, FRS, FBA. Professor Villere is the archaeologist whose famous adventures in Tunisia and Algeria were the subject of his several successful novels. Although he is now retired, Egyptian Hotels Ltd. has spared no expense to bring the Professor from his residence in Cyprus to present his most famous excavations at Carthage and Tamanrasset to an enthusiastic crowd. Afterwards, the Professor joins us for dinner.

Over an excellent repast at Celestino's, Professor Villere shares a great many more personal details of his experiences in the Maghreb and those of his "tribe," as he calls them.

"Please tell us," we ask, "where is your brother Jack now?"

"Jack? Yes, yes, Jack, you know, he believed that the French military police might come to arrest him since he had chosen to ignore Joubert, but he changed his name again and returned to Casablanca. The French government seemed to have forgotten all about him after the city was destroyed; perhaps they assumed he was dead, or they just didn't care. He told me he inherited a small business in Algeria of some sort, a little tavern or something, which he sold, and with those proceeds and the money I gave him, he opened a nightclub and casino in Casablanca. It was a rather enormous success. But that was many years ago. He may be retired now; we haven't spoken for some time."

"It seems like Jack might have become friends with Ahmad, is that right?"

"They might have, indeed, but the opportunity never arose. Once Abd al-Hafid became the Sultan of Morocco, there was a great resurgence in resistance to the French, especially in the border regions between Morocco and Algeria. Even though he was not Sharif, Ahmad was able to put together a haraka in the Wadi Saoura with more than two thousand well-armed warriors. They massacred a whole outpost of French soldiers near Colomb-Bechar. After that, well, Ahmad attracted so many followers and the haraka got so large, nearly twenty thousand men, that the French had no choice but to send the whole damned army after him. There was a huge battle in the foothills of the Atlas Mountains which lasted eleven days. Many, many people were killed on both sides. I was later informed that Ahmad was killed in that battle."

"And yourself, after your journey to the 'Telouet Kasbah' to give Queen al-Kahina's necklace to Madani El Glaoui, did you finally get to return to Carthage, Professor?"

"Eventually, I did, yes. Tom Childers had returned safely to Algiers from the Sahara with a mountain of artefacts and treasures for the antiquities museum, even after setting up a permanent exhibition in Tamanrasset, so we had to get all that in order first. But Tom and I did return to Tunis, and we re-opened the Palais d'Hamilcar. He and I worked together for many years and trained many archaeology students there together. Tom even went over to Tangier for me to prepare the Antiquities Museum where the 'Emeralds of the Garamantes' were initially displayed."

"Are they no longer on display there?"

"I understand that, after a time, it was decided that the security at that facility was not adequate to safeguard them, and a decision was made to transfer those precious heirlooms to the Louvre."

"But Tom, is he still at Carthage?"

"No, no, I'm afraid not," the Professor answers quietly. "I suppose people began to lose interest in Carthage around the time that Tutankhamun's tomb was discovered by my friend Howard Carter. That was in the early '20's. Of course, Père Delattre stayed to work on Carthage until he passed away in '32. I believe Tom is somewhere in Mesopotamia now."

"But didn't Tom see Bella again? I thought they would eventually get married."

A darkness passes over Doctor Villere's face, and he is silent for a moment.

"Bella died, I am sorry to say. She returned to Fez to visit with her friends for a time, and then was on her way to join us in Algiers, traveling alone across the Tell Atlas. There was a flash flood, near Tlemcen. She drowned in her tent."

"Oh, how awful!"

"It was a great loss, yes. Thousands of people across the Maghreb mourned her death. General Lyautey personally arranged for the building of a tomb for her; it's in a little village near Tlemcen. I went to visit her there once, many years ago; it's a lovely little marabout's tomb with a white dome. I hope it's still in good condition."

Tamanrasset

Our dinner concluded, the aging professor somberly mounts the stairs to return to his rooms as we step outdoors to the hotel's porch to enjoy the evening air. Abd al-Hafid, as we recall, turned out to be a very unpopular Sultan, far too religious for most and still burdened by the country's debt to the European banks. He only ruled for a few years and was finally forced to sign the agreement which turned Morocco into a French Protectorate. Lyautey was then promoted to Resident-General of Morocco, and he persuaded Abd al-Hafid to allow another of his brothers, Yusef ben Hassan, to become Sultan. But that was all many years ago now, long before the Great War.

Notes

This novel is a work of fiction inspired by actual persons and events. The character of Renwick Villere was based on Byron Khun de Prorok, a Hungarian-American amateur archaeologist and author who discovered the tomb of the ancient Tuareg queen Tin Hinan in 1925. The character of Isabel Pedersen was inspired by Isabelle Eberhardt, a Swiss explorer who moved to Algeria in 1897, converted to Islam, and married an Algerian soldier; for a time she worked for French General Hubert Lyautey, but she died in a flash flood near Aïn Séfra in 1904. The character of Jack Villere was based on the French Foreign Legionnaires whose memoirs inspired a genre of adventure novels such as "Beau Geste" by P.C. Wren and countless "pulp fiction" stories. The character of Ahmad was based on the resistance leader in the Western Sahara Ahmed al-Hiba. The character of Hamza was based on Hadj Mohammed Mesfewi, a serial killer who murdered dozens of women in Marrakesh and was executed by public entombment in 1906. The character Jilali al-Zerhouni was based on the "Pretender" to the throne of Morocco known as Bou Hmara who was ultimately captured by Abd al-Hafid and put to death in 1909. A number of persons, such as Reverend Père Alfred Delattre, French General Hubert Lyautey, Paul Gauckler, Lèlla Zeyneb, Abd al-Hafid, and Muhammad al-Kattani, have been fictionalized for this story.

Tamanrasset

The action of the story takes place against a backdrop of events that occurred in Morocco and Algeria between the years 1900 and 1908. These include the Doui-Menia attack on French Foreign Legion forces near Igli in 1900; the French bombardment of Figuig and the Battles of Taghit and El Moungar in 1903; the Pericardis abduction in 1904; the Shura held by Sultan Abd al-Aziz and the First Moroccan Crisis arising from Kaiser Wilhelm II's visit to Tangier in 1905; the Algeciras Conference of 1906; the murder of Émile Mauchamp and the French bombardment of Casablanca in 1907; and the abdication of Abd al-Aziz in 1908. However, the novel is not intended to be a historical record of those events, and they have been adapted to the story. For further information, the author refers readers to the following non-fiction sources of information about those people and events: *Resistance in the Desert*, Ross E. Dunn (1977); *Lords of the Atlas*, Gavin Maxwell (1966); *Conquest of Morocco*, Douglas Porch (1982); *Mysterious Sahara*, Byron Khun de Prorok (1929); *A History of Modern Morocco*, Susan Gilson Miller (2013); *The French Foreign Legion*, Douglas Porch (2010); *The Passing of Morocco*, Frederick Moore (1908); *The Wages of Virtue*, by Capt. P.C. Wren, I.A.R. (1916); *Baedeker's The Mediterranean*, Karl Baedeker (1911); *A Search for the Masked Tawareks*, W.J. Harding King (1908); *A Soldier of the Legion*, C. N. Williamson and A. M. Williamson (1914); *Life in the Legion*, Frederic Martyn (1911); and *Travels in Morocco*, James Richardson (1860). The verses recited by Mrs. Beaton are from "The Siege of Carthage: An Historical Episode" by S.H. Sleigh (1880).

Epitaph

Farewell dark Maghreb, Empire of the Moors, mayst thou remain yet many years immured, impenetrable to the things that are new!

Turn thy back upon Europe! Let thy sleep be the sleep of centuries and so continue thine ancient dream!

May Allah preserve to the Sultan his unsubdued territories and his waste places carpeted with flowers, there to do battle as did the Paladins in the olden times, there to gather in his rebel heads!

May Allah preserve to the Arab race its mystic dreams, its immutability scornful of all things and its grey rags; may He preserve to the Moorish ruins their shrouds of whitewash and to the mosques inviolable mystery!

From *Au Maroc* by Pierre Loti (1890),
translated by Frederick Moore in
The Passing of Morocco (1908)

About the Author

Edward Parr is a retired attorney now living in New Orleans. He studied playwriting at New York University and worked with artists Robert Wilson, Anne Bogart, and the Bread and Puppet Theater while staging his own plays Off-Off-Broadway, including *Trask*, *Mythographia*, *Jason and Medea*, *Rising* and an original translation of *Oedipus Rex* before pursuing a career in law and public service. His previous works of historical fiction include the award-winning *Kingdoms Fall* series, three espionage thrillers set during the First World War. He has always had a strong interest in expanding narrative forms, and in his novel writing, he explores older genres of fiction (like the pulp fiction French Foreign Legion adventures or early espionage fiction) as inspiration to examine historical periods of transformation.

Other Novels by Edward Parr

Kingdom's Fall – The Laxenburg Message

Kingdom's Fall – The Korniloff Affair

Kingdom's Fall – The Wieringen Proposal